Books by B. V. Larson

STAR FORCE SERIES
Swarm
Extinction
Rebellion
Conquest
Battle Station
Empire
Annihilation
Storm Assault
The Dead Sun
Outcast
Exile
Gauntlet
Demon Star

REBEL FLEET SERIES
Rebel Fleet
Orion Fleet
Alpha Fleet
Earth Fleet

Visit BVLarson.com for more information.

Edge World

(Undying Mercenaries Series #14)
by
B. V. Larson

"I hate the Roman crowds… if they all had one neck, I'd hack it through."
—Emperor Caligula, 41 AD

-1-

After Abigail Claver left me, I spent a few months relaxing. It was a wonderful feeling. My folks were happy, and Etta even came back down to Georgia Sector to visit. Breaks between deployments were usually good times, and we all enjoyed this one.

In my long and storied life however, I've come to learn that such moments were always short-lived. It's just part of the nature of things that when the universe seemed whole and hale and full of promise, fate liked to swoop down and take a sudden shit on your head.

"James? *James?* I know you can hear me." I knew the voice well. It was my tribune, one Galina Turov.

"Aw *damn…*" I whispered, looking down at my tapper. Someone had finally found me.

Hiding from one's own tapper is quite a feat. You should try it sometime. I mean, the damned thing was embedded in my forearm, so avoiding it was nigh on impossible—but that never stopped a man like me from trying.

My efforts to block my tapper began months back. First, I'd turned off every notification service, every tracking app, and every location finder I could without performing physical surgery. That was just the beginning, however.

1

Winslade had shown me his tapper about a year ago, and he'd wrapped it in honest-to-God aluminum foil. Now, if you ask me, that was straight-out ingenious. After having seen this extreme effort on his part, I'd been itching to try it myself.

Accordingly, along about mid-September, I went for it. I built myself a tape-and-glue wrap for my tapper, covering that whole section of my arm with foil. To pretend I wasn't a weirdo, I followed up with a layer of sports tape, the kind you wrapped up your ankle with after taking a fall in football.

For about a week, it worked like a charm. Not one damned message got through to me. My parents took the trouble to relay things I really needed to know about—messages from Etta and such-like.

It was heaven to be off the grid. But with all such miracle cures, it had failings. One critical flaw was based in my own lackadaisical personality. You see, I tended to let things go, if letting them go was at all possible. Few things in my life couldn't be left until tomorrow—or better yet next week.

So, after having built my contraption and taping it down, I pretty much forgot about it. I went back to my daily habits without another thought on the topic. This included sleeping, eating, exercising and bathing—with the wrap in place.

It was this last one that got me. Soaking something in water and rubbing at it—that can do all kinds of damage. Just about any adhesive eventually slips off with the application of enough sweat, soap and water applied over time.

I sort of noticed this degradation of my wrapping over the weeks, and I made a few small efforts to pull it tight again. This was like pressing a band aid back into place after it started to curl up and get dirty.

Due to my minimal maintenance, strips were dangling and flapping by the end of the third week. Since it still seemed to work, I ignored the damage and led my life of leisure and seclusion. I watched projected shows on my ceiling, boated around on the Satilla River and pestered girls in the pool halls of Waycross. Somehow, I felt confident the good times would never end.

But today was a dark day. My arm had started talking to me again. Somehow, Galina had not only managed to call me,

2

she'd pressed the override that allowed superior officers to invade the privacy of their underlings, bypassing my option to answer.

"Dammit James," I heard her muffled voice. "I know you're there listening. Don't pretend you're asleep, it's only three pm."

"Huh…" I said, frowning at my filthy, wrapped-up arm. Even after a shower, the adhesive seemed to attract black Georgia dirt like flies to a cow pie. "Is that you, Tribune?"

"You know damned well who it is. Stop fooling around. I have an assignment for you."

I winced, and I honestly considered doing the whole "I can't hear you right" routine. But, after a heavy sigh, I accepted the fact that such tactics were bound to fail. Galina was many things, but she wasn't a woman who gave up easily.

Grumbling, I began to unwind the tape, then tore off the foil. Galina's surprised face watched the world as it was revealed in streaks.

"What the hell did you do? Stuff your arm into a roll of foil?"

"That's exactly right. I was eating some leftover chicken from last night, see, and—"

"Shut up. I don't care. You have a new assignment."

"Sir, the legion has been deactivated, I checked only a week back."

"I know that. Don't you think I know that, McGill? I run Varus."

"Yeah… so what's this about?"

"We've chosen some of our best officers to participate in an exciting new experiment."

I blinked once, then twice. "Have I been volunteered for something awful, sir?"

"Not at all. This assignment amounts to an expensive vacation—on the Moon."

This threw me. Oddly enough, I'd been to a couple dozen star systems—maybe more. But I'd never been on the Moon.

Without thinking about it, I began to smile. "The Moon, huh?"

3

Galina smiled as well. "That's right. The Moon. You've never been up there, have you? I checked."

These days, the Moon wasn't just a simple gray-white rock in the sky. It was a vacation spot for millions of visitors from Earth. It had become almost a pilgrimage to go up there and see the sights. For most people, it was the only place outside of Earth's atmosphere they'd ever been.

In addition to the touristy spots, there were a whole bunch of experimental bases up there on the Moon. It served the government and military as a testing ground for weapons and the like—after all, when you had no atmosphere and precious few inhabitants, anything goes.

My face faltered as I thought about this. I realized I wasn't going to be stirring a Moon-fizzy in the crystalline craters, or attending the bounding Moon-races they held every day for the tourists. No, I was probably going to be on the *wrong* side of that rock—the dark side.

Walking outside and blinking in the sunshine, I gazed overhead. The Moon always looked kind of weird in daylight. It was a ghostly blue-white disk hanging over the roof of my shack.

The Moon…

"Centurion McGill? Damn you James, is that your ass I'm looking at?"

"Uh…" I said, lifting my arm back up to my face. "I was just having a scratch. Sorry."

"Get yourself up to Central. Your contract has been reactivated. You fly at nine a.m. tomorrow. Don't be late, or I'll send the MPs."

"I'm sure you will, sir," I said, losing interest.

I shaded my eyes and stared up at the sky again. It was kind of weird to think I'd be going to the Moon in the morning. Despite all my concerns, a smile tugged at the corner of my lips.

After all, how bad could it be?

4

A day later, I strapped myself into a seat aboard a Hegemony lifter. The spacecraft was one of those older, louder jobs. It shook like a palm frond in a hurricane as we left the Earth and plunged upward into the sky.

"Feels like your ass is coming out of your ears, huh?" shouted a noncom who sat next to me. Hegemony types rarely got off the ground, and he seemed bemused by the launch.

"Nah," I told him. "For a Varus man, this is positively homey."

His nametag identified him as "Bevan" and he had an accent that told me he was some kind of brit. Welsh, maybe— but I didn't really care where he was from.

A minute later, I nudged him with my elbow. "I've heard on good authority that you dirt-huggers have spines that are shorter than what's natural. A full two centimeters shorter on average by retirement, they say. Is that right?"

He looked at me like he smelled shit. "How the hell could that be true?"

"Well hog, it's simple physics. You've spent all your years under the cruel force of continuous gravity. Makes a man hunch over eventually."

He seemed bemused again. "I know a few things about physics. I doubt your story—but I suppose it's possible."

That was kind of an odd response for a hog. I'd expected outrage and loud denial, but Bevan seemed like a thinking man.

This surprised me, as Hegemony didn't often put uniforms on men like that.

Shaking his head, Bevan turned away and stared down the long line of jump-seats. Not all of them were full, and I had the feeling this fellow was already sorry he'd sat next to me.

"Apparently, gravity sours a man's attitude as well," I remarked, but he still didn't reply.

I decided to stop poking at the hog and turned to my tapper. It was in better shape now, with all the aluminum foil peeled off. There were just a few tape stains on the inside of my arm to show that I'd ever covered it up in the first place.

The hog started spying on my tapper when I brought up my orders from Central. They were simple enough: I was to get on this lifter and head out into space.

"If you're really a Varus man," the hog said at last, "not some internal security spook, you must know the real reason we've been ordered up to the bloody Moon."

I glanced at him, and I seriously considered making up some cock-and-bull story to scare the bejesus out of him—but I didn't. I decided to go with the truth. After all, I'd already messed with him from the start, and he hadn't gotten pissed off. That kind of self-control was rare in a hog, and it deserved some civility.

"I've got no idea what Central has in mind for us, if that's what you're asking. It'll be something grim though—you can count on that."

He nodded and grunted unhappily. Then he tried to go to sleep, and he actually managed it. I was impressed. Usually, it took a real starman to sleep on a lifter as it flew up into orbit, ground-pounders were too freaked out.

The lifter coasted in freefall for a time, then thumped into something big. The lights flickered and motors whined. We docked onto the belly of another ship, but they didn't let us out of the troop module. We stayed strapped in and the sensation of acceleration began again—but more gently.

"What the hell is happening now?" the hog asked me.

"You scared?"

"No," he lied. "Just bored and annoyed that they aren't telling us what's happening."

"This is no commercial flight. There's no peanuts, ginger ale or cute stewardesses up here. We're no better than cargo. You don't tell a side of beef which market he's heading for, do you?"

The hog was wide awake now. He looked around, and he was kind of twitchy.

"You think they'll shut off the air? To test us, or something?"

"Maybe."

"How can you tell?"

I reached down and popped his harness button. He immediately began to float and curse at me.

"Looks like we're in the clear," I said. "If this were a death-test, they'd lock us down and we'd have to cut our way out of our harnesses."

The hog flailed around. We were in a near freefall, with only a bit of acceleration to send him drifting toward the aft of the lifter, but I could tell right off he wasn't an accomplished spacer. He flapped around with his arms, and he tried to grab the back of his seat, but missed. He kind of smacked it. That sent him into a mild spin.

"Whoa!" he said, flailing around. "McGill you cunt, get me down!"

Sighing, I popped my own harness, hooked an ankle under my seat and reached out with one long, long arm. I caught him by the breathing hoses and pulled him back down. I tossed him into his seat and sat down myself.

All this activity had garnered the attention of a primus-ranked hog girl. She came swooping by, and I was impressed by how easily she moved in zero-G. You could tell right off this wasn't her first rodeo.

"What's going on here? Veteran Bevan, why are you out of your seat?"

"Well... I was just trying to figure out the harness, sir."

The primus looked him over coldly, then turned her unsmiling eyes on me next. "And you... McGill, isn't it? I might have known. I was told to expect trouble from your direction. Straighten up if you want to stay alive on the Moon,

7

Centurion. No one will shoot at you up here, but there are still plenty of ways to die."

"Looking forward to it, sir," I told her in a cheery tone.

Shaking her head, she drifted away. She tossed us a sour glance over her shoulder every now and then.

"Veteran Bevan, huh?" I asked. "How come she knows you?"

He slapped at his nametag and rank patches. "Maybe she can read. And you're McGill? I've heard about you."

"All good, I hope."

He grinned. "Not exactly…"

"Hey, nice of you not to mention I was the one that set you loose. You're okay—for a hog."

Oddly, he seemed pleased with my backhanded compliment. I'd always harbored the theory that hogs were people who wanted to be real legionnaires, but who, for one reason or another, had decided to play it safe. Bevan definitely seemed to be in that category.

In my long history of meeting up with hogs, I'd never gotten along with them well. But Bevan seemed okay so far. He had a sense of humor, and he lacked the stick-up-the-butt attitude most of them had.

The rest of the flight to the Moon was pretty dull. It took six hours in all. I'd forgotten how big the Solar System could be if you didn't have an Alcubierre warp drive to cheat with.

After a long flight, the tug—or whatever it was that had picked us up in Earth orbit—finally released our lifter and tossed us toward the Moon's surface. There weren't a lot of windows on a lifter, but we used our tappers to get an external view. The stark, gray-white surface of the Moon shined up into my eyes so brightly it made me squint.

"I thought we were landing on the dark side," Bevan complained.

I laughed. "The dark side of the Moon isn't really dark. At least, no more than the side that faces the Earth. They call it that because normal Earth people have never seen it. The Moon is tidally-locked with Earth, meaning it always shows the same side to us no matter what."

8

He nodded as if he got it, but I suspected he didn't. This didn't bother me. I was a well-practiced man when it came to living in ignorance and pretending I understood things.

We landed in a huge crater, which I recognized from what little study I'd done on the topic. "That's Aitken basin under us. The biggest crater on the Moon. It's one of the biggest impact craters in the entire Solar System, actually."

"You mean that entire dark circle at the southern end? That's like a quarter of the Moon's face."

"Yep. It's about six thousand meters deep, with eight thousand meter high walls around it. Must have been a real shocker when they first saw it way back in the nineteen hundreds."

"An impact crater? What hit the Moon hard enough to make that big of a dent?"

I shrugged. "No one really knows."

We watched as we came in for a landing, and Bevan seemed to study the place with growing unease.

"I just realized something," I said. "I never asked what *you* know about this mission."

He glanced at me sidelong. "They found something up here," he said. "That's all I know."

"Found something? Like what?"

"Like... something they'll only talk about in whispers. Something they don't want to tell the public about."

"Something bad?"

Bevan shrugged. "I guess."

"Why are you here, then?"

"I've been puzzling on that point. Why a Hegemony veteran? Why not some kind of nerd in a white coat?"

I nodded, looking around. If the truth were to be told, most of the people in sight on the lifter fit that description—nerds from the labs and vaults deep under Central.

"You got a specialty of some kind?" I asked him. "Some reason they might want you along?"

"Well... back in college, I got the easiest degree I could take. That's how I chose it, actually."

I snorted. "You finished college, huh?"

"Yes, with a degree in ceramics."

9

"Seriously? You're, like, some kind of a pot-maker?"

"There's more to it than that."

"I'm sure there is…" I said frowning. "You're sure that's all that's special about you? You're not some kind of physics geek or anything?"

"Hardly. What's your story? What are you good at?"

"Hmm… I've met lots of aliens. Tons of them, on many worlds."

"Huh… some kind of diplomat, then?"

"Nah. Mostly, I shoot them all."

"Oh… I see then."

We shut up as we made our final approach. The lifter drifted ever lower, sinking down, down, down, into that deep crater to land.

Both Bevan and I frowned at our tappers and the shaking vehicle around us. We watched the instrument readings, many of which were in the yellow warning-zone the whole time.

When the creaky old spacecraft finally crumped down onto solid rock, we unclenched our jaws and buttholes in relief.

-3-

The sparse crowd exiting the lifter wasn't met with much fanfare. A bored crewman waved us toward the unloading ramp, which was whining open by now.

"Better put your visor down, fool," he told Bevan, who hastened to obey.

To our surprise, we didn't step off the lifter into some kind of terminal. It wasn't even a docking bay for cargo. Instead, we were treated to an amazing vista. We were outside on the surface of the Moon. The barren landscape was all harsh whites and grays, with deep shadows in every crevice that was sheltered from the sun. To me, the base looked like a bunch of egg crates flipped over and painted white.

We followed the crowd toward what appeared to be a stack of modules. I could see the modules were all interconnected with spindly white-painted metal struts and walking tubes.

We soon reached the base and walked into a dark opening, entering one of the multisided chambers. Once the big door came down behind us, the crewmen did some quick pressure-checks then immediately opened their helmets with a sigh.

With flipped-up visors, some scratched their cheeks and noses while others puffed on stims. A few poured water into their sticky eyes. One of the worst things about living in space was being enclosed in a helmet all the time, unable to touch your own face.

The spacers ignored us. They talked among themselves. Bevan tried to turn on the charm anyways. "You guys really pour water into a spacesuit? Doesn't it pool up down around your arse?"

The nearest of the men sneered and made no reply.

"Come on," I told Bevan, and we left the sullen workmen behind. "These guys are hard-bitten spacers. They're used to long hours and breathing their own stinks in a spacesuit for days at a time. Such men are rarely in a good mood."

We kept walking, and we passed into the interior of the base. Still, no one greeted us, or gave us any instructions. As far as I was concerned, this suited me just fine. I didn't like being ordered around all the time. If there wasn't anything around that needed to be shot with my rifle, I'd just as soon be left alone.

I took the lead, hopping along as I always did when traveling on a low-gravity rock like the Moon. The gait was almost like skipping, or shuffling. Each hop sent me two meters or more down the passage.

Bevan seemed nervous, but he stayed on my six. He was stuck to my ass like he was glued there.

"Shouldn't we find someone in charge?" he asked.

"What? No way... I'm looking for a bar."

"A bar? Seriously? Do you think they'll even have one up on this rock?"

I laughed. "Don't worry, they've got one. The first thing all spacers build on every outpost is a bar."

"What could they use for booze? I mean, if the quartermaster isn't cooperative?"

"They'll ferment their own fingers if they have to," I told him.

"Charming..."

We soon found a ramp that led down into the wall of the crater itself. There in the darkest corner of the base, I spotted a bar. It didn't even have walls, and the tables were just empty barrels with fiberboard planks on top.

We were in a hollowed-out area dug into the side of the crater walls. With the bare rock of the Moon visible, I could tell by the circular marks on the walls these chambers had been cut out of solid rock with energy tools. The air was bitterly cold down here, but at least there *was* air.

The people at the makeshift bar looked surprised to see us. I figured they were all part of the permanent crew, and they weren't accustomed to entertaining visitors in their dusty pit.

Ignoring the unfriendly stares, I grabbed a stool and sat on it like I owned the place. Bevan reluctantly sat next to me. Our seats were nothing special, just discarded spools that had once been wound tight with cables.

"Are you sure we're supposed to be back here, McGill?" Bevan asked me in a whisper.

"Nope, probably not. But I need a drink after traveling all day."

Finally, a woman sauntered near and looked at us quizzically. "You boys lost?" she asked.

"You selling hooch?" I asked her.

She smiled. "The best on the Moon."

"Then I'm in the right place. I need two drinks, pronto. Give me your worst stuff. Anything, as long as it has a kick."

"Our special brew is like rocket fuel—but more toxic."

I smiled. "That sounds perfect."

She eyed us doubtfully again. "We don't take Sector money here. You've got to have Hegemony credits."

I laughed, and I touched my tapper to her wrist, giving her a hundred credit tip up front. She lightened-up after that. "Two drinks on the way."

I caught her deftly as she turned toward a line of urns and spigots. "Hold on. Those two drinks are for me. You didn't take my friend's order yet."

Bemused, she turned back to Bevan. "What will you have, sugar?"

"A beer—if you've got one."

She nodded and left.

Bevan looked nervous, but when we finally had a few drinks in us, he relaxed a notch. "This place is weird," he said. "Not like I expected. How can everyone be so dirty up in space? I always thought it was kind of sterile up here."

"You thought wrong. Hot water is always rationed in space, and we humans tend to bring our biology with us wherever we go."

After I'd finished my second drink, I was feeling pretty good. The waitress came up to us, but Bevan tried to wave her away.

"We've had enough. We're on duty… technically."

She ignored Bevan and looked at me sternly. "Are you James McGill?"

"Who's asking?"

"Your boss-lady is, from the look of it."

She showed me her tapper, and I saw Galina Turov's face glaring up at me.

"McGill? Your ship arrived over an hour ago. The briefing is already over."

"The briefing…?"

I glanced surreptitiously at my own tapper. I realized I'd put some aluminum foil over it during my trip up from Earth. That had become a habit of mine lately when I wanted to get some sleep—but I'd forgotten to unwrap it when I got to the Moon.

"Oh…" I said. "Where should I go now, Tribune?"

"Get your ass upstairs to the conference room. Now!"

"Yes sir."

Standing up fast, it took a second to regain my low-gravity balance. Bevan was whining about something, but I didn't pay him any attention. I paid the tab and left.

-4-

On my way back upstairs, I noticed Bevan was still following me around like a puppy dog. I thought about ditching him, but I didn't have the heart.

"Say," I said gently, "don't you have a job to do? I mean, someone to meet up here?"

He looked kind of sly, kind of furtive.

I began to frown, becoming suspicious. "Aw, come on. Don't tell me…?"

"Yeah," he said at last, "I was told to follow *you* around. I thought you would have noticed by now."

"I did notice, but I thought you were just pissing your pants. Is this really your first time out in space?"

"Yes—and the pants-pissing is for real."

We studied one another for a second. Normally, when I found out I had a hog spy befriending me and tailing me, I took offense. Sometimes, such unlucky persons found themselves dead shortly thereafter. This being the Moon and all, any number of accidents might befall an inexperienced man like Bevan. He might find himself short of breath for example, or frozen solid—or both.

Maybe it was the alcohol, or maybe it was the fact he seemed out of his element, but I found I didn't have the heart to kill him. Instead, I took in a deep breath and let it out slowly.

"Bevan, you just don't go around following a man like me under false pretenses. Many a hog has found himself being crapped out of a revival machine for less."

"Really? Shit… Look, I didn't ask for this. Like I say, I'm only a veteran who—"

"—who studied pottery back in school. Yeah, I heard all that. Who told you to spy on me?"

"It's not *spying*. Not at all. Think of me as more of a friendly escort."

"An escort? I pay for those, and they're never as ugly as you are."

He chuckled nervously.

"It was Turov who hired you, right?" I asked him.

"I can't say."

Annoyed, I grabbed the nearest uniform I saw drifting by. The spacer inside it scowled at me, and he levered back his arm to punch me—but the blow never landed. Seeing that my fingers were as thick around as flashlights, the spacer thought the better of taking a swing at me.

"What do you want, dirt-sider?"

"Some directions," I said. "Where does the brass sleep on this rock?"

"You mean the officers?"

"What do you think?"

Scowling, he pointed up a ramp. I let go of him, and we climbed up the ramp into the upper levels of the base. Soon, we found the officers' level, and the place looked nicer. I got past the sentry robot because I was a centurion. I vouched for Bevan, and he kept tailing me.

"Uh… McGill? If you're reporting to Turov, I don't really have to be—"

"Shut up. You wanted to tag along. Don't go chicken on me now."

He shut up and followed me sullenly. We soon found Turov's quarters, which doubled as her office. I hammered on the thin door, and it felt as if it might dent under my fist like a cheap tram's hood.

"What the hell?" Turov demanded, snatching open her flimsy door. "Oh… there you are. About time you reported in. Why did it take so long?"

"We made a few necessary stops," I explained.

Turov's eyes slid to Bevan, then back to me. "Come in, I'll give you a briefing."

I jerked a thumb toward Bevan. "You sure we still need your sheepdog? He got me here safe and sound."

"You knew he was under my orders?"

"Of course."

She pursed her lips, looking surprised. "In that case, I'm shocked he's still alive—but yes, bring him in here. He's part of this."

We both followed her into her tight office. When we encircled her computer desk, our knees bumped together underneath it. There wasn't much free space inside Moon bases, it seemed. I guess just keeping these modules warm and full of breathable air was a struggle.

"I suppose you're both wondering why you're here," she began. "I've only recently been assigned to this mission myself. The real reason we're all here is below us—and it's something of a mystery."

"What kind of mystery?" I asked.

She sighed. "We've found an object below the base that shouldn't be there. I was tasked with forming a team. I don't know much else, other than the fact Central has been calling up all kinds of people to examine it. They're excavating the bottom of this crater deeply."

"I know that the Aitken crater is deep," I said. "We've got to be at the lowest spot on the Moon already. I suppose that if you wanted to dig deeply enough to find something interesting, this would be the place to start."

"Yes…" she said, eyeing me oddly. "What would *you* expect to find, McGill?"

I shrugged. "Maybe ice from a comet. Probably from the one that smashed into the Moon and made this big dent."

"A good guess, and that was what we found at first. Some of the initial excavation was done to provide water for this base."

"There you go."

She shook her head. "No, there we don't go. We've found something else... a hard surface underneath all the layers of dust, rock and ice."

"What is it?" Bevan asked, speaking up for the first time.

"We're not sure what it is. It's very dense material. Very hard. Possibly... artificial."

She had our attention now. Bevan and I looked at each other, and my face split into a wide grin.

"Spaceship!" I shouted. "An honest-to-God alien spaceship? Buried on the Moon all this time? That is *sooo* cool!"

Galina shushed me.

Bevan looked alarmed. "Is McGill right? Is that what we've found—a spaceship?"

"No one knows. Not yet. That's why we brought in a hard-materials expert."

"Hard materials?" I asked, glancing at Bevan. "Clay pots, more like. They break easy."

"Don't play the fool, McGill. If you figured out Veteran Bevan was working for me, you must have checked up on his record."

"Uh..." I said, certain I'd done no such thing.

"The first thing you must have discovered is his intense study of puff-crete. He's an expert in the field, actually."

I glanced at Bevan. He shrugged. I knew then he'd been less than honest with me all along. He was no dummy seeking a beer and working as a noncom hog. He was more of an engineer.

"How come you're only a veteran, then?" I asked.

Bevan scowled. "Making new kinds of puff-crete is interesting, but technically it's not legal to produce the stuff. When I got out of school, I found no one wanted to hire me. Just the stink of it was too much. Hegemony, private companies—no one wanted any part of working with a man who'd spent years stealing another planet's monopoly. I didn't know it going in, but everyone fears an angry lawsuit. They didn't even want me on their payroll, in case it looked like they were trying to break Galactic Law."

18

"Huh… okay. So you joined the hogs?"

"Yeah. They wouldn't take me as an officer, but I was trying to get into the officer ranks eventually. My degree would actually help me then. They don't care what it's in, just that you have one."

I turned back to Turov. "Let's get this straight. You guys found a hard surface deep inside the Moon, so you called in an expert on making hard surfaces. I get that—but why am I here?"

Galina looked evasive. "Well… if we can get inside, you see, we'll need someone to explore… right?"

My mouth sagged. I finally got it. I'd been volunteered to investigate a buried alien spacecraft.

After the initial shock wore off, I found myself beginning to grin widely. "Sounds like fun!"

Galina smiled in relief. "I knew we'd contacted the right man."

-5-

After a few hours of watching a pack of nerds operate a drilling machine, I found myself getting bored.

The worst part was wearing our bulky spacesuits. They were the kind of suits that could heat and cool themselves as well as provide oxygen. This meant two things: you couldn't just lie down and a take a nap with that big backpack-thing behind you, and two, you could hardly tell the women from the men.

With nothing to look at, eat, or do, I forced myself to listen to the nerd conversation. Bevan was right in there with the rest of them, talking technical stuff and generally boring me to death like the others.

"This is remarkable," he said for about the tenth time, scraping at something in the bottom of a dusty hole. "I can't even scratch it. A diamond-tipped drill bit should be able to mark anything—even puff-crete."

"So, this material is denser than puff-crete?" Galina asked him.

"It's harder, certainly. We'll have to get a sample to measure the density."

"How can we get a sample if we can't cut it?"

Bevan shrugged and began working a chemical kit full of smoky acids. Fumes rose from the hole, and I got the feeling it was a good thing we were all wearing breathing equipment.

This kind of thing went on and on as they scratched and scraped a big area of moon rock away from the crater floor. As they labored, they created a trench line that went for a hundred meters or more across the bottom of the pit. At that point, it ran into the two far walls.

"It's still going," Bevan marveled. "The same surface, a hundred meters of it. So smooth and flat… If it's a ship, it must be a big one."

"I'm starting to think this isn't a lost ship at all," Galina said. "I think it's a base. That would make more sense—a buried base on the Moon."

"Who could have built it?" Bevan asked. "There was a time when the Asian Block and the Americas were racing to occupy the Moon…"

"Yes, yes, but it can't be their work. They didn't have materials like this."

Bevan nodded. "You're right. Earth had nothing like this until we imported it from other worlds. We've only recently learned to duplicate puff-crete in labs."

"Due to your dangerous work?"

Bevan shrugged.

Galina narrowed her eyes at him. "I can see why no one would hire you. You're a loose cannon. If the Nairbs audit Earth someday, you could be construed as evidence of willful patent theft."

"I don't *sell* puff-crete. I study it."

Galina wagged her finger at his faceplate. "You don't know the Nairbs like I do. They won't care about that distinction."

"The lady's right," I said, walking toward them. "Planning a crime and doing a crime—that's damned near the same thing in any Nairb's book. They'll convict and punish for either one."

Bevan looked annoyed. I'm sure we weren't the first people to admonish him over the nature of his life's work. He went back to scratching in the trench on the crater floor while I took stock of things.

"Bevan seems to be out of ideas," I told Galina. "What are we going to do next?"

21

"There have been thoughts…" she said, looking at me speculatively.

"Uh… like what?"

"Like blindly teleporting a man down there—to see how deep this surface goes."

"Hell's Bells, woman! You're talking about a straight-up perming. How would you get some poor fool back if you got no response at all from him?"

"You know how. I'm talking about using the casting device. We could fire you at this surface, transmitting your body a hundred meters down, perhaps. If you lived, you could report back until you stopped living. At that point, we could print out a new soldier."

"Uh… hold on. You want to cast *me* into this rock? Firing blind?"

Galina shrugged. "Don't be such a baby. We can always print out a new McGill. The casting device can watch you, and it can penetrate any distance or obstacle. Just make sure you die after ten minutes, and we'll make a new copy. No perming required."

"You're not the one dying and risking it all."

"Of course not. We all have our critical roles to play in this drama. Yours involves penetration of the target. Bevan is here to study and identify the husk of this thing—you are here to explore the unknown."

I sighed. I realized there was no way I was getting out of this one. "Where do I hook up?"

"To teleport? Not so fast. The crew is coming up from Central to do the honors of casting you."

"Spooks from Central? And you say they're bringing up the casting device? That's a big load."

"It's become more manageable in its current form."

"That reminds me, why didn't you guys just use a set of gateway posts to transfer me up from Earth? Why do it all the old-fashioned way with a lifter?"

Galina's eyes slid around to see who was listening. "You're always so nosey—but I'll give you an answer. This… ah, *surface* has odd properties. It interferes with gateways somehow."

"What? And you're planning to use a casting device to penetrate it? Why do you think the casting machine will fare any better than a gateway did? I'm going to be doubly-permed."

"Your cowardly attitude is becoming embarrassing, McGill."

"Look, I don't mind dying. You know that. As long as the pay is good, or at least there's a just cause in it for me, I'll die a dozen times while people watch. But perming... that's another matter."

"All right," she said, looking disgusted. "I'll get someone else. There has to be another legionnaire with balls somewhere on the Moon."

I caught her elbow lightly as she brushed past me. She didn't like that. After all, she was my superior officer—but she was also my occasional bed partner.

"Not so fast. We might be able to work something out. Just you and me."

I gave her my best smile, but she frowned back.

"Are you serious?" she demanded.

"I'm always serious about... uh... private moments."

"You chose Abigail Claver over me last year—among others. I'm not interested."

"I get that, but don't you want to know what's under this big slab of rock you've found?" I stomped on the dusty surface for emphasis.

"I do, but you can forget about getting any special treatment from me."

She marched away, and I watched her go. Even inside that spacesuit, you could kind of make out the shape of her. It was a good shape.

Bevan walked up, eyeing me curiously. "You know the tribune pretty well, don't you?"

"Word got around, huh?"

"Even among us hogs, yes."

Right then, I knew he wasn't *really* a hog. Not a committed hog, anyway. Never had a true Hegemony puke been born who would call himself what every other man on Earth called him every day.

23

"Have you met Floramel?" I asked him.

"Who?"

I explained that Floramel was a tall, weirdly pretty woman with an unbeatable brain. He seemed intrigued.

"She's a big shot in Central's labs, is she? And you know her?"

"Almost as well as I know Galina."

He laughed. "I see… well, if you don't mind putting in a good word from me—I mean, I wouldn't mind transferring out of the uniformed set into a research group that better fits my talents."

"That's what I was thinking. I'll see what I can do."

-6-

Floramel showed up on the next shuttle. Instead of getting herself lost and finding a bar, she moved immediately to the secret excavation area under the base.

She put her hands on her narrow hips when she spotted me. Her expression was guarded, but curious. "McGill?"

"Hiya Floramel! Fancy meeting you up here! This Moon base is like a vacation spot, isn't it? Just like those online ads always tell us."

She pursed her lips briefly. She didn't always get sarcasm, but she'd begun to expect such responses from me.

"No," she said. "It's not charming in the least. But I find this mystery to be more stimulating than some low-gravity playground. This is an important scientific expedition. What I'm puzzling about is why anyone thought it a good idea to include you."

I was pretty sure I'd been insulted, but I kept my smile firmly in place. "I've got someone with a big brain who you should meet. His name's Bevan."

I introduced my pet hog then, and Bevan seemed shy but competent. Floramel studied him, then consulted her tapper.

She was kind of rude like that. She began doing a full background check on Bevan using the grid, prying into every detail of his life while he stood right there in person. After a minute or two, she looked up.

"Your research is interesting. We could use your perspective on this project. Who recruited you? Not McGill, surely?"

I'd been about to claim credit for Bevan, but I realized she wasn't going to buy that now.

"Tribune Turov found me," Bevan explained. "I have… unique qualifications, and I was already under government contract. She was able to contact my superiors and transfer me to her legion temporarily."

"What?" I demanded. "You didn't tell me that! You're a Varus man now, official-like?"

"Uh… I guess so. It's only a short-term contract, I'm working as an auxiliary, you see—"

"And to think I was calling you a hog and figuring out how to kill you—you should have said something, man. I'll have to make it up to you later. We'll have to party professionally whenever we get out of this freezing hole."

Floramel studied me. "I'm still not sure why you're here, James."

I explained Galina's plan for my one-way ticket into the ground, and she nodded. "I'd hoped that wasn't the reason. I'd considered security, or specialized knowledge—but no. Of course, you're here as my guinea pig."

"That's exactly right." I grinned, but she looked troubled.

Floramel and I had a long history, and she'd often felt guilty about my mistreatment in the past. While guilty feelings and a ten-credit piece wouldn't get you a cup of coffee with Galina, Floramel was a gentler soul. She didn't like perming her friends, not even by accident.

About then Floramel's team began to filter in, and they went to work on the trench. They set up all kinds of gizmos and big lights. They had drones, too, but they couldn't fly due to the lack of air. They crawled over the roof and the dirt, using cameras on stalks to examine every inch of the place.

I expected Etta to show up, but she didn't. I asked Floramel about it when she was reviewing her notes.

"What about my girl?" I asked her. "She's still part of your team, isn't she?"

26

Floramel blinked down at my hand. I'd touched her arm, and I knew that kind of thing freaked her out. I let my hand slide away from her, and she looked up again.

"Etta is upstairs setting up the casting device. If you want to talk to her, please wait until she's finished with her work for the day."

"Don't worry," I said, striding away. "I won't be any trouble at all."

Marching off, I found ramps going up and soon reached the upper decks. Etta was in one of the only open areas, setting up what looked like a dentist's X-ray machine.

"Do I sit right here in this death-seat?" I asked, fooling with the headrest and the folding arms on the chair.

"Daddy? Oh God, don't tell me you're involved in this!"

Etta hugged me, and I lifted her in the air. It had been a few months since I'd laid eyes on her.

"You've got this thing wired by now, don't you?" I asked her. "Looks way smaller than before. What happened to that big white ball of light in the cage-thingie?"

"Oh... you're talking about the alpha unit, right? We've moved on two or three generations since then. This chair— well, it sort of forms the plasma ball in the middle of the person, rather than having them walk into it. That makes the reaction much more stable. The person isn't moving, see, changing shape and position as the computer is trying to scan them and lock on. This way, we're able to get a good impression faster, with less chance for error and with a much smaller field size."

"Uh... okay. You've miniaturized the whole thing by having your victim sit in a chair. I get it."

She nodded, but then her face fell. "I don't want to watch you die again, Dad."

"Aw now... there's no problem. When it comes time, you just shut your eyes and have one of your assistants mark me down as dead."

She closed her eyes, shook her head, and looked a little sick. I didn't talk any more about it. I'd learned over the years that dwelling on someone's fears just made them grow bigger.

27

Sighing in resignation, she adjusted her reclining dentist's chair-thing to fit my massive frame. She had to dial out every setting to the max so I could fit comfortably. Once she did that, I climbed onto the seat to try it out for size.

"This is pretty comfy," I declared.

"I'll be back in a minute, Dad."

Etta left, and I do have to admit that I dozed off, just for a second.

"McGill?" Galina's voice rang out, interrupting my thoughts. "Are you asleep on that thing?"

A sharp, rude blow struck me in the shoulder. I'd taken off most of my spacer's suit and stretched out on Etta's little electric chair, making myself at home.

"Sleep? Hell no!"

Staying on the chair, I reached up with my hands, stretching and yawning luxuriously. Galina made faces at me while I did so. She leaned over me when I'd stopped squirming around.

"We've got trouble downstairs, in the pit," she said. "Come with me. I want you to see something."

"Uh… okay."

I got up and gave Etta a pat on the head. She was under the chair with a power-driver in her hand. "Dad? Where are you going?"

"Duty calls, girl. Don't worry, you'll get to fry my bacon in your chair soon enough. Very nice of you Central types to make it so cushy. Almost makes me look forward to the glorious moment of disintegration."

Etta looked baffled at first, then she saw who had me in tow. Her face shifted to a mix of amusement and disgust. No doubt she figured I was being dragged away into a personal encounter with the tribune. I grinned at her, enjoying the confusion and hoping she was right at the same time.

Unfortunately, Galina hadn't come to drag me away to her quarters this time. She really did take me down to the pit.

"There's something wrong here. I don't like it," she said.

"Uh-huh."

When we got down there, I found the excavation had continued in my absence. *Damnation*, Floramel's team had moved a lot of dirt! I must have been asleep for an hour or two.

"Wow," I said, reaching up to scratch my head. My glove bonked into my helmet, as I was back in my full kit again. "The floor has a crack in it."

"Yes, it does," Bevan said. He seemed excited—more excited than before, even. "I thought we should do more than dig out a single trench, you see. We dug around the entire region—or most of it. It was then that I found this mark, right here."

He walked me over to one far wall of the circular chamber and pointed. There was indeed a crack there. It was just a hairline, and all squiggly, like a crack in an eggshell.

"That led us into digging along the demarcation. We found, after getting some drilling bots to work this area, that it merged with a much larger disruption of the surface."

Bending down, he picked up a loose chip of debris. "You know what this is, McGill?"

"Uh… a piece of Moon rock?"

"No. It's not rock. Nothing like this has ever been on the Moon—or it shouldn't be."

"Yeah?"

"That's right. And here's another, and another. I've sent several chips to the lab. The results aren't back yet—but I already know what they are."

"You don't say?"

"They're collapsed matter. At least, partially collapsed. Here, take this one."

I reached out and plucked the eggshell-colored chip from his hand. It fit into the palm of my hand with room to spare—but it was surprisingly heavy. "Feels like a chunk of gold—or lead."

Bevan smiled. Right then, I could see a hint of the mad scientist he really was in those wide, staring eyes of his. "Yes, it weighs about that much. A kilo at least, for a chunk that's only a few centimeters in diameter."

"That's pretty cool," I said vaguely, tossing the chunk down onto the pile of loose earth.

Bevan stared at me like I wasn't getting it. I got that look a lot. Shaking his head, he picked up the chunk again and waved it in my face.

"Don't you get it, McGill? We're on the Moon. We're only experiencing one sixth of Earth's gravity—meaning this chunk is *way* heavier than it should be. A rock this size made of solid gold wouldn't weigh more than a few grams here."

My jaw sagged for a moment as his words sunk in. He was right. The rock weighed at least ten times as much as it should. It was *impossibly* heavy for its size.

"Uh…" I said. "Is it collapsed matter? Star-stuff?"

"It has to be."

My jaw sagged, and I looked around. I spun full-circle, on my boot heel.

"I know what this is," I said in a hushed tone. "I *know* what we've found."

"That simply isn't possible," Galina told me when Bevan and I confronted her with the truth. "Don't even try to sell me this bag of Georgia horseshit, McGill. I'm not a fool."

"It's true, sir. We're standing on top of a Skay."

She crossed her arms and glared up at me. "Look, it just doesn't make sense. For one thing, a Skay is made of condensed matter, I give you that much. But that means it has a higher gravitational pull. We should be pressed up against this thing, not almost floating at one-sixth Earth's gravity."

Bevan leaned forward. "I looked into that. Then I checked with McGill—the gravity of a small Skay is similar to that of our Moon."

"What? Why?"

"Well, it is dense, yes… but it's also hollow. That means it has a gravity equivalent to a normal body of similar size."

Galina's eyes darted around. She was thinking about it, and I could tell she didn't like what she was thinking.

"You've been inside these things, McGill…" she said quietly.

"Yes, several times as a matter of fact."

"You're telling me this could be a dead Skay? How? It's our Moon, for God's sake! It's been around for a billion years!"

"Maybe," I said. "But the empire has been around for a long time, too. How long has it been since the Skay owned our

31

very own Province 921? You know they used to. The Mogwa took it from them. They fought here and lost some of their brothers."

Galina's pink tongue flirted with her lips. Her eyes were flashing around, her breathing seemed elevated. You could tell by the steamy puffs on the inside of her faceplate. She was beginning to believe—and she was beginning to become fearful.

"How did it get buried in rock? For all this time?"

I shrugged. "Who knows? Maybe it collided with Earth's original satellite and kind of merged with it. Or maybe it died here and collected millions of years' worth of dust and comets and asteroids... until they covered it up. Like one of those mammoths they find now and then under a glacier."

She was staring fixedly at the surface now. Workers with machines were sweeping and vacuuming up more and more loose Moon dirt. The revealed surface was undeniably smooth up until the ruptured area.

Galina pointed to the damaged region. "If it's so hard-shelled, so ancient—what could have cracked the surface like that?"

Bevan walked to the area and examined it closely. Now and then, he picked up a rock sample and pocketed it.

"Something hit the Skay hard—hard enough to kill it. I doubt fusion warheads could do this. Antimatter, maybe? Or something more exotic?"

"That's great. This is simply unbelievable," Galina said, talking fast the way she always did when she got excited and scared. "I think we should bury it again. Right now—while we can."

"What?" Bevan said, standing up straight and approaching the two of us. "We can't do that. This is a fantastic discovery."

Galina wasn't listening to him. I could have told him that. She was in one of her strange, scary moods. Her eyes darted this way and that, and I knew she was having a whole lot of dark thoughts all at once.

"Uh... Tribune?" I asked, becoming concerned.

In the meantime, Bevan approached us and began to make his ill-fated pitch. "We must study this. It's such an amazing

32

opportunity. Imagine! We'll rewrite all of Earth's history. We'll see the past in an all-new way. We weren't just annexed by the Galactics, we were part of the Empire from the beginning. I'm sure they never thought we were significant enough to bother with until we developed advanced tech of our own, but—"

Galina stepped toward him suddenly. Her finger came up, and she pointed it at his nose. "Do you know what you are, Bevan?"

"Um… I like to think of myself as a man of science. Sure, I'm not the greatest mind to walk the Earth—or even the Moon, but—"

Her finger began to wag. "Wrong. You're what people call a loose end. A frayed bit of thread that can't be allowed to unravel everything else."

"Huh?"

Galina turned to me. She glanced down at my sidearm. "Do it."

Our eyes met, and I blinked in surprise.

"Aw now, come on, sir. He's the nicest hog I've met in a decade. Let me just explain things to him."

"You've gone soft, McGill. I'm disgusted."

So saying, Galina took my pistol out of my holster—I could have stopped her, but she was my commanding officer after all—and she aimed it at Bevan.

Shocked, the slack-jawed hog lifted his hands in the air.

"Put your hands down, you idiot!" Galina told him.

He did so, looking around in bewilderment. "Sir, if I—"

"Shut up. Take that drill from the ground—yes, that one. Hand it to me."

Galina took the drill, and she put it to her knee. She buzzed it for a few seconds. The spot on her tough spacer suit was torn through. The diamond bit had done its work. She handed the drill to Bevan and put that free hand on the leaking hole.

"It's frigging freezing," she complained.

"Look, sir," Bevan said. "I don't know if you're feeling well, but that was self-injury. You'll have to take that to the medical people upstairs—and you might want to take a sedative, or something."

33

"What? Do you think I have PMS? You're an even bigger fool than I thought."

"Galina, come on," I said, trying again. "Cut him a break. You hired him, after all."

"Yes, and that was a huge error. I can't fix it the easy way. Not now, McGill. This genie is going to be stuffed back into its bottle—with or without Veteran Bevan's help."

Then, she lifted her gun toward the hog again. "Step closer to me," she said. "Take my weapon. Go on—take it!"

I could have told him to run, but it probably wouldn't have mattered. Bevan reached out a shaking glove—and Galina shot him in the faceplate. His helmet vented and bubbled redly. Exposed to the frozen airless void inside the chamber, his blood began to boil before he hit the deck.

I put my hands on my knees and bent over him. "Bevan? You dead yet? Wave a finger or something if you're in pain—I'll finish you off."

Bevan didn't do or say anything intelligible. He sort of curled up and shivered a little.

"That was plain mean, Galina."

"Shut up. It was necessary. Rest assured, I'm not going to blame you this time. I take full responsibility for this fuck-up, McGill."

"Well… that's a nice change."

Nodding, Galina turned to address the scientists. "Call security. This man attempted to assault me. He's an assassin, I suspect. See? Look at my leg. I might have asphyxiated."

I sighed. Her lies were often like that, ham-handed and over the top. As a near professional liar, I found her amateur efforts embarrassing at times.

But she stuck with it. She had turned off her suit audio, but she played the video to some goons sent down from the upper decks. They looked baffled, but her rank saw her through. I probably wouldn't have gotten away with this kind of blatant bullshitting—but she did.

Once Bevan had been properly disposed of, Galina demanded that the crews cover up what they'd found. They did so in a dazed fashion.

Following her and fretting, I left the chamber at the bottom of the Moon crater. I felt kind of bad about Bevan, to tell the truth. Sure, he was a hog and he therefore served Hegemony and all—but his heart hadn't been in it. That had been clear from the start.

8

"I tell you, that killing just didn't seem right to me, sir."

"You big hypocritical baby. You kill people all the time—especially hogs. Often, you do it just for fun."

"Well... yeah. But Bevan was different. He's never going to understand why you did that to him."

Galina laughed. It was an evil sound. Right away, my radar went up. I got the feeling her dark plans hadn't yet fully played out.

"You're right, McGill," she said. "He's never going to understand what happened to him—his data, in fact, is going to be tragically lost."

I got up, and I grabbed her arms. Surprisingly, she didn't start sputtering and hissing threats. She looked kind of turned on, in fact.

"Get out of that stupid suit," she said.

She unzipped hers, and I watched as she did it. Galina Turov was a startling woman. She often blew hot and cold, like a Spring day in Denver. She was pretty, too. Really pretty. Every time she got a wrinkle or something, she got herself killed and revived young again. In all likelihood, she was the best damned looking woman I'd ever been with.

"Uh..." I said, eyeing her as more and more undergarments and finally skin was revealed.

She *was* turned on, I realized. She'd killed a guy, and she figured she'd solved a big problem at the same time. When I

36

grabbed her she'd interpreted it as a sign that I was thinking the same way.

Now, I'll be the first to admit I'm not a proud man when it comes to taking advantage of a lady's good mood. Over the decades, I'd come to understand a fella had to move when the girl was in the right mental zone—but this was just too much.

I let go of her and straightened. I turned away from her.

"What's this?" Galina asked, circling around to face me again. "Are you having some kind of breakdown?"

"It's just not right. You're talking about perming Bevan, aren't you?"

She shrugged. "Probably not... I'll just have his data lost for a month or two. When he comes back, he'll be back pushing a mop around Central somewhere. I'll have someone edit his files, deleting everything recent."

I sighed. I knew she could do what she was talking about. That was wrong, sure, but it wasn't as bad as perming the poor little hog.

"Are you feeling better now?" she asked. "Now that you know I'm not going to perm your little pet?"

"Yeah... you promise?"

She looked furtive for a moment, then shrugged. "Will it improve your mood?"

"Sure will."

"Okay then, I promise."

I gave her a half-smile, and I let her paw at me again for a minute. Finally, after putting on a show of being sulky, which seemed to drive her half-crazy, I grabbed her and gave her what she wanted. When it was over, we lingered, embracing and sharing beads of sweat.

"It's been a long time," she said. "Are you glad to be with me again?"

"Kinda."

"Oh for God's sake, stop moping."

She climbed off me and showered. I didn't join her, as there wasn't room for two—but I watched her. I had to admit, she could put on a great show in a showering tube if she wanted to.

When she climbed out, I took my shower, and she began talking a mile a minute.

"Killing Bevan isn't the end of it. We'll have to come up with a good way of getting Floramel and her crew off this rock. Have you got any ideas as to how to manage it?"

"Why not just shoot her, too?"

Galina snorted at me, pulling a bra up from the floor and over her hips. I was never sure how or why women did that.

"That would be hard to explain," she said. "We'll have to do something less direct."

"We? What do I have to do with this?"

"Well… Etta is here. She's part of the team. Don't you want to be involved?"

A dark look came over my features. I didn't answer her right away. She was turned away from me at that moment, fussing with her shoes. I took that opportunity to step out of the shower tube and stand over her, warm water running off my lengthy person.

I put a heavy, drippy hand on her shoulder. She startled and turned around. She caught the look in my eye—and she froze.

"I didn't mean anything by that," she said, almost whispering.

Galina knew me well. She was a stone-cold killer—but so was I. When a person—*any* person—whispered a threat concerning my family, well sir, their lives weren't worth spit. And Galina knew that.

"I didn't mean anything, James. Get ahold of yourself."

I sucked in a breath, and I nodded. Then I faked a smile, for good measure. My hand lifted off her shoulder, which was wet after my touch.

"Of course you didn't," I said in a mild tone. "Have you got another towel handy?"

A few minutes later we were hopping down the passageways of the Moon base. I'd given Galina my best suggestion—she hadn't liked it, but she'd understood right off it was her best shot.

We moved to where Etta was setting up the miniaturized casting device. She told us Floramel wasn't there. She'd gone to the LIDAR room.

Frowning, we made our way to the science center. Floramel was indeed there, working on the equipment.

Modern LIDAR was an amazing technology. It was most often used these days to mine for minerals or find archeological sites on distant worlds. Today, it was operating in a new capacity.

"There you are," Floramel said when we entered. "Etta said you were looking for me. I hope I'm not about to have a startling accident."

Galina narrowed her eyes like a cat when you flick its ears.

In truth, the remark had surprised me as well. Floramel wasn't like she used to be. She wasn't as innocent about the dark ways of Earthlings. She obviously suspected what had happened to Bevan wasn't entirely straightforward.

"I only defend myself when I'm attacked," Galina said.

"Of course, Tribune. What can I help you with?"

Turov ran her eyes over the LIDAR equipment. "What are you doing in here?"

Floramel turned back toward the glowing screens. "It's quite surprising, but the science crew here has focused primarily on the crater walls—did you know that?"

"No, but it makes sense."

"Yes, to a degree. The crater walls are already disrupted, they're easy to dig into and full of water and minerals…"

"What is your point, Floramel?"

"My point is they never dug down into the depths of this crater—they've never focused all their beams downward to do a full scan of what's underneath this base."

"Are you doing that now?" Galina asked in a falsely sweet voice.

"Yes. My team has discovered that you've ordered the excavation work filled in. We're naturally curious about mysteries, so we decided to take a look at what we were missing. Do you know what we found? What our scanners have revealed?"

Galina compressed her lips. "I'm sure you're going to tell me."

"Look here."

Floramel swept a long arm toward the monitors, and our eyes followed the gesture. A blue, white and gray scan began to scroll by. There were lumps, a lot of them. They were shaped into rounded modules.

"Looks like eggs in an egg-carton," I said, staring at the image and scratching my chin.

"Well said, James," Floramel said. "We believe these are ancient bodies."

"Uh… what kind of bodies?"

"Not of men, clearly. See the spherical trunk, the numerous limbs?"

I squinted. I'd seen X-rays and the like before. They were always hard to make out for me.

"They're not men?" Galina asked. "What are they?"

Floramel turned slowly toward us. She had a device in her hand.

Instantly, Galina bared her teeth in rage. "That's a deep-link pick-up! Who are you spying for?"

Floramel pretended to be startled by the object in her hand. "Oh, so it is. I've been using this to transcribe all my findings. Everyone in the labs down at Central is very curious about the anomalies you've discovered on the Moon."

Galina's hand strayed to her gun again. I reached out a seemingly gentle hand and clamped onto her wrist. She couldn't draw her gun if she'd tried.

"Just tell us what they are, Floramel," I said.

She nodded, and she pointed back to the scans. "Six limbs. All with similar appendages. One bulbous body, with an equally bulbous head on top. These beings were soft, but they were also agile and intelligent."

"Wait a second," I said, staring. "You're not serious?"

"What, what?" Galina demanded in frustration.

I turned to her. "She's saying they're Mogwa. She's found a vast burial ground of Mogwa—dead soldiers, probably."

"That's exactly right, James," Floramel said, flashing me a smile. "Everyone down at the labs in Central is buzzing about this discovery."

9

"That giraffe-necked bitch!" Galina complained as we left the LIDAR center. "I should have gotten rid of her when I had the chance. How did I ever let you convince me to bring her back to life last year?"

"Uh…"

Galina stopped suddenly, and she whirled to face me. Her head was full of evil thoughts, I could tell. "She did something like this to you back then, didn't she? Something pissy and superior—no wonder you clubbed her to death."

"Clubbed? Look, Galina, I never—"

"Okay, okay. You threw a punch, maybe, and fractured her skull by accident—whatever. I don't want to hear about it. But I will say, after today, I can understand how you could have been brought to such a point of rage."

I rolled my eyes, deciding it was best just to change the topic. The truth was Etta had murdered Floramel, not me. I'd been universally blamed by everyone involved, however, partly because I'd never offered a good explanation. It was just one of those things parents got caught up in to protect their kids sometimes.

"She's planned it all carefully," Galina went on, half talking to herself. "Sure, I could have her killed in a dozen ways—but it wouldn't change the situation. She's alerted Central, and those lab-rat nerds will be frothing to come up here and investigate what we've found."

"Yeah... but aren't you the least bit curious yourself? I mean, a Skay ship and graveyard full of Mogwa? It's quite a story."

"It's a nightmare. A worst-case scenario for all of us."

"How so?"

"James, I know your brain doesn't always work right. But just try this one time, okay? Lay out for me what's likely to happen over the next month or two."

"Uh... more scientists will come up here from Central?"

"Right, good. Keep going. I'll ready a fire-extinguisher in case your head begins smoking."

I shrugged. "I don't know. They'll poke around, dig down to the Mogwa graveyard, maybe. They'll take pictures and samples."

"Right, right. And who will they tell about this?"

"Probably not the news grids. They'll want to keep it secret. But the Hegemony bigwigs will learn of it."

"Of course they will," she said. "The political animals always sniff out something new. What will they do?"

"Uh... they'll fight over who gets to examine the tech? Become legalistic over who owns what, and what we should tell the Galactics?"

There, she put her finger up into my face. "There you go. Finally. You have struck upon the problem."

"Huh...? What do we care who wins a turf war over a bunch of fossils?"

"No, you idiot! They'll tell the Mogwa! *Someone* will do it. Just as your stork-like ex-girlfriend blabbed to Central today, they'll tell others—nonhumans, I mean."

"Oh... I suppose that could happen. So what?"

"So... Imagine this, a long lost expedition of heroes has been discovered on Earth's back porch. The Skay seem to have been here, at war with Mogwa. What will happen if this news makes it to Trantor?"

"Hmm... they'll probably send out a delegation—of Nairbs."

"Exactly. And what will the Nairbs think of all this?"

"It will be some kind of violation. Some kind of permit will be missing, or maybe there will be salvage laws involved..."

My faced changed as I considered it. The Nairbs were a race of bureaucrats that served the Galactics. They were overzealous in every respect. No violation, technicality or harmless accident was too small to be blown out of proportion by them.

"They'll climb all over us and blame us for something…"

"Yes! Now you know why I shot Bevan."

To my surprise, I found myself nodding and following after that nasty little woman. I didn't like her methods, but she wasn't crazy like most people thought. She was crazy like a fox—a murderous she-fox, that is.

"What are we going to do now, Galina?"

She chewed on her lower lip. "I don't know yet. It might be that there's nothing we can do. This disaster might be something that can't be controlled."

"Uh… there's something else," I said.

"What?"

I showed her my tapper, which was buzzing in vibrate mode. There was an incoming message there from Floramel.

"A booty call?" Galina exclaimed, grabbing my arms with claw-like fingers. "I'll kill her. It's not even noon yet."

"No, no… she says she wants me to continue with the mission—to explore the inside of that cracked Skay."

"Fat chance of that. I'm your legion's commanding officer."

"Yeah, but… read this part."

I fingered my arm, scrolling down to the final sentences. Galina read the words there, and she began hissing something awful.

Praetor Drusus, a top dog among Earth's defense officers, had backed Floramel's request. I'd been ordered to go on this mission, under the personal guidance of Floramel herself.

Galina was quite unhappy about this development, of that I had little doubt.

"That vicious skinny witch!" she complained. "I'll get her for this!"

"No doubt you will, sir," I said in what I hoped was a comforting tone, but she didn't look comforted at all.

"And you!" she said, turning on me. "You're going down there to investigate—but you're not going to screw this one up. Drusus insists I can't rely on a single man. I'm to activate your best squad of commandos."

"Oh... like who?"

"I don't know what he means. That crowd of clowns and retards you always operate with, I suppose."

"Like... Carlos? Harris?"

"Yes, yes. Whatever. I've sent my approval in a text. Activate whoever you wish. They'll be placed under your command."

"But if I'm using the casting device—"

"We're talking about arrangements for *after* that step. You'll go down alone at first."

"But why bother to bring in a whole team if I've already checked it out?"

She rolled her eyes at me. "Think, McGill. If we're standing on top of a dead Skay and a Mogwa invasion force, you won't be able to scout all of that in one ten minute trip, will you?"

"I guess not..."

"No. The best you can do is find a safe place to set up gateway posts. They'll operate even through walls of star dust."

"Okay then... When do I go?"

She looked at me again, making an effort to focus her roving eyes. I could tell she was thinking hard, and most of it wasn't about me at all. "You'll go immediately. There's no time to waste. Make up your team roster, and then report down to the casting chamber for your first solo mission."

Sighing, I did as I was ordered. Things were not going in the direction I'd hoped at all. Instead of rekindling on the romantic Moon, my near future involved being kicked around and most likely killed a lot.

My list of commandos was short, and I kept it down to just assholes and essentials. The assholes on the list were people I didn't care to save from this vicious mission, which was most likely going to kill us more than once. The essential people were... well... essential. People I couldn't do a good job without.

Carlos was number one on my list, naturally. There'd never been born a bigger half-useful irritant than him. He would be my bio specialist, the team medic. Harris was my supporting officer. I couldn't very well take Barton or Leeson, they didn't deserve to be brought out of a nice furlough for such a cruel duty.

Cooper was an easy choice for my scout. He was a Ghost Specialist, and a good one—but he was also a smart-mouthed shirker.

When it came to my weapons man, the choice wasn't as easy. I didn't want to take Sargon. He was too friendly. Nope, I chose Washburn, a big dumb guy who'd never stopped talking about how cool he was since birth.

After that, the choices thinned out. Most of my heavy troopers were reasonable and law-abiding. Still, I manage to scroll through names and come up with seven more that fit the bill. All of them were gruff and unforgiving men and women.

The last spot in the team was reserved for possibly the most critical role: that of tech specialist. As we would be investigating alien hardware, I knew my techie would be even more important than usual to my mission success.

In the end, I was torn between Kivi and Natasha. Overall, Natasha had superior skills, but Kivi was more pleasant to be around...

Hmm... I *almost* chose Kivi, but in the end I sighed and tapped on Natasha Elkin's name. I felt bad doing it, but I consoled myself with the firm knowledge that she would be overjoyed. Death sentence or not, she'd have been angry if I'd chosen anyone else to go on this crazy safari of exploration.

Confirming the list twice, I transmitted it to Central. All the people on the list would be sent a notice, informing them they were reactivated and summoned immediately. In my mind, I could almost hear all the cursing going on down on Earth as those fateful texts were transmitted about a minute later.

With that done, I moved to my daughter's little death-chamber she'd set up. She looked up warily when I entered.

"I got the message," she said. "You're really going to go first? Again?"

"Yup."

"Daddy, listen. You can just send one of those flunkies you called up. I'll tell you what, I'll inject you with this."

She held up a dripping needle, which I eyed warily.

"Uh…"

"It's no big deal. A purgative, that's all. You'll throw up everywhere, and you'll run a fever for a few hours. After that, the team will have arrived. You can send whichever loser you wish at that point."

Etta seemed happy with herself and her scheme. The whole thing alarmed me. What kind of a daughter had I raised?

Of course, my mind was able to immediately answer that question. Etta had never been terribly civilized. She protected her own, and everyone else could damned well choke on it.

The needle in her hand dripped one more time. I stared at it like a man eyeing a snake.

"I'm going to go on the first jump," I told her. "Don't worry, I'm good at it."

She tossed the needle down into a metal tray where it clattered and bounced in the low Moon gravity.

"I knew you would say that. You're always playing the hero."

"I live up to my responsibilities… most of the time."

Sighing, she strapped me into her compact death-box, and I stretched out on the seat.

"Hey, this is pretty comfy. You sure I don't have to get naked or anything?"

"Not anymore. You can carry some minimal equipment, too."

"My suit? My rifle?"

"Both. Enjoy."

She strapped me down and started the reaction. As she did this, Floramel came into the chamber quietly. She watched the proceedings with interest, but without interrupting.

"Good luck, Daddy," Etta told me, and she threw the final switch.

The room dimmed then brightened. A blue, flashing light grew and grew. The flashing became faster and more intense every time it strobed on and off. I knew it was the casting field, building up energy.

Something unexpected and new happened next, however. It started as a burning white fire in my belly. This sizzling light expanded, seeming to crack loose from my guts. It shined through my suit, as if my body had turned to liquid fire.

I was screaming, I'm pretty sure, but it came out as hoarse grunts of pain and fear. I knew what that white light had to be. Before, when I'd been casted, I'd walked naked into a contained violent field like this one.

Now, with improvements made after years of study, these science pukes had managed to make the reaction start *inside* my own person. That way, I didn't have to walk into it—it formed inside me instead and grew outward to engulf my sad-sack body.

Floramel walked closer and stood beside Etta. Neither one spoke or shed a tear. But they didn't look happy about my torment. At least I had that going for me, I told myself.

The field engulfed me a moment later, and the universe vanished—or maybe I did. It was hard to tell the difference.

-10-

"What's his score?" asked a gruff voice.

"Don't have it yet," said a much softer, feminine voice. "He's not breathing on his own."

Alarm bells went off, drifting in my head. I felt hazy, distant—but I knew something had gone wrong.

I'd died, I guess. That much was clear. I knew the stink and sickness of a revived body, coming to life for its first time. It wasn't like being born, it was more like being Frankenstein's monster as he's shocked into life.

Dying wasn't the bad part. I'd expected to die down there, wherever I'd been cast into the crust of the Moon. The freaky part was I couldn't remember *how* I'd died. I was a blank. One minute, I'd been in that chair being eaten by a ball of white light—then I was here.

"I've got something now," said the girl. "Independent movement—looks like he's going to be okay."

"I need a score."

"Call it an eight. I'll go with that."

"Good enough. I'm off-shift. Get him dressed and up to the officer's deck for a debrief as soon as you can."

"Will do," said the sweet one.

I didn't recognize either of them. Permanent Moon base spacers, probably.

For a time, I struggled to breathe, to get my limbs moving. Another person came into the room and looked me over.

"That's him. I'd recognize that big lump of stupid anywhere."

Carlos. That had to be him. What was he doing here?

I opened my eyes a crack, but closed them again. The room was painfully bright. For a few seconds, I was drifting again. The sensation was almost pleasant.

Then I heard Carlos—I heard what he was telling the sweet-voiced girl. "...yes, yes, seriously. That's what they call him. That's what everybody calls him—especially the ladies."

"Leather-dick?" she asked. "Why would anyone call him that?"

"*Old* leather-dick," Carlos corrected her, "with emphasis on the *old*. Why that loving nickname? Well, first off he's been around for decades, dying and coming back like some kind of demented vampire."

"Really...?"

"As to the rest of it, I'm not entirely certain as to the history of the leather-dick nickname, but I'd guess it has something to do with his infamous promiscuity. He's a righteous goat around women, see. Some people say that's because he's undergone too many revives, and he's... well... a little nutso."

"Ah..."

By this time my hand, still shaking and dripping with slime, was reaching for his throat. With my eyes cracked open painfully, I could barely see his round-faced form, standing over me. He was probably ogling the bio-girl and grinning at her, not watching me.

To my surprise, my fingers made it to his throat, and I got a firm hold on him. I clamped down immediately, as he was a trained fighter. He hacked and slapped at my wrist, trying to break the hold. My fingers were rubbery, or he wouldn't have had a chance. As it was, there was a struggle to be had.

"Centurion?" the bio asked with her sweet voice. She didn't seem all that alarmed.

My eyes were still bleary, but I could detect a cute girl's voice right-off. It was a skill of mine.

"...urgh..." I said, or something to that effect.

49

"If you want to kill him now, it's a good time," she said quietly. "I'll run a private recycle and have him back at his post in an hour."

Carlos was growling, straining. Finally, he managed to get my long, thick fingers away from his windpipe. He stumbled away, choking and gasping.

"Uncalled for, McGill!" he wheezed. "Uncool!"

With a serious effort, I sat up and tried to stand. I swayed, and both Carlos and the bio-girl took a step back. No one offered to help me stay on my feet—people rarely did when I was in a murderous mood.

"Give me some clothes," I said.

Carlos grabbed a coverall and threw it at me. "I'm supposed to escort you up to the brass on the observation deck," he said. "Fortunately, I'm in a good mood. I won't report you for this assault, Centurion."

"Damn straight you won't," I told him, and I staggered by—brushing him out of the way.

As my vision was clearing up, I finally got a good look at the girl with the sweet voice. She looked as nice as she sounded, but I could tell she wasn't. She'd known Carlos was full of shit and been as ready to off him as I was.

I smiled at her, and she smiled back.

"Dawn?" I said, squinting to read her nametag.

"That's right, Centurion."

"What happened to me?"

Her smiled faltered. "I... I don't know. You were on some kind of mission. They say it went wrong—and you died."

"I figured out that much already. Thanks anyway—hey, what if I went to that little bar dug-out of the crater wall later tonight? Would you be interested in coming with me?"

I sensed motion off to my side. Carlos was undoubtedly making obscene warning gestures. I ignored him. His time would come.

"Well... maybe. Check back when my shift ends."

Nodding, I walked out.

Carlos followed along, grumbling. "You just had to do that, didn't you? Chicks like that always go for you—always. The sweetest, most innocent women can't wait to be defiled by—"

50

My hand clamped onto the back of his neck. He struggled a bit, but I was getting my strength back.

"Listen up Specialist Ortiz, unless you want to take the next ride on that casting couch the lab people have cooked up, you'd best shut the hell up."

That did the trick. Carlos seemed alarmed, and he actually shut up. Oh sure, he kept on muttering to himself about tyrants with leathery dicks all the way to the observatory, but I didn't mind. He'd gotten the message.

"What *did* happen to me?" I asked him as we approached a pressure door with an old-fashioned wheel lock in the center of it.

"No one knows. That's the real story. They sent you down there to what appeared to be an empty chamber—but you never came back. The casting machine lost contact with you—you were damned lucky they didn't just call it a day and declare you permed."

I nodded. "I'm kind of surprised they brought me back. They must have something else in mind for plan B. Oh, and by the way, why are you being a prick today?"

"What? About the leather-dick stuff? That was all in good fun."

"Sure, right… you're pissed because I volunteered you for this mission, aren't you?"

"No, no, why would I feel that way? I love the Moon. I love breathing my own farts in this helmet all day, and I look forward to my turn at the casting couch. I can't wait to be transported into solid rock."

Ditching Carlos at the door to the observation deck, I entered the meeting place alone. The wheel spun with a squeal, then it swung open on big hinges with a metal-on-metal groan. Inside, I followed a short airlock tube that led to the observatory itself.

The view was spectacular. Spread out on every side were perfect vistas of stark black and white. The surface of the Moon was down low, a glaring motionless expanse. The rugged crater walls stood farther out, like cliffs looming over a dead sea.

51

But it was the sky above me that took the prize. Overhead, the observatory was constructed with a perfectly clear crystalline dome. It looked like I was really out there, just standing on the Moon fully exposed to open space.

I gaped overhead, staring at a heaven full of fat stars.

Finally, a voice called to me.

"McGill?" Graves said in his gravelly tones. "Stop gawking and make your report."

When I brought my eyes back down from the heavens, I noticed the officers sitting in a circle around a glimmering desk. I walked over to them and slumped into a chair.

"Well?" Graves asked.

I eyed the group for a few seconds. Turov wasn't there, so that left Primus Graves in charge. The rest of them were Varus officers, all primus rank. I knew something about all of them, and from the disgusted looks on their faces I figured I wasn't going to be receiving any commendations for my valiant service. Not today.

"Not much to say," I told them, spinning around in my chair and gazing up at the spectacular sky again. "I got cast into the middle of the Moon and promptly died. I don't remember jack squat."

"The trace feedback we got suggests that you landed—but the casting device never synched up."

"Maybe the techs screwed up then?"

"Maybe… but it's never happened this way before. We couldn't even read your vitals. After the timer ran out, we had to make a hard call. By all rights, we should have declared you permed—but we didn't."

"Why not?"

Graves shrugged. "Because you were *probably* dead—and we needed a guinea pig. If your old self is still down there, puttering around, you'll know what to do the next time."

I brought my eyes down to the circle of faces again. "Uh… the next time?"

"That's right. Unless you want us to execute you right now and call it good, you've got to go back down there and discover what went wrong the first time."

"Outstanding," I said, slamming my palm down on the computer table hard enough to leave a dent in the aluminum bezel. "I don't like leaving missions half-done."

Graves smiled grimly at the others. "See? He's up for more. McGill almost always is."

"There's one tiny thing I'd like to ask for, however."

Graves' smile soured immediately, and he turned back to face me. "What's that, McGill?"

"Don't send me to the same spot. Send me down to the petrified Mogwa area instead."

"What good will that do? There's no critical tech there. It's more of a mass burial site than anything else."

"Right. But it has a story to tell. All mass graves do."

Graves looked like he was sniffing dog shit, but he didn't argue. "Go on."

"I think there's something wrong with the first LZ. Send me to a different spot. I'll make my report from there."

"Well... all right... what the hell. If you can at least prove the equipment is working right, we'll have made some progress."

"Thank you, sir. Uh... where did Tribune Turov go off to?"

"She said she was suddenly called away to Earth."

"I see... Did this summons come a few minutes after she found out my mission failed and I was buried in rock?"

Graves squirmed, just a little. "It might appear that way. But I'm sure Tribune Turov had good reasons—"

"—I'm sure she had *excellent* reasons, sir. The very best. Now then, when can I expect to enjoy another jaunt into the blue?"

Graves worked his tapper for a full minute before answering. "Tonight. Report back to the casting couch at around ten p.m. They'll be ready for you then."

I stood up, and so did Graves. With a startled glance at Graves, the rest of the lounging, primus-ranked officers did the same.

Graves saluted me sternly. "Thank you for your service McGill... in advance."

"I wouldn't miss it for the world, sir."

"Dismissed."

53

I left them then, and they fell back to jawing about budgets and security. They didn't seem to care much if I lived or died—but at least Graves knew what he was asking me to do.

-11-

Since I had a few hours left to live, I hunted down the adjunct bio named Dawn who'd revived me. She seemed surprised at first, but soon she was smiling. I talked her up then down again, and she finally let me take her to the only dive bar on the base.

"You like this stuff?" she asked, sipping her rocket fuel dubiously.

"It grows on you."

We talked, and we laughed, but we didn't have time for much else. Right about when I might have made a move, my tapper went off. The unwelcome craggy face of Primus Graves stared up at me from my forearm.

"The schedule has been updated, McGill. You're launching at 2100 hours. Get downstairs half an hour early to suit-up."

"What's the hurry, sir?"

"Central wants answers. We've got to get a valid report from the depths of that hellhole before morning."

"In that case, I'm your man!"

Looking up, I saw disappointment on Dawn's pretty face. I reached out a big gloved paw and put it over her tiny hand.

"Don't worry, I'll be back before you know it. We'll have breakfast—or lunch, maybe."

Her mouth smiled, but it flickered out. "Are you really going to smash yourself into Moon rocks again? That seems unfair. Can't they get another victim?"

"Don't even talk like that, girl. I don't want anyone else stealing my glory. Whatever is lurking under our feet right now, I want to see it first."

She laughed, and she kissed me.

Damn. I was really going to be missing out. I sure hoped I didn't get myself permed before I could find my way back to her.

Marching down to the casting chamber, I whistled a happy tune. Floramel was down there waiting, and Etta too. They both looked like pissed cats. Their arms were crossed and their chins lowered.

"Uh..." I said. "Is it time for me to plug in?"

"No," Floramel said. "It's time for your daughter to stop being an obstructionist."

"The circuits aren't clean. They aren't tested. We brought them up here in a hurry, fired a man off and killed him."

"He's right here, Etta. He's unharmed and ready to go again."

"My father's sanity notwithstanding, the system isn't... isn't... it's not safe yet. I have to run a full diagnostic, and that will take well into the morning. So—"

Floramel shook her head. "That's not how events are going to proceed. Etta, you are relieved of your duties until further notice. Now, exit the lab before I call for security."

"Whoa!" I said, stepping forward. "Ladies, ladies... let's not forget ourselves."

"We almost permed you last time, Dad," Etta said. "You don't want to know how close it was."

I heard a dangerous note in her voice. Only a father of a girl like Etta would recognize it. By Earth standards, she wasn't entirely right in the head. In fact, she'd already killed her boss Floramel once in the past. No one knew about that, but the truth worried me sometimes, late at night.

Sure, sure, I was a stone-cold killer myself. I'd killed all sorts of people—most of whom needed a good killing on a regular basis. But even a man like me doesn't want to see that kind of behavior in his own daughter. Somehow, I wanted her to be different than me.

My mind fast-forwarded through the tense words the two women were still spitting at each other. They were like alley-cats getting ready to throw down on the spot. I didn't think Floramel had any idea what she was getting into. Sure, she was technically in authority—but that didn't mean squat to any McGill when push came to shove.

"Hold on, hold on," I said. "I've got a solution that will please everyone."

Floramel glanced at me. "What's that?"

"This time, how about we don't try to cast me into the sphere through those stardust walls. Instead, you can airmail me to that other site, where you found the Mogwa graveyard."

They both blinked at me.

"Have you got approval for this change?"

I nodded. "Graves okayed it just a few hours ago."

They both looked dubious, but at least the yellow light of murder was fading in Etta's eyes.

"That wouldn't be as dangerous, would it?" I pressed. "See, if you send me to that relatively shallow destination, we'll be testing the equipment and making sure it's working. If the strange properties of this big ball we're all standing on are the cause of the trouble, we'll know it when things go right this time out."

"Going to the Mogwa ship wasn't even suggested in the briefing I attended earlier today," Floramel complained.

"Don't worry about that. Just check, I have approval from Graves."

I flicked the last few minutes of my conversation on the observation deck from my tapper to hers. She listened to it, then she looked up, surprised.

"I… I guess that changes things."

"Yes," Etta said, stepping closer to us both. "It's a great idea. I'll get the time I need to run diagnostics, and even if the machine does glitch—we'll be able to recover you. There's no reason to think the casting device won't get a good lock on your signal inside the Mogwa ship. It's only a few hundred meters down, and the rock is quite normal. You could go there safely with a teleport suit if you had to."

57

"There, see?" I asked, throwing my arms wide. "No need to fret! Let's get started."

I walked up to the device and began screwing with the straps and things. I whistled a cheerful tune while I did it.

Both the women watched me, then eyed one another stiffly for another minute or so. But soon they began moving and cooperating again. There was a frosty chill in the air, but at least I no longer believed Etta was plotting her next murder.

Floramel left eventually, and Etta slid a helmet over my head. It had more wires attached to it than an old-fashioned Christmas tree.

"You still don't have to do this, Dad," she complained.

"I surely do! Not only am I following orders, I *want* to go. Aren't you curious to find out what's really down there?"

She sighed and hooked me up. About twenty minutes later, Floramel came back and the two women watched me light up inside. My guts turned into a ball of plasma—or whatever the hell happened to a man when that infernal machine fired up— and I vanished into nothingness.

-12-

I have to admit, when I opened my squinched-shut eyes and realized I wasn't being shat out of a revival machine again, I was kind of surprised.

My breathing was loud in my ears. That's a normal thing in a spacesuit, but it seemed magnified. I realized after a second that the effect was due to the utter silence around me. I was in an underground tomb, after all.

Flipping on my suit lights, which I'd neglected to do before I jumped, I saw two pillars of bright light shine out of my chest plate.

Dust. Swirling gray dust, and darkness. A few odd shapes loomed.

I turned on more lights—every light I had, to be honest. I hadn't been down in the guts of the Moon for more than thirty seconds, but I was already feeling a little creeped out.

Turning this way and that, I bumped my helmet into something. It was the roof. Reaching up a gloved hand, I ran it over a smooth, curved surface. It looked like metal, but it was burnished with dark stains.

Had a fire stained the roof with black soot long ago? It seemed that it had.

Looking down at the strapped-in dead aliens, I did a slow scan, taking in everything. All around me were dusty, ash-covered lumps. The lumps were big, maybe the size of a small man or a large dog. I took a step to the nearest and brushed off the drifting gray stuff.

It really was ash, mostly. Underneath, I found a burnt body. The alien was a Mogwa, I could tell that in an instant.

Moving from mound to mound, I confirmed a dozen of them—then guessed there were a few hundred more in the chamber. They were all Mogwa troops. Some were burned, others intact. Either way, they were all long, long dead.

"What happened here?" I asked aloud. "And how did you poor boys manage to get yourselves buried in the crust of our Moon?"

The dead rarely answer our questions, and it was the same with these guys. They lay mute in their ash heaps. It was up to me to determine their fate.

"I'm assuming you ladies up at the base can hear me," I said as I walked around. "I'll give you a running report on what I find down here."

"We can hear you, McGill," Floramel's voice buzzed in my earpiece.

I almost jumped out of my skin. "Wow! That's new tech!"

"Just an improvement," she said. "The casting device holds a pathway open to your location after transmission. After years of experimentation, we've managed to make the communication link go both ways."

"Makes sense…" I said, relieved to know they could hear me. It made my survival much more likely. "Anyways, I'm walking among Mogwa soldiers. Dead ones. They're buried in ash. The strange thing is the roof of this ship—I'm assuming it's a ship, or a capsule of some kind—is curved and scorched. It seems like there's a big crease or dent down the middle of it."

"Try finding an exit."

I searched for maybe three long minutes. At last, I found a hatch I could open. Crawling out, I discovered a shocking thing: the Mogwa ship was lodged in the mouth of the Skay. It had been partially crushed, probably during an invasion attempt. The hatch I'd chosen led out to the vast, hollow interior.

I slid off the Mogwa ship's dented hull and stood next to it. Looking around, I realized I had to be walking around on the interior hull of the Skay.

The place was dark—really dark. It was near total blackness for dozens of kilometers. That, more than anything else, indicated to me that this Skay was well and truly dead.

"It's confirmed," I said. "This is a Skay, it has to be. I'm walking inverted—meaning the gravity is enough from the hull of the alien vessel to keep me adhered to it."

"So odd..." Etta said, speaking up for the first time. "It's strange to think our Moon has been a dead enemy wreck all these years. Imagine all the star-struck lovers who've looked up at the Moon and felt romantic. What a shock this will be when they find out."

"They aren't going to find out," Floramel said sharply. "Not unless Central wants them to."

The women finally fell quiet after that, so I had a look around.

"This Mogwa ship is kind of like a lifter, but somewhat smaller. It might hold three hundred soldiers, not a thousand like one of our landing vessels."

"Forget the ship. Look around at the Skay. Is there any sign that some of its subsystems could still be operational?"

"Uh... I doubt it. This thing has been buried here for thousands of years. Maybe millions."

"So far, our analysis places it at around ten to thirty thousand years of age."

"Thirty thousand, huh? Back far enough that we would have forgotten... Has it always been our Moon, or did this Skay crash into an older natural satellite, or what?"

"It seems likely that it did collide with Earth's original Moon, making it larger. The material from that smaller body has encrusted the Skay and perhaps other strikes from various asteroids and comets over time—"

"Wait a minute," I complained. "I thought our Moon was billions of years old. Scientists have always said that."

"Well..." Floramel said, hesitating.

"Dad," Etta said, "you should know by now that scientists always make up theories based on observable data, but it's largely guesswork. Not long ago, some of the best minds on Earth were convinced that the Moon would be so thickly covered in dust that the Apollo landers would sink into it like quicksand and vanish."

"Ha ha!"

Floramel cleared her throat, clearly unhappy with this turn of the conversation. "Let me point out that the clock is ticking, James. Also, I might add that Earth scientists aren't fools. Rocks returned to Earth were correctly dated to a billion years or so back—it was only the composition and original size of the Moon that was incorrectly calculated."

"I'll say," I said, and I checked my chronometer. I'd wasted a good eight minutes climbing around and yakking. "I'll have to find a convenient place to die soon…"

"No you don't—not yet," Etta said quickly. "We've updated our tech in that department, too. You've got at least half an hour."

I whooped. This version of McGill had some juice left in him.

Using some boot-jets I'd brought with me, I soared up into the dark heart of the Skay and did some pinging. There wasn't much light, and my suit lights couldn't shine for thousands of meters. But I did have some basic LIDAR gear that gave me a few pings of information.

"There's a large structure ahead, a few kilometers from the landing spot where we found the Mogwa ship. I'm going to go check that out."

After several minutes of skimming over the pitch-black surface, I came to a battlefield. There were Mogwa invaders and Skay defenders everywhere. Thousands of them were locked forever in violent embraces. The Skay creatures were similar to those I'd seen before back on Armor World, but with a flavor of their own.

These things resembled big bears with metal claws and cameras for eyes. They were constructs of flesh and metal, I knew. Every Skay created cyborgs designed to be as deadly as possible. Every individual Skay seemed to have its own version of such defensive creatures, unique to their own interior worlds.

"Looks like this was a full-scale invasion," I told the girls. "The Mogwa must have cracked open the Skay and gotten in somehow. They tried to storm the Skay's organs with ground troops—but I guess they failed to escape when it died around them."

"Yes..." Floramel answered, "the carnage looks terrific. Any signs of life?"

I snorted. "You just told me it's been thirty thousand years."

"Right, but machines like the Skay don't die easily."

Troubled, I soared onward over the battlefield. It was a strange, eerie sight to behold. A vast struggle with all the bodies still here, frozen in time and vacuum. They hadn't even rotted in many cases. The lack of air and the low temperatures had kept them looking fresh.

To my surprise, something came at me out of the hanging gloom. It looked like a wall at first—a vast wall of stacked grit. I hit the brakes hard, but almost slammed into it.

"Holy shit! I almost offed myself!"

"Careful, Daddy."

I skirted the wall for a bit, getting an inkling of what it was. Soon, I was certain.

"I've seen this kind of thing before. It's a Skay cooling tower."

"A what?" Floramel asked.

I described it to her, and she seemed intrigued. "You say you once did battle with a Skay inside such a cooling tower?"

"That's right."

"Why haven't I read that in a report?"

"It must be classified, or something."

Floramel snorted in irritation. The truth was, she had a high-level security clearance, but it didn't quite reach far enough to be privy to the secrets of the Skay.

Working from memory, I searched around the base of the tower. Soon, I found a crumpled hole. It was half caved-in due to the efforts of the Mogwa soldiers I'd been gliding above, but after climbing over them into a tunnel, I managed to get inside the tower.

Memories came flooding back as I slogged up and up through the spiraling tunnels. I felt puffs of air hit my spacesuit now and then—the Skay still held an atmosphere of sorts—but I kept on climbing.

"...McGill... interference... probably should... back soon."

"Uh..." I said, taking what I could from Floramel's transmission. "I'll kill myself real soon, I swear. I just want to see the CPU again."

"...doubtful... time allows... signal strength low."

"That's right, I'm doing just fine. Hold onto your panties, I'm almost there."

Soon, I came out into a wide open area. It was the center of the heat pipe that I'd been climbing through. I'd only seen such a place once before, and I hadn't made it out of that situation alive, either.

Down below me there wasn't any hot breath coming up in the way of a greeting. I'd been broadcasting, too, trying to get the Skay to wake up and talk to me. It hadn't made a peep so far.

The air was cold. I could feel it through my suit.

"Ah well. This thing is well and truly dead."

I opened my faceplate then. A frosty breath puffed down into my suit—or maybe the heat all left my suit, flowing out and mixing with the ancient frozen gasses of thirty thousand years past.

I'd braced myself for a big stink—but it didn't come. The centuries had changed the odor of the battlefield outside to a dead, neutral scent.

"I'm going to jump!" I broadcast. "Can you still hear me?"

There was no answer.

"Ladies?"

There was nothing. The thread signal they'd used to communicate with me had died completely.

Maybe I was out of time. Hopefully, they wouldn't get all persnickety and call me permed. Getting worried, I decided to hurry things up. It was time to die.

I stepped to the very edge of the cliff and teetered there for a second, looking down. Right then, I got the biggest shock of this McGill's brief lifetime.

A gloved hand came up over the edge of the cliff I was standing on, and it grabbed the ankle of my left boot. I don't mind telling you, it scared the bejesus out of me.

-13-

"James?" I asked, recognizing the glove.

It was mine.

A familiar face came into view. That old rat-bastard McGill, the previous incarnation, was laboriously climbing the cliff face.

"Hey," he said. "I wondered if it would be you. No breaks at all from the brass, huh?"

"None whatsoever. At least they didn't call me permed when you disappeared."

"Yeah... give me a hand up, will you?"

I hesitated. His gloved hand was reaching high, wavering. If I grabbed it, he could yank me right over and off the cliff.

Shrugging, I took his hand and hauled upward. If he wanted to pull me over the edge, well, so be it. I'd hold on and we'd both die. That would at least ensure there wouldn't be a third McGill born up on the Moon base, giving us further headaches in the future.

He didn't pull me down. Instead, he scrambled up to stand on the ledge beside me.

Panting, he nodded to me. "Thanks. You're all right for a McGill."

"So far, I feel the same way."

I think some people wouldn't get along with a copy of themselves. They'd just rub each other the wrong way. Two

Galinas, for example, or two Winslades—it just didn't bear thinking about.

"You got anything to eat?" McGill asked me.

I handed over the contents of my pockets. There wasn't much there. Some cough drops and a half-eaten sugar-bar. He took and ate them.

"I suppose eating some spit from my future self is harmless," he said, chewing methodically.

"I suppose."

After he'd finished his meal, we both sat down on the ledge. Our boots dangled over the edge.

"Did you find anything interesting down there?" I asked him.

"Not really. This Skay seems to be about as dead as they get. There are some automated systems still going—but nothing to indicate it can be brought back to life."

I checked my tapper and did some math. "What do we do now? The next McGill will be coming out of the oven any time now."

The other James shrugged. "I know. Seems like a big waste. I've been down here for twelve hours wasting time. I hung out here, because I knew you'd be coming—it was the first thing I thought to do, after all."

I nodded. If there was one person in the universe who could predict my next move, it was another James McGill.

"Want to do it together?" I asked.

He nodded, and we both got to our feet.

We didn't sing, or hold hands, or nothing like that. We just jumped at the same time. We hurtled down into the void. The stale dead air blasted up into my face, moving faster as we fell.

It was a long way down. Wanting to get it over with, I turned on my boot-jets, aiming head first for the bottom. Beside me, the other James did the same. I could see the flare of his jets, two blue plumes like mine, not far away.

We sailed down into utter blackness, speeding up every second, aiming into the unknown and yearning for a quick, painless death.

* * *

"McGill?" asked a sweet voice. "Is that really you? Again? Do you know that I haven't revived anyone all week except you—twice now?"

"…urble…" I said.

It was Dawn, and her voice released a flood of relief that coursed through me.

I'd made it back to life. Did she say it had only been twice? That news made me feel better, too. There was no third James McGill lurking.

"His signs are good," a male orderly said. "Should I get him off the table?"

"There's no hurry. Give him a second."

The orderly mumbled something.

"What's that?" Dawn said sharply.

"I said maybe I should leave you two alone."

"Fine then, get out."

He left with poor grace. I couldn't blame him for feeling jealous. Dawn was a hot little number.

When I could talk and sit up, I smiled at her. "I'm glad to be back. I didn't think I was going to make it."

"You weren't. They were arguing about leaving you permed, the last I heard, until that radiation blast went off. They figured no one could have survived that."

I blinked at her. "Uh… what radiation blast?"

"Were you already dead by then? That thing—that ship, or whatever is under our feet—it sent out a signal. It was a *strong* one. A single blast of radiation that was so strong it fried a lot of circuits all over the base."

I squinted and thought that over while she suggested various dinner plans. I said "uh-huh" until she stopped talking. Then I gave her a kiss on top of her head before I left, and I marched straight up to where Graves had been holding court on the observation deck.

But when I got there, I was in for a surprise. Graves was there all right, with his crowd of primus-ranked courtiers. Unfortunately, they were all stone dead.

68

Keying my tapper, I contacted Dawn. "Hey... you might want to check your revival queue again. Your break is over, girl."

She was quiet for a second, then she started cursing. "Our dinner date is off, McGill, sorry. Do you know how they all died?"

"Not for certain, but I've got some ideas..."

I walked over to the thin crystalline walls of the observation deck. I poked at them gently. They were solid enough, and good at keeping out stray cosmic rays. But apparently, the glass couldn't keep the blast of radiation that had been released by the Skay under our feet. It had fried all these officers while they sat in their chairs.

Borrowing a cup of coffee from the table circled by dead men, I sipped it gratefully. It was only lukewarm, but scavengers can't be choosy.

I waited around the observatory, poking at things and admiring the view. I managed to get a pretty good look at the computer data from the radiation blast, and I talked to Floramel about it. I showed her the circle of bodies, but she didn't seem overly impressed. She'd seen a lot of death in her day.

"Intriguing... we've been tracing the signal. It's not just a radio burst, nor just a gamma burst. It was more than that."

"Yeah? Like what?"

She looked up at me out of her tapper. She licked her lips and seemed uncertain. "It was a deep-link transmission too, James."

"What? You guys can trace those? I had no idea," I lied. Natasha and I had recently figured out deep-links could be traced, but we'd never managed to do anything with that information as yet.

"That's classified. Don't pass it on."

"How could I, when I barely understand how it works in the first place?"

"Good enough then... the trouble is, James, I did manage to find out where the radiation was targeted."

"Well girl," I said, "don't keep me in suspense any longer. Where did it go?"

"Toward the galactic center—toward the Core Worlds."

69

We looked at each other for a few seconds. "Uh…" I said. "Do you think it might actually be heard that far out?"

"Not the normal radiation. That will take millennia to travel the distance. In fact, I think they probably sent a signal like this out thousands of years ago. Without the deep-link element, however, it must still be on the way."

"How's that?" I asked, baffled.

"Our galaxy is about a hundred thousand lightyears across—you know that, right?"

"Sure do," I said with a confidence I didn't feel at all.

"Well, at this range away from the center, it would take about thirty thousand years for such a signal to get from here to the Core Worlds in normal space."

"Ah!" I said, catching on. "So, if the Skay sent out a signal before, it might be getting there right about now."

"That's what I'm thinking."

"Huh… that's wild. Anyways, what makes you think the Skay might have sent a message out before?"

"All those dead combatants around the central tower that you found made me think of it. What could have killed them? What could have killed them *all*, in the middle of a deadly struggle?"

"Uh…" I said, and my poor mind was a total blank for a few seconds. Then, I thought I had it. "A burst of radiation? Like the one I triggered? Like the one that fried poor Graves, here?"

"Exactly."

Floramel signed off, and I sipped another coffee. It had gone cold, but I didn't mind. I was thinking. Thinking hard.

Graves showed up about a half hour after I reported him dead. He walked in, and his mouth twisted up into an unpleasant snarl when he saw me.

"McGill? I might have known."

"Take a seat, sir. Oh wait… I'll just push the old Graves out of the way for you. Sorry about that."

He watched impatiently while I moved the corpse out of his chair. It was a longstanding rule of courtesy among legionnaires that a man shouldn't have to deal with his own

70

corpse. In Graves' case, however, I got the feeling he didn't care.

He sure didn't bother with the other bodies before he sat down and went to work on the battle computer embedded in the conference table. Whenever one of the other dead primus-types got in the way, he kicked over their chairs.

As it seemed like he was in a sour mood, I took it upon myself to tidy-up, loading the corpses on a floater and programming it to carry them down to Blue Deck. Dawn might not be happy to see that cart-load of death, but that was part of her job, after all.

"Did you kill me, McGill?" Graves asked after he'd reviewed all the reports and discovered that a burst of radiation had done the deed.

"Not on purpose, sir. I'll swear to that."

He didn't look at all happy with my answer. "Right... you did something that killed me and my entire staff. I would have you up on charges, but I don't think they would stick."

"Aw now, don't talk like that, Primus! It's embarrassing!"

"What?"

"Real legionnaires don't fret about who killed who. Not in an accidental situation, at least."

"You're right... if it *was* an accident."

There it was. Yellow suspicion filled his eyes. I swear, every time something went a little bit cock-eyed in this legion, everyone came looking for me.

"Wasn't me, sir," I said, crossing my chest. "Cross my heart and hope to die."

"You already did die—all of us did."

"Right... well, sir, if you don't need anything else, I'll be—"

"Sit your ass down. I just got Floramel's report about the signal, and its direction."

"Uh... oh... that."

I sat down with a sigh. We went over data and reports all over again. I tuned out all the boring details, as I already knew the important parts. The dead Skay had sent out some kind of urgent message. Probably, someone out there had heard that call for help.

Maybe they would come looking, or maybe they wouldn't. Either way, there wasn't a damned thing me or any of Graves' flunkies could do about it. To my way of thinking, we should all just have a beer and stop worrying about it. What was done was done.

But no, that's not how the brass ever looked at the universe of events. No, they had to jaw and complain and carry on for hours. In fact, by the time I was finally dismissed and sent packing, every one of Graves' seven dwarves were back at it, each having arrived about a half hour after the last one.

Each of them demanded to hear the whole story over again, which was pure torture for me. They all carried on and complained. What little of this I listened to eventually created a gray wave of sheer boredom between my ears.

-14-

A few days went by after the Skay sent out that fateful signal. Fortunately, the expedition team seemed so upset about the threat from the Core Worlds they mostly forgot about me.

I took this rare opportunity to goof off and made the most of it for a few days. Dawn and I had our second date, then a third one, and we were planning our fourth when an unwelcome interruption dashed our plans.

Galina Turov has a small fist, but she can hammer nails with it when she wants to. She gave the door to Dawn's tiny cabin three short thumps, then threw it wide open.

Startled, the two of us began pulling on clothing, and Dawn's face reddened. She was about to yell, but she recognized the rank insignia and swallowed instead.

"Tribune?" she asked in that sweet voice of hers. "Is something wrong?"

"Damned right something is wrong, and that overgrown ape in your bed is in the middle of it all, as always. Adjunct, take my advice: You should stay away from McGill. He's driven more officers insane than you've enchanted with those tiny boobs of yours."

Dawn pulled up her clothing a little higher. Her smart-cloth straps cinched over her bare skin by themselves.

"What can I do for you, Tribune?" I asked in a cheerful tone.

Galina gave me a shot of her death stare. "For starters, you can remove the tape and foil from your arm and report to duty, Centurion."

As I began peeling off the fresh cover I'd put over my tapper, Galina did a U-turn and stalked out the door.

Dawn watched me with big eyes. "You told me your arm was injured."

"And so it was, little lady. But it's all healed-up now. Protective bandages are miracle-workers, aren't they? I'll tell you what: I'll be right back after this is sorted out. Don't worry, and keep the bed warm for me."

Dawn looked a little put out, but she wasn't outright pissed. That's how sweet she was. She was a breath of fresh air after putting up with huffy Varus women for decades.

Stumping along down the passages, I followed Galina. She moved fast and never looked back at me. By the time we reached her office, my clothes had knit themselves together again.

"McGill," she said, waving me to a seat. "I want you to explain how you triggered Earth's possible extinction—yet again."

"That's a sheer exaggeration, sir. The worst we should expect would be an investigation party coming out from the Core Worlds. There's no way even the Galactics will blame us for this mess. After all, the Mogwa and the Skay fought here many centuries ago."

"It would seem that you're not up on current events, are you?" Galina asked. "Graves? Enlighten him."

"If you would refer to the memo of yesterday, 0500 hours, McGill."

"Uh…"

Graves looked at my tapper. I hadn't bothered to take the last of the tape off yet.

"That's a violation, soldier. You're not even on leave."

"Just a mistake," I assured him. "My tapper was growing a few crazy hairs, and it was itching something awful. The bio people suggested I—"

"Wrap it in tin foil?" Galina interrupted. " Is that what that girl told you to do? We will investigate. I'll have your little friend arrested, if it's true."

I glanced at her in alarm. From her behavior, I hadn't really gotten the idea she was jealous—but maybe I'd thought wrong.

"There's no need for that, sirs," I said, tearing the remainder of the foil and tape all off with a single, ripping sound. "See? It's only bleeding a little. It works fine!"

I poked at my sore arm and found the memo Graves was talking about. It flooded into my inbox along with about a thousand other messages, but I kept the things that came from Graves in a separate folder.

"The Chief Inspector of Province 921," I began reading aloud, "hereby informs the servile inhabitants of Earth that an investigatory commission has been dispatched from Trantor…"

I trailed off, as it got worse from there. I looked up at the two officers in alarm. "Nairbs? They're sending out a commission of Nairbs?"

"Oh yes, and that's not all," Galina said. "The Skay sent us another message, just today. That's why I was ordered to come back here from Earth. Somehow, the stink of this has been traced back to me personally. I don't like that, McGill. I don't like that at all."

"Uh…" I said, "I don't seem to have that one."

"It's top secret. Here, read it."

She flicked her hand over her tapper, transmitting the message in my direction. It was a violation to send me a secret document, but I wasn't going to report her.

I began reading again. Before I was halfway through, I slumped back into my uncomfortable seat.

"The Skay are coming too? We're talking about hosting two Galactic investigation teams?"

"That's right," Graves said. "They both want to learn what happened in every detail. The Mogwa are calling this a salvage situation—that means they want to steal the Skay ship and tear it down, spying on everything."

"And the Skay are calling their dead brother 'a missing citizen.'" Galina said. "They say they lost a soldier in an old war, and they want him returned."

"Ha! What are they going to do with our Moon? Take it out and bury the thing in space somewhere?"

"It's no laughing matter, McGill," Galina told me. "Think about it: if either one of these aliens gets their way, they'll be confiscating our Moon."

"Uh... that's bad."

"Yes, it is. No more tides on Earth. Losing our moon will disrupt our climate, maybe even our orbital path. The planet will probably survive, but it will be drastically altered in the process."

I stared at them. Right off, I could tell that neither one of them was joking.

"Damnation..." I said. "That *is* bad. Real bad."

"Yes, it is," Galina said. "Is there anything you could say or do that might be remotely helpful?"

"Hmm... I've got just one question: Why do you think they're making such a big stink out of this? I mean, I thought the Mogwa and the Skay had signed a treaty concerning Province 921."

"Treaties are meant to be broken, McGill," Graves said.

"Yeah, but... this could mean a whole new war between them."

"It may come to that," Galina said. "We shall see."

"How long do we have? Before the Nairbs get here, I mean?"

"The Nairbs?" Graves asked. "Don't you mean the Galactics themselves?"

"Oh well," I said, "I figure they might send a few representatives, but the Mogwa don't like to leave the center of the galaxy. They'll send the Nairbs to do most of the investigating."

Galina lit up the wall by running a finger across it. A map of the galaxy glowed into life. It only showed our local region, from the Orion Arm of the Milky Way to the center. Trantor, the Mogwa homeworld, was clearly marked in red like a gleaming eye.

Between the blue dot that was Earth and the gleaming eye that represented Trantor was a single contact. It shined with a golden hue. Galina tapped that fleck of gold. "This is the investigation team, as far as we can determine."

I whistled long and low. The golden dot was maybe a third of the way out toward Earth already.

"As you can see," Galina said, "we have only a few more days."

"Jeez… I had no idea our sensors were this good. A few years back, we could hardly tell what was coming at us."

Graves and Turov glanced at one another. Turov cleared her throat, and Graves turned toward me.

"That's an inappropriate observation, McGill," he said.

"Inappropriate? How so? It's as plain as day, Primus. Anyone with half a brain—"

"Anyone with half a brain would know when to shut up!" Galina interrupted.

I gawked at her for a moment in surprise, but then I nodded. "Right. Sorry. Hush-hush and all that. Don't worry, I'm not the kind of clod-hopper to go blabbing about us having illegal long-ranged sensors—leastwise, not in front of the Galactics."

"Good. You'll need to keep your brain turned on throughout the coming ordeal."

"Uh…" I said, eying her. I couldn't see how asking for a clarification could be considered "inappropriate" so I continued. "How am I involved in all this—exactly?"

"You're the only one who's actually been down there," Graves explained, "down inside the dead Skay, that is. You're our only witness, and Central has decided not to send anyone else inside after the debacle concerning the SOS signal you somehow triggered."

"You think they're going to want to talk to me then?"

"Absolutely. It's keeping me from sleeping at night."

"Huh…"

They fell to talking about strategies and what should and should not be said aloud during the investigation. I stopped listening after a while, as I found their ideas impractical.

I knew from long experience with the Nairbs and Mogwa that you couldn't really predict how such conversations were going to go. To do so was to risk getting surprised and tongue-tied. I preferred to wing-it—that was both a lifelong goal and a firmly held belief for me.

"McGill?" Graves barked at me.

"Huh?"

"What do you plan to tell them? We have to give them something, and now that you've heard our prepared statements, we'd like to hear yours, if it's not too much to ask."

I looked at them both. My lower jaw sagged open, but I snapped it shut again. For a few seconds I was a blank—but then I had it.

"I'm going to tell them about the pitched battle down there. The battle I saw was full of heroes from both sides, locked in combat for all time. I'm going to suggest that they make a memorial out of this hallowed ground—a place dedicated to the bravery of those long lost souls."

They blinked at me for a second, but Galina caught on first.

"You mean… to make our Moon some kind of monument? To their battle?"

"Exactly that, sirs."

They chewed that over for a few moments, and at last Galina nodded. "I like it. If they go for it, they won't try to steal our Moon."

"You've got the idea, Tribune."

The corners of her mouth tugged upward. It was almost a smile, almost an expression of hope, but it didn't last long. And as for Graves, I could tell he wasn't buying it at all.

"The Skay are machines. The Mogwa are heartless bastards. I'm not expecting much in the way of romantic notions from either of them—or from the Nairbs."

"We'll see, sir. We'll see."

-15-

The time passed quickly as the alien investigation team drew closer. Each day, Galina held a long meeting in her office. I was bored stupid during these events, but I couldn't think of a way to get out of them.

In the evenings, however, I found Dawn was very relaxing to spend time with. She wasn't like a legionnaire woman. Not at all. Not once, for example, did she attempt to murder me. It was like a breath of fresh sweet air just to share her company.

Galina, however, didn't seem to be as taken with the girl as I was. She kept coming up with reasons why I should be doing something else.

"McGill," she said out of my tapper, calling at ten-thirty one night. "I think we need you to come up to the observatory."

I sighed, and Dawn rolled her eyes. She and I were having a nice glass of wine together. I hated wine, but for Dawn I sipped and pretended.

"Uh... Tribune? Can't that wait until morning?"

Galina became instantly annoyed, no doubt divining my reasons for the delay. "No. Get up here now."

Shrugging, I gave Dawn a kiss goodbye and left her with her hands on her hips. Suddenly, she moved to the doorway and blocked my exit.

"Hold on," she said. "I know what this is. You're going to her, aren't you?"

"Uh... yeah. That's what she said."

Dawn narrowed her eyes. It was one of the first times I'd ever seen her with a pissed look on her face. Galina really was working her magic. Could that be intentional? I wasn't sure.

"I mean," she said, "I know about you and the tribune."

"Are you crazy? Don't go listening to rumors and idle gossip."

"Every woman in your legion told me about it. They made a point of it."

"Well... damn."

"So, it is true? Is she making up reasons to order you to the observation deck at midnight?"

"It's only about ten... and besides, lots of people go up there after hours. We did one night, remember?"

"People don't go up there anymore. Everyone is afraid after Graves and his team got fried."

I scratched at my ear. "Yeah, well... I've got to be going. If this meeting doesn't run too late, how about I come back here and—"

"Forget it."

That was that. I was all but kicked out of Dawn's apartment.

Annoyed and stomping my feet a little, I headed up to see what the hell was so damned important. To my surprise, Galina actually *did* have a reason to talk to me.

"The expedition is arriving early," she said, displaying their status.

I stared at the star maps, dumbfounded. "How did they jump like—what? Five thousand extra lightyears?"

"I don't know, but we've seen Galactics do this sort of thing now and then. Central suspects they have highways, of a sort. Something like our gateway posts, but larger, able to transmit an entire spaceship over great distances."

"Why don't they just set up posts like that out here in our province? They could be here in minutes instead of days."

Galina made a pffing sound. "Because such contrivances are expensive. There's nothing they want out here, nothing worth trading for. Who would bother to build infrastructure out to Earth? It would be like building a bridge from New York to Antarctica. Pointless and expensive."

"Oh…"

"Anyway, they will be here about lunchtime tomorrow. I want to go over our script with you one more time. You must have the limits of what you can say, and what you can't say, clearly in mind."

I groaned aloud.

She took out a scrap of plastic computer paper and shook it at me. I took the document and pecked at it with my finger. It scrolled and listed countless things. Overall, the list was almost insulting. For instance, I was to make no mention of having killed various Mogwa in the past—as if I was that stupid.

There were a few things, however, that stood out from the rest.

"This is mostly made up of things I can't say."

"Of course."

"Like… I can't talk about our casting device? Really?"

"No. Absolutely not. Imagine if there is another planet somewhere we are unaware of that has developed such technology. Perhaps they have a Galaxy-wide monopoly on it. Do you want to explain to Nairbs why we're indiscriminately violating their patent laws?"

"But we don't know of any such race."

"So what? For the Nairbs, ignorance of the law is no excuse."

"Yeah, but we're not ignorant of the law, we're ignorant as to whether someone else has invented such a system."

Galina rolled her eyes at me. Women did that a lot when they spoke to old James McGill.

"Listen," she said, "they don't care. There's nothing fair about it, naturally. They don't care about that, either."

I nodded, knowing she was right. I hadn't laid eyes on a Nairb in years, and I really wasn't looking forward to this occasion.

"Okay… So the story is we used LIDAR and a very accurate jumpsuit to get me into the Skay's mouth. That's all I know."

"Good. Let's move on to item forty-six."

The briefing went on like that until midnight. At that point, I began to get antsy. If I could slip away from my tribune, I might still be able to talk my way back into Dawn's place for the night.

But Turov was just getting started. I could tell she was full of energy, mostly out of desperation. The big bad Galactics were coming, and it was the last-minute cram session for our coming exam.

"Are you really falling asleep?" she demanded after a trip to the canteen downstairs.

"What? No, no," I lied.

"Here's a beer. Wake up."

I drank my beer, and I did perk up. We talked a bit more. Finally, she noticed I was stargazing again and not listening to her. She kicked me, and I grunted.

"I need more beer."

"You'll get none. You'll pass out if I give you another. I know you."

"It sure is a wonderful view. Too bad most of these Moonies are too scared to come up here anymore and enjoy it."

"Yes," she said softly, sitting nearby. "It is nice."

She was close. Within grabbing range. Frowning at her, I began to hold suspicions again. "Why is it just you and me up here?"

She shrugged and smiled. "Don't you like it that way?"

I stood up, aghast. "Dammit! I knew it! You're just jealous about Dawn fooling around with me."

"All right, fine," she snapped. "Get out of here. Go back to your childish tramp."

Muttering, I went downstairs. I gave Dawn a try, but she wouldn't open the door. It was about one-thirty a.m., so I couldn't really blame her.

I slept alone, and I slept angry. Galina had done it again. She'd made a play for me, and in doing so, she'd scooted another girl out of the way. She'd made sure I wasn't getting anywhere tonight.

I thought about storming over to her quarters and yelling at her—but I didn't dare. She was a tricksey woman. I knew if I went to her, she'd pout or walk around half-dressed or something. Knowing myself equally well, I realized I couldn't chance it.

With a final, irritated sigh, I fell asleep.

-16-

At something like four-thirty in the morning, the whole Moon base went crazy. The Nairbs had jumped closer to Earth again, and they were arriving *way* ahead of schedule.

"McGill!" Graves shouted through my tapper. "Get out of bed, man! They're here!"

My eyes snapped open. They were bloodshot and dazed—but I was awake in an instant.

They were here.

That could only mean one thing: the Galactics had come to town. But which ones, exactly, had arrived? I had no idea, but a visit from our alien overlords was never a good thing. It was always like the pope had decided to come to dinner, and you were passed out naked when he showed up.

I skipped my shower, figuring I'd smell like a dirty ape to any Galactic whether I scrubbed or not. Scrambling to get my suit on, I rushed out the doorway and down the passage beyond. Spacers dodged, cursing, when I charged right through them to get to the dockyard.

"There you are," Graves said, shaking his head like it was noon or something. "Always a day late and a dollar short, aren't you McGill?"

"That's my creedo, sir."

"Well, shut up and stand still. With any luck they won't even ask about you. Sateekas didn't come—neither did Xlur or any of the others we know of."

My lips clamped together tightly, keeping myself from blurting facts. Sateekas had been more or less deposed the last time he'd come out here as governor. Xlur, on the other hand... well, I'd permed him. I wasn't proud of it, but there it was. Not everyone knew or acknowledged that dangerous bit of history, so I tried to keep it as forgotten as possible.

Instead of a wobbly Mogwa, a pompous Nairb was the first thing to pop out of the docking chute. Like all his kind, he resembled a seal with partly transparent skin. You could see his organs in there, pumping and oozing around. It was just as disgusting as it sounds, too. He was essentially a green blob of snot.

As Tribune Galina Turov was our most senior officer present, she stepped forward to greet the Nairb. The slime-ball backed up and reared a little, as if alarmed by her approach.

"Hello Inspector," she said, sounding like she were greeting a long-lost friend. "So magnificent of you to come all the way out here from the Core Worlds. Province 921 is at your service."

The Nairb eyed her coldly. I don't think I'd ever seen them eye anyone in any other manner—except maybe when they'd been angry with me.

"You are the ape-creature labeled 'Turov?'"

"Yes, that's me. I'm sorry, but our full delegation isn't scheduled to arrive from Earth until tomorrow. You surprised us with the speed of your ships."

"That is by design, human. No inspector should arrive when expected. Violations are often covered up if the suspect is given advanced warning."

Turov blinked twice, but she managed to hold her hands clasped to her belly and her face was locked in a grin. "Of course, of course. Tell me, what can I do for you while we wait for the arrival of the Earth officials from Central?"

"Wait? There will be no waiting. These proceedings will commence immediately."

"But, ah, sir... I don't have the authority to—"

"I possess all required authority. Are you refusing to answer my questions?"

"Not at all, Inspector! Not at all!"

Whoa! This Nairb was loaded for bear. I was taken aback, and Galina was too, I could tell. I'd never seen one of these green pukes so angry right out of the gate. Usually, it took a half hour of talking to me to get them into such a state.

"My prosecution probe will wait for no one," the Nairb continued. "Any Earth official will suffice for my purposes—you're all equally guilty in any case."

"I was only suggesting that—"

"Cease offering suggestions. To save time, you can consider them all to be rejected in advance."

Turov blinked again. I could tell her hands, which were still clasped against her belly, were starting to squeeze together and press against her gut with tension. With an effort, she drew a breath and spoke again.

"In that case, Inspector, tell me what you wish me to do."

"Finally, you respond with proper subservience! Your reluctance to submit to my authority up until this moment has been noted, Turov. Although such behavior is technically not a crime, it is frowned upon, and it may distort my judgment if you don't discontinue your attempts at obfuscation."

As she hadn't been given a command yet, Galina just stood there staring and gulping in shallow breaths of air. I didn't envy her. I knew she had a temper, and she had to be visualizing a ritual slaughter of this nasty alien even now. The good Lord knew I was.

The Nairb humped forward a few slappy steps. Behind him, a couple more Nairb underlings followed. They looked around at us warily. Maybe they'd heard a few things about us vicious border-aliens.

"I am the new acting prefect of this Province," the Inspector said. "My Mogwa mistress is waiting in the ship until I've cleared some formalities."

Galina nodded, but she still didn't speak as no one had asked a question. Believe me, that's hard to do when you're tense. Just try it sometime.

"First question:" the Nairb said, "are any of the humans in this chamber armed? If so, this is unacceptable."

We glanced around at each other. We were pretty much all armed, naturally. We were military, after all.

"We can and will disarm all our personnel," Galina answered, "if it will make our new lord more comfortable."

"That will suffice. We will wait and observe."

Galina made frantic gestures to Graves and I. Stiffly and with plenty of shaking heads and big frowns, we all passed our service pistols out into the passageway and ditched them.

"Make sure you don't drop mine," I warned. "It's got a hair-trigger. I shaved it down some."

"That's against regs, McGill," Graves grumbled, but I ignored him.

When we were done, the Nairbs seemed somewhat more relaxed. I could have told him his newfound lack of concern was pointless. Nairbs had thin skins and even thinner skulls. Against any Nairb, my fist was as deadly a weapon as a gun.

"Excellent," the Nairb said. "Now, question two: is there a being here known as 'the McGill?'"

Turov winced noticeably. I, on the other hand, took in a deep breath and grinned. It was always nice to be recognized.

"I'm right here, Inspector sir!"

The Nairb swung his sensory organs around to face me. "Ah, yes of course. You're unnaturally large for the species. A mutant, I presume?"

"Some would say so, yes."

"Interesting… Lord Sateekas, former admiral and former governor of this province, requested that we seek you out. Now that your presence has been confirmed, I can continue."

"Let's hear it. I'm all ears."

The lead Nairb ruffled up like a pissed parrot and shook himself. "Impudence is rife in your behavior patterns already. This shall be an easy judgment."

"Uh…"

"You stand accused, human, of murder in the first degree. That is, murder which was premeditated and intentional."

"Murder? What? That's crazy talk!"

The Nairb sidled closer. His nose lifted higher, like a finger-sniffing dog. "You dare to deny your actions? That is a further crime, an implied perjury."

"No, no! I'm just confused. We humans are dumb, you know that, right?"

The Nairb stared at me. "Clarify your meaning, human."

"I was just baffled. I don't know about any murders I might have committed that could be coming back to bite me in the ass right now. Sure, I've shot down my share of aliens in combat zones—but as a soldier and an enforcer, that's my job."

"Is it your job to assassinate your rightfully appointed provincial governor?"

"Uh... no."

"Then let me ask you this directly: did you, or did you not murder Governor Xlur on Trantor?"

I was unable to answer right off. I opened my mouth, but hesitated. Nothing I could say right now sounded all that good—not even to me.

"Further," the Nairb went on, "as this act of murder was visited upon a member of a higher quality species, the scope of the crime and magnitude of the associated punishment is amplified. Your entire species, should you be found guilty, will share in experiencing justice as it is dispensed."

There was a buzzing that rose up from the circled group of humans. They'd been tense at first, but the more the Nairb kept talking about species-wide responsibility and shared guilt, the more their faces sagged.

"But... why? Why punish everyone?"

"Because they gave birth to you. When an insect from a hive attacks an innocent, you can't just destroy that single member—you'd never locate it, for one thing. No. Anyone meting out justice would dispense it liberally, eradicating the entirety of the dangerous nest."

"Oh yeah, I guess you're right about that..."

Galina seemed to be having some kind of a conniption at this point. "Inspector, please let me intervene and speak on the behalf of all humans. We don't accept McGill as a member of our species. In fact, we reject him. We abhor him and his grotesque behaviors. We—"

"Your statements are unhelpful. As members of his species, you all share guilt and all must stand trial at his side. In the scope of Galactic Law, you are all responsible for his actions."

Galina closed her eyes and gritted her teeth. I figured she was close to losing it, and we'd only just gotten started.

-17-

At this point, I got an idea. No wait, calling my random doodling thought an idea would be too grandiose. It was more of a vague notion than anything else—but it was all I had in my otherwise empty head, so I ran with it.

"Mr. Nairb, sir?" I began, "Mr. Nairb? Aren't we getting ahead of ourselves just a bit?"

"I hardly think so. Your long evasion of justice has led us with utter finality to this inevitable endpoint. I will confess I've spent too much of my lifetime on this case—the 'McGill Mysteries', as they are known in the Core Systems."

"You call my adventures the McGill Mysteries? Really? So, you're saying I'm famous all over the galaxy, aren't you? That's pretty cool!"

The Nairb seemed confused by my remarks. "While the ambient temperatures in this region of space are lower than in the Core, I fail to understand how the relative motion of molecules has anything to do—"

"Sorry, sorry, 'cool' is just an expression. Anyways, what I'm talking about is the critical find we've got right here on the Moon. We're standing on top of a dead Skay's corpse—you know about that, right?"

The Nairb ruffled himself up. "What you speak of is simply one more mystery layered upon all the others," he said officiously. "I will admit a single positive outcome, however. This fresh diplomatic crisis provided me with the authority and the budget to pursue your case all the way out here to the fringe provinces."

"Ah-ha!" I said, jabbing a finger at him. The Nairb ducked away, his floppy green head dodging my gesture. Maybe he'd heard a thing or two about me. "I get it now! Until this latest scandal blew up, no one cared enough to let you come out here to do your investigating. Is that it?"

"Essentially, yes. Now, let's get back to the proceedings—"

"Damn straight we will. You see, first off, the most important thing going on in this province is this here dead Skay. The McGill Mysteries are nothing in comparison."

"There is some truth to your statements. However, I'm in charge, and I've made a choice. I'm going to handle your depredations first, not—"

I waggled my finger at him. "Ah-ah-ah, hold on, Mr. Nairb. Think for a second: if you try and convict me, you'll have to execute me—hell, you might find yourself itching to kill everyone in this room!"

"That seems highly likely," the alien admitted.

"Well then, if we're all dead, how in the heck are you going to question us about your primary mission?"

The Nairb opened his nasty trap, but then he closed it again. He didn't say anything for a few seconds.

"You see there?" I asked him. "What you've gotten yourself into is a set of irrational priorities. It's real common when folks get all riled up about one small thing. They tend to forget about the rest of their jobs. You've got to keep your eye on the big picture, Mr. Nairb."

The Nairb twitched a little. "All right. You are correct— logic dictates that you must be questioned about the Skay's demise first."

"There you go. Have at it, boy, ask away."

"Firstly, what part did you play in this latest tragedy? Did you kill a Skay and hide its body inside this satellite?"

I sniffed and drummed my fingers on the table. Watching me, the Nairb shifted itself about quizzically.

"What are you doing, human? Is that finger-tapping some kind of code?"

I laughed. "No sir, I'm refusing to answer."

The Nairb stiffened and turned toward Turov. Good old Galina looked kind of upset—as in she appeared to need one of those spacer's diapers I'd heard so much about.

"Is this being under your command?" the inspector asked her.

"Nominally, yes, Inspector."

"Then command it to cooperate."

Galina turned toward me. "James, I don't know what your game is, but I hereby order you to confess your individual and entirely non-Earth-related criminal actions to the inspector."

I sniffed again, and lifted one hand to inspect my glove. It was frayed at the thumb, so I tucked in some of the threads. I took my time doing it, too.

"James…" Galina said, her voice taking on a hard and desperate edge. "Talk to the nice Nairb, please."

"Why should I?" I demanded. "I mean, I'm already as good as dead. What's my incentive to help this alien do anything?"

The Nairb shifted around and flapped his flippers in astonishment. "How grotesquely ill-mannered this beast is! How have you tolerated its continued existence up until this late date?"

"I ask myself that quite often," Galina said, and then she turned back to me. "Bargaining, eh? I see. Let me put it to you this way, McGill: You are a criminal. You must be punished—but maybe your punishment could be in some way lessened. Perhaps, just possibly, the nice inspector will ease up on the level of shared guilt involved here—"

"No!" interrupted the Nairb. "There will be no reduction in the punishment, or in the scope of the suffering!"

I threw my hands high. "You see?" I asked Galina. "What's the point? Why help this nasty green blob? We're screwed anyway. Let him figure out what happened to the Skay. Let him replicate all our research, and if he gets one iota wrong, let him explain that to his masters back on Trantor."

"What possible details—?" blurted the Nairb.

I rounded on him next. "This mess is all yours now, Mr. Nairb. It's your baby. You can blow us up, and then you can explain the dead Skay to your Mogwa overlords any way you want to."

91

"I don't find this scenario enticing."

"Neither do I." I went off into a rumbling laugh. "I'm sorry, it's rude to laugh at the misfortunes of others, but I'm thinking about all the burnings and beatings you're going to enjoy after we're gone. Just think what your underlings will say—if any of them survive, that is. 'What a fool. He took his best and only alibi and erased it. He might as well have killed and buried that Skay himself.'"

"Alibi? I think you're confused, human. I require no alibi. I'm not the guilty party here."

"You sure are! You were charged to come out here and investigate the dead Skay. That's *your* job, snot-bag! You're not supposed to be here for some personal witch-hunt. When they figure out you blew your mission to indulge yourself in vindictive fantasies, why, they'll fry you like bacon!"

The Nairb looked confused, but he also looked worried. I'd called his bluff, and he didn't know what to do.

The trouble with Galactics from the Core was their insufferable arrogance. They were accustomed to roll-over-and-play-dead type aliens. They usually ruled over everyone, and no one ever challenged them. Certainly no one lower on the food-chain than they were would dare. That all changed when they met up with one ornery human named McGill.

"Perhaps torment will alleviate this situation," the Nairb suggested. "After a taste of real punishment, you'll be induced to explain your role in harming this Skay, and confess your other sins. Afterward, as a reward, you will be provided with a clean, painless death. Are you amenable to this approach, creature?"

I crossed my arms and shook my head. "To be honest with you, I'm not that impressed by torture. I have to warn you, I've been tormented to death more times than I can count. You'll get nothing that way—except maybe some lying. I do like to do some lying, when I'm pressed to it."

The Nairb looked to Turov in alarm. "Is this true?"

She nodded. "That is definitely true."

"What an obstinate animal. What will entice you to cooperate, McGill-creature?"

At long last, my face broadened into a smile. The Nairb was coming around. He'd finally gotten the picture. He wasn't the one in charge—not until he got his investigation of the Skay all figured out.

I crooked my finger at him. "This way, Mr. Nairb. Come with me—and bring that delegation of barking seals with you. I'll show you all what we know and why we know it."

Suspicious, but also curious, the Nairbs waddled and humped their way after me. Galina followed along, looking no less reluctant than the Nairbs. She sidled up to me, passing the pack of aliens in the passages. This wasn't difficult to do, as they moved slower than a herd of fatties in a donut shop.

"McGill," she hissed when she got close. "What are you up to? You can't show them our casting device! It's not even legal!"

I paused and gazed down at her. "Do you want me to do it now, or later?"

"Do what?"

"Kill them. Kill them all. That's the only other option."

"No, damn you! I want you to make up some elaborate lie and get them to believe it."

"Hmm…" I said, starting to walk again. "That's not so easy. This Nairb knows me real well. You noticed that, didn't you? How can I get him to believe anything I say?"

"You're supposed to be some kind of masterful liar."

"That I am, but lying to a nasty critter like our dear Inspector, here, isn't so easy. He's naturally suspicious, and anything I say will be suspect."

"Well then, what are you doing? Why take them down to—?"

"Sir, I'm cooperating. He'll believe what he sees. It won't be me telling him, it will be his own eyes and ears—if they've got ears."

Utterly dissatisfied with my answers, Galina didn't seem to be able to come up with a better idea. What she did was step aside and make some very urgent calls on her tapper. In the meantime, I led the Nairb delegation down to the teleport room.

When we got there, I was in for a surprise. Some spacers were lifting and hauling away the casting couch, as I called it. In its place, they were setting up a pair of gateway posts. Etta herself was on the spot, fiddling with the posts and aligning them.

"Daddy? Are you going down there again?"

"I think so. Where do these posts lead to?"

"The guts of the Skay, you remember?"

"Uh… sure. But how did you get another set down there?"

She smiled. "Think about it. You can now carry objects with you while casting. We also have teleport suits, and valid coordinates to safe landing spots."

"Oh… so you sent some flunky down there to set up the posts?"

She stood up and flicked at her own teleport harness. I hadn't even noticed she'd had that on.

"Damnation, girl! Those things are dangerous.'"

"I made it back okay, Dad. We had all the recordings from your trip, and everything's dead down there. I wasn't in any danger. Now, let me calibrate these posts."

The Nairbs were squawking and circling around me by this time. I looked around, but I didn't see the governess they'd mentioned.

"Hey guys, did you forget to invite the lady Mogwa along? I figure she might like a look around in person."

"She's not a trusting individual. She's still waiting in her ship."

"Oh… well, her loss I guess. Let's get started."

The Nairbs barked and slapped the rock floor all around me. Their leader addressed me. "Human, what is the purpose of this delay?"

I pointed to Etta's gateway posts. "You see this gateway here? We're all going to take a look inside the Skay in person."

At this suggestion, the Nairbs reared up a little in alarm, reminding me of a herd of caterpillars. "Why would we consent to such a thing?"

"In order to be sure, of course. Are you really going to take my word for anything at this point? Of course not. I might be lying—and I probably am. But, if you can verify my story with your own personal orbs, you can rest assured it's true."

The flapping Nairbs circled around, sniffing, clicking and barking about the gateway in their own language.

"What are they saying?" I asked a translating girl.

"They're questioning their own sanity at trusting advanced human technology."

"Ah, right. Tell them we bought these on the open market."

It took a few minutes, plus a few demonstrations where I walked back and forth between the posts to show them I wasn't killed or nothing. Finally, their brave leader tried the posts. He came back humping through the posts again in a hurry.

"That is a most inhospitable environment!"

"Sure is. Now, if you'll kindly follow me, I'll give you boys the full nickel tour."

Still complaining and crowding around, they followed me into the gateway. One by one, their bodies vanished between the two glowing posts. Each transmission caused a flash of light and a crackling sound that always reminded me of one of those really big bug-zappers.

-18-

We'd made a few smart changes since my last foray into the depths of the Skay's guts. Instead of arriving at the Mogwa landing ship, for example, we arrived close to the cooling tower.

There, laid out around us by the thousands, were the dead and desiccated corpses of two armies. Both the Skay constructs and the Mogwa soldiers immediately captured the attention of the investigation team. They chattered and used instruments that I couldn't even identify to record and relay all their findings back to their ship.

I wondered who was receiving all that data. I rather suspected it was the Mogwa in charge. So far, she hadn't dared to show her nose among humans. That was extremely wise of her, and it spoke of a deep knowledge of me and my kind.

The Nairbs, on the other hand, soon lost their natural fear and disgust at being surrounded by two armies of the dead. They flapped and squawked, humping from one horrific scene of carnage to the next.

"Hey, uh..." I said. "If you don't mind my asking, what's so exciting, Inspector?"

The lead Nairb turned in my direction. "The nature of the find is unexpected. We'd understood there would be a dead Skay—but there are so many Mogwa here as well. That changes matters entirely."

"How so?"

"Initially, we'd planned to lay claim to this vessel on the basis of salvage rights. That would allow us to tow the ship to one of our home ports and dissect it in detail. Even though the ship is extremely old, the technological capabilities of the ship aren't all that different than those of a modern Skay. They rarely make technological advances."

"Why's that?"

"The Skay are inferior. They're AI-driven, and thus relatively unable to grasp the power of scientific method and advancement."

This statement amused me, but I didn't let on. To any human's way of thinking, the Nairbs and the Mogwa suffered from the same calcified approach to science. They were supremely confident in their traditions—and they'd turned technological development into one more tradition. Why experiment and find a better way to build a star-drive, for example, if you assume you'd already built the best possible? That was the attitude I saw over and over again among the Galactics.

"You're exactly right, Mr. Nairb," I said with finality. "The Skay are *totally* inferior. They should never be allowed to mount the throne of the Empire."

When I said this, it elicited a strange reaction. Every Nairb present, whether he was scanning with some strange device, or poking at a corpse, turned as one to look at me. They all fell silent, and they all stared.

"Human," the leader said, humping up to steps closer. "How is it that you're aware of the succession crisis at the Core?"

"What? Did you Nairbs think no one knows about that?" I laughed. "You can't go and have decades of civil wars without word getting around as to what all the fighting is about."

He narrowed his nasty eyes. "Who, exactly, informed you?"

"Uh... Xlur himself did, actually. He told me when I visited Trantor."

The Nairb seemed dumbfounded. "You accuse the dead of an act of treason... possibly, this could be construed as an additional crime. Slander on top of murder. Attempting to sully the name of your victim is an extenuating circumstance, and it must—"

"Hold on, hold on! *Someone* must have told me about the war, right. Xlur knew the facts himself, didn't he?"

"Of course."

"Well then, who else could have done it? Who else have I had contact with who might have spilled the beans?"

The Nairb looked baffled. That was good, as he was barking up a dangerous tree. The truth was that Grand Admiral Sateekas had told me the story, and I liked him. Of all the Mogwa I'd ever met, he was the only one I had any respect for. I certainly didn't want to get him into any trouble. We humans had done enough to ruin his life and career already.

"Upsetting…" the Nairb said finally. "Let's get back to the matter at hand. We're excited about these discoveries as they strengthen our case. The Skay lost a single member of their species, but the Mogwa have lost thousands of lives as well. The presence of their physical remains should sway the intergalactic courts in favor of the Mogwa."

"Because the hulk is on your property, and the Mogwa can call it a war memorial if they want to?"

"Precisely."

"Let me ask you something else, Mr. Nairb. Who runs these intergalactic courts? Are they fair and impartial?"

The Nairb drew himself up, lifting his nose a few centimeters higher. "Of course they're impartial. In this jurisdiction, they'll be operated by Nairbs such as myself. Only the most vaunted and aloof of my people achieve the great honor of becoming a district judge."

"Uh-huh," I said, unconvinced. In my limited knowledge of such things, judges were just like anyone else. They saw what they wanted to see. That said, a Nairb would probably be more impartial than your average human. They were very fussy creatures.

The group of Nairbs soon tired of the battlefield full of dead. They wanted to see more of the Skay. That's when I pointed out the big cooling tower.

"Right over there is our next stop. That's the CPU of this whole monster, buried under that miles-high tower."

With great excitement, they humped in my wake. I took big steps and led them up the path I'd traveled just the other day.

"Is this safe?" the Nairb leader asked me.

"Normally, it wouldn't be anything like safe," I admitted. "The Skay have these nasty guardian creatures, see—kind of like giant termites—that tend their towers. They'd attack us for being so close."

"Fascinating. This must be a critical center of the Skay's physiology. That's why the Mogwa were attempting to assail it when they all perished, isn't it?"

"Uh-huh, stands to reason. Now, watch your step, we're coming out to a big open area."

Slapping and barking all around me, the Nairbs were soon peering in every direction and running their scanners eagerly.

"You can see what a big benefit this find would be, right?" I asked. "So much tech, so much intel... just in case your masters ever have to fight the Skay again, that is."

Their eyes were yellow with greed. That's when I smiled, and I pretended to trip.

"Whoa!" I shouted, sliding off the edge. I reached out big hands and clung to the side of the cliff, right under their flippers. "The rim is so old, it crumbled under me! Quick, pull me back up!"

The Nairbs shuffled backward in unison. There wasn't a hero among them.

"You must save yourself, human. Even on this planetoid, your weight is too great for any of us to lift."

"Come on, come on!" I shouted, making a show of scrambling and ripping up chunks of the paper mache-like material the tower was made of. "Give me a hand, here!"

Not a one of them moved to help.

After grunting and scrabbling a little more, I pretended to lose my grip and fall. I screamed on the way down just to freak them out.

-19-

I awoke to the gentle stroking of kind, small fingers. It was Dawn, and she was whispering in my ear.

"How did you manage to get yourself killed again?" she asked.

"Some would say it's my best and only talent."

She sighed and helped me off the table. Soon, I was staggering through the Moon base. I hadn't been alive for more than a dozen minutes when my tapper buzzed again. It was Graves.

"McGill? Did you do it again?"

"Uh… yeah. I died, if that's what you mean."

"Not that, you crazy bastard. Did you set off the signal again?"

Slowly, a smile appeared on my face. "I might have, at that."

Graves had discovered the nature of my gamble. As the Nairbs had seemed dead-set on putting me on trial, well, I figured I owed them some payback—in advance. I'd decided to give the Nairbs a thought gift: one heinous death, no charge.

"Dammit, McGill. You can't go around killing whole parties of Nairbs!"

"I did nothing of the sort, Primus. The expedition was dangerous. I told them that at every turn. I also asked—no sir, I *begged* those green snot-bag bastards to pull me up to safety.

They refused. Whatever happened afterward, that was on them."

Graves sighed heavily. "The whole delegation was fried. They aren't happy about that—but oddly your presence is being requested again. Something you showed them seems to have piqued some interest."

"Yeah? Are they all revived again and freshened-up?"

"No, this time the Mogwa governor wants to talk to you personally."

"Is that so?"

A few minutes later, I found myself face-to-face with my very first lady-Mogwa. Unfortunately, she wasn't a pretty sight. In fact, she was kind of horrible to gaze upon, if the truth were to be told.

Mind you, there's never been a Mogwa hatched that was a looker. They were strange beings with six limbs that could be operated either as arms or legs. Like chimps, they could pick up objects with any of their feet-hand things that terminated their appendages. When they walked, it was with an odd, churning gait.

Toss in a half-dozen eyes, a bulbous black thorax and some body hair, and you didn't have yourself an elegant creature.

The Mogwa lady went a step further, however. She had a pouch on her belly. The thing squirmed a little now and then, and I thought maybe there was a mini-Mogwa in there. It was enough to make you want to retch.

But if I'm anything, I'm good at covering up reactions when I have to. I grinned at her like she was Miss Universe and bowed deeply when I came into her presence.

"Glorious Queen!" I said, belting out the words. "What can I, your humble servant, do for you?"

"You can stop getting my investigators killed for one thing," the Mogwa said in a harsh tone. "And don't call me Queen, either. I'm Nox, your rightful governor."

"Yes ma'am! Governor Nox it shall be, your worship. By the way, I'm truly sorry about your Nairbs. That was an accident. If they'd only helped pull me up—"

"Yes, yes, I know. I witnessed the farcical events remotely. Your fall triggered the same powerful beam that alerted us to the presence of this Skay in the first place. What triggered it the first time?"

"Uh…" I said. "I don't rightly know. Maybe when we breached the walls after so many years and started poking around—"

"All right, whatever. It hardly matters. The Nairbs are dead and good riddance to them. I'll be sorry when they're revived."

"Well then… what else can I do for you today?"

"You were summoned into my presence to confirm certain facts that I gathered while watching you speak with my slaves. Firstly, did you speak with Xlur personally, the former governor of this rogue province?"

"Yes sir, I certainly did on a number of occasions."

Nox looked me up and down, then nodded. "I can't see why he did it—but Xlur seems to have made a number of errors involving Earth. It's most peculiar."

"Let me take this moment to convey our heartfelt condolences concerning Xlur. We were distraught when we heard he'd taken his life. All of Earth mourned."

"Absurd. Mogwa do not take their own lives. Not even when faced with an infinite existence filled with pain and suffering. Xlur was murdered, plain and simple. The only question is: who did it?"

"Uh…"

Nox flapped a hand-thing at me. "Don't worry, human. I no longer share the bizarre paranoia of my Nairb investigators. I've behaved with an overabundance of caution since my arrival due to their silly warnings. After remotely witnessing all your interactions… I felt the fool. Not once did you perform a threatening act. Your only crimes thus far have been acts of boobish incompetence—but certainly your kind represent no danger to my person, or this commission."

I nodded, and I smiled. It was a real smile this time. All my efforts and chicanery had managed to convince this lady Mogwa she was safe around us. That was a start. A very good start.

"Governor Nox," I said, "do you think I murdered Xlur?"

She hesitated for a moment. "It seems unlikely. At this point, I'm starting to believe that another Mogwa did it—

blaming the crime upon you as you were on hand. Either that, or some outside force did the deed."

"Like a Skay agent, maybe?"

Nox laughed. "The Skay are too big to operate as agents of any kind. The idea is preposterous. Don't you think we'd notice a moon-sized figure lurking around Trantor?"

"Oh... no, that wasn't what I meant. I'm talking about a normal-sized agent. Perhaps from another race among their planets. Surely, they have handy humanoids that live as their slaves? Couldn't one of them be convinced to act on behalf of the Skay?"

Nox looked troubled. "What you say is possible... a grim thought. They might have advanced enough to possess such a spy network at this point in time. But why would they choose to kill Xlur?"

I told her then about the poison—the bio-terminator the Skay had been so anxious to get hold of. The truth was I'd sold it to them personally in order to buy peace—but I threw accusations and innuendo at everyone else I could think of to get her off that scent.

My tapper buzzed a few times while I was telling my tale, but I ignored it, giving my wrist a shake to disconnect.

"Disturbing," Nox said when I'd finished. "I'd heard about such a bio-agent, but I'd been told by Mogwa Defense that wasn't a serious concern... I'll have to look into its efficacy. Still, to get back to your point, human, such a motivation would be sufficient. I'm not sure how Xlur fits into the picture—other than being the highest authority here in this bestial province."

"That's exactly it!" I said. "Xlur was in charge when the poison was discovered and handed over to the Skay—whoever did it. He had to be involved in some way. I guess now that he's dead, we'll never know the truth."

Nox waggled several nasty fingers at me. "Not true! My army of Nairbs shall be thorough in the extreme. We'll get to the bottom of this mystery!"

"Excellent," I said, pretending to be happy. "One last thing, Governor? The Nairbs seemed so convinced I was guilty of countless crazy crimes. Things I could never even dream up on

103

my own. Is it possible that Earth could still serve you as your enforcers? We've done a bang-up job of protecting this province for decades, you know."

"I know no such thing. There's been nothing but warfare, strife and skullduggery out here at this lonely outpost."

I spread my hands widely. "It's the frontier, ma'am. Not the Core Worlds. Things are wilder out here."

Nox made a farting sound. I thought maybe she was sighing in defeat. "This is worse than I thought. I'd assumed it would be a punishment-post—but it's worse, far worse."

"Uh... might I ask why you were assigned here, my lady?"

"That's highly impertinent."

"Sorry, sorry. Curiosity got the better of me."

Nox eyed me for a moment. Most Mogwa I'd met were very reluctant to talk to slave-races much. But she seemed different. She seemed to like to gossip and complain about her place in the universe.

"I... I was assigned to mate with a warlord I didn't favor. He was from a low caste, an ugly old thing."

"Like Sateekas?"

"Worse. He wasn't even brave or competent. In any case, my refusal to award my attentions to an old fool put me into disfavor. When the next unpleasant post came up, it was dumped upon my person. The next thing I knew I was laden with the grim task of managing this flaming latrine of a province."

Her bitterness came through loud and clear. Managing our slice of space had always been a punishment among the Mogwa. It was like being assigned to a military base in Greenland or something.

For a few seconds, I considered asking her something else. I opened my mouth, then closed it again with a snap.

Unfortunately, she noticed this.

"What is it, human? What were you about to confess?"

"Uh... well ma'am, I couldn't help but noticing your pouch. Are you... uh... with offspring?"

"Rude in the extreme," she said, shuffling around so her pouch was barely visible. "But you are correct. I'm carrying a newborn."

"Ah! Congratulations! I'll make sure there's a celebration with cake and ice cream and—"

"Shut up. There will be no celebration. My child has been exiled, just as I have."

"Oh… sorry about that."

Nox heaved another long, farting sigh. Like all Earth's rulers, she was absorbed by self-pity. As far as I could tell, the Mogwa all preferred to live on their home planet, Trantor. Trillions of them lived there. Being assigned anywhere else meant you were a pariah.

Right then, my tapper started buzzing again. I ignored it, going so far as to put my hand over it. Whoever wanted my attention, they could damned-well wait a minute.

"All right, human," Nox said. "This interview is at an end. I've decided that your existence will continue as long as it is useful to me."

"That's very generous, ma'am!"

"Yes, it is. You owe this leniency to the urgings of a friend of mine: Grand Admiral Sateekas."

Suddenly, everything clicked in my mind. Sateekas! Of course!

He'd long since gone back to Trantor to retire, but he was too much of a wily old goat to leave well enough alone. He was probably still active in politics back home. Maybe when he'd found out that Nox was to be our new governor, he went to her and spoke a few kind words.

"We surely do miss Sateekas," I said truthfully. "He was a pleasure to serve under. He was, in my estimation, the bravest Mogwa I ever met."

Nox studied me for a moment. "Just so," she said. "Very well then, I will return to my ship. When the Nairbs are revived, I will inform them as to my decisions."

"Thank you, ma'am. I—"

Right then, none other than Tribune Galina Turov burst into the room. She had sticky hair, puffing breath, and a wild look in her eye.

"Tribune?" I asked. "Did you just come from the revival machine?"

"Yes, you imbecile. When that second blasting signal went off, I was in the observatory!"

"Ah-ah," I said, nodding toward Nox suggestively. "Let's not have a scene in front of our new lady. Let me introduce you to Governor Nox of Trantor."

Nox eyed Turov thoughtfully. She was a thinker, I could tell. Most Mogwa's were smart schemers. They weren't like humans. They didn't seem to have a working class of underlings. They were instead a broad society of smart, hard-working, struggling, self-pitying, heartless bastards.

"You are the superior officer here?" Nox asked.

"Yes," Galina said, controlling her breathing and her mood with difficulty. "I'm Tribune Turov."

"Ah, Turov... Of course. I've read of you in Xlur's reports."

Galina suddenly looked wary. "All good, I hope?"

"Not in the least. However, I was just about to retire to my ship. I've completed a stimulating conversation with the McGill, and I don't wish to spoil it with another less pleasant interaction."

"Ah then, please go and rest for now. We will all pray for your comfort." Galina said these words with bitter sarcasm, but I didn't think Nox picked up on that. She wasn't used to human inflexions yet.

Nox left us while we stood silently at attention. When she was gone, I whistled loud and long.

"That was intense," I said. "You're happy you missed it, I guarantee you."

Galina was breathing through her teeth. "Did you get me killed on purpose?"

"Uh... no. I had no idea you were lounging around in the observatory, sir. Last I knew, Graves liked to hang out up there."

"He did. But he wasn't happy about the place after you fried him a week ago. I took over the spot for its ascetic beauty."

"It sure has a pretty view."

She waved a finger in my face. "You have ruined it for me forever. In fact, I hate the Moon now. I was *burned*, James. I

106

felt it—I can remember it. It was like being trapped in a microwave."

"Oh... I'm sorry." I lifted a hand and put it on her shoulder in a comforting fashion, but she brushed me off.

"You dick, I'll never believe you didn't do that on purpose."

"Listen, Galina... I did get myself killed. I did set off the signal again—but I did all that to kill the Nairbs. I had no idea you would be hurt."

"Why did you do that?"

"I admitted to a few very interesting things while the governor listened. Then I decided it was time to get the Nairbs out of the way. Sure enough, the governor emerged from hiding, and I got to talk to her personally."

"Such scheming..."

I shrugged. "It's all good now. She's convinced I didn't kill Xlur. She's not going to punish Earth."

Galina's eyes searched mine. "You're doing it again, aren't you?"

"What?"

"You always do things like this, James. You killed everyone who got in your way, and then you romanced some nasty, pregnant alien! I'm disgusted!"

"She's not pregnant. That's a pouch, see. She's carrying a baby Mogwa in there."

Galina shuddered. "Whatever. I... I need a shower."

She stomped off, and I watched her go. She had a nice walk, even when she was on the Moon and angry. The thought of her in the shower got my mind to wandering.

Was she so pissed off because I'd upstaged her with the Mogwa? I wasn't sure. That was reasonable on the face of it, but there seemed to be something else. Something personal.

She was hurt, I think, because I was carrying on with Dawn instead of her. That didn't make any kind of sense, but I thought it was true.

Hmm. The situation was going to take some thinking about.

-20-

The next day I was walking around the Moon base like I owned the place. To my way of thinking, I pretty much did.

"McGill?" Adjunct Bevin asked me in a whisper when he found me at breakfast. "How do you do it?"

"Uh… do what?"

"Things like pissing on Galactics and getting away with it. Not to mention shagging half the chicks on every base you're assigned to—stuff like that."

"Whoa, whoa! First off, nobody has touched any Galactics. You forget all about that, and you should never speak of it again, okay?"

"Right, right, sorry. I'm sure it's some kind of crime to even utter such words."

"It sure as hell is. Secondly, I've only got one girlfriend on this base, and that's way less than half of the women on this big-ass moon."

Bevin twisted up his lips. "Come on, mate. Carlos has been talking to me. I know how you operate."

Carlos. Of course.

"Don't ever listen to that bitter, jealous little man. He's just mad because I, uh, I once interfered with one of the girls he liked."

"You mean Specialist Kivi, right? He told me all about that, too. I met her—what a hot package. I can hardly blame you for hitting on her."

I blinked at him. "Kivi is here? On base, you mean?"

"They all are. Your crew. The teleport squad you were supposed to invade the Skay with has finally arrived. I guess they won't be needed now. They'll probably send them back to Earth. Too bad, in Kivi's case."

I stood up and left my breakfast half-eaten.

"Cheers," Bevan said. The minute my back was turned, he stole my food and helped himself.

Hardly noticing, I went in search of my "crew" as Bevan called them. I found them below decks. They'd been given quarters in the least hospitable part of the facility—the basement they'd dug out when they'd originally found the Skay's hull.

"Here he comes at last," Harris said as I walked up to the group. A full squad sat dejectedly on a pile of emergency gear. It looked like they had a heated tent and few other amenities.

"Wow," I said. "I can scarcely credit my eyes. How did you ladies score these first class accommodations? Did you have to bribe the dock boys to put you up down here in the Moon dust?"

They all looked like they smelled a sewer. Perhaps they did—they'd been cooped up in their suits for a full day now.

"Centurion, sir," Harris said, "I was chosen to lead this sorry-ass platoon until you arrived. Now that you've decided to join us, I fully and gratefully relinquish my command—"

"Whoa! I'm not here to relieve you, Adjunct. I'm here to take stock of an operational asset. Are you all ready to march into combat in ten minutes flat?"

They looked around at one another. A few of them scratched at their suits, but that was pretty pointless. It was like trying to scratch an itch through a sleeping bag. These spacesuits were just too bulky.

"Not exactly, Centurion," Carlos said. "We've been kind of busy breathing our own farts since we got here."

I whirled around to face him. My eyes were wide and staring. "There you are, my favorite specialist. You'll be happy to know I've got a very unique duty for you to perform tonight, Ortiz."

Right off, Carlos looked worried.

Cooper laughed aloud, catching both our expressions. "Whip his ass, McGill! He's been as funny as a butt pimple since we got here."

"That's an accurate assessment, sir," Harris chimed in.

I could tell Carlos had been working hard to make friends from the very start. That was just his way. He'd never been killed without someone privately cheering when it happened.

Reluctantly, Carlos gathered his kit and followed my crooked finger. We walked out of the pit and up to a higher level of the base. At least it was clean up here, all metal instead of raw rock.

"Carlos, what is your frigging problem?" I asked him.

"What do you mean, sir?" he asked in a tone that told me he knew exactly what I was talking about—and he didn't care.

"You've been going around telling people stuff you shouldn't be talking about."

"What? Is your ego stung, McGill? All I did was warn a few innocent women. If that—"

I grabbed him and gave him a shake. He broke free, and we squared off.

"No, you idiot," I said. "I'm talking about mouthing off about Galactics. I just spent all frigging day getting our new Mogwa governor off our butts."

"What? You did? The governor is here? And you talked to him?"

I hesitated. "Yeah, I talked to the governor—and he's a she this time, by the way. I had to do it just right. They found out some things, see. Some things that went wrong back at the Core Worlds."

Carlos squinted at me. "You went to the Core Worlds?" he said, figuring things out immediately.

That was the trouble with trying to talk to Carlos. He wasn't as dumb as he seemed. Worse, he had a sixth sense when it came to lies, secrets and scandals. To top it all off, he had the biggest mouth in the legion.

"That doesn't matter," I told him. "The point is I can't have you talking to anyone about what you heard, or you think you heard. Forget all that stuff for the good of Earth."

"For the good of McGill, more like," he said, laughing. "But yeah, sure. I get it. You don't have to spell it out. You like your privacy. You like your free-wheeling ways with the ladies. As your humble specialist, I shouldn't get in the way of your happiness."

"Dammit, Carlos, just don't talk about dead aliens—not to anyone."

"No problem, Centurion..." he said, then he nudged me with his elbow. "But you have to tell me, did you nail her?"

"What? Who?"

"You know. I bet you had to get down on all fours to do it, didn't you? I bet you threw up afterwards, too. All that hair and those eyes looking everywhere at once. Gives me the creeps."

I blinked at him for a few seconds, then I noticed he was grinning and I got it.

"I didn't screw the Mogwa, Carlos. That's just sick."

He laughed. "I didn't think so, but then you had that funny look in your eye when you mentioned it was a lady Mogwa, and I began to wonder. Part of me said: 'yeah, sure, why wouldn't he? He's McGill after all.' But then, my rational brain rejected the idea. I mean, I know you're a goat, and all, but even—"

I grabbed him by the scruff of his spacer suit and gave him a shake. It wasn't much of a punishment, but he stopped talking. If he'd been out of that helmet, I might have punched him.

"You hear the crap coming out of your mouth right now? That's what I'm talking about! No more talking shit about aliens!"

Carlos grumbled, but he did finally shut up. I left him there and walked off in irritation. A moment later, I realized he was following me.

"Don't you have to go back to your platoon, Specialist?"

"Aw come on, McGill. It sucks down there. When those dogs at the docks saw we were a full combat unit, they ordered us to camp in the dirt under their precious base. It was like we weren't good enough to walk on their rattling ramps and sleep in aluminum modules dug into the side of a frigging crater. Oh

111

sure, they talked a good game about the overuse of their oxygen and state of their carbon dioxide scrubbers—"

"Whatever. Shut up and follow me."

Eagerly, Carlos trailed in my wake. "Where are we going?"

"The bar, I guess. I need a drink."

"Cool. If you want to get me drunk, I'll be easy tonight. I swear it."

That was Carlos in a nutshell. He was the most annoying asshole of a friend I'd ever had. Somehow, he'd never quite pushed me enough to ditch him, but I'd thought about it more than once.

We'd joined up together, enlisting in Legion Varus on the very same day. We'd also died our first times together—we were like brothers, in a way. No one else could figure out why I put up with all his shit, but it was due to our long history, I guess.

We had a few drinks down at the spacers' bar. Carlos became happy, then buzzed. He hit everything that even looked like it was a girl under that baggy spacesuit. I mulled over my beers, thinking hard.

Three females were on my mind tonight. Galina, Dawn... and Governor Nox. The last one was the most important.

Sure, I'd thrown her off the scent. She'd been talked into barking up various other trees instead of the one I was perched in.

But that Nairb of hers... her chief investigator. He'd made a career out of hunting me down. I knew he'd never give up. Never.

Along about five beers later, my tapper began to itch. I took a second to look down at it, and I realized it had been buzzing and filling with red messages.

I poked and swiped through the most recent of these, and Galina's face popped up. I grinned, immediately entertaining certain ideas. After all, when a lady calls a man relentlessly after quitting time... well sir, sometimes that can be a good thing.

One look at her panicky face melted my fantasies in a hurry. She wasn't hot and bothered—she was freaked out.

"Uh… what's wrong, sir?"

"McGill…? McGill… you did it again. You really are a moron."

"Huh?"

"The second message you triggered—it's been received. Another ship is coming out from the Core Systems."

"Yeah, so?"

"This time, James, it's one of the Skay…"

She said a bunch of other stuff, but I didn't listen to any of it. I just drank my beer and said "uh-huh" now and then.

Finally, at long last, I knew what Galina was upset about. The Skay weren't like the Mogwa—they were worse. A lot worse.

21

Governor Nox summoned Primus Graves, Tribune Turov and little old me to a meeting the next morning. To top it all off, we were ordered to meet on Nox's ship.

That was unusual. Most of the time, the Mogwa acted like humans were dirty animals. They didn't like to see us aboard their ships any more than a housewife wanted to see a herd of goats in her parlor.

Right off, we all suspected we were walking into an execution. Galina was fully convinced of this.

"It's the only thing that makes sense," she said. "We all know McGill is guilty of any sin any of us can imagine. So, they've been digging a little deeper, and they found something very ugly. Whatever it is—they've traced it back to him. To top that all off, we're both his immediate supervisors."

Graves perked up at this. "You think that's why we're tagging along? To suffer the same fate as McGill?"

"It seems likely, doesn't it?"

"That's a good thing then. If they keep the executions down to just McGill and the next two officers in his direct chain of command—well, we'll be getting off lucky."

"I don't call that good luck," she snapped. "Earth might, perhaps—but *I* don't."

"Ladies, ladies!" I said, putting up what I hoped were two big calming hands. "Let's not lose it just yet. Let's hear what our most excellent Governor Nox has to say."

114

They fell into a moody quiet, and we followed the lit arrows on the deck to a large chamber. Stepping inside, we found Lady Nox holding court with six Nairbs. These lesser beings were scattered around the base of her throne-like chair. None of their twitching noses were lifted higher than her six nasty-looking feet.

"Humans," Nox said, "we have unfortunate news."

"What's that, Governor?" I asked loudly.

Nox slid her eye-groups over me, then moved them to Galina.

"I was under the impression that you were in command here, Tribune."

"I am indeed."

"Very well. Tell your beasts to be silent until called upon."

"Gladly."

Galina turned and drew her sidearm. Nox shrank back a little, and the Nairbs squirmed.

"You were asked to leave all weapons behind!" the Nairb chattered.

But Galina aimed the pistol at me, not the Galactics. "McGill, be silent on pain of death."

I almost opened my big yap to say "yes sir," but I stopped myself with my mouth hanging wide.

Galina nodded in approval. "Excellent. You can be taught to take instructions—but only at the point of a gun. I shall remember this moment fondly."

She turned back to Nox and holstered her weapon. "What can we do for you, Governor?"

Nox relaxed a fraction. She eyed us the way a child might look at scorpions in a glass cage. "You are here to be instructed. There is another ship coming out from the Core Worlds."

I almost opened my big yap and said something like "we know all about that" or something equally improper. Fortunately, I was able to quell the impulse.

All of us stood there with stony faces. I was probably the only one who even twitched a little.

"Do you know anything about this ship?" Nox asked quietly.

Galina looked evasive. "We do now, your Excellency. Is there anything else you can tell us?"

Nox looked like a black widow as she crouched on her throne. Her eye groups scanned us carefully. Nox looked at us each in turn. She tilted her head toward the Nairb next. The Chief Inspector waddled forward a few centimeters.

"The enemy vessel is headed to the border of Province 921 and Province 926. This is a ceasefire line between the Mogwa and the Skay empires."

"Uh..." I said, not getting it at all. "Why the hell are they flying out there?"

Quick as a cat, Galina drew her pistol and put it against my temple. It seemed to me like she *wanted* to shoot.

Nox watched this with interest.

"He's spoken out of turn again, my Lady," Galina said. "Should I execute him?"

"It would be the sensible thing to do... unfortunately, I have plans for him. Taking drastic action now would upset them."

Galina nodded and she put her pistol away again.

I glanced down at her in alarm, but she didn't look me in the eye. There it was, a hostile attitude showing itself. It wasn't just my imagination. She was pissed off at me.

"To answer your poorly-timed question, McGill," Nox continued, "we've analyzed their target, and we believe there is reason for concern."

None of us said a thing. I didn't even move a muscle. I'd come to this meeting feeling kind of floaty after a half-dozen rocket-beers, but now that buzz was draining away. I was sad to feel it go.

"Explain it to them," Nox snapped at her top Nairb.

He lifted his snout high and addressed us. "The approaching Skay vessel is headed toward the 91 Aquarii star system. It's our belief they intend to create a border incident there. We've already laid claim in district court to this satellite—and they know it. Oddly, they have not bothered to do more than file a stay of judgment—that's an entirely illegitimate action, of course, but it will tie things up for quite some time and—"

"Get to the point, Inspector," Nox interrupted.

The Nairb ruffled himself before beginning again. "The point is that they're irritated and see it as in their best interests to push back in some way. The Skay are programmed to overcome all obstacles and to meet aggression with aggression. In this case, they see themselves losing something of value. Accordingly, they seek to make a claim of their own in the 91 Aquarii star system."

"How so, overlords?" Galina asked. "I'm not sure I understand how they can make the claim stick, if the system in question is clearly in Province 921."

"That's the problem," the Nairb continued. "Star systems move, you know. They travel at many thousands of kilometers an hour. Because of this, over the centuries, one system might move enough to legally be located in a different province."

"Ah..." Galina said. "So, the 91 Aquarii system borders their space?"

"It's worse than that, I'm afraid," Nox said, coming back into the conversation. "It's on the very edge. Half in, and half out of the two provinces. It is, in effect, transitioning into Skay territory."

"It is customary to wait until a star system has fully shifted to lay claim to it," the Nairb explained, "but we fear that in this instance the Skay will try to press ahead with an early claim— years before it would be appropriate."

Galina nodded, and she shrugged. "Well, that is a problem... but I don't understand why it would be so great a loss. After all, there are thousands of stars in our province. One more or less—"

"You seem profoundly unaware of the economics of your own home province," the Nairb interrupted. "Let me enlighten you: 91 Aquarii produces a product that you use quite frequently. I believe it's called a revival machine."

Galina stopped. For once, it was her mouth that hung wide. "Really? They're going to take an inhabited world? One with an invaluable trade good?"

"That's right," Nox said. "I see that you finally grasp the difficulty you're facing. If the Skay successfully press their claim, they'll own the local means of production of a critical piece of technology."

"Well... I guess we can still buy them—from the agents of the Skay."

Nox made some blatting sounds. I knew from long experience with the Mogwa that she was laughing at us.

"Not so, unfortunate slave. They are irked, as we said before. They have no use for revival machines themselves, being planet-sized machines. They'll probably cease production."

"They might even eradicate the factories on the planet in question, just to be difficult," the Nairb chimed in.

"That would be... terrible," Galina said with real feeling.

"Yes, most regrettable," Nox said. "Well then, if you've heard enough, I'll be leaving now. Our mission here is complete."

"But... Lady Nox! What about the enemy encroachment? Aren't the Mogwa going to challenge this intrusion? You said they were breaking with custom—"

Lady Nox appeared unconcerned. "It is unfortunate, but if we get to keep this hulk we're all standing on, it will be worth it."

"But what can we do? We can't let them take away our revival machines! Every legionnaire death would be... permanent."

Nox flipped a foot-hand at her in dismissal. "That's not our problem, is it? You've been informed, now please withdraw. I've completed my obligations here, and I wish to cast off as soon as possible. Good day, beasts."

Stunned, the three of us walked off the Mogwa ship. Each of us was thinking hard, but no one wanted to speak our thoughts aloud.

Not while the Mogwa might be listening.

118

22

"This is total *bullshit!*" Galina said, striding around the conference chamber in a fuming rage. "I won't stand for it. Even if I have to destroy that Skay by myself!"

I knew, of course, why she was in such a tizzy. She'd gotten very accustomed to her everlasting fountain of youth and beauty. Every five years or so, she made sure she died and came back to life as fresh as a daisy. There was probably no perk in heaven or earth she'd fight harder to keep.

"Permed..." Graves said thoughtfully. "Every death, a perming... That will change everything. All our training regimens would have to be reimagined, reworked. It will be a logistical nightmare at the very least."

Galina whirled on him. She had a crazy light in her eyes I knew too well. "That's all you can think about? Your frigging training routines?"

Graves shrugged. "We'll adjust. All militaries played under such rules in the past. We'll just have to relearn how to deal with permanent losses. We'll have to be more careful, that's all."

Galina went back to strutting around. I watched her body move with increasing interest. Somehow, when she was really pissed off, she seemed more sexy to me.

"I'm not going to get permed because some damned toaster-oven became miffed!" she raged. "We're going to go out there to fix things... somehow."

Finally, I perked up. She was talking about disobeying orders. Discussions like this, where other officers considered going off into the weeds, well sir, that was the sort of thing that got me out of bed in the morning.

"Uh... Tribune?"

"What is it, McGill?"

"I've got an idea."

She whirled around and looked me in the eyes. I could tell she was hungry, desperate for a solution.

I began to open my big mouth, but she put a hand up to stop me. Her eyes slid toward Graves.

"Primus, you are dismissed."

"Sir? Aren't we going to write up a report for Central about this—?"

"Go have your ears tested. You're *dismissed*."

Graves wasn't stupid. He glanced at me, then back at Turov. He shook his head and made a disgusted face—but he left without another comment. That was Graves for you. He didn't approve of shenanigans, but when he got a legal order, he followed it.

When he'd left, Galina came at me like a whirlwind. "You'd better not be bullshitting this time, McGill. This is *big*. This is no joke. This will ruin *everything*!"

"Don't I know it, Tribune. Just sit still and listen for a second."

Then I told her my plan. As I did so, her eyes widened, then narrowed again. After a while, she looked disturbed.

"I don't like it," she said.

"Why not? It's foolproof. You know she can do it—if we ask her."

Galina licked her lips and thought it over. "Okay. I'll brief Drusus. I'll mention it to him."

"Uh... with all due respect, sir, that Skay is on the way here. It will be parked in orbit in a week or so. We don't have much time."

She flashed her eyes at me. "Meaning?"

"Let me come along to help convince Drusus."

She heaved a sigh. "All right. Let's go."

Without another word to anyone, we left the conference room. Then we left the Moon base. Using some gateway posts, we headed down to Central as fast as we could.

A pack of hogs greeted us. We found ourselves in the midst of a puff-crete bunker. Several guns were aimed our way.

Turov stepped forward and shouted some orders at them. Once they'd figured out we were who we said we were, the guards lowered their weapons and escorted us to the elevators. We were pretty deep, several hundred floors under Earth's military headquarters.

"Why are they more jumpy at those gateway posts every time I come here?" Galina asked me once we were in the elevator.

"Uh… well sir, that might have something to do with me."

Over the years, I'd used the gateway station to get to Central in a hurry on a number of occasions. Drusus had even referred to this as a bad habit of mine. Often, during these unexpected visits, I became a little rough with the hogs that were posted there all day to greet travelers.

"Of course," Galina said. "You hate hogs, don't you?"

"Not all of them. Some hogs are just like regular people. Take that Bevan guy, for instance. He's not so bad once you get a beer or two in him."

She shook her head. After a few hundred floors went by, we made it up to where the top brass lived. We had to wait outside while Drusus held court with a dozen senior defense people. We were cooling our heels outside his office, under the nose of a disapproving staffer. Even the staffer was a tribune. Seemed weird to me, being so high-ranked and working as a secretary, but that was life in Hegemony for you.

"What do you think they're talking about in there?" I asked Galina in a harsh whisper.

She didn't answer. She just gave me a funny look, so I asked her again. "What's more important than Earth losing her revival machine supplier?"

Galina made a hand signal, but I still didn't get it.

"Huh?" I asked, scooting closer.

She repeated the gesture furiously. "This means: *shut the hell up*," she hissed at me.

I got the message at last, and we waited quietly until we were called upon. The flunky tribune escorted us into the big man's office, and I whistled right off, long and low.

"Damnation! Look what you've done with this place, Praetor! I stand impressed!"

The office had changed somewhat. It had always been kind of overly large and fancy if you asked me. A private air car that came down a shaft from the roof sat in the center of the room, as usual. There was a waiting area, a giant conference table, and a massive computer-desk.

But the newest item was a shrine of sorts. A whole row of statues all lined-up along the north wall. These statues were life-sized effigies of various aliens we'd encountered. There was a saurian, a Peg, a Nairb and even a Mogwa. Some of them, down at the end, I couldn't identify.

"Glad you like my new gallery, McGill. I find these statues give foreign visitors something to talk about. They always gravitate toward them and want to talk about them."

"Huh…"

I walked along the line, examining the statues with interest.

"I don't have much time for idle talk today, I'm afraid," Drusus said. "So, if you'll please come to the point of your visit, we'll try to cut this short."

"It is rather important, sir," Galina said. "James and I have just met with the Nairbs and the Mogwa governor of our province."

"I'm aware of that. I have a recording of the proceedings, in fact."

We both looked at him in surprise.

"Don't be alarmed, but you must realize that such high-level interactions must be monitored. The only reason you were allowed to have this appointment was because we don't have the end of it. We only have the beginning with the Nairbs and your first introduction to the Mogwa governor—Nox, I believe her name is?"

"That's right," I said. "You think she did something to mess up your recording?"

122

Drusus shrugged. "It's possible. Now, please fill me in, and be on your way. There's another Galactic citizen incoming from the Core systems, and we—"

"That's why we're here," Galina interrupted. "We know what it is, and what it wants."

We told him about the Skay that was incoming, and the fact it was headed for 91 Aquarii, not Earth. This was immediately troubling to Drusus.

"That makes a lot of sense..." he said. "We've been puzzling over the Skay's flight path for hours. Thanks for answering that one. But, why would such an advanced power be interested in 91 Aquarii?"

"Because they wish to claim the star system," Galina explained.

"What?"

We relayed the details of the situation, and he became ever more worried. After a few minutes, all of Drusus' confidence and brusque attitude had vanished.

"They're going to *claim* 91 Aquarii? Where our revival machines are manufactured? Who would license the technology to us in such a case?"

I shrugged. "Either the Skay... or no one. Most likely no one. Maybe we could petition and get one of our worlds on it."

Drusus bared his teeth. "We've tried to duplicate the science here—just in case. The lab people here at Central have worked on the project. Unfortunately, they've failed miserably. There are some elements that are beyond our science. The odd thing is that the 91 Aquarii inhabitants themselves don't seem to be all that sophisticated. As I understand it, they lead a violent, nomadic lifestyle."

Having never been out there to that particular border of our province, I knew nothing about it. But that fact didn't keep me from shooting off my mouth as usual.

"You've got nothing to worry about, Praetor sir. Just pack up old Legion Varus, and send us on our way."

"What the hell are you going to do out there? Fight the Skay?"

"Uh… well… probably not that. We've got a truce going with them. But, maybe we could do some negotiating for Earth."

Drusus laughed. "When it comes to diplomacy, Legion Varus wouldn't be my first pick, McGill. Sure, you've been involved in more first contact situations than I care to admit. But this would take a delicate touch."

"We had another thought…" I said, glancing at Galina.

She nodded to me. Drusus watched this interchange with interest.

"There is another option, sir," I said.

"Out with it. What have you two cooked up?"

"Maybe we could… uh… *trade* for the revival machines. On the black market, so to speak."

Drusus opened his mouth to tell me I was crazy, that there was no magical supply of revival machines handy. But then he thought the better of it and closed his mouth again. He put his hands behind his back and walked around, pacing.

"You're talking about the Clavers, aren't you? We know they have a supply of revival machines from somewhere. No one else in our province does, to the best of our knowledge."

I nodded seriously. "That's right. We figured that if one supply dries up, well sir, you've got to find a new supplier."

"Even if you were recently at war with that same shady, illegitimate merchant?"

"Even then. It's all a matter of desperation, sir. How much do we want these machines?"

Drusus nodded and massaged his chin. "All right. We're going to take a shotgun approach here. There isn't much time before the Skay arrives. Turov, you'll load up your legion within twelve hours. You'll fly to 91 Aquarii, and you'll see what can be done."

"Twelve hours' notice? The standard is forty-eight, sir."

"Yes. Rush it. If you can't scrape them all together, leave some behind. Take a set of gateway posts. We'll transmit them to you en route."

She nodded appreciatively. "I won't let you down, sir."

Drusus looked at me next. "Can you contact the Clavers, McGill? We've… well… we've lost them."

"I thought we cut a deal with them way back. Didn't we normalize our relations after the war?"

"Theoretically, yes. But the contracts didn't go through at the Hegemony Council. Apparently, there were political problems."

"Hurt feelings over the various invasions and such-like? That's petty, but I guess I shouldn't expect better from a pack of hog bureaucrats."

"In any case, do you think you can find them?"

"I'll give it a try, sir—but I'll need access to a deep-link rig. Full access, no restrictions."

Drusus studied me through narrowed eyes. I didn't think he entirely liked what he was seeing, but he nodded at last. "All right. Do what you have to do. Pursue all avenues. We've got a few more tricks up our sleeves back here at Central, too."

"Uh… any chance you'll be informing us about those along the way?"

"None whatsoever."

I nodded, unsurprised. "All right, sir. Looks like we've got to saddle-up and ride to 91 Aquarii."

"Godspeed."

That was it. We got the bum's rush out of his office, and we soon began working our tappers, contacting key personnel.

Legion Varus was mustering out again, and we were doing it as fast as we could.

23

Eleven hours later, we pulled out of orbit on a new ship.

A few years back, we'd been assigned the battlecruiser *Berlin* as our legion's transport. That had been kind of cool, flying on a warship, but *Berlin* couldn't hold our full complement of troops. The ship had always felt cramped, and it had a general lack of amenities.

Finally, after years of wrangling about budgets, Legion Varus had been assigned a truly worthy vessel. *Dominus* was similar to our original ship *Legate*—but it was better.

Dominus was what the Fleet pukes referred to as a force-projection transport, whatever that meant. In practice, she was a flying space station. She had sufficient cargo space to hold our entire legion, plus a supporting legion of Blood-Worlders—but that was just the beginning.

The improvements were many. *Dominus* was faster, bigger, more comfortable and chock-full of weaponry. She had not only one set of broadsides, but two. There were thirty-two fusion cannons in all, half of them mounted on each side of the vessel. She also had an array of missile pods and six small mass-drivers for point-defense.

What really impressed me, however, was the fighter bay. She carried six honest-to-God squadrons of heavy fighters to go along for the ride.

I whistled long and low when I first laid eyes on her. "Damnation! I'll eat my cap if this ship isn't the best-looking monstrosity of titanium I've ever seen!"

Galina, riding with me on a lifter loaded with troops, eyed *Dominus* as we approached her glorious belly. "She is quite striking. She's a super-ship worthy of her name."

After we docked and boarded, we counted heads. Less than half of Legion Varus' full complement of troops was aboard. As it had turned out, mustering up thousands of troops took longer than twelve hours.

Those who had made it aboard were marveling at the ship. I received compliments from everyone, even Carlos.

"Buddy, I don't know who you had to blow to get this rig—and I don't want to know. But whoever it was, rest assured, it was worth it."

"She's a beaut all right," I said good-naturedly, knowing he meant well.

Dominus got underway just after midnight. Even the act of shipping out was an experience. The ship kind of thrummed when she pulled out of orbit. You could just feel the power coming right through the deck plates, vibrating your feet inside your boots.

Galina invited me to a late dinner after that, as neither of us had had a chance to eat much. After accepting her invite with a tap of one finger, I whistled as I went to her cabin. I don't mind telling you, I was in high spirits. I'd even begun to entertain certain ideas… but she wasn't there.

As I hammered on her door, my tapper buzzed again, and she smiled up at me. "You didn't read my entire message, did you?"

"Uh…"

"Come down to Green Deck. The forest isn't fully grown out yet, but I ordered the engineers to let me in anyway."

Shrugging, I high-tailed it down to Green Deck. Every transport ship had such a zone, a place that served as both an exercise chamber in the day hours, and a recreation area by night. Back on *Berlin*, there hadn't been any room for such an extravagance. Here aboard *Dominus*, however, there was more than enough space.

I found the big doors of the number seven portal wide open when I arrived. The cool green world inside was lit only by fake starlight and the occasional phosphorescent mushroom. I walked inside and raised my hands to my mouth, cupping them to bellow for Galina.

A tiny hand touched my elbow.

I spun around, one hand going to my pistol—but I paused. There she was, smiling up at me.

"Always ready to kill at a moment's notice, hmm?"

"Absolutely."

"Come on, I've brought us a basket."

I followed her into the gloom. The big doors with a giant seven painted on them swung shut with a clang. We were all alone on a brand new Green Deck.

"The trees aren't fully grown yet," I said, looking around. "The tallest is no more than five meters high."

"Yes. It will take another few days for them to reach maturity."

For the sake of our human psyche, the Green Deck was bioengineered to grow lush but hollow plants of every variety. As the forest was often damaged, the rate of growth had been accelerated. You could actually *hear* the genetically enhanced plants rustling as they nudged taller every few minutes. The trees were really stalks of feral grasses, designed to grow at unheard of speeds. Pipes pumped liquids up from the deck underneath a thin coating of soil, feeding the growths a continuous ooze of water and nutrients.

We walked to the best spot in the park-like chamber. It was a forested area surrounding what amounted to a rocky swimming hole. Galina led me to a boulder near a waterfall and opened up her basket. I reached out to dig in, but she slapped my paws away.

The first thing she pulled out of the basket was a bottle of sparkling wine. We poured it into cups. She sipped while I gulped.

"This is lovely, isn't it?" she asked. "So much better than that dusty old Moon—or that cramped warship, *Berlin*."

"You've got that right."

She finally handed me half a roasted chicken. I started chewing immediately, as I really was hungry. She stuck to the wine.

"James," she said, "let's say for the sake of argument that we can't stop the Skay."

"Uh-huh." I said, chomping and plucking bones out of my mouth.

"Just how do you plan to contact the Clavers? I mean, no one else can do that, you know? We're underway aboard a transport at this point. How do you plan to reach them...?"

I licked a few greasy fingers before answering. "Don't worry about that. I'll get ahold of them. You'll see."

As my hand reached into the picnic basket for the other half of the chicken, she snapped it closed on me.

"Not good enough," she said. "How are you going to do it?"

I glanced up in surprise. "Is this idle curiosity, or...?"

"James, I *really* want to secure a reliable supply of revival machines. I don't want to be left dead or old or anything horrible like that. This is important to me, and I want to hear the details."

"Oh... right. Well, don't worry. I'm planning out some special engineering tricks. When the time comes, I'll reach out and find a Claver. It can't be that hard!"

She squinted at me. "Why are you being so evasive? Can it be that you're still secretly in touch with that bitch, Abigail? I should have known."

"Uh..."

"She's an evil woman, McGill. You should steer clear of her kind."

"Don't I know it," I mumbled, but Galina didn't seem to get my meaning.

Galina's eyes were glittering dangerously. She was looking around at the fake forest and the fake stars. Suddenly, those eyes landed on me again. "Call her right now. I want to see you do it. If you're bluffing, I'm going to have to pursue other options."

"Oh... well... I can't really do that right now. Give me a few days."

I was stalling, and we both knew it. The trouble was, I couldn't contact Abigail any more than Galina could. I couldn't get in touch with any of the Clavers using my tapper, and I didn't have Abigail's deep-link ID to send a ping out to her, even if I did have the gear. All along, my plan had been to get Natasha to help me with all those messy technical details.

Galina glared at me. Her mind was churning. At last, she sat back and nodded. "Okay. I get it. You don't want me around when you talk to that little witch. I get it."

"Uh… hold on, Tribune—"

"No, no. Don't play me for the fool. Our picnic in heaven is done."

She stood up and walked away, taking her basket with her. Grumbling, I followed her. All fantasies of enjoying the rest of the evening with her had been banished from my mind in an instant.

-24-

The next day I was in a bad mood. I got up early, around 0530, and rousted my troops for a hard day of physical training.

"PT already?" Carlos complained as he staggered out of his module. "We just got aboard this monster ship. I haven't even explored the observation deck, or the squash courts, or—"

"Shut up and fall in. Harris!"

Adjunct Harris trotted up and glowered at Carlos. "Is Specialist Ortiz giving you a pain, sir? I haven't kicked him for an age now, and my boots are itching."

"He's getting to that point. Take over, Adjunct. Get these lazy, yawning troops into line. We've got to whip them into shape."

Harris took a step closer. "How long do we have, sir? To whip them up, that is?"

"A week, maybe two, tops. This new ship is fast, and we're not sparing the engines. We've got to figure we'll be deploying planet-side a few days from now."

Harris whistled and shook his head. "That's not enough time. Many of these boys are hanging over their pants with an obvious paunch. At least thirty of them have a beer gut. May I make an unpopular suggestion?"

"What's that?"

"Let's get them killed. Most of them, anyway. Then we'll pump out a lean, trim unit after that. It'll save time."

The irony of the suggestion didn't escape me. He was talking about leaning on the revival machines. It was almost reflexive for Legion Varus officers to do so. Most of our problems could be easily solved by recycling anyone that wasn't performing at their best.

Soon that capability might be lost to us. At the very least, they'd start rationing revives, no longer allowing us to wear out machines with frivolous use.

Harris didn't know about any of this, of course. He hadn't been briefed yet—I wasn't sure Turov planned to tell the rank and file at all.

"All right," I said. "We'll think about that. For right now, I want to work them hard. See who's in good condition and who isn't. Make a list."

Harris grinned. He liked making up death-lists—as long as there was no chance his name would be on it.

"Good call, Centurion. Good call."

He trotted off and began drilling the troops. They really were in sorry shape. It was partly because we'd called them up with no warning at all. Oftentimes, the legion got some kind of advanced warning about a coming deployment. That gave a man a few weeks to get his wind up—but not this time.

After an hour of exercise, we broke for showers and breakfast. After that, we got serious.

Heading down to the ranges, we found them full of units with commanders who'd had the same idea.

"Here comes McGill," Centurion Manfred said loudly with a Brit accent. "Late to the party as usual, eh mate?"

I walked up and hammered Manfred on the shoulder. He smiled up at me. That's what I liked about Manfred. He wasn't anywhere near my height, but he was just as broad across the chest as I was. He could take a big fist to the shoulder without crying about it.

"My boys have already run a 5K," I told him.

"Really? They look kind of fat to me."

My grin soured. "Yeah… about that. Maybe you can help me out, and I can return the favor?"

"Go on."

I explained the situation. How we had only a few days to prepare our men. Manfred looked concerned.

"How do you know all this? The brass hasn't shat down so much as a single pellet of hard data into my lap yet."

"Uh... let's just say, I'm in the loop this time out."

Manfred nodded sagely. "Banging Turov again, are we? I stand impressed as always."

I shook my head. "You're as bad as Ortiz."

"What? I won't have that! Those are fighting words, McGill!"

He said this very loudly, taking our private conversation up to a level that could be heard by the men around us. Several glanced our way.

My face went slack for a second. I was honestly surprised by the look of anger and outrage on Manfred's face—but then I saw him wink, and I finally caught on.

"You Brit wanker," I said with equal volume. "That's what I said, you're as bad as Specialist Ortiz!"

A few around us sucked in a quick breath. Carlos might be my friend, but he was a renown asshole of the highest order. Being compared to him had been an insult in our cohort for decades.

"You take that back, or you'll eat my boot, McGill!"

"You can't kick that high, midget!"

We traded insults, then jostled each other, then threw punches. It was fun. I was impressed not only by how hard Manfred could land a fist on my ribs, but also with the punishment he could take in turn.

Finally, standing back from each other and panting, we noticed our adjuncts had come to circle around.

"I thought you two were lovebirds, McGill," Leeson said.

"Don't let him get away with that crap!" Harris said in my other ear. "Put him down by surprise!"

Barton was the last of my people to weigh in. "Sir, Manfred's adjuncts want a word with you—that probably means they're calling for a duel. What's this all about, Centurion?"

Fistfights, duels and even large-scale brawls were commonplace in a rough outfit like Legion Varus. Not only

133

were we surly, bad-tempered and mean—we were close to immortal. When a man knew he couldn't be killed permanently, it tended to make him push things further when he lost control of his emotions.

My face was red, and my right eye was mildly swollen. I stabbed a finger in Manfred's direction, and it was easy to play the part of the pissed-off officer.

"We came here to shoot—but this pug beat us to it. That's fine, but then he starts in with the insults."

"That's right!" Harris said excitedly. "He compared McGill to Carlos, straight-up!"

The crowd muttered and surged a little. Everyone knew that was a strike below the belt.

Naturally, I knew Harris' game. He was egging me on. He wanted to see me duel. The first clue was he'd reversed the direction of the insult in question—after all, I was the one who'd compared Manfred to Carlos, not the other way around.

Harris loved duels—when he wasn't involved. Nothing made him happier than to watch another man catch a beating. But today, things weren't going to go quite the way he planned.

I lifted a fist in the air. The groups fell quiet. I boomed out my challenge then.

"These fleet-loving snots from Unit Seven don't want to let us do any target practice today," I shouted. "But I don't accept that. I'm hereby calling them out."

"Uh…" Harris said. His face fell, and he looked around in alarm. "What the hell…?"

"That's right," I roared. "We'll have our target-practice. I hereby challenge Unit Seven to tactical action down on Green Deck—right the fuck now!"

"Oh shit… you've got to be kidding me, McGill," Harris complained, but I ignored him.

My eyes locked on Manfred. After a dramatic pause, he swaggered closer. "Challenge accepted, McGill. You and your fat-assed load of cowards will serve well as moving game for my boys. Your team and mine, one hour from now, Green Deck. Light suits and snap-rifles only—no armor, grenades, or other heavy gear."

"Got it. Challenge accepted. You'll be face down in mud inside of ten minutes, Manfred! Mark my words!"

"Bravado from the doomed."

And that was it. My troops and Manfred's were both cheering, baring their teeth and shouting boasts.

The exception was the handful of adjuncts and veterans on both sides. They looked concerned, and more than a little baffled. How had this fight mushroomed so quickly into an outright mini-war?

I'd never tell, and I was pretty sure Manfred wouldn't either.

-25-

Aboard *Dominus*, the Green Deck trees were quite a bit taller than I remembered from *Legate*. What's more, they'd grown significantly since last night. Despite this, most of them hadn't yet reached their full height. I got a few complaints about that from the various custodians and wannabe hogs who were Fleet crewmen. It was their job to care for and maintain this new Green Deck, and I could tell they didn't want to see it get torn up before it'd even had the chance to fully grow.

I didn't care at all about their petty problems. I contacted Graves, told him what I was up to, and got immediate approval.

"That's excellent, McGill," he said. "Innovation as usual, I've come to expect it from you."

"Uh... thanks, sir."

"The praise is well-earned. The primus council has been meeting today on this very topic. How do we get a good training in to sharpen our troops with only a few days to spare? You've got an answer, and it's flexible, with no prep-time needed."

He waxed on, telling me how he planned to have units pair-off, staging fights all up and down the legion. I soon grew bored and began to wonder when he'd say "dismissed" and get off my tapper screen.

"All right then, all I ask is that you damage no more than an acre of territory on Green Deck. Do you think you can do that? There are a lot of other men that need to water those plants with their blood."

"Sure thing, Primus. An acre is plenty of room."

"Excellent. Proceed with my blessing."

Armed with the name of our Blood Primus, I was able to brush aside the grumbling Fleet losers who seemed to think they were growing out Green Deck to be their personal vegetable garden. Choosing the big gate number seven, I led my men onto the field of honor with loaded snap-rifles and little else. I'd chosen gate seven because I knew the lay of the land from there, having scouted the area the night before with Galina.

"Out that way," I said, "toward the center of the combat zone, is a small lake with two waterfalls. They're each bigger and nicer than *Legate* ever had, too."

"That's great, McGill," Leeson said, "but where is the enemy?"

I shrugged. "I don't know. I doubt he knows, either. We just agreed to meet each other out here. He probably chose one of the other gates, and he's wandering around looking for us."

My troops fanned out, and we began patrolling. I deployed Della and Cooper to scout ahead. They were my ghost specialists, and they both had camo suits. Unfortunately, as we'd agreed not to use advanced equipment, they couldn't activate them. Essentially, they were recon on foot.

"This sucks," Carlos said loudly. "Kivi can't even launch her drones? Seriously? No buzzers? Nothing?"

"That's right," I called back to him. "Now shut up, or I'll send you forward to probe the grass with your dick."

We walked around for longer than I expected without meeting the enemy unit. Harris followed me closely.

"This is the biggest Green Deck I've ever seen," he said.

"Sure is."

"Excuse me for saying this, Centurion, but this scenario doesn't seem super well worked-out."

I glanced at him. "Who said it was a scenario? This is a straight-up duel. The challenge was publicly accepted."

"Excuse me again, Centurion, but that's total horseshit. It took me a few minutes to figure it out, but after our discussion about our troops state of readiness, and the fact this fight came out of nowhere between you and your only friend in Legion Varus—"

"Stop right there. You're starting to irritate me with this subversive talk. Try to come up with more solutions and less bitching, Adjunct. You'll live longer."

Harris stopped talking for a bit. He was frowning hard, thinking it over. "How about we break the unit into squads? Send the half that need, uh, *servicing* right toward the center. The rest of us will turtle up somewhere and wait."

I thought that over. It seemed like as good a plan as any. "All right. Who leads the lucky half?"

"The two adjuncts who aren't talking to you, of course."

I glanced back and saw Leeson and Barton. They looked paranoid but clueless. Harris and I grinned at each other.

"You have been keeping in shape..." I told him. "All right."

We broke our squads up, and I did a bit of last-second shuffling around. Barton and Leeson were baffled, but I told them I had a secret plan. That was the God's-honest truth, but they didn't get it at all, fortunately.

Once all the lame-footed fatties were grouped up, I ordered them to go stake out the waterfall area. They'd be hard to miss there.

In the meantime, Harris and I took the better half of our troops and positioned them in a strong defensive area. It was a cluster of boulders with a slight rise all around. The foliage was thick here, and it would provide good cover. We took up a circle of firing positions and waited.

It didn't take too long before the fireworks started. Out near the center of the deck, where the lake was, a rattling sound began. A moment later, the forest lit up with flashes and ripping sounds.

"Snap-rifle fire in the area around the lagoon," Della said in my ear. "Leeson reports contact at ten O-clock, Centurion!"

"You don't say... hold your position, Ghost." I turned to Harris. "Have your men hold their positions, Adjunct."

"With pleasure."

We hunkered down and listened. Checking out my HUD, I watched as my fighters blinked red, then went dark one or two at a time. At first, I was smiling. Our plan had worked flawlessly. Manfred was out there chewing up those that needed a good recycling.

But after a dozen were down, I began to frown. A rustling at my side revealed Carlos.

"What the fuck, McGill?" he asked. "Why are we sitting here with our fingers in our butts? We have to go help them!"

"It's all part of the plan, Carlos. This position is great defensive ground."

"So what? Morale will be in the toilet after this. All those guys down there are feeling abandoned, and the rest of us up here are feeling like cowards."

I looked at him, and he looked back. I could tell he was serious, and worse, I knew he was right.

"McGill," Della said in my ear. "Our troops are dying. They're pinned down and encircled. What are we doing holding back like cowards?"

"Shit..."

I spent a hard moment reflecting on her words. "How many of the enemy are attacking?"

"Looks like Manfred's full unit. They outnumber our boys two to one."

"Goddamn it..." Dark thoughts began to enter my mind. What if Manfred had decided to screw me? What if he'd lost interest in trimming the fat? Sometimes, when faced with real combat, men reverted to their natural instincts.

"Harris! Mount-up! Della, Cooper—yeah, I know you're out there staying quiet, Cooper—engage them with sniper fire and try to slow them down. Draw them north, if you can. We'll be there in a minute."

"Uh..." Harris said, "are you sure about this, sir?"

"Move!"

Cursing, he rushed off to get the troops on their feet. He didn't have to work too hard, as they were all itching to charge.

Two minutes later, we were running through the thin, crackling trees and stomping them down. The whole forest shook with our passage.

But I wasn't too worried about being detected. Manfred was having too much fun slaughtering my troops for that.

When we got there, we found Manfred's unit had entirely encircled our lesser half. Leeson was cagey, however, and he'd chosen the best defensive ground he could. His back was to a cliff between the two waterfalls, and his troops were spread out along the shoreline behind any scrap of cover they could find.

Manfred, on the other hand, had fanned his troops wide in a half-circle. His people were advancing, firing steadily, pinning down my smaller force. Both sides were nailing each other now and then, but my troops were naturally taking the worst of it. By the time we got there, at least thirty of my men were down, and maybe a dozen or so of Manfred's were floating in the lagoon.

We circled until Manfred's troops were directly between my two groups.

"Hit 'em," I said to Harris and the rest. "Hit 'em hard, right in the ass! Go, go, go!"

We didn't shout and roar. Not this time. We simply walked forward, blazing automatic fire at the enemy's exposed flank. Ten of them were down before they knew what was happening.

Wild shouts and sounds of rage met our ears. Manfred's unit separated by platoons, trying to get out of the trap. They peppered us with fire, making us duck and take cover—but we kept up the attack. Soon, the lagoon was choked with bodies. Manfred's troops reached the safety of the shoreline and dragged their wounded into the cover of the trees.

"They're ducking under the water, sir," Harris said. "Using their suits to breathe."

Grim-faced, I dug a grav-plasma grenade off my belt. I lobbed it into the middle of the lagoon. The concussion sent up a white geyser, and Manfred's men scrambled toward shore.

Sure, I'd cheated, but as I saw it the enemy had cheated first.

Barton led a counterattack then, coming out of her defensive position. I saw no sign of Leeson—then I noticed on my HUD that one of my adjuncts was clearly down. Barton was in charge of the second half of my unit—or what was left of it.

"Let's crush the right side," I said. "They're stuck climbing a wall there, no easy way out."

Veering right, we advanced toward a platoon of Manfred's people. Seeing this, Barton did the same. We were soon pressing into the trees, killing them hand-to-hand in some cases.

Manfred himself came up and rushed me, roaring when I waded up onto the shore. He must have been waiting there for me.

"You fucking twat!" he shouted. "Draw your blade if you have the balls!"

I threw up one arm, fist held high. "Hold your fire! This prissy Brit is all mine!"

As most of Manfred's troops were dead, the rest threw down their arms. At a signal from Harris, our boys slung their rifles. Everyone gathered around, relieved the fight was over.

But it wasn't finished for me and Manfred. Not yet.

He was well and truly pissed. I could tell. His anger seemed misplaced from my point of view, but everyone sees battle through their own eyes.

We squared off, with nothing between our skin and two blades but a centimeter of tough cloth. We weren't wearing our combat armor, and we hadn't yet been issued the new stuff we'd learned to make from the Rigellian bears.

Our knives glinted, and I caught a yellow gleam on his blade. Was that flame?

Backing up a step, I dared a glance over my shoulder. "The forest is on fire?" I asked.

"Yes, you fool. You're the one that threw grenades to get my troops out of the lagoon."

I whirled back to him. "So you lit up the trees?"

He grinned. "One trick deserves another. Graves won't be happy."

Suddenly, I got it. Graves would blame me for turning his precious Green Deck into a smoky ruin. It was a foolproof form of revenge. No matter how the battle turned out, I was going to take a ration of shit from the brass about this.

Already, the distant roof was turning black with soot. The trees were weak, it seemed, more vulnerable to fire since they were so young and frail.

"They don't put in the fire retardant until they're full grown," Manfred informed me. "Or didn't you know that, you long-armed wanker?"

That was it. I charged him. We went into a clinch, grabbing for each other's wrists. I got in one stab, nailing him in the shoulder before he clamped onto my hand and pushed me back.

Unfortunately, he'd gotten in a poke under my ribs. My guts took it, and I felt a sick explosion in my belly.

I wasn't out yet, not by a long shot. We grunted and strained, slashing at each other when we could. Our body types were quite different, but we were well-matched. He probably had the greater strength in close due to his short-limbed leverage, but I had the bigger frame, the greater weight and reach.

Snaking an arm around his neck, I managed to draw my blade under his chin. I'd cut his throat. Gore flew everywhere, and he mouthed raspy curses.

Most men would reel from the shock of such an injury, but Manfred was what he sometimes called "a tough old bird." He put both hands on his knife handle, and he drove it at me.

I tried to keep him away, but he got in close. I was losing strength from my wounds, and he had the powerful arms of a gorilla. I stabbed him in the chest and arms a half-dozen times—but he rammed that knife home anyway. The thrust was unstoppable. I took it in the chest, and I knew even as he slumped down from loss of blood, that I was well and truly screwed.

Standing tall, I lifted my knife over my head. Blood dripped from my fist, and the blade ran with reflected flames. The whole damned forest seemed to be going up now, all around us.

My troops cheered, but it was a half-hearted thing. They could see I wasn't in good shape.

Disappointed by their lack of enthusiasm, I staggered two steps toward shore before flopping down in the mud. Bubbles and bloody foam oozed out of my lips as I died.

-26-

When I got out of the revival machine, I wasn't pissed. After all, Manfred and I had both done a number on each other. We were friends underneath, and real friends didn't let one night of murderous rage get between them.

After returning to life, my habit was to take a shower, sleep a bit, then maybe find something to eat. Knowing Centurion Manfred well, like I did, I was aware his habits were somewhat different.

I found him in the officers' pub, with wet hair and a sour look on his face. He had a mug of beer in each hand, and when he saw me, he slid the one in his left paw across the bar.

Catching it with clumsy fingers, I sat on a seat beside him and took a big gulp.

"Nice of you to save me a mug, Manfred."

"You're daft, McGill. I was drinking two at a time."

We grinned at one another and went back to drinking.

After a solid killing, Manfred liked to drink. I figured it was his way of ignoring what had just happened. Everyone had their own way of dealing with death in the legions. If you didn't have a few mind-tricks like that, you wouldn't last long.

"Graves is looking for you, you know," he said after we'd drained a few.

"I kind of figured."

I was making a point of ignoring my tapper. It was buzzing, and vibrating and generally carrying on—but I wasn't in the mood.

Manfred looked down at his, reading it. I could have told him that was a mistake. Graves was a master at souring a man's gut.

Manfred frowned. "He says he'll remove your teeth, your balls and your rank buttons if you don't contact him right now."

I sighed heavily. "All right, all right."

Poking at my arm, I faked a grin. "Hello Primus, sir. Damn if that wasn't a fine idea you had about matching up two units on Green Deck. We had a blast. What's more—"

I broke off as Graves began an angry tirade.

"Why, no sir!" I exclaimed. "Manfred didn't intend any excessive destruction. Sure, he lit that forest on fire but—what's that, sir?"

I glanced up at Manfred, who had been grinning at my distress. Now, his face had transformed into a glare. "You prick," he whispered.

"The primus wants to talk to you, Centurion. Apparently, they had to open the dome and expose the whole deck to space in order to suck out all the oxygen. That stopped the fire right-quick." Whistling long and low, I shook my head. "Damn boy, when you punch yourself in the nuts you go all out—you'd better answer that."

Manfred's tapper was buzzing now. I poked at it to wake it up. I was only trying to be helpful, but Manfred took offense and slapped my thick fingers away.

"Get off!"

Chuckling, I paid the bar computer with a brush of my tapper. Draining my third beer, I headed for the exit. Manfred wasn't good company all of a sudden, and it seemed likely to me he would be tied up for a spell.

Walking out, I stretched and yawned. All that beer on an empty stomach hadn't made me sick, but it had made me a little sleepy. I headed down to the mess hall, grabbed a few items to snack on, and then found my bunk. I fell onto it gratefully.

Sleep was not for the wicked, however. Not tonight, not ever.

"McGill?"

It was my tapper. The damned thing was talking to me in the dark—again. At least it wasn't Graves peeping at me. He was probably still too busy making a chew-toy out of poor old Manfred.

That thought made me smile, so when I put my big face into view of the camera pickup, Galina Turov at least got to see me at my best.

"I'm glad you're so happy to see me," she said with false warmth. "You wrecked all of Graves' plans—you know that, don't you?"

"Just a little high-spiritedness, sir. You see, once a fight breaks out among the boys of Varus, there's no telling—"

"I know what you did. You wrecked Green Deck. Did it occur to you that no one can use it now? We'll probably arrive at 91 Aquarii before it's grown in fully."

"Well now, that sounds like poor planning to me. Why couldn't these Fleet pukes grow out the deck before we even got aboard?"

"They were saving budget money, I'm sure. They didn't seed it until they knew they had a legion to carry."

"That sounds about right. What a miserly bunch. Penny-wise is pound-foolish, my father always says."

"I'm sure he does, whatever the hell that means. In any case, I was wondering if you'd made any progress toward contacting the Clavers."

"Uh… I sure have!" I said with certainty. The truth was I'd forgotten all about it in the excitement of the day. "Don't you worry your pretty little head about it. I'll have Claver on the line the minute we decide the 91 Aquarii campaign is a bust."

"That will possibly be too late. Get on with it, and report back to me as soon as you have made contact—sooner, if there are any positive developments."

"Will do, sir. Now, how about a nightcap? I was just lying here bored and wondering—"

"Forget it. Contact Claver. Turov out."

I sighed and waited five seconds before heaving my carcass out of bed. After all, I could sleep the next time I was dead. Searching doors and tapping on a few, I looked for Natasha.

She wasn't in her bunk asleep, naturally. As her superior officer, I could have simply done a trace on her location with my own tapper—but I didn't dare. Things like that were automatically flagged by tech specialists. Not only would Natasha have been warned by her defensive software, but every other mouthy little tech would know about it, too.

Kivi was the problem creature in this scenario. Sure, we hadn't hooked up for a long time, but there was always hope for the prospect on any new campaign. The one person in the world she seemed most jealous of was Natasha. If she knew I was looking for her at around midnight... well, I could kiss all my fantasies goodbye for the next year or so.

I finally found Natasha down in the quartermaster's storage room. Every unit had their own supply man, who was sometimes a specialist, or other times a veteran. They were always people who were slower and fussier than the rest.

In this case, I didn't see the quartermaster at all. Instead, I saw only Natasha squatting over some kind of gear.

Clearing my throat, I got her to spin around on her haunches and almost fall on her can. That was a dead giveaway. She was up to something that was against regs.

"Oh! Hello, Centurion. I didn't hear you come in."

I nodded sternly, putting on my serious officer's face. I stepped inside the store room and had a look around.

There was gear of every kind in here, but mostly the unusual stuff. There were medical kits, two communications dishes, and a lot of extra buzzers.

Her body was between my eyes and whatever she'd been working on. I pretended not to notice. Picking up an auto-wrench, I waved it around and smiled. "Found it," I said, and I moved to go.

Relieved, Natasha turned back toward whatever she was illicitly working on.

"Hold on," I said, turning back around again at the door.

"Yes?"

"I just had a thought. You remember that private project we were working on last year—on the way out to Glass World?"

She blinked for a second in surprise. "You don't mean—?"

"That's right. Something about aligning light. About recording shimmers in oceans and such-like."

"I remember… what about it?"

"Well, I'll tell you what. If you don't want to go on report for your little midnight excursions—"

"Hold on, McGill," she reached out a hand to touch mine. "James... You can't tell anyone about that."

"Don't I know it," I said, having absolutely no idea nor interest in whatever the hell she was up to. "The brass would be pissed, wouldn't they?"

She stared at me furtively. "You're not asking me for a date or something, are you?"

"Huh? Oh… no, no. I'm asking for you to work on something for me. I want you to press on with your... uh... your detection equipment. In particular, I want to be able to read an ID from a message. An old message, maybe."

She blinked at me. "What?"

"Well, if you can figure out what a deep-link message is saying, you'd think it would be even easier to trace back where it's coming from, right?"

"Oh… I see. Maybe…" she said, looking down.

Was she a little disappointed? Maybe she wanted a date. Natasha and I shared a strange, long history, after all. But now wasn't the time for fooling around. I put such thoughts away for later. Right now, I needed her help. If anyone could reach the Clavers, Natasha could.

"Let me know if you figure anything out. All of this," I said, waving my wrench around to indicate the entire storeroom, "I never heard a thing about it. Okay?"

"Okay…" she said, almost whispering. "Thanks, James."

"Sure thing. Goodnight."

"Goodnight."

As I yawned and staggered back to my bunk, I felt a sense of pride surging. That had been a job well done, if I did say so myself. Natasha would work like a beaver chewing on a fencepost until she solved my problems for me.

Contented with this certain knowledge, I fell asleep until dawn.

-27-

Graves finally caught up with me at breakfast.

"There you are, McGill. Don't think that I'm unaware you've been dodging me since your latest revival."

"Uh… why would I do that, sir?"

Graves glowered at me. "Because you don't want to talk about that jackassed stunt you pulled yesterday on Green Deck. You told me there would be no more than an acre's worth of damage. Well, the entire deck was a total loss."

"Really? That's a shame, sir. A *damned* shame. Did you know they had two waterfalls this time? And that lagoon… it was as pretty as a sapphire shining under that fake sun."

"McGill, listen to me: this is exactly the kind of wasteful behavior that must stop if we're going to operate effectively without revival machines. You're going to have to clean up your act, or I won't be able to use you on future campaigns."

"How's that, sir? After all, we've still got plenty of the machines aboard."

He sighed and sat down opposite me. "Let me educate you on the subject of economics and human psychology."

"Oh… not that, sir. Please. I'll eat my greens, I swear."

Half of Graves' face twitched up. For him, that was the equivalent of a wide grin—but it didn't last long.

"Listen," he said, "if we lose our revival machine supplier, everything is going to change very quickly."

"How do you figure?"

"Because a lot of people rely on them—important people back home."

We stared at each other for a second, and I started to catch on. "Are you saying these machines aren't just reserved for the legions? That some political types back home use them?"

"Of course they do. Every rich, privileged shit-heel back on Earth has access to them."

"But... I don't think that's legal, sir. Or ethical."

Graves laughed. "Even you have cheated with them, haven't you?"

I stared stupidly, pretending I had no earthly idea what he was talking about—but I did.

A decade ago, I'd noticed my parents were in failing health. I'd rigged up a way to copy them, kill them, and then get them revived again. No one knew about that, no one but Natasha.

Or at least, that's what I'd thought. But now here was Graves, giving me a hard stare. Did he know? Crap...

"Okay," I said, "I can understand the appeal of printing out a limb or an organ—even a whole body of some fat VIP when he gets too drunk and crashes his government aircar. But why would that mean we'd have to change things? These units we have aboard right now are good for years. With any luck, we'll still be pumping out legionnaires with them when I retire."

Graves shook his head slowly. "Forget that. The moment the big boys at the top find out our supply is threatened, they'll hoard whatever is left for themselves."

"Really? But how could they explain—?"

"Oh, sure," Graves said, leaning back. "They'll talk big about a strategic reserve, or some such malarkey. But the fact is the important people will still get revives, while grunts like you and me will be face down in the mud—permanently."

I was beginning to see his point. The change would come faster than I'd assumed. Graves had me frowning now, and I'd been in such a great mood only moments before. He was a wizard at making a man glum.

"Uh... what do we do to fix this?"

"We stop fucking off, for one thing. We don't take the resources we have for granted. We shape-up, and we run this legion like professionals."

"That's a tall stack of change, sir."

"Indeed it is. Do I have your cooperation?"

"You were never without it, Primus. I hereby swear to fly as straight as an arrow from now on. You have my word on that, something everyone in space knows and trusts. You can take it to the bank!"

Looking unconvinced, he stood up. "There's a general officers' briefing on Gold Deck at 1300 hours. Be there."

Then he left me in peace, and I finished my breakfast. It was a dismal way to start your day, contemplating such big issues.

The day dragged by until 1 p.m., when I went up to the meeting. There was a sorry spread of food to be had, and it wasn't even a proper lunch. Just a few chips, dips and stuff with toothpicks in it. I filled the biggest plate I could find and found a seat to start munching.

Manfred came in and sat down next to me. He bummed some of my snacks off me, and we watched the proceedings begin.

Tribune Turov strutted out onto the stage first. In her wake was her zoo-legion sidekick, Sub-Tribune Fike.

"Gentlemen," Turov began. "I'm here before you today to explain what we know of the situation on the ground at 91 Aquarii. The most important fact is that the Skay ship has not yet arrived. With any luck, we will beat them to this prized star system. That alone, however, won't guarantee anything."

She made a subtle spinning motion with her finger. I knew the gesture well. She was signaling Fike to take action.

Like a trained seal, he went to the big wall behind them and began to pull up a full diagram of the star system in question.

I was immediately disappointed when Fike started the info-dump. Usually, Galina herself would turn away and do this part. She often had to stand on her tippy-toes to reach the corners of the huge screen area. This gave everyone a highly advantageous view of her posterior.

Today, there was no such luck. She kept on yapping, and Fike showed us his lumpy rear to the disgust of many.

"When did Fike turn into Turov's butt-monkey?" Manfred asked me, but I shushed him.

Galina began talking, and I tried hard to pay attention. "The 91 Aquarii system is on the very edge of known space. It's on the border between Province 921 and Province 926. The most important thing about this border is it separates vast zones of space owned by the Mogwa and the Skay."

I knew all this. We all did. We shifted in our seats and stared, hoping she would get to the point.

"Here is a visual of the movement of the star system. Over the past decade, it has crossed a boundary line. As it continues, it will soon be entirely in Province 926. By custom, the moment it does the system will be seized by the Skay."

My fist came up and pushed into my right cheek. Even eating chips wasn't going to keep me awake through this one.

"Most of you know all of this," she continued, "what you *don't* know is the nature of the planet and its inhabitants. Fike?"

Fike touched the display, and it lit up nicely. A pack of skinny humanoids wrapped up in strips of cloth appeared.

"Heh," I said. "They look like mummies."

A number of the officers around me rumbled with laughter. They *did* look like mummies.

"That's enough disrespect," Fike said sternly. "These people live on the bright side of the planet. They're nomadic, of course, like the entire population. Their brethren don't allow them to enter the shadowed zone, or the night side, of course. Arguably, they're the least fortunate of all three tribes, but—"

"Ahem," Galina cleared her throat importantly. "I believe you're leaving out some vital information."

Fike frowned. "The basics? Is that really needed? All of the background information was distributed to everyone's tapper hours ago."

Galina nodded. "Yes… but that doesn't mean anyone read it."

Fike released a puffing breath, showing his disgust. "The officer core of the Iron Eagles would have—"

"Yes, yes, I'm sure they would all have book reports ready here at the meeting, just in case. But these unfortunates aren't from the Eagles. They were all rejected by your former outfit. So, if you wouldn't mind?"

Grumbling disapprovingly, Fike swept his hand over the image on the big screen, quickly swiping left to right to back up the presentation. Soon, he was at the beginning of it.

Manfred leaned over to me. "Did you read the report they sent out this morning?"

"What report?"

"That's what I thought."

Fike began to drone again. He started off with the description of the star system itself. 91 Aquarii, was in the constellation of Aquarius from Earth's point of view. It was a triple-star system, with a binary center and a long range small third star that orbited the other two at a significant distance.

"Sounds just like Alpha Centauri," I said aloud.

Fike glanced up. He was somewhat irritated with the interruption, but also glad that at least someone was paying attention.

"Yes," he said, "it's similar to that, although the core double-stars are very close—even physically connected. This makes them somewhat less stable and their output of energy is much higher. The first exoplanet discovered in this system was a gas giant, suspected in 2003 and confirmed in 2020. Since then, a smaller and more habitable planet has been located in the system. That planet is our destination."

"What do we call it?"

"The local name is unpronounceable. Our astronomers call it 91 Aquarii e—but I'm sure you'll come up with something more catchy soon. It's an arid planet without oceans. The local gravity, atmosphere and general composition is similar to a dry, stony version of Earth."

"Sounds nice so far."

Fike frowned at me. "Just keep listening. I'm almost finished with the happy-talk. The planet is in a life-allowing orbit around its double-star. It's well-positioned for liquid water to be stable and even common. The poles are lightly frosted with ice, and the equatorial region is hotter than the rest of the world—however."

"Here it comes," Manfred said beside me, and I steeled myself. There was always something shitty about any world Legion Varus got shipped out to. Always.

"What makes this world different from Earth," Fike continued, "is its damnably slow rotation period. One local day takes just over a standard year to go by."

There were some gasps from the crowd. Apparently, I wasn't the only one who hadn't done his homework.

"That's right," Fike continued. "A damned whole year. That means any given spot on the planet is in daylight for about five months and then dark for about five months. For about one month at either end of that sequence, it's either dawn or dusk."

The imagery swam on the screen, and we saw the world. It looked kind of yellow-orange, like a lemon-flavored version of Mars.

"There it is, that shadowed zone," Galina chimed in, and she finally turned toward the screen. She began stretching and tapping at it. This made every male in the chamber look a little happier.

"Yes..." Fike said. "As you can see, about forty percent of the planet is dark and freezing at any given time, while another forty is blazing hot and sunny for months. The shadowed zones along the edges—that's where things are pleasant, but where that region is slowly shifts day to day. Our Earth rotates at around seventeen hundred kilometers an hour. 91 Aquarii rotates at about five kilometers an hour—a walking pace."

Galina spun her finger at Fike again, but this time she did it faster. She wanted him to hurry things up.

"So you see," he began summing up, "the inhabitants have divided into three tribes. One inhabits the bright side, one the dark, and the last lives in the glorious middle."

"The shadowed zone," Galina interjected.

"The shadowed zone is the most pleasant of the three, and those who dwell there are dominant. It's these folks who managed to invent the revival machines. They have an advanced culture—but it is, by necessity, nomadic."

"That's really weird," I said loudly. "Show me the freaks from the dark side. Are they mummies too?"

Fike shook his head and skipped past a few screens of his slide show. Suddenly, a lumpy four-legged creature crouched on a patch of ice and black rock. It was as thick as the bright-siders were thin. Instead of a mummy's rags, he wore heavy furs. In fact, he was furred from what I could tell. A mangy coat of hair grew all over him to protect him from the cold.

And the eyes—the eyes were the worst. They gleamed yellow like some kind of a wild thing that's been drawn to a campfire in the wilderness.

"They wear furs, they have eyes adapted for night vision, and they're vicious. The night-siders are probably the most dangerous and uncivilized of the lot."

I hooted and pointed. "He looks like a werewolf! We've got mummies by day and werewolves by night!"

The group busted up laughing. Even Graves let his lips twitch upward before scowling at me.

"And the third tribe rides herd on them all," he said, flipping to another image. A tall man and a tall attractive woman stood side by side. For a second, I thought they were humans—but they weren't.

The differences were subtle. For one thing, they had eyes that were too big. For another, there were tufts of fur on them, here and there. On humans, you only saw hair on the head, plus some body hair. These guys had more. Their shoulders, for instance, had small epaulets of carefully combed hair.

A few of the officers present winced and hissed. Not me, however. I kind of like the lioness look of the female. The male wasn't anything special, but he seemed mighty proud of his shoulder-patches.

They wore clothing as well. It was a normal combo of shirts and pants.

"These shadow-zoners are definitely humanoid. They're well-adapted to a life in perpetual twilight. It's these people who invented the revival machines we rely upon in the legions."

My hand shot up at this point, making Fike frown. "What is it, McGill?"

156

"Why'd they make them?" I asked.

"What?"

"Why'd they invent revival machines? I mean, if they've got it so good, if they run the show on 91 Aquarii—why did they go to all this trouble to patch themselves up?"

Fike pointed a finger at me. "Ah-ha! A good question at last. We've determined that it's because of the extreme bloodshed on 91 Aquarii. Due to the existence of the three distinct tribes, and the perpetual requirement for nomadic behavior, there is a constant struggle going on. Essentially, these three tribes are in a permanent state of war."

"And the shadow tribe decided they wanted to live again, huh? That's really something."

The briefing went on after that, but I didn't pay it any heed.

I was thinking too hard inside my own head to listen to Fike or Galina. This was going to be really something. Three sides in a permanent war? On a planet that rotated as slowly as molasses in winter?

Then there was the Skay. What would that monster out of space demand? When the Skay arrived, it was surely going to stir up the local pot.

I began eyeing the female Shadowlander again, and I felt a twinge of interest in her. She looked smart, pretty and exotic. At the very least, she might make a suitable companion for a man like me.

We were dismissed, and Galina slapped me on top of the head as the meeting broke up.

"Hey, Tribune," I said good-naturedly.

"Stop drooling over that creature."

"What?"

"The Shadowlander. She's not likely to want an ape like you. Her native males are civilized and distinguished-looking. You, McGill, are a brute. You'll remind her of a vicious night-sider."

There she was again, acting all jealous. I hadn't even gotten off the ship yet, but she was seeing every woman as a rival. Oh sure, there were plenty of reasons from our shared past for her to feel jealous, but to me it seemed premature for her to start in before we'd even reached the planet in question.

"Uh... I don't even know who you're talking about... wait a second! You don't mean that freaky shadow-lady, do you?"

"Yes, of course. I saw how you looked at her."

I laughed and faked a shudder. "Don't be crazy, girl! I'm not into alien tail. I'm into humans, you know that."

"Yes... I do. But I also know how your eye wanders when something interesting goes by."

I tilted my head speculatively. "Sounds like someone wants a date tonight, huh?"

"Think again."

"Don't you like your men to be a little… brutish?" I asked, giving her my best smile.

She thought about it. She honestly did. Finally, she sighed. "I don't know why I should care one way or the other about that Shadowlander."

"It's because you're lonely. I've got the fix for that." My big palm slapped down on the table. "Done! It's a date. See you at eight."

She started to turn away, but I stood suddenly and kissed her. She pouted, but she was kind of smiling, too. She didn't meet my eye.

"Eight," I whispered in her ear. "Don't forget."

"All right, eight… if you don't get killed again by then."

I thought that was an odd and rather cryptic message to give me under the circumstances, but a man like myself couldn't afford to look a gift-horse in the mouth. Accordingly, I ducked out before she could change her mind, or I somehow managed to blow up our plans.

Whistling as I marched down the passageways, I found myself to be in an excellent mood. I had a hot date scheduled tonight, followed by a planet full of interesting women to conquer in the morning. What could go wrong?

Returning to my module, I found my whole unit was in turmoil. Word had gotten out that we would be dropping in the morning.

"Hey, Harris," I said, grabbing his arm. "Who spilled the beans?"

"About the drop? You did." He grinned and walked off to shout at a recruit who was packing the extra barrel for his rifle the wrong way.

Alarmed, I checked my tapper. It was true. I'd meant to forward the briefing from my tapper to Adjunct Barton's. I often did that when there were too many details to learn. Barton was the kind of woman who *loved* details. She couldn't get enough of them.

But instead of targeting Barton alone, I'd actually hit the mailbox of every officer and noncom in my unit. It was a disaster, as they were busily spreading the word to other units.

"Damn…"

159

My first thought concerned the date I'd just set up. If word of this had gotten out… well, it would be hard to cover all my bases by eight pm.

I began walking fast and picking up steam. Soon, I was trotting after Barton. I caught up with her and crooked my finger. She followed me into my office.

"That briefing you sent me," she said, almost out of breath, "there hasn't been enough time to react to it. Can you confirm that we're flying into the 91 Aquarii system late tonight, then dropping on their capital in the afternoon? Doesn't that seem extreme?"

I blinked at her for a few seconds. Sure, I'd figured out that we were arriving tomorrow, but I hadn't read any of the other documents. This whole business about dropping on a capital immediately was news to me.

"Uh… which capital?"

"The Shadowlanders, of course. They're the only ones who don't have a completely nomadic society."

"Oh yeah."

Barton frowned at me. Her gloved hands slid up to rest on her waist. That was a bad look from any woman.

"Did you read *all* that stuff you sent me?"

"Well… it was kind of late, see. So I wanted you to check through the details and brief me."

"So that's what this 'meeting' is about? Don't you usually have Natasha do your homework for you?"

"You're doing fine," I said, but I was beginning to frown myself. This wasn't going well. I didn't want Barton losing respect for me. That was the trouble with spending decades in space with the same group of people. They got to know all your tricks after a while.

Barton looked down at her tapper. "All right, to summarize, we're arriving at around 0400 hours ship time. We'll cross the system at sub-light speeds for another eleven hours. At that point, we should be within striking distance of the planet itself. We'll drop, secure their capital and demand immediate submission to the Empire… Heavy-handed, like I said."

"What do you think about the plan?"

160

She looked up, puzzled. "What do I think? In what regard, sir?"

"Will the Aquarii people fight or give up? Are they even *capable* of fighting?"

Barton looked troubled. She lowered her tapper and looked me in the eye.

"They'll definitely fight. The whole planet is at war most of the time, anyway. To me, this opening move seems like a huge mistake. Turov is trying to impress these people, to overawe them so they won't be any trouble. But I don't think it will work."

"Yeah? Why not?"

"Because they *constantly* fight among themselves. It's their culture to do so. They've been struggling for thousands of years. That's why they invented the revival machine in the first place. They die often. In their culture, a boy isn't even considered a man until he's fallen in battle at least once."

"Hmm..." I said, thinking she might have a point there. Turov's plan could work well on a peaceful world. What's more, they could probably defend themselves against our level of technology. She might believe she was going to be pushing around bumpkins, but these people were smart enough to build revival machines we couldn't duplicate yet. They had to have effective weaponry.

"James," Barton said, touching my arm. "Go talk to Turov. You know her well. Convince her that this is the wrong approach."

I grunted unhappily. Sure, I knew Turov pretty damned well. One thing I was sure about was she didn't like people telling her that her plans were dumb. That was doubly true if they actually *were* dumb.

Scratching my head, I grumbled something and walked away. My date at 8 pm was looking pretty bleak all of a sudden.

Dinnertime came and went. As soon as I'd eaten, I headed over to Galina's quarters.

A wannabe hog stood guard in the lobby. He was Fleet, not part of Legion Varus, so I didn't have much respect for him.

161

There was no one else around except for one clerk at the duty desk. He had his feet up and his eyes on his tapper. He snapped to attention at my approach, but then sagged back into his seat again when he saw I was only a centurion.

When faced by flunkies, my instinct is always to ignore them utterly. Accordingly I walked on by, not even bothering to smile or make eye-contact.

The hog-like guard approached and intercepted me. He'd been ordered to keep the riffraff off Gold Deck, especially after regular hours had ended.

"Sorry sir," he told me with practiced regret, "Gold Deck is closed at this time."

"Check your roster, hog," I suggested.

His fake affable smile transformed into a twisted mask of anger. Now glaring, he lifted his tapper and poked at it.

"Here we are: Centurion James McGill, known troublemaker. Banned for life. Approach with extreme caution."

My jaw sagged low. "Banned for life? What the—?"

He began laughing then, lowering his arm and grinning. "Sorry sir, just having a little fun. But seriously, there is no list. I'm under orders to keep out anyone under the rank of primus. There've been entirely too many people wandering up here with their petty problems."

"Says who? Who gave you these orders, Veteran?"

He grinned. "Tribune Turov herself, sir."

It was my turn to be annoyed. Thinking things over, I believed the hog-boy. Those snotty words sounded like they'd come out of Galina's mouth all right.

Lifting my tapper, I contacted her directly. She answered after the first buzz.

She was out of uniform, as I'd hoped she would be. I couldn't see much more than her head and shoulders, but I could tell she was wearing something low-cut and silky-looking. Her hair was down, and she'd put on some extra makeup if I wasn't mistaken.

"You're late, McGill. I don't like being kept waiting."

162

"That's what I figured, sir. Could you inform this former hog, the unfortunate you left in the elevator lobby? He's misinformed."

I turned the tapper toward the guard. Galina didn't look any happier to see him than I did. Before she said anything, the hog caved. He looked like he might wet himself.

"I'm sorry, sirs! McGill is on his way, Tribune!"

"Good," Galina said. "Now, go back to playing hallway monitor."

"Have my orders changed, sir? In regard to this man, I mean?"

Galina seemed to think about it. "I don't know yet. Dismissed."

The hog gave me a strange look as I sauntered on by. He said something about not having believed the rumors.

"What's that, Veteran?" I asked him sharply.

"Nothing, Centurion! Nothing at all."

Nodding, I continued on my merry way. There were quite a few twists and turns. Her quarters were located at the very back of Gold Deck—by design, no doubt. Her door was both hard to find and as distant as possible from the lobby.

Reaching Galina's door at last, I tapped politely a few times. But she didn't open up right away. After all that fuss with the guard, I'd gotten a little steamed up.

"Come on, girl," I boomed, banging my big fist on the door. "Stop playing games and open this door. I know you can see me through the cameras."

She still didn't open the door. Annoyed, I stepped away and flipped off her pinhole camera.

But then, before leaving, I hesitated.

Galina hadn't given me any hint that she was going to pull something like this. She'd been dressed up all sexy-like, and she'd been annoyed I was taking too long to arrive. None of these behaviors seemed like she was in the mood to play some kind of coy game.

"Hmm..." I said, frowning at the door. I reached out and tried the handle.

It was locked, but the latch broke easily in my grip. I pushed it wide open and stepped inside.

163

There she was, wearing a frilly nightgown of that satin stuff she liked so much. She would probably call it a kimono or a robe—but I called it a provocative, easy-access excuse for clothing.

None of that was alarming. What stopped me dead in my tracks was her position, and her pose. She was face down, head to one side, lying on the floor. Her nails were freshly painted a bright red, but I knew in an instant that the pool of liquid surrounding her pretty person on that deck wasn't paint—it was blood.

-29-

I could tell in an instant the angle of her neck was wrong—it wasn't natural. Her neck was broken, and there were stab-wounds in her back.

Now, when any normal man is confronted by his dead girlfriend on the ground, he might well shout and approach. He might kneel down and try to help her—but long years had shaped my mind differently.

I didn't cry out or piss myself or anything. Instead, my eyes slid from side to side. A knife appeared in my hand. The blade glittered silver-white, reflecting the overhead lighting. I didn't even look at Galina—I looked for her killer.

There wasn't much to her quarters. Everything was nice, mind you, with a main room, a separate bedroom, a walk-in closet and a private bath. It was a studio apartment, essentially. Back on Earth, it would have been considered upscale. Here aboard a military ship, it was the equivalent of a palace.

Still, it didn't take too long to search the place. As I stalked around, I touched the emergency button on my tapper and held it down for five long seconds. I'd always thought five seconds took too much time to summon help, but I supposed it helped prevent accidental alarms going off every day.

The first man to reach the hanging door was the hog-candidate I'd irritated back in the lobby. He was fast on his feet, and at least he knew his job.

He came barreling in, swore up a streak when he saw Galina on the deck, and then fumbled out his sidearm.

"Centurion McGill! Drop that knife! Submit to arrest immediately!"

I glanced at him. I was standing at her private computer now, tapping at the sensors. I put my knife on the table. It clattered there, and gouged the surface. Just touching a mono-filament blade to a solid surface often gouged it up something awful.

"There's no blood on my blade, Veteran Daniels."

"What?"

"Check it out. Someone stabbed her and broke her neck."

"I can see that, McGill. Didn't take you long to get angry did it?"

I looked up from the computer. "How's that?"

"I've heard a few things about you. None of them good. They call you a predator, you know that?"

"Who does? Your hog buddies back at Central?"

His face reddened. "I'm talking about the women in this legion."

"Aw, come on. I chase skirts, but I don't murder them. Too much trouble."

Daniels stepped forward. His pistol was out, and his other hand was raised high in a defensive posture. I made no move on him.

"What are you doing on her computer? That's against regs, McGill."

"Don't I know it... here, I've got something."

I flipped the screen flat, so it merged with the desk. That made the software kick in and expand the video I'd found. I touched the controls, making it jump forward ten seconds.

"Is that her security footage?" he asked.

"Sure looks like it. Let's see who came to dinner before I did."

Doubtfully, Daniels stood with me and peered at the video. For several jumps in time, nothing happened—then a figure appeared.

And I do mean *appeared*. One frame, it wasn't there. The next, there was flash of blue-white light, kind of like a small

166

jolt of lightning. A figure stood in the center of her quarters, wearing a dark cloak and hood.

"That's a woman," Daniels said.

I nodded in agreement.

A moment later, Galina stepped into view. The taller woman attacked her immediately. She didn't say anything or give any warning. She just quickly and efficiently murdered Galina.

"She stabbed her in the heart, then twisted her neck just to make sure?" Daniels asked.

I nodded.

The moment the deed was done, the assassin adjusted what must be a teleport harness of some kind. She built up a charge, and her image began to strobe.

The assassin was startled when my fist began to hammer on the door. I could tell she could hear me, and she crouched. She reached for her harness and gave it a quick twist.

My fat finger stabbed down and paused the action. I zoomed in.

Before I could watch the rest of the vid, however, a bunch more security people rushed into the place. They were all Fleet-types, and they had guns drawn. Behind them, belatedly, was a bio team. I could have told them they were too late. There was nothing left for them to do other than collect the body.

"Hold on a second," Daniels told the excited shore-patrol stooges. "McGill found her like this—he's onto something."

"Stand down, Daniels!" an ensign ordered. "Get away from that console, McGill! You're tampering with evidence, and that's a whole separate charge!"

Ignoring these new irritants, I gestured to Daniels. I pointed at the screen and zoomed in to check out the hooded figure's chest. "See that? Standard jump-harness. She didn't have time for a full charge. She jumped early."

"McGill, I'm placing you under arrest," the centurion said.

Stepping around the table, I pointed at Galina's body. "Our commander was just assassinated. You're the one interfering, because the assassin is still aboard this ship—but probably not for long."

167

The centurion blinked at me and then Galina in confusion. "Replay that video, Daniels."

He began to do so, but I didn't feel like waiting around. I brushed past the growing pack of cops. Damn, these boys weren't too quick on the uptake.

"McGill, come back here! I've got questions for you! Damn it man, this is my job."

"And you're doing shitty work tonight. If you want to arrest, torment and execute me later on, you can. But I'm going to find that assassin."

"How are you going to do that? She could be anywhere on this ship, according to you."

"Nope... she'll be trying to charge her harness."

"Where?"

"Down on Gray Deck, dumbass."

Complaining, half the cops followed me. Others fussed over the body, like they were going to find fingerprints or something. They really didn't seem to like my intrusion on their turf, but that was just too frigging bad. My date and my evening had been ruined, and I wasn't in the mood to take any crap from a pack of desk-jockeys.

I reached Gray Deck a few minutes later. By this time, I'd alerted both Graves and Sub-Tribune Fike. They were in my chain of command, and they needed to know what had happened.

"Let me get this straight," Graves said, speaking out of my tapper as I marched along with sweeping strides. "You went up to see the tribune—inappropriately, I might add—and found her dead when you got there?"

"Not against regs, sir. We're only two steps apart in rank now, both officers."

"Sometimes things that aren't strictly forbidden are considered bad policy, McGill. Your actions tonight are officially frowned upon."

I rolled my eyes, but I didn't argue with him. He was just pissed off that we had a leadership crisis a few hours before our ship was due to arrive at 91 Aquarii.

"If you want to know more, sir, meet me on Gray Deck."

Rudely, I disconnected the channel and contacted Natasha. She was the best at tech puzzles, and I knew her personally.

"Sorry James, I still haven't cracked the code yet," she said sleepily.

"What? Oh, that... I'm not calling about that."

I filled her in quickly, and she agreed to meet me on Gray Deck as well.

By the time I got there, Graves was waiting. Natasha arrived soon afterward.

"Followed by the cops everywhere you go, as usual," Graves complained, seeing the Congo-line of Fleet pukes in my wake.

"What? These guys?" I jerked a thumb over my shoulder at the disgruntled pack. I could tell they were still itching to arrest me. "They're in this hog-look-alike contest. They're trying to sway the judge with tonight's performance, but you know me. It takes more than a pretty face to change my vote."

Graves waved away my words. "Let's get down to it. There's no one here. None of the techs have seen anything."

"Huh..." I said, looking around. "Where did she go, then?"

Graves and the cops fell to talking. I paced and ignored their rude suggestions concerning my possible guilt. Everyone cast random glances in my direction, as if they thought I was the murderer, and I'd concocted an elaborate ruse to throw them off. That sort of thing had happened before, but in this case it was pure slander.

"Hold on..." I said, playing the video again. This time, when we got a glimpse of the woman under the hood, I zoomed in to see her face, rather than what she was doing with her teleport harness.

"She's a looker," Daniels admitted.

Everyone glared at him, so he shrugged and shut up.

"That face..." I said, jabbing a finger at the screen. "Long and lean, kind of mean-looking. She reminds me of someone..."

"She looks like one of those people from the dominant tribe on 91 Aquarii," Natasha said.

"You're right," Graves said. "You think she really could be a Shadowlander? Here, on our ship, while we're warping through space?"

I nodded. "She could have come here if she got the coordinates from someone. Hell, I've done stuff like that myself."

Graves looked like he smelled shit, but I didn't care. I knew those missions had been classified, but this was the here and now.

"All right," I said. "If she's still aboard this ship, what's she doing?"

"Sabotage? More assassinations? We should contact Fike. He's next in command."

Just then, Fike arrived and gave us all a stern look. "Contact Fike about what?"

They explained the theory that we had a roaming agent from the Shadowlander tribe aboard.

I got bored and moved on. I didn't want to waste time sticking around to listen to it all again.

"Where's McGill?" Fike boomed suddenly as the door slid shut behind me. "You men let him slip out? What's wrong with you?"

That was all I heard, as I was on my way to Blue Deck next. Nothing was going to stop me.

-30-

Blue Deck was quiet, but it was guarded by some stern-eyed orderlies. The nature of the bio people in the legions had always been a bit strange. They considered themselves to be above the rest of us. They acted more like an aloof priesthood, tending to their strange machines in hidden rooms, than the blood-and-guts biological repairmen they really were.

All this meant next to nothing to me. I had a long history of bypassing silly rules made by silly people.

To keep things rolling, I arranged for Carlos to be on hand and greet me at the door. As a bio-specialist, he was allowed onto Blue Deck whenever he felt the urge. He came out of the big doors, scooted past the guards and came to talk to me in the passageway in low tones.

"McGill, do you have any idea what they'll do to me if they find out I'm sneaking you onto Blue Deck under false pretenses?"

"They'll have to sew them back on first, Carlos. Open that door! She's probably getting away even now."

Sighing, Carlos showed his credentials to the guards and led me into the clinic area. That part was no big deal. Anyone could walk onto Blue Deck and get service, as long as they had an appointment.

Unfortunately, in my era, just believing you needed some medical help wasn't good enough. Not anyone could just up and go to the doctor because they were feeling poorly. Our tappers monitored all our vitals, and something had damned-well better be wrong with the numbers they reported over the grid before any medical person would waste their time and money on some hypochondriac.

In the past, I knew this system had often been used to deny services. If you were sick, but not sick enough to be seriously ill, well, you could just frigging wait it out until you were *really* sick—or else you got better on your own.

Still, when we walked into the place the first set of guards didn't blink an eye. Carlos was a bio specialist, and he had the right to march a man into the clinics. The next step would be harder.

We didn't bother with the wards, the examination rooms or the dispensaries. We made a beeline for the back of the place, where they kept the serious equipment.

At the next set of doors was another pair of guards. These men weren't like the white-suited beefcakes at the entrance, no sir. They were armed and armored. They didn't look like they wanted spit from us, and they watched our approach with growing suspicion.

"Veteran!" I boomed at the nearest of the two. "Open that portal! We have reason to believe there's trouble inside."

"Excuse me, Centurion," the noncom answered, "but who the hell are you?"

So far, so good. He hadn't recognized me right off. If he had, he'd probably never let me pass. You see, I was a man with a particular reputation, a reputation that didn't spark trust in guards and the like.

"Are you aware there's an assassin aboard?" I demanded. "Our tribune was murdered moments ago."

He shook his head, and I showed him my tapper. There the video I'd stolen from Galina's security system played. He watched the critical moments.

"Wow, what can we do about it?"

"Let us into the revival chambers. We have reason to believe the assassin is in there."

The guard hesitated. "Okay," he said at last.

He turned around, but the other man stopped him. "We've got to call this in. We need permission to let two unknowns into the sanctum."

"Yeah—yeah right," the first man said.

Right there, that second guy had made a terrible error. The first guy had been reasonable. He'd been doing his job, but he'd been willing to bend the rules under extreme circumstances.

The same couldn't be said of the second guy. He was a stickler. I hated those types, and so did Carlos.

The rules-lawyer had his back to Carlos. He was frowning at me, as I'd done all the talking up until this point. I could have told him from long experience that you didn't turn your back on any bio specialist. They were among the worst of all the sneakiest bastards alive.

The stickler stiffened as a syringe penetrated a port on the back of his armor. Just as a testament to the unfair and dirty nature of all bio people, they'd lobbied to have ports embedded at strategic locations in all our armored suits. This was supposedly so they could do their jobs, helping the injured and such-like.

In practice, they could break-and-enter at will. The ports would only open at the touch of a member of their anointed priesthood, while even an officer like myself couldn't open those same ports on his own suit of armor. It was all sheer evil in my book.

"What—?" the victim grunted, then he kind of stiffened up and pitched forward on his face.

The other guy wasn't slow on the draw, I'll give him that. He had his hand on his weapon, and he had it out of its holster in a flash.

Unfortunately for him, I had my bigger hand on top of his. When the gun went off, it shot a bolt down into his armored foot. The metal covering his toes sizzled. I think the boot had stopped most of it, but not all, judging by the bared teeth and growling sounds coming out of the guard's face.

After that, Carlos and I made quick work of him. We beat him down, stuck him with needles—the works.

"Too bad about him," I said. "He was a reasonable man."

"Send him flowers in the morning. Come on, McGill."

Carlos managed to get the portal open with an emergency code—again, something that bio people aboard ship generally had access to—and we raced inside.

We got lots of hateful looks and even a few snarls from the staff inside, but they didn't try to stop us. There was blood on our hands, after all, and even the bio people knew enough about the animal nature of Legion Varus troops to stand clear.

We rushed to each of the of the revival chambers and threw open the heavy steel portals.

"Is everything all right in here?" I demanded.

"Get out!"

That was the universal outcry, but we hurried on, determined to check them all.

At last, I came to the one unit we had aboard ship that serviced the Blood-Worlder types. The Zoo legions needed a bigger revival unit, a machine so grotesque, so disgusting with dripping fluids and stench, that it could successfully give birth to a creature the size of a squid, heavy trooper or even a giant.

There, we found trouble. The staff of saurians were face down, tails stuck up—they tended to die like that when struck down by surprise.

"Oh, shit…" Carlos breathed. "Look at the *machine!*"

I did, and my horror grew. Now, I'm not an expert in these matters, but I could tell when a giant puddle of dark, blood-like fluids had pooled up under the outsized revival unit that something was very wrong.

The machine's flappy mouth hung open, dribbling and slack. It looked dead to me. Now and then, the whole thing shivered a little, but that was it.

We approached, ready to fight, in case the assassin was still in the place. Out from behind the machine a figure emerged. He staggered unevenly.

It wasn't any Shadowlander agent, however. It was another saurian. I knew him well.

"Raash?" I asked. "Are you okay?"

"No…" he said. "I have failed in my duties. My charges… they are all dead. I should die as well."

"Hold on a second. Where did the agent go?"

He pointed with a scarred up arm. "They are in the next chamber. Be warned, McGill, there are several."

We rushed out of the place and moved to the next chamber. It was the last one in line, and I knew in an instant why it was special.

The sign over the door said *VIP Chamber. No admittance.*

It was the room that they used to revive top officers and other important people. By all logic and reason, they'd be reviving Galina in there right now.

-31-

The portal was locked.

"Get this open!" I ordered Carlos. "I don't care what it takes!"

"You owe me, big man."

Carlos went to work on the lock, using every password he'd ever stolen from his superiors. In the meantime, I put my big mug up into the triangular window to have a peek.

There they were. Three of them, all wearing teleport harnesses and dark cloaks. Around them on the floor were the dead staffers. The bio-people had put up a valiant but hopeless fight to defend their sacred cow.

Fortunately, the revival machine didn't look damaged. In fact, the three aliens weren't trying to kill it—they were working it.

The machine's mouth fell open as I watched. There was a nasty splash of fluids as the water broke, then a pair of bare feet hung out into the steamy air. They were feminine feet, and I knew who they belonged to right off.

"Galina... hurry it up, Carlos! I think I know what they're up to."

"Just give me a second. I steal passcodes whenever I can—it's a hobby of mine. But the systems keep making people change them."

He typed in another code, but the door just beeped and rejected him. Carlos cursed.

Noticing my scrutiny, one of the aliens walked near.

It was the same female I'd seen before. The one that had killed Galina in the first place. She looked at me with curiosity, and I glared back. I made threatening motions, telling her visually what I was going to do to her scrawny neck if I got inside.

She seemed unconcerned, and she went back to cutting Galina's umbilical cord. I watched as she was lifted, helpless, and held aloft in the arms of her assassin.

"What? Are they going to just kill her again?" Carlos asked. "What's the point? We'll print out another one."

"Just get the frigging door open."

"I can't. This one is special—I don't have any code that can open it."

Frustrated, I looked through the portal again. I watched as the trio worked the console on the machine. They seemed to be doing something—something evil.

"Damnation," I breathed. "I think they're erasing her."

"What?"

"Her body scans, her engrams… they're hacking that unit. I don't know how, but they're messing with her files."

"No surprise there. They built the damned things. Wouldn't you put some special backdoors into the software if you'd designed our revival machines?"

I didn't answer. Instead, I hammered my closed fist on the portal. The aliens barely glanced at me.

When they were finished with their dirty work, they gathered together, holding Galina like a ragdoll. At least I could tell she was alive. She was feeble, like all newborns, but she was trying to struggle with them. Watching her like that… it made me angry.

"I'm going to rip you little weasels apart when I get in there!"

There were shouts down the hallway now. It was Fike and his team of crack patrolmen, no doubt finally catching up with us. I didn't care. I just stared at Galina and her captors. I was having some really violent thoughts right then, I don't mind telling you.

"What's that light?" Carlos asked.

I realized he was right. There was a glimmer and it was growing. The bluish light flashed rhythmically. It quickly became blinding.

"Oh crap, they're getting away," Carlos said.

I was banging on the door and raging—but it didn't help. Fike and his team arrived, telling us to stand down and other nonsense. When they peered into the chamber however, their attitudes changed. They pushed us out of the way and worked the door, but long before they could get it open the aliens had teleported out and left us behind.

When they were gone, Fike grabbed me and shook me. He was big enough that this action wasn't a joke, but it wasn't impressive, either.

"Damn you, McGill. Where are they taking Turov?"

"I don't know. I couldn't stop them. All these hogs got in the way."

Fike turned his eyes toward the bio people. He'd just experienced the frustration of being unable to open an important door on his own ship.

"You're right. This double-security nonsense on Blue Deck is bullshit. This ship belongs to Legion Varus—and to my support legion. Why do they need all these heavy portals and guards if they only serve to stop friendly troops, not real enemies?"

Carlos and I raised our eyebrows in appreciation. Fike was talking sense. That was a rare thing when it came to members of the brass.

To our further surprise, Fike left us alone and began kicking ass all around the place. He'd been on the spot during the actual kidnapping, I knew that was the key. Without that critical personal experience, he might have blamed the messenger for strange goings-on. Instead, he blamed those who had actually failed to stop the security breach.

The long and the short of it was I found myself at a meeting of brass up on Gold Deck about an hour later. The ship was in an uproar, and Fike had summoned all the key players to a conference room for what amounted to a group-spanking.

"All right. Let's get this straight. It's not entirely making sense to me."

Graves spoke up. He was the only one with the rank and the balls to do so under the circumstances. "We were attacked. Our tribune has been taken hostage. It's simple enough, the natives of 91 Aquarii have given us *casus belli* to declare war on them."

"That's true, but I want to understand their reasoning, Graves."

Graves shrugged. The enemy's reasons weren't interesting to him. He wanted to get down to the business of destroying them and have done with it.

Fike was staring at me all of a sudden. I lowered my tapper and looked dumb. It didn't work, he stepped closer anyway.

"McGill... you knew what was happening. How did you figure it out?"

"Uh..." I said. "It wasn't anything special. Someone killed Turov, so I checked the security vids. When I saw that the assassin was fooling with their teleport harness, I knew they were adjusting the target coordinates—but not by much. Most rigs have a single button to return home, so I figured they were jumping to another spot aboard our ship."

"Then you tried to catch her on Gray Deck, because you figured maybe her charge was low?"

"Yes, but I was wrong. They went to Blue Deck instead."

Fike nodded. "Why did they go down there? Why didn't they just kidnap Turov in the first place?"

I shrugged helplessly, but someone else cleared her throat. It was Centurion Evelyn Thompson. She was a big-wig on Blue Deck, which is why she'd been invited to the meeting. She and I had a history—but that was years back. Still, she made a point of not meeting my gaze.

"Centurion Thompson?" Fike asked. "You've got something to add?"

"We've been doing our own investigation. Mind you, we haven't had time to figure everything out yet."

"Of course not. Continue."

She began reading from her tapper. It had to be a prepared statement. That made me wince.

"The Shadowlanders from 91 Aquarii manufacture our revival machines," she began. "As you know—"

Fike made a spinning motion with his finger, indicating he wanted her to get to the point. I could have told him that sort of thing wasn't in Evelyn's nature, but I didn't want to be rude.

"They hacked into the VIP unit—somehow," she said. "We still aren't aware of how such a thing could be done. But, speaking as to their motivations—"

"Centurion," Fike said, "Turov is missing, and we're about to make planetfall over a hostile world in... less than two hours. Can you please get to the finish line?"

Evelyn stiffened. "Certainly. I'm trying to say that they killed Galina—our tribune, that is—in order to trace the packets carrying her engrams. Once a person dies, you see, there's a burst if at all possible to make sure the victim remembers as much as possible—like flushing a buffer, or closing a file."

"Yes, yes..."

"So, Galina's death essentially led them to the revival machines, which they vandalized. When she was reborn, they stole her physically and also erased her file—which was up on the console at that point. What it all means is that we can't print out a new copy of her."

"And if we do so anyway?"

Evelyn shrugged. "It will be a Galactic crime."

"So they took our leadership, and they apparently wanted to be thorough," Fike said, nodding. "We can't get her back without negotiating with them. She's a hostage, essentially. They must be looking for leverage in any upcoming conflict. It's diabolical..."

My hand shot up.

Graves glowered, but I ignored him. Fike flicked his eyes to me, and finally, with seemingly reluctance, he called on me. "You have something else to add, Centurion?"

"Just this, sir. I've been studying up on the Shadowlanders. They're in constant conflict with the other tribes on their world. In order to maintain order, they frequently hold hostages from ruling families. The bright-side people and the night-dwelling types are all controlled in this fashion."

Fike appeared surprised. "You researched this? On your own?"

"I surely did, sir."

That, of course, was a bald-faced lie—but Fike bought it. Natasha had done all the grunt-work concerning 91 Aquarii cultures and habits. She'd come up with this business of hostage-taking, and it had sounded good, so I'd decided to run with it. It never hurt to impress the new boss once the old boss had moved on.

After all this nonsense about research, Evelyn and Graves both looked at me suspiciously. They both knew me better than Fike did, but they didn't say anything.

"All right..." Fike said, "all right... I'm starting to get the picture. They think they have an edge on us. They think we'll back down under the threat of a single permed leader. What fools. This is Legion Varus!"

"Uh..." I said, not liking the new direction of this talk.

Fike ignored me. "We'll invade full-force. We'll show these insects what it feels like to be crushed under a boot heel. As you said Graves, they've given us a firm reason to attack. Once we're in control of the star system, we'll deal with the Skay from a position of strength."

I glanced over toward Graves. He was no longer frowning at me. In fact, I figured he no longer gave two shits about me and my truth-bending ways.

He was beginning to suspect what I already knew: that Fike enjoyed the taste of command. With Turov out of the way, this campaign was his baby. He couldn't even be blamed for it, as the aliens had struck the critical blow.

I realized as the meeting dragged on into tactics and landing zones, that the Shadowlanders probably believed they'd prevented a war. Ironically, they'd ensured there would be one. If they dared to perm their captive, Fike would be overjoyed. He'd be given free rein to run wild, wrecking their planet.

The part of the situation that bothered me the most involved Galina herself. I hadn't liked seeing her like that, all naked and drippy and helpless. They'd carried her off right from under my nose. The truth was, it had gotten my blood up. I wanted some pay back—and I wanted Galina back, too.

-32-

We came out of warp into the 91 Aquarii star system a few hours later. We didn't bother to hail anyone, or make other friendly gestures.

Dominus was in a decidedly predatory stance. We approached the world in question with our gun-ports hanging open like the mouths of panting dogs. Our missiles were fueled and armed, sizzling in their silos.

For some reason, Fike had posted me up on the bridge to watch the festivities. I'm not sure if that was because he'd liked the initiative I'd taken in chasing the alien invaders around the ship, or if he just wanted someone to blame things on if everything went tits-up. But it didn't matter much to me, either way. I was glad to be allowed onto Gold Deck without having to make up some kind of pretext.

Captain Merton was commanding the ship, the same as he had done for the battlecruiser *Berlin*. I'm pretty sure he hadn't wanted the job, but he hadn't been given a choice.

Merton was all right in my book, but he didn't like Legion Varus or Galina Turov. He'd wanted out of the transport business entirely. Unfortunately for him, in the Earth Navy, you took the assignment you were given.

"Sub-Tribune Fike?" Merton said for at least the third time. "Their planetary traffic control is demanding we contact them immediately."

"Ignore that. It's just bluster. They've got no defensive missile bases, no fleet."

"Yes, sir… but I must point out that 91 Aquarii is inhabited by over a billion citizens of Province 921. They have rights, sir."

"They have *nothing*," Fike said emphatically. "The Skay think they own them already. To me, they're on the border. They're not our citizens, they're in no-man's land."

Captain Merton looked Fike up and down disapprovingly. I thought for a moment he might answer the call anyway, going against Fike. Technically, he was in operational command until the planetary assault phase began.

In reality, however, Fike had all the cards. Turov had proven that to Merton during our last campaign, having him murdered when he went up against her. He'd spent some days on ice after that, as dead as a mackerel. Galina had told me she wanted to give him some time to think things over.

Merton stopped looking at Fike and turned away, eyes front. He shut his mouth, forming a tight bloodless line with it. I could tell he wasn't happy, but he wasn't willing to put his balls on the line for a principle—not again.

Fike seemed mildly surprised when the ship's captain backed down, but he recovered quickly. "We'll wait until they have something interesting to say."

Dominus continued to stalk forward. We glided silently, and I knew we must be intimidating to the locals.

Finally, when we were only a million kilometers out and beginning to brake for orbit, we got a different call. This time it wasn't traffic-control, continuing their dull mantra about regulations and the necessity of clearly stating our intent. Instead, it was a private, encoded transmission from the planet's surface.

"Sir," one of the Gold Deck flunkies said, turning to glance first at Merton, then Fike. "Sirs, someone from the surface is hailing us."

Merton's face was stone. He stared at the view screens as if he hadn't heard the flustered ensign. Fike stepped forward into the gap.

"Pipe it up onto the screen. Let's see what we've got."

A face appeared, bigger than was natural, taking up a meter of the forward wall. She was attractive, but kind of alien-looking. I knew her in an instant. She was one of the Shadowlanders, one of those who'd invaded our ship.

I took an involuntary step toward her. Fike eyed me and put a hand on my shoulder.

"Is this the one? Is this the bitch that dared to attack our ship without provocation?"

Now I knew why he'd let me up here. He'd needed an eye witness.

I shook my head. "I don't think so. She's similar, but older. Maybe a relative. Maybe they all look like that—I don't know."

Fike nodded. "Good enough. Ensign, open the channel, let her talk."

The woman's eyes shifted. They swept over us. She was able to see and hear us now.

"Earth ship," she said. "You have invaded our space in the manner of a striding warrior, but you are sworn to protect us. Why would you behave in this fashion?"

Fike took center stage, and her cold eyes fell on him. "I'm Tribune Fike. I command this expedition. You people attacked us during our approach. Know that I've ordered our shields to be raised. You won't invade this vessel again."

The woman looked concerned. "I'm Kattra, and I rule the Shadowlanders. I might be called a queen in your language, although I was elected, not chosen by birth. Hear my words: we did not attack your ship, Fike."

"Lies!" Fike shouted. He made a pin wheeling motion with his arm. "Send them the video file. Play it live!"

A nervous ensign complied. A sub-screen opened next to Kattra's looming face which showed three figures—clearly Shadowlanders—swarming and abusing a revival machine. Saurian attendants lay dead at their feet.

"Ah," Kattra said. "I see there is a misunderstanding. Those agents were sent to repossess what is ours."

"What? You mean the revival machines?"

"Yes. It is within the scope of our contract to end our lease-agreements at any time. Earth's government refused our

185

polite requests, so we took it upon ourselves to perform this action. Check your contracts. You will see the matter was agreed to decades ago."

Fike blinked in confusion. It was possible that the woman was speaking the truth, at least the way she saw things. Hegemony had a zillion contracts with a zillion other worlds to provide valuable alien trade goods like the revival machines. These arrangements were necessarily complex and held in secret.

"We don't have a copy of any such contracts aboard our ship," Fike complained.

"Ah—then we are at an impasse. Perhaps if you are still confused, you can wait a dozen of your short days. A committee of Nairbs is coming here, I understand... along with others."

So, she knew about the Skay. What else did she know? I was intrigued. These Shadowlanders had looked kind of simple from the sparse intel we had on them, but I was beginning to think they were anything but.

Fike was becoming frustrated. "All right. Fine. Explain this action then."

Another video began to play. We saw an agent killing Galina viciously, then kidnapping her fresh revive shortly afterward with two others.

"Another misunderstanding," Kattra said. "The female you displayed ignored our demands to return the revival machines, which began before you left Earth. Further, she was engaged in the unauthorized use of one of these machines when my agents arrived on the scene."

"You mean she used the machines after you killed her?"

"Yes, of course. They were forced to make an arrest."

Fike was pacing and fuming. "Such bullshit... Where is Galina Turov, you pirate?"

Kattra turned her head to one side, as if hearing a translation. "A pirate... that is an insult, yes? You call us lower beings. You should know we aren't bandits, not like the bright-siders or the vicious creatures who dwell forever in the dark half of our world."

"Yeah, yeah, whatever. You're a frigging pirate all right. A pirate queen. Now, listen to me: you can't just pop aboard our ship, kill and kidnap our commander, and expect mercy. Prepare to be attacked and conquered if necessary."

"If necessary? What action on our part might prevent the irrational fit of rage you describe?"

"Return to us what is ours. Immediately."

The woman turned away, talking to her subordinates off-camera. Finally, she looked back toward us. "Very well. Your talk and threats are brutish, but I think we shall make an effort to appease you. Lower your shields so we can deliver what you require."

"By teleporting?" Fike asked, thinking it over. "Hold on."

He turned to the crew. "Can you Fleet-monkeys make it so only a small part of the ship is unshielded?"

"We can, Sub-Tribune," Captain Merton said. "But I would advise against it. They might send up a bomb or something."

Fike gave him a feral grin. "That will give us all the more reason to destroy them. Expose something we don't need. The crew quarters, for example."

Merton made a disgusted face, but he huddled with his officers. He turned back less than a minute later. "It's done."

"You hear that, pirate lady? We opened up—"

"Yes, we detected the shift in your shielding. The package has been sent. When you have verified the contents and found them satisfactory, please contact me again."

The screen went blank.

Frowning, Fike turned toward the crew. "What did they send? Is it Turov? Where is she?"

"We're scanning for anomalies now, sir... no, it's not Tribune Turov. The computer isn't showing her aboard—dead or alive."

"Well, what the fuck—?"

Captain Merton put up a fat hand. "There's an energy release. A reading has spiked on deck seven."

"Deck Seven? That's the Legion officer's mess! If you brought a bomb aboard and let them set it off in the middle of my men, Merton—"

I almost laughed, despite the tension of the situation. Merton had made his own interpretation of what a "useless area of the ship" might be. Apparently, he'd decided it was Fike's own lounge.

"It's not a bomb. Someone came aboard, and they're teleporting again now."

Fike grabbed the captain by the tunic and shouted in his face. Spittle flew. "You spiteful jackass. They've sent us a bomb or another agent attack. God only knows what's next!"

"My actions were taken under your orders!" Merton fired back.

I had to admit, I was going to have to award the point to Merton on this one. Fike was more of a trumped-up primus than a real tribune. His legion was made up of dumb-ass mutants and the like. He'd never been in command of a serious operation that had to deal with something bigger than a single infantry battle on some planet or another. We were now in the realm of diplomacy, negotiations and space battles. Fike was out of his league.

A blue-white glimmer began on the bridge then, and people scattered. Whatever the Shadowlanders had seen fit to send our way, it was popping into existence right in the midst of us all.

The Varus men roared and drew weapons. The Fleet pukes ducked and shrieked.

As I was close to ground zero. I stepped closer. I'd dealt with things like this before, probably more often than anyone else aboard *Dominus*.

Any kind of teleportation attack was terribly hard to stop. The key to them was surprise. Unless the attack was an automated bomb, it could be dealt with.

I didn't think it *would* be a bomb. There hadn't been much time for the enemy to transport a drone attack aboard and have it be smart enough to port again, coming to our bridge. That sounded like the work of a trained agent. I'd seen such Shadowlanders at work, and I figured I was seeing it again.

When the agent arrived, I was first on the scene with my pistol in her face. I'd once gunned down a full squad of squids who'd invaded Central this way. On other occasions, I'd slaughtered Rigellian bears and even humans. The key was not to hesitate. You had to shoot the enemy down before they could get their bearings and take action.

I knew all that, but still, I hesitated. The Shadowlander was the one I'd seen before. She was the one I'd raged at, the very same alien woman who'd kidnapped Galina only a few short hours before.

By all rights, I could have shot her down. I had every reason and opportunity to do so—but I didn't. Why not?

Well… she was kind of cute.

"Freeze!" I shouted. My big face, big hand and pistol were all up in her personal space.

"I submit to capture," she said.

Baring my teeth, I gripped my pistol. The other Varus men circled around, surrounding her with an angry circle of pistols in tight fists.

She looked around slowly, her eyes sliding from side to side. "I will disarm myself," she said, reaching up slowly and unfastening her teleport harness. It slid away to the deck. Then, she unbuckled her gun belt and let it drop as well. A long dark pistol with a slim barrel clattered on the deck, along with a wicked knife that spilled out of its sheath. Was that the very knife she'd used to murder Galina? I kind of figured that it was.

"All right then," Fike said, stepping forward and waving his troops back.

They all stood down, except for me. I kept my pistol trained at the agent's pretty head.

Fike glanced at me, but he didn't order me to change my stance. Maybe he figured I had the right to be paranoid.

"Identify yourself and… ah…" Fike said.

I knew what the problem was right off. The alien woman hadn't stopped stripping things off. In fact, she'd opened her tunic, which was kind of like a wetsuit, and she let it peel away from her body. The empty sleeves were flapping below her waist, and she didn't seem to have a stitch of clothing on under that. Not even a bra—nothing.

"That's not entirely…" Fike said. He stopped with his mouth hanging open.

The woman was still undressing. She pushed the wetsuit down over her hips, which were kind of skinny, but nice enough to look at. A moment later, she stepped out of her suit as naked as a jaybird.

"Uh…" Fike said. "Why are you stripping down?"

"Tradition. Exchanged captives are always taken nude. There is no other way to ensure they aren't armed somehow. Isn't it the same with your people?"

"Well… not always… you can just—"

"Hold on," I said, putting up a hand. "If I might have a word, sir?"

Fike blinked at me. "What is it, McGill?"

"I strongly suggest that we need to respect her alien culture, sir. This lady operates under different rules than we do. If we don't take her surrender under her own terms, she might feel free to break other agreements we have with her and her people."

"What? That's nonsense."

"It isn't, sir. I've dealt with a stack of aliens. They've got all kinds of weird ideas. It's best to play along."

Fike sighed. "All right, whatever. You take charge of her. Transport her to the brig under guard."

I tried not to grin. "You can count on me, sir."

Someone snorted nearby. I thought it was Captain Merton. He knew me better than Fike did, so I didn't take offense. He could think whatever he wanted to. I would declare to anyone who asked that I was determined to protect my ship from this dangerous lady-alien. I'd swear to it, in fact.

Taking the agent by the arm, I turned to go.

"Wait a minute," Fike said as if something had just occurred to him. "Who are you?"

He was addressing the agent, so she answered him. "I'm Helsa," she said.

"Does that queen bitch Kattra think giving us a hostage is somehow a valid payment for all that your people have done?"

"It is a beginning, a peaceful gesture. It's tradition for two powers in dispute to exchange hostages at the outset of negotiations. Is it not the same with your people?"

Fike snorted. "Not for the last thousand years or so. Take her out of here, McGill."

Helsa stared at Fike as I walked her off the deck. Then she turned her head quizzically to one side as she eyed me. The behavior reminded me of Kattra who'd done the same thing on the big screen earlier.

"Uh…" I said, having a thought. "You're not by any chance related to Kattra, are you?"

She looked up at me next with those big eyes. "I am. It is she who trained me to kill with efficiency. She's my mother."

"Oh…" I said. "Oh shit."

-33-

Now, to set matters straight, I've known and consorted with any number of scary women—but even by my standards, Helsa was a special case.

"So... you're like, an assassin, right?"

She had one of those Imperial translators embedded in the bone of her skull, right under her left ear. She listened to it a moment before nodding in agreement. "That would be an appropriate term. Also, heroine, or adjudicator, are titles that come close to the mark."

"Hmm..." I said, thinking that her people's idea of a hero must be different than our own. "But you like... kill people, right?"

"Not always. Often, a mission involves the destruction of enemy assets or the gathering of critical intelligence."

"Okay, so you're a spy. An agent who works for your mom."

"Yes! These terms are more accurate."

Helsa was finely built, which was easy to notice as she was alongside me in the nude. She had a fine way of walking, too. Her nudity didn't seem to bother her in the slightest, so I didn't make a big deal out of it, and I tried not to stare too much. She padded along in bare feet like it was the most natural thing in the world.

"Are you an honorable girl? One who's not likely to try to escape?"

"These questions are in direct conflict," she said.

"Uh…" I said, puzzling out her words.

"Whoa!" Veteran Daniels exclaimed. We'd reached the elevators by now, where he was still posted to pester people. "Who's your new girlfriend, McGill?"

"She's a prisoner, funny-man. I'm taking her down to the brig."

"*That's* the prisoner?" he asked in a disbelieving tone. "Only you could get away with something like this."

"Like what?"

He made a flippant gesture with one fat hand. "She's obviously harmless. Yes, I can see she's an alien. Pretty close to human, but those ear lobes are too long. Her eyes are kind of spooky, too."

He stepped forward and put his fat hand on Helsa's wrist. She looked at the hand quizzically.

By this time, I was getting pretty tired of Daniels. "Back off, hog. I'm taking her down to the brig."

"No you're not. I've got orders from Fike. He wants you back up on Gold Deck."

I grunted unhappily. Daniels took custody of the girl with obvious relish. His whole face lit up as he walked her onto the elevator.

The pair turned to face the doors and Daniels touched a button. I noticed that Helsa was frowning at Daniels' hand, which was still latched onto her wrist. It was a new expression, one I hadn't seen before on her face. I could tell she was irritated. Daniels had seen fit to keep ahold of her, and he didn't seem to understand she could be dangerous.

As the elevator doors shut, I thought about warning him. I really did. But something evil inside me kept me from doing so. I figured that if Daniels lost a few fingers on the way down to the security deck, well, he kind of deserved it.

Whistling loudly, I returned to Gold Deck. Fike was having a powwow with Captain Merton, who still looked like he smelled shit.

"All right, Merton. Pull your ship up to high orbit. We can't drop from there, but we'll be out of range of any defensive guns they might have."

"I told you before, Fike, the locals lack any kind of space-based defenses."

"Yes you did, and you were wrong. They popped agents aboard *Dominus*, and you almost lost her due to incompetence. I repeat: You'll move to high orbit, ready to swoop back down into landing range with fifteen minutes' notice."

There went good old Fike, making friends again. I recalled he had a talent for pissing off other officers. Winslade had outright hated him at first sight.

Captain Merton nodded his head stiffly. I could tell he didn't love being ordered around on his own bridge—no captain ever did.

The two men noticed me, and Fike gestured impatiently for me to speak up.

"Sirs," I said, stepping forward. "Did you want me for something, Sub-Tribune Fike?"

He turned slowly toward me, and his eyes darkened. "What are you doing here? You couldn't possibly have delivered the prisoner to the brig so quickly."

"Uh... Daniels took over to do that, sir. He said it was done under your orders."

"You're mistaken, McGill—or you're lying. I don't care which it is. If you've lost that girl already, it's your ass."

Fike turned back toward Merton, and it was about then I realized I'd been screwed. I raced for the door and thumped down the passages. By the time I reached the elevator, however, it was too late.

Daniels was facedown with his own knife planted in his spine. For good measure, that fat hand he'd been too eager with had been sliced off.

It was a clean cut. One stroke, no-fuss, no-muss.

"That girl knows how to handle a blade," I said aloud with honest appreciation. "Etta herself couldn't have done better."

I was inside the elevator car then, and a tiny sound caught my attention. I whirled, my hands coming up into a fighting stance.

There was the girl, stuck to the ceiling like some kind of spider. Her feet were braced, her legs and arms splayed. She was able to hold herself up there—maybe her palms were sticky or something.

Helsa aimed a pistol into my face. It was Daniels gun. I cursed, realizing I'd been distracted by the body and the knife. I hadn't even checked to see if she'd armed herself.

"This elevator is programmed to ignore my biometrics," she said calmly. "Move the body, close the door, and take us to Green Deck."

Shrugging, I did as she asked.

"Why'd you kill Daniels?"

"I found him unpleasant."

"Uh... but not me?"

"You are less disgusting. Less weak and obvious in your motivations. I sense in you a strange combination of honesty and duplicity. I'm mildly intrigued."

I put my hands on my hips and looked up at her. She wasn't even straining to maintain a pose that no human could manage. That was bizarre, but I'd dealt with plenty of aliens before. They were full of surprises. For all of that, I'd never met one that couldn't be killed—or fooled.

"I thought you said you were an honorable agent. You're our prisoner, right? I demand you accompany me to the brig until we decide what to do with you."

She gave me that quizzical tilt of the head again. "Would you submit to such treatment?"

"Uh... probably not. But this was all your idea—your mom's idea, I mean. Listen, are you going to cooperate or not?"

"There is little you can do about it at the moment," she said.

"Wrong."

So saying, I stepped up, reaching high with my, long, long ape-arms, and plucked her skinny ass off the ceiling.

She fired the gun at me—or rather, she squeezed the trigger. But it didn't go off.

"Biometrics," I explained as I set her on her feet and removed the gun from her hand.

"You're strong, and brave, and tricky. But you're not fast."

So saying, she swept up a foot toward my privates. If I hadn't been wearing a cup, I might have been stunned—but most military men wear protection for moments like this.

My foot moved next, and I swept her feet out from under her. I didn't put her down hard. I caught the back of her head so my knuckles took the blow instead. This left me kneeling over her.

Helsa was breathing hard. She looked kind of pissed. "You humiliate me."

"That's my intention, girl."

A hard little fist came up and cracked me one on the cheekbone. It would have hit my nose if I hadn't turned my head.

I stood up, and she bounced to her feet like a cat.

"You don't want to go and get me riled," I warned her.

Her eyes darted down to Daniels, who was still soiling the floor of the elevator.

"You're not like him. He was slow, stupid, distracted and a poor fighter."

"Yeah, well… Daniels' isn't a legion man. He's just a kind of cop. He stays on our ships—he doesn't fight for a living."

"Ahh…" she said, as if finally understanding. "You are a true warrior of Earth, then?"

"That's right."

"In that case it was an insult when your commander ordered such a poor specimen to take custody of an agent. He thought very little of me."

I blinked in confusion. "You mean you didn't change that order? You didn't hack Daniels' tapper and get him to take custody of you?"

She spat on the dead man. "Of course not. I wouldn't lower myself to be pawed by such a creature. Besides… I don't have the skills to hack your tech."

"Yeah…" I said thoughtfully, thinking of the gun and the elevator buttons. If she couldn't operate basic equipment, there was no way she was capable of sending a message that imitated a legit order.

We got to Green Deck then. Helsa took a step, but I barred her way with one thick arm.

"Why did you want to come here?"

"I was told you people keep a facsimile of Earth aboard your ships. I wanted to see your flora and fauna."

"Huh… well, we don't have much in the way of fauna. A few birds, maybe. What we do have is a lot of pretty plants. I could show you that."

"I'd like that."

She stared at me with those big eyes. Damnation, this girl was trouble. All naked and wide-eyed like that, I felt an urge to indulge her wish—even if she was a murdering alien.

"Just a second. I'm going to check Daniels' tapper."

Leaning over the corpse, I noticed for the first time that she'd knifed his tapper too.

"Did you do this? You can't perm him that way, you know."

"Of course not. But destroying his implant means he'll never remember what it was like to touch me. He might not recall meeting me at all."

"Huh… vindictive little thing, aren't you?"

"I am an avenger. That is one of the most appropriate terms in your language for my occupation."

Mumbling something about petty vengeance, I led my peculiar companion onto Green Deck. I showed her around for a few minutes—but the detour was a mistake.

"What the hell is this?"

It was Kivi. I could hardly think of a more unwelcome girl to meet up with right about then. Raising her arm, she took a couple of quick snapshots with her tapper and scowled at me.

At Kivi's side another trooper raised his big hand. It was Veteran Sargon.

"Hey, McGill," he said.

"Hey, Sargon."

I knew what it meant when Kivi led a man around by the nose on Green Deck. Sargon was either about to get some, or he'd already done so.

None of this changed Kivi's reaction to Helsa. Her lip curled like a snarling wolf.

"Disgusting, McGill. Positively disgusting."

"What?"

"Tell me your little naked friend here isn't an alien from the planet below?"

"Uh… can't do that, I'm afraid."

"I know you work fast, but this is ridiculous. We've only just arrived. How did you get a native up here so quickly?"

"She just sort of… popped in on me."

Kivi shook her head, grabbed Sargon's hand and led him off into the trees.

"Who was that woman?" Helsa asked.

"Nobody. She's just one of my support personnel."

"Strange… she was so familiar in her speech. You say she's your inferior?"

"Yeah… well… we've known one another a long, long time. On top of that, she's off-duty."

"You should discipline her. Will you do so?"

"Uh… maybe later."

"I would like to watch."

I laughed. "I'll see what I can do. Now, let's take you down to the brig."

Suddenly, her hand came up, and I flinched a little. I don't mind telling you, I expected pain—but it didn't come. Instead, she sort of caressed my arm with her fingers.

"I thought when you agreed to bring me here… I thought we would mate."

Standing still, I blinked a few times. I considered it. I honestly did.

At last, I sadly shook my head. "Nope, not today. Come on."

She followed me dejectedly. She stepped behind me as we exited Green Deck, but I spun around and grabbed her wrist.

Her hand was on the hilt of my knife. I almost hadn't felt her touch. She was a sneaky one, that was for sure.

Helsa looked at me in honest surprise. "Will you slay me now? Or abuse me?"

"Nope—but you're walking ahead of me from now on."

Helsa took the lead. I marched her pretty, naked little butt down to the brig. I couldn't even properly enjoy the view as I kept thinking she was going to pull something else—but she didn't.

When I handed her over to the Fleet security-pukes, they all looked angry.

"What took you so damned long? And what did you do to Daniels? He's away from his post, and his tapper isn't responding to any pings."

I glanced at Helsa. If these wannabe hogs found out what she'd done, they might put her in a straightjacket or something.

"Daniels and I are great friends," I told them. "We played a little game in the elevator. You'll find him in there."

The cops narrowed their eyes at me, but they let me go. With any luck, they'd blame me for Daniels' death. Since he probably wouldn't remember what had happened, that would work out just fine for Helsa.

Unconcerned with the regulations they read out to me, I left them mid-sentence and made my way upstairs again. The brig was always on one of the lowest decks, down near the engines, where it was hot and humid.

They took custody of Helsa arrogantly when I left. All of their pissing and moaning about Daniels had left me in an uncharitable mood, so I didn't warn them about the seemingly harmless Helsa.

I figured she'd school them on her Shadowlander ways before too long.

-34-

The next morning we dropped on the planet at 0600 hours. It was a fine morning for an invasion, and my troops looked like they were perky and raring to go—all of them, that is, except for Kivi.

She was still butt-hurt about meeting up with me and the naked Helsa. She was spreading venom about it to every female who was interested—which meant pretty much all of them.

"And he had her by the arm, too. Leading her around like a dog. I'm surprised he didn't make her wear a leash and collar."

"Now, now," I said, walking up behind her. "Let's not be spinning those tall tales, Specialist. We're about to drop."

The women surrounding Kivi gave me odd glances. I couldn't read their expressions as I wasn't good at that. But they didn't look happy. Even Moller was giving me a weird look.

Annoyed, I hammered my big palms together repeatedly, making a loud booming sound designed to interrupt every conversation in the module. "All right people, saddle-up. We're heading down to Red Deck."

"What?" Leeson complained. "No breakfast?"

"That's right. Leeson, you're with me. Moller, ride herd on the new recruits."

That got them moving. Instead of slouching and bitching, they started grabbing up gear and flooding into the passageways.

Leeson caught up with me just as I'd ordered. "McGill? The deck arrows haven't even lit up yet. Are you sure we're supposed to board the lifters already?"

"That's what I said," I spoke with utter confidence. "Fike's new. Maybe he forgot to push the button."

Just as I said these words, the floor under our feet lit up. It was stroke of luck, really.

"There we go," Leeson said. "I should have known."

I nodded sagely, as if it was all a choreographed operation. Glancing back along the line, I saw they were really hustling now. The unit moved at a ground-eating trot. We weren't in parade-step, but we stayed together due to long practice.

A face back there caught my eye. It was Natasha, and she was running, pushing her way up among the platoons.

Internally, I groaned. Kivi had probably gotten to her, telling her about Helsa. Damnation, these women had to get over this kind of thing—but I knew in Natasha's case that was pretty much hopeless. The girl had been hung up on me for over two or three decades now.

I picked up the pace. As I was in the lead and in command, the entire column was soon pounding along, passing over the deck with startling speed. Every now and then, a hapless crewman stumbled into our path, and we pretty much ran him over. Varus legionnaires were all business when the call to action finally came.

Daring another glance back, I saw Natasha was still gaining on me. *Shit*. That girl was persistent. I figured that if I made it to the lifter first, we'd get wedged in our seats, and she'd be unable to catch up to me and deliver whatever heartfelt message was simmering in her mind just now.

Taking a chance, I glanced down at my tapper. I'm well-known as a man who might leave a text message drifting for a week or more before I got around to reading it. Today was no exception, as there were no less than forty-one unread messages in my queue.

I'd almost made it to Red Deck and rushed aboard our assigned lifter when there was a snag. Another cohort had beaten us to the loading zone.

"You're early, McGill," a sour-faced Primus Collins told me.

Collins was mean-looking, and she had a long scar over her face. She'd never gotten her body-scan files updated to get that fixed. I guess that was because she thought the scar looked kind of cool. To me, it had ruined her face.

"Stand down," she ordered. "Stay off Red Deck for five more minutes."

Sighing, I stood aside and tried not to pant. I'd run down here for nothing.

Moments later, a gasping Natasha came trotting up behind me. She poked at my back persistently with a finger.

"Hey! What kind of bird is pecking at my backside?" I asked, turning around on her. I pretended to be glad to see her. "There you are, Natasha… did you know you're panting hard, girl? Did you let yourself go during that last furlough on Earth?"

She shook her head, and she crooked a finger in my direction.

I knew she wanted me to lean close. Hesitantly, I did so. A few of the troops guffawed.

"He's gonna kiss her!" Carlos howled in delight. "Right in the middle of a drop! Watch and learn, boys!"

Both Natasha and I straightened our spines immediately. We stopped leaning close.

"Frigging Carlos," Natasha complained. "Come on James, step out of the main passage. It's important."

I hesitated, but at last I followed her. I could tell after that run she wasn't going to give up easily. I might be able to shine her on this time, but she'd make sure she got her chance to speak her mind at some point. I figured I might as well get it over with.

Sighing, I followed her into a ready room that was empty. A few hooting sounds followed us, but I cut them off when I shut the door.

"What is so wildly important, Natasha?" I demanded.

"Did you read my messages?"

"Messages? I sure did!"

She twisted up her lips. "No, you didn't. Well, they weren't very specific, anyway. I wanted to be as vague as possible, so we wouldn't get into any trouble."

"Uh-huh…" I said, not getting whatever she was hinting about. I'm not terribly good at taking hints about anything. Just ask anyone.

At least I was beginning to figure out this wasn't about Helsa at all. That was a relief.

"Anyway, as you've probably figured out by now, I cracked the code."

I almost said "what code?" like an idiot. It was *that* close. But fortunately, a dim bulb lit up in my sorry brain, and I realized what the hell she must be talking about.

"The deep-link? You managed to crack the deep-link com system? What message did you intercept?"

"None, really. I just hacked Captain Merton's bridge console and downloaded a standard report he sent back to Central. After that, it was easy. After he transmitted the message back to Earth, I ran a program to look for patterns. It was like having the combination to a safe. All I had to do was dial it in, and—"

"Okay, okay. So, we can listen to anything we want?"

"Well… not really. We can listen to Earth fleet official communiques now—but that's all. If some aliens, like these Edge Worlders here, were to send a message with their own encoding we'd have to break their code first."

"Oh… Still, that's pretty cool. But why did you work so hard to get here? To tell me about this? Why couldn't it wait until after we dropped?"

"It's about the content of Merton's message."

"So what? Is he asking for permission to perm me or something?"

She looked around furtively. Then, she gestured for me to lean close. I obliged her, taking off my helmet. Her hot breath warmed my ear.

"Captain Merton has called for help. He told Central that Fike is out of control and out of his depth with this mission command. He's asked for a personal retinue of guards and a new commander—preferably someone of imperator rank."

"Huh..." I said, chewing that over. "I guess he got spooked when Fike threatened him on his own bridge."

"More like he got pissed."

"Hmm... okay. That is good to know. I can see why you didn't want to broadcast it over any open channels. I can also see how this project has real possibilities..."

Natasha eyed me with her pretty blues. She knew me well, as well as anyone, and she could tell where my mind was going.

"James? Aren't we going to turn this tech over to Central? I mean... it's a big deal."

"It is. I happen to know that the nerds inhabiting the basement under Central have been working on exactly this kind of technology."

"Oh, right... your daughter Etta works down there."

I looked at her sharply. "I didn't say it came from her. I've got lots of friends down there."

"Of course. Don't worry, I'm as guilty of espionage in this case as you are—I'm probably more guilty, because I actually did it."

I nodded, and I pointed down to the floor. The red arrows were blinking again. "We've got to board the lifter. Keep this under your helmet for now, will you?"

"Yes, Centurion."

We walked back out of the alcove and found most of the unit was staring at us. Money exchanged hands, and Carlos began to lead a loud clapping session. To my chagrin, Leeson and Harris joined in.

"That's right people, give it up!" Carlos shouted. "That has to be the quickest, hardest hook-up I've witnessed in a dozen lifetimes. I stand in awe, Centurion. Sheer awe."

Brushing past them all, I strode toward the lifter. I didn't meet anyone's eyes or make any denials. In my wake, Natasha was sputtering and growling about a "pack of lies," but I could have told her that it was hopeless.

At times like this, it was best to let the troops think what they liked. Besides, I didn't see how this particular moment could damage my reputation. I was already infamous for horn-doggery.

-35-

The lifter fell away from the bowels of *Dominus* with a gut-wrenching lurch. We dropped down, screaming into the atmosphere at the highest speed and sharpest angle the pilot dared. The external hull heated up with friction, rising to something north of twenty-five hundred degrees C.

Bouncing and shivering in our seats, we felt the heat penetrate the hull. The air inside the lifter became stuffy, and we all sealed our helmets. Then the jump seats under our asses got toasty. Despite being heavily insulated in our suits, it became mighty uncomfortable before the pilot pulled up and slowed his dive.

Swooping down around the capital city of the Shadowlanders, we made our grand entrance in style. Twenty lifters, full of Legion Varus and our supporting pack of auxiliaries from Blood World landed in unison. What a grand sight it must have been from the ground.

We encircled the town the moment the ramps went down. Trotting outside by the thousands, we met no immediate resistance.

The Shadowlander city was interesting in appearance. It was really a vast collection of large fabricated domes. Surrounding this was a hastily built defensive bulwark. A carved pit was the final defense, dug some twenty meters deep.

"Looks like a frigging fortress," Harris said.

"Yeah, but modern weapons can easily crack those flimsy metal walls," Leeson said. "They probably built them to hold off the primitives."

Looking around, I saw it was true. There were two major gates leading in and out of the town. One went toward the brighter side of the planet. In that direction, the sky was permanently lit up a bright pink. In the other direction, where the second gate opened, the road led into twilight. A purply darkness hung there.

Every month or so, the Shadowlanders picked up their entire town and moved it to a better spot as the sun grew too bright overhead. Like every soul on 91 Aquarii, they were nomads by necessity. They truly lived on the twilight edge of their world.

"Standard rules of engagement, people," I told my unit over tactical chat. "If someone takes a pot shot at you, you have permission to return fire—but don't pop off at any locals without verifiable provocation."

"That's no fun," Carlos complained.

I gave him a dark look, and he grinned in return. The truth was, I'd had about enough of him already on this campaign, and he was skating on thin ice. Of course, in his case, that didn't mean he'd change his ways. I'd have to kill him if I wanted some peace and quiet.

That gave me an idea, so I smiled back at him. "I've got a job for you, Ortiz. You're going into town at the head of our column."

"How's that? I'm a freaking bio. I'm supposed to pick up the pieces *after* you grunts screw things up."

I shook my head. "Not today. You're trained in xenobiology, right?"

He snorted. "I took a class once, but I forgot everything they said years ago."

"Good enough. You're my expert on local customs, diseases and other dangers. Get up there to the front line and tell me what we can eat, where we can safely walk—all that crap."

Carlos looked disgusted, but he knew he was outranked and outmaneuvered. He walked ahead of the unit with the light troopers, holding a snap-rifle tightly in his hands. I hadn't watched him hold a rifle like he meant business in years, and it did my heart good to see it.

"About time you put the fear of God in that pug of a man," Leeson said.

"He's a member of your platoon. Why don't you fix him?"

Leeson laughed. "Fix him? That's rich. Carlos will figure out a way to be annoying even after he gets himself permed someday."

I couldn't argue his point, so I dropped it.

Graves gave us the signal to advance once everyone was safely on the ground. Behind us, with a fiery whoosh, twenty lifters rose back up into the sky, leaving us behind.

As we approached the makeshift city, I saw the locals eyeing us. They didn't look scared, and they didn't look friendly. They kind of reminded me of Dust World colonists. You could tell just by the way they stared that they weren't entirely civilized.

They weren't entirely human, either, but I suspected we shared some kind of ancestor. I hadn't expected to find anything like a human this far from Earth, but it had happened before.

History hadn't been kind to humanity, not even in our home region of the galaxy. Long ago, various aliens had visited Earth. Our home planet had been regarded as a wilderness until a few thousand years back. Bored travelers had picked up specimens now and then, transporting humans to serve as slaves, exhibits, or to be dissected. Now and then, especially among the Cephalopod worlds, we discovered colonies of humans that had diverged somewhat from our own genetics, but who were still recognizable as cousins. 91 Aquarii was that kind of planet.

"There's no army, nothing," Harris said. "These guys have teleporting agents, but they're losers when it comes to a stand-up fight."

"Ah-ah," Leeson said. "Watch that kind of talk. They're more technically advanced than they look. They're also sneaky. Keep your eyes peeled."

I took Leeson's advice to heart. Helsa had taught me just how sneaky these Edge World people could be.

Graves and his unit walked in the lead of our cohort. We were right behind him, backing him up in case he needed it.

When we reached the glinting metal walls, a delegation of aliens came out to greet us. I recognized their leader, who was stern but attractive. It was Kattra, Helsa's mother.

She nodded to Graves and put her hands together in a movement that reminded me of an earthly monk. As I wasn't able to hear their talk, I stepped closer. My intrusion earned me some reproachful stares, but the legion Varus people stepped aside. After all, I was a centurion and my connection to the brass was well known, even if it was often scoffed at.

"...and we bring you greetings from Earth as well," Graves was saying when I got within earshot. "Your planet and your people should consider themselves to be a welcome protectorate of Earth from now on. We'll see to your security and well-being."

"Protectorate?" Kattra spat out. I didn't think she liked the word. "Are you saying you rule here now?"

"Not at all. We're representatives of the Empire. We're officially Enforcers for the Mogwa, we serve their will here in Province 921. Therefore, it's our job to defend any planet that comes under attack in this vast region of space."

Graves wasn't good at diplomacy. In fact, he was usually awful at it. But I thought he was doing a good job today, candying up what essentially amounted to an annexation.

Kattra, however, wasn't buying his nice words today.

"We don't want your protection. We're capable of defending ourselves."

Graves spread his hands wide. He was still on his best behavior, but I could tell he was becoming annoyed.

"Look, Queen, it's our job to defend worlds in this province. We're going to do our job, and since we have approval from the Galactics, we don't need your permission. Naturally, we'd prefer to do this with your full cooperation."

Kattra's eyes narrowed into slits. She slewed them from side to side, taking in our vast array of troops, armor and guns. Her eyes finally landed on Graves again.

"Now I understand why you didn't simply park yourselves in orbit and wait for the Skay. You're here to conquer, not to protect. Your disdain for us is evident in everything you do, human."

"Um... how's that? Have we offended you in some way?"

"Your insults are numerous. First, your top command Fike doesn't come himself. He sends a lapdog instead. That is your first insult."

To me, that part seemed like basic common sense. After all, these crazy people had already killed and kidnaped Galina. What would they do if they could reach Fike? God only knew.

"Secondly," Kattra went on, "you land with a force of thousands to talk of peace and protection. You seem to believe we are helpless. Trust me, we are not. To a Shadowlander a show of strength such as you've performed here today is an act of foolishness. A wise fighter never displays his troops. He strikes suddenly, unexpectedly, leaping close from the deepest shadows of our creeping sun."

I could tell Graves was getting annoyed. I was something of an expert on that subject, as I'd arguably annoyed him more times than any other man alive.

"Listen up, Kattra. I'm not here to negotiate or kiss your ass. I'm here to inform you concerning the realities of this situation. Do you understand me?"

She eyed the armored line of troops for a moment. At last, she inclined her head. "I understand fully. It is *you* who are confused. 91 Aquarii will determine her own fate. Nothing you can do or say will change that. Soon, the Skay will arrive. They will take ownership of our planet, and all will become clear. In the meantime, I will pay you back for your disrespectful words."

Saying this, Kattra produced a glowing length of blade. It was a force-blade, one that was intensely bright. She stepped forward with speed and grace, thrusting the bright shaft of energy at Grave's belly.

Graves was no slouch. He grabbed her wrist, twisted and threw her to the ground.

There, she gazed up at him with a feral smile. "I always carry a secondary blade that is as dark as the first is bright."

Graves blinked, then he staggered.

We all saw it then. A jagged black line had appeared, cutting diagonally across his belly. Kattra's second blade had penetrated his metal armor as if it were paper.

Kattra had gutted Graves. He was dead on his feet.

Rushing forward, I shot her. She saw me coming, but she didn't look fearful. She didn't even look surprised.

Graves' bodyguards, wankers all, stood around and aimed their weapons at the dead woman. A lot of good that did anyone.

Graves was struggling to keep on his feet. He looked at me, and his teeth were gritted. He lifted a finger and pointed toward the glinting metal walls.

"McGill... burn down that town..."

"Is that an order?"

"No, but I want you to find a way to do it."

Those were his final words. After that, he fell on his face and shivered in his death throes.

-36-

A few primus-types came running to the scene after it was all over. They fussed over Graves and Kattra, who were both as dead as doornails.

Primus Collins was among this useless gaggle. She'd never liked me, but today she looked like she wished I was dead in the dust instead of the two who lay at her feet.

"What did you say to her?" she demanded.

"Me, sir? Nothing. I just put a little punctuation on the argument, if you get my drift."

Collins nodded slowly. "You shot her. A leader of a planetary government. Why have you been allowed to keep breathing for so long, McGill?"

"Your question has been the topic of many lively conversations, sir, and that's a fact. But don't worry. I wouldn't get too fussed-up about all this. These people invented revival machines, after all. She'll pop right out of an oven somewhere after this, and we'll do the same for Graves. No harm done."

Primus Collins looked at me as if I was crazy. Her tapper was buzzing though, so she turned away to answer it. After a short, tense conversation, she turned back around to face me. She had the kind of grin on her mug that I knew pretty well. It was a vengeful look, I was sure of that much.

She flicked her finger over her tapper and transferred the call to me. "Tribune Fike wants to talk to you, fool."

"Uh… thanks," I said to her, then I addressed my tapper. "Hello?"

"McGill? This is Tribune Fike. Did you just murder a foreign dignitary? Again?"

"Yes sir, sort of. In my defense, I'd like to point out she was in the act of killing Graves at the time."

"I don't care about Graves. I don't care about you, either. What I care about is our source of revival machines. Do you get that? You've set this mission back!"

"Uh…" I said, wondering if that was why Graves' security team had done nothing to help.

"Listen, next time a Shadowlander tries to kill you, deflect the blows if you can. Take them if you can't. We have to convince these people we're strong, but we're on their side."

"Sure thing… Maybe I should take off my armor and walk naked into their town, sir? Would you like that?"

Fike's face darkened. I could tell right off he didn't like my remarks. The man had no sense of humor. None at all.

"McGill, here are your new orders: since Graves is dead, and your team is on the spot, you will walk your unit into that city. Recon the place and send back a live vid-stream. If they want to tear you apart for vengeance, they have my blessing."

"That's mighty—" I began, but he'd disconnected. "Shit…"

Harris was lingering nearby at this point. He always seemed to sense when important matters were being decided that would shape his near future.

"So what's the deal, McGill? Are we storming this town and slaughtering these uppity peasants?"

"Even better! We've been ordered to march in there and recon the place."

Harris narrowed his eyes. "We? As in this legion, or this cohort, or…?"

"As in us. 3rd Unit, the best and the brightest of Legion Varus."

"Oh for fuck's sake…"

He wandered off, and I watched him go. He was right, of course. We were royally screwed. But I'd never been a man who liked to kick off a suicidal mission on a negative note. I rousted my troops and led them into the city with fanfare. I didn't tell anyone else what the story was, but Harris had a big mouth. Leeson was soon on my tail.

"You just had to go and kill that woman, didn't you?" he asked me.

"You're breaking ranks, Adjunct. This is a combat mission."

Grumbling, he withdrew to his platoon of specialists. My unit was a mixed-forces formation, meaning we had a platoon of heavy troops, led by Harris, and a platoon of lights led by Barton. In the rear of the force was Leeson's group. It was made up of weaponeers, ghosts, bio people and techs. They did all the jobs that took a bigger brain than average to complete.

We walked into the sprawling city of domes unopposed. No one attacked us—they didn't even talk to us. The locals moved out of the way and watched our column go by. They didn't look terribly impressed, or terribly friendly. I'd seen their flat, lizard-like stares before. It was impossible to know what they were thinking, but I was pretty sure it was something unpleasant.

Something about the Shadowlander attitude made my skin crawl a little, I'll admit. I found myself wishing that our newly discovered personal armor was in mass-production by now—but it wasn't. We'd worked on the project since we'd discovered the secret to making Rigellian armor back on Glass World, but I'd heard from Etta that the investigation team had hit some snags. Mostly, they didn't have enough Vulbites to make the suits in quantity. Back on Dark World, there were billions of those overgrown centipedes to do the work by mandible. But on Earth, we only had about a hundred cooperative specimens.

Naturally, they'd tried to reproduce the material artificially. So far, they'd failed to do so. That meant that every suit of armor took days to make, and there weren't enough to cover a legion's worth of troops yet—if there ever would be. At the moment, they were as rare as the pig-Latin version of the Gutenberg bible.

Marching around in suits of regular old layered steel and titanium seemed half-assed to me now, but I suffered with it. After all, there was nothing else I could do.

Or was there?

"Leeson, send your ghosts up here!" I said in tactical chat.

A moment later Della appeared on my right, while Cooper materialized on my left. They'd both approached with their stealth gear on and activated.

"Creepy native trash," Cooper said. "After what they did to Graves, I'm surprised we aren't going house-to-house, burning them out."

"No such luck," I said. "Listen-up. These domes are organized with winding roads between them."

"Dirt paths, more like."

"Whatever. You and Della have a new mission. Della, you swing out to the right of us, one road over. Report back any ambushes forming. Cooper, you're to do the same on the left flank. Neither of you are to engage the locals, or touch anything. Got it?"

Della vanished without a word and moved away. Cooper, on the other hand, hesitated. "What if I find something interesting?" he asked me.

"What? Like some farmer's daughter?"

"No, no, like piece of tech we could use. A special item that would be of real value."

"No stealing, no looting, no giving them a hint you're around. A ghost is useless if people know you're lurking around."

Grumbling, he vanished and moved away as well.

The streets were dry and dusty, but there was a film of moss growing on everything else. The moss flowered and grew bulbs of fruit here and there. Most of the Shadowlanders lived off the stuff.

This mossy carpet was very successful on Edge World. It essentially grew continuously, creeping forward with the same slow pace as the local sun. It completely covered new land that was just thawing out as the cold night-side rolled into the warmer twilight. On the other edge of the shadowed lands, where the bright-siders dwelled, the relentless sun burned the moss, causing it to shrivel and die at an equal rate to the growth.

The end result of the situation was the nomadic life of the Shadowlanders. They followed the growing moss, ate of its bounty and then left their refuse behind for the bright-siders to pick over.

The streets themselves were lined with metal huts and domes. These dwellings were all hastily constructed, but they weren't artless shacks. Wicker baskets surrounded each quaint building, and I knew that when the time came again to migrate, the Shadowlanders would load everything they owned into these baskets and cart them off to a new region, driving away any night-siders who'd dared to remain in a warming slice of land to forage.

After we'd advanced a few hundred meters down the narrow streets, one of the soldiers knocked over a clay urn, which spilled out about fifty gallons of oil on the street.

"You dipshit! Don't wreck stuff!" I shouted at him. In immediate reaction, Veteran Moller cuffed him. There was a resounding clang and a fresh dent in his helmet.

The men were more careful after that. There wasn't much chatter on tactical, as nothing much was happening. The farther we went, the more the natives seemed to gather around, but they weren't doing much. They were just watching us—staring, mostly.

The people themselves looked a bit primitive. They dressed in thin sheer cloths—which was a pleasure in the case of the women, but kind of cringe worthy on the men.

"What am I looking for exactly, McGill?" Cooper buzzed in my earpiece.

"You'll know it when you see it."

Soon, the main street widened, and we were able to share the road with other local traffic. The buildings here were fancier, prefabs made of white metal that gleamed in the permanently purple sunlight.

Harris fell into step with me a moment later. He had his rifle up, and the muzzle tracked with everything his eyes fell on.

"You notice something, McGill?"

216

"What?"

"You see all those grav carts?"

I looked around. There were a lot of natives wandering around with gravity carts, which allowed a man to float a heavy load a meter or so off the ground. They were quiet, efficient systems for transport.

"So what?" I asked. "They've got to carry their stuff somehow."

"Sure, but why are all the carts going in our direction? And why is every load covered by a blanket or something?"

I blinked twice while I absorbed his statement. After a moment, I realized it was true.

On a normal city street, one would expect half the carts to be coming toward us, while the rest were moving away from us. But that wasn't the case here. All of them were flowing in one direction—right along with us.

We were flanked on both sides by dozens of covered carts, and I already knew that I wasn't going to like whatever the hell was under those blankets.

"Unit halt!" I called out on tactical chat. "We're going to take a break and regroup."

This caused my men to mill in some confusion. After all, you didn't take breaks in the midst of an enemy city while on patrol—at least, my boys didn't.

But the test proved effective. The people walking the gravity carts slowed a bit, but then they continued on after a moment of uncertainty. It was almost as if they had someone giving them instructions using headsets or bone-phones or something. As I continued to watch, I became more sure that they did have a coordinator I couldn't see.

"McGill!" a new voice buzzed in my helmet. "Why are you halting your march?"

It was Fike. I cursed quietly. I'd forgotten he was watching on live feed.

"Sir," I said quietly. "There's something wrong here. I smell an ambush."

"Good. Walk on into it. That might make them feel better."

I bared my teeth, but I managed to keep my tone civil. "Roger that.'"

We marched a few more meters up to another intersection. We were pretty close to the center of town, by my best estimate.

"Unit," I said, "take this left fork right here. Cooper, we're advancing toward your position now, give me a sit-rep."

My helmet buzzed for a second.

"Cooper?"

When there was no response, I quickly flipped through the vital signs list. Cooper was dead—so was Della. I should have gotten a warning about that, a beep or something, but I hadn't. Could they have hacked my HUD? These guys didn't look like tech wizards, but I knew they'd invented revival machines, so they couldn't be rubes.

Looking around, I saw there were more gravity carts than ever. They'd followed our turn, and they were all carrying something covered.

"Heavy platoon! Turn around and uncover the loads on all those carts! Move!"

Harris had been waiting for this order. He rushed toward the nearest cart, kicking it over with one big boot. That was a rude approach, but I hadn't been specific on how to follow my orders.

What rolled off that flipped cart surprised me—but in retrospect, it probably shouldn't have.

-37-

"Ambush!"

A moment after the warning went out, the things on the carts went into action. They rose up with deliberate slowness, casting aside their concealing tarps and blankets.

They were automatons, drone troops of the sort we'd outlawed on Earth decades ago. Each had a somewhat man-like upper body, but with three black metal bulbs where the head should be. They reminded me of a praying mantis seen close-up.

Their bodies were sleek, black metal. The bulbous sensors that served as eyes were made of blue polymers. Underneath the torso, they deployed legs that looked like a collection of telescoping spikes. In short, they were technological nightmares.

Earth's history had always been a gruesome epic of warfare, bloodshed and plain old murder. Along the way, we'd developed some pretty awful ways to kill each other. One of those we'd experimented with and discarded some time ago was the drone-trooper.

In history class, I'd been fascinated by the old files. Earth's drones had been built to more or less human dimensions, so they could use standard human weapons. That had worked out well, as the combatants didn't have to retool their factories to make specialized guns and such-like.

A drone always had certain advantages over humans—but disadvantages as well. They could be mass-manufactured, for instance. They also came with a heavy price tag, and they broke down fairly often.

According to the history I'd been taught, as far as you can trust any of the stuff they teach kids in schools, Earth had abandoned this kind of soldier after some experimentation during the Unification Wars. Unpopular from the start, the drones were said to be too expensive, and they caused a lot of unemployment.

They were ditched once and for all when the revival machines came into vogue. With that sort of tech, you could print out a man faster than you could build a drone, and for a fraction of the cost. Overall, that economic argument won in the end.

The same series of events hadn't occurred on Edge World, it seemed. It was ironic that this planet, despite being the inventors of revival gear, had gone another way with their military. I guess it was just a case of different strokes for different folks.

Once the drones had stood tall, reaching their full height the streets lit up, and the scene transformed into a wild firefight. Streams of countless bolts and bullets flew in both directions, but most of them were coming from our side.

The *things* rose until they loomed over the humans and Shadowlanders. Gunfire ripped into the drones, but the majority of the fire was deflected by armor.

I sent Harris and his heavies at them with morph-rifles and powered shotguns. My troops blasted the rising drones hard, which sent the cart-drivers running. A few of them caught a stray round as they fled, I couldn't say I regretted it.

"Take them down fast!" Harris admonished his men.

He was charging with the heavy troopers, and he seemed frantic to attack the drones as fast as he could. It was a rare display of bravado and ferocity on his part, and I for one was glad to see it. Still, most of the drones were unlimbering and climbing off their carts without much hindrance from the shower of explosive pellets. They were armored, and only a few of them were destroyed.

Unfortunately, I soon learned that Harris wasn't being efficient and on-the-ball—he was desperate. Once the drones got to their feet and unlimbered their big beam weapons... well, the nature of the battle shifted.

"Down! Down!" Harris screamed. "Kiss the dirt!"

I fell onto my chest, but I was a little slow. Others were even slower.

Those that didn't get down fast enough caught one of a dozen sizzling rays of heat that passed horizontally over the roadway. When these air-shimmering beams struck anything flammable, that object exploded into a gush of fire. Worse, when one touched an urn of oil, there was an explosion of burning liquid.

That's when I realized the urns were part of the trap.

"Those skinny, sneaky bastards," Leeson complained in my ear, "they lined our route with urns and filled them with oil on purpose!"

His complaint was undeniable. The urns popped in rapid succession and went up like bombs. Each one gushed orange flame, black smoke, and screaming men. It was as if they'd dumped napalm on the town.

"Take cover!" I roared, backing into a side alley and firing bursts at handy targets, "Take cover! Leeson, get your weaponeers on those drones! Knock them out!"

Leeson's men, God bless them, were already in action. They had their belchers out and they targeted the drones one by one. The drones returned fire methodically, and they took each other out on a one-for-one basis.

The drones became increasingly terrifying as we kept fighting them. They weren't entirely man-like, I saw that now. They stood taller than men, and they had three legs rather than two. Rising up to about four meters high, they moved on their telescoping tripod assemblies like walking spiders.

The top part of them was equipped like men, with two metal arms and their large death-ray weapons that plugged into their torsos. Whatever powered the drones also powered their weapons.

"Barton!" I shouted. "Attack with your lights!"

"Sir, we're trying, but snap-rifles aren't doing shit against these things. They're mostly ignoring us."

"Charge in close! Get under those tripod legs. Cut their wires with your knives, take a leg out, blow them up with your grav-grenades—whatever it takes. That's an order."

"Yes sir!"

That was Barton for you. She was the best leader of a light platoon I'd ever met. Most light leaders didn't like their jobs, which all too often involved suicidal tactics.

Not so Barton. She took a deep breath and charged when you told her to. No hesitation, no regrets. She always did her best with whatever she had.

Today was no exception. She rushed in with her troops behind her. Right there, she demonstrated her superior approach. She knew damned well that her troops were the least experienced and most skittish of legionnaires. Many of them would not reenlist, returning to Earth instead with hellish tales of their experiences in the legion.

The only way to lead such troops into battle was by taking risks yourself. Barton did so without relish, but she was elite to the core, you could just tell when you watched her.

She rushed under the sprawling legs of the first drone, and she sliced a metal tube from the hip area over her head. This sent up a gout of steam. The drone sagged, one of its legs dipping low and dragging in the sand. Two more of her troops came in behind her, and they took the drone down using the same tactic. They sawed with their diamond-sharp blades, severing vital lines and toppling the drone.

Leading her troops toward their next victim, her luck ran out fast. This drone had learned that these thinly-clad soldiers weren't harmless. It dipped an arm low, with wicked speed, and lanced her through with a curved length of metal that looked like an insect's killing spike.

In a moment of final vengeance, she did manage to set off her grav-grenade, destroying the drone and two of her troopers who were sawing at its leg hydraulics. The death made me smile. She had gone out in style.

When the last of the drones was destroyed, we huddled in the flaming streets and took stock of things.

222

"What have we got? Harris, you still alive?"

"Yes, sir. I've got nineteen heavy troopers I'd call effective—but Jamison is kind of burned up in his armor…"

"Good enough. Leeson?"

"Four weaponeers are still in the fight. Most of my bio people and techs are still alive. They scattered like hens when the firefight started. Both my ghosts were fried—that means the enemy can see through stealth, sir."

"Noted…"

"McGill? McGill! Report, Centurion!"

It was Fike again. How could I have forgotten about that asshole?

"Sir!" I said, tuning to his frequency. "Good news! The locals set up a little welcome-wagon for us, but we—"

"Why the fuck are the streets on fire, McGill? I walked away from the orbital console not fifteen minutes ago to attend a meeting aboard ship, and when I returned to examine the scene I learn that you've laid waste to the town!"

"Now hold on a second, sir. The enemy did that to themselves. Review the vids."

"I don't have to. I should have known that sending you into a hot zone would result in monumental destruction."

"You've got the right end of that, sir," I agreed. "A Legion Varus man is really only good for one or two things—and neither of them is called 'diplomacy'."

"All right… withdraw. Pull back the same way you entered, double-time. We'll have to come up with another approach. Fike out."

These were welcome orders, and we followed them with gusto. We raced out of the burning town, dragging our wounded along with us. Long before we reached the entrance, a lifter came roaring down and squashed a half-dozen people's homes.

We hustled aboard and lifted off with a gush of flame and radiation. I thought the extraction was a little rude, but I appreciated the gesture from Fike. Maybe he wasn't such a bad sort after all.

-38-

Thousands of Legion Varus troops, along with a full supporting legion of Blood-Worlders, had surrounded the Shadowlander town. It looked like a siege—because it was.

Our lifter didn't take us back up into space. Instead, it did a little hop out of the middle of the Shadowlander town and landed at the encircling Legion Varus encampment.

"Fike's really going for it," Leeson said. "I hope one of those cute agent-girls doesn't come along and assassinate him, too."

I glanced at Leeson, who grinned back. It was really inappropriate to be talking in such a manner about our new CO, but everybody was doing it anyway.

Fike was untested at this level of leadership. He knew how to handle an op, sure. He'd even led large formations of troops in support of several campaigns. All of that was fine and dandy, but true responsibility for a campaign on an interstellar level was something else again. Not since distant times, back when the Earth hadn't been fully mapped out yet, had local military commanders been saddled with such vast freedom to screw up.

An Earth legion commander was on his own—literally. In most cases, he was hundreds of lightyears and weeks of travel time from home. There were faster-than-light communications options, but they weren't continuously monitored from afar. Because of the distance and time-lag in our chain-of-command,

224

the officer in charge on the ground had to make independent decisions that were both political and military.

A leader who was good at such things was valuable indeed, but in Fike's case, the jury was still out.

"You think Turov would have done better?" I asked Leeson.

He frowned, taking the question seriously. "I don't know. She's more of a chicken-shit schemer, but Fike seems more emotional. More prone to give an order while snarling."

I thought Turov could be quite emotional at times too, but I knew what Leeson was talking about. She was hyper-focused on not letting things go wrong. That led her to take fewer risks—and make fewer mistakes.

Fike, on the other hand, had ordered me to march into that damned town with no clear mission. That had led to a deadly encounter. The flames and destruction in the midst of their town would never have happened if Fike hadn't pushed things. The Shadowlanders had felt threatened, so they started a fight.

Walking off the lifter with the few of my troops who'd survived, I was surprised to see who was waiting for me at the bottom of the ramp.

"Centurion McGill," Fike said, "this way."

He turned his back, and I glanced at Harris and Leeson. They looked surprised, but they didn't take long to recover. Leeson made a kissing motion, perhaps suggesting I should do some kissing-up. Harris, on the other hand played with the hilt of his knife and flashed his eyebrows up and down in my direction.

Was Harris really suggesting I murder Fike? That was just like him. He was full of drastic ideas that would cause other people to risk their lives and careers.

"Uh… Tribune Fike, sir? Weren't you up on *Dominus* just a few minutes ago?"

"I was. We've set up some gateway posts, and I came down the moment I saw what was on your vids. I need a full report on those non-standard drones you fought."

"They were non-standard all right."

While we walked to the command bunker, I began describing the nature of the robot troops we'd encountered. By the time we reached the gloomy shade under the bunker, I got to the part about the death-ray.

Fike stopped, looking at me in concern.

"So, they blasted their own town, setting it alight?"

"As God is my witness sir, that's what happened."

He nodded thoughtfully and pushed open some swinging doors. I followed him, and we parked ourselves around a battle computer. It glowed between us, being the relative size and dimensions of a pool table back home.

"Let's look this over," he said, bringing up maps photographed from orbit by *Dominus*. "Essentially, they hit you in the center of their own town. They fought on their own ground, heedless of damage or loss of life... it was almost suicidal."

"That's about the size of it, sir."

"What do you think of these drones? Were they locally built or imported?"

"Uh..." I said, thinking it over. "I'd say they'd almost have to be imported. They have decent organic tech, but those things couldn't be made in a mobile dome. Constructing those metal nightmares would take too much in the way of specialized industrial machinery."

"Right... our techs have sampled the moss carpet that wraps the rotating edge of this world. They say it has DNA traces that match up with any revival machine. That all makes sense—but not these killer robots."

"Well sir, I would put to you that the Shadowlander people must have plenty of Galactic credits to spend on imports. Their revival machines don't come cheap, and Earth can't be their only big buyer. They've got to be spending the money on something."

Fike wagged a finger at me and nodded. "That's a good point. It makes sense, but what I can't get over is their willingness to take casualties like that in the midst of their civilian population."

I shrugged. "Pretty easy to pop out a reprint of any citizen that dies, I guess."

Primus Collins pushed her way to the edge of the battle computer then. Her face, under-lit in the bluish glow from the big screen, looked even less pleasant than usual. She eyed me like she'd spotted a turd in her kitchen.

"I've found Bevan, sir," she said. "He wasn't easy to locate."

Surprised, we all regarded the man she had in tow. Reluctantly, Veteran Bevan took a spot along the rim of the big computer.

"Hello mate," he said to me. "It's been since the Moon, hasn't it?"

"Damned right it has. Glad to see you're still breathing, Bevan."

"He won't be for long if he doesn't start becoming useful," Primus Collins snapped.

"All right, Bevan," Fike said. "You're an expert on alien tech—at least that's what people keep telling me. Review today's action."

Fike played back the battle in the streets of the Shadowlander city. Bevan watched in alarm. He winced and sucked on his teeth in appreciation as the battle unfolded.

Finally, Fike paused the action and made a spinning motion with his fingers in Bevan's direction. He was demanding a verdict.

"They're drones, obviously," Bevan said. "They must be an Imperial make, they can't have been built locally on this world."

"Where are they from, then?" Fike demanded. "Who sold them weapons like these?"

Bevan shook his head. "They're not from our province. You can't get gear like that anywhere in 921."

He looked up at us, and we all stared at him.

"So..." Fike said, speaking up first. "You're saying the Edge World people are already in contact with the merchants of Province 926? That they're trading with other worlds in the Skay province?"

Bevan nodded. "They must be."

We all stared down at a single frozen frame from the fight. One of the alien-made drones had rammed a spike home, lifting a dying trooper in the air. A spray of blood flew wide from the victim's abdomen. It was a gruesome and shocking reminder of the enemy abilities.

We didn't know much about our new enemy, but we knew they had weapons we'd never seen before. Suddenly, this campaign was looking much more dangerous.

-39-

Fike pulled off his helmet and rubbed at a carpet of stubble on his wide jaw. "I've got to report this to Drusus," he said at last. "We've lost our commander, and we're dealing with shit I've never seen before…"

Right then, for the first time, I approved of his decision. Turov might have pressed onward, working blindly toward whatever disastrous finish awaited her, but not Fike. He wasn't that stubborn—or maybe he wasn't quite as good at denying reality as Galina was.

The brass wanted to plan in private, so they kicked me and Bevan out of their bunker. Blinking in the slanting sunlight, we walked out into the gleaming twilight of the alien sun.

"Isn't it weird how that sun just hangs under the horizon, never getting any darker or brighter?" I asked.

"Actually, it *is* getting brighter. Only at a very slow rate."

"I know that. But it doesn't seem to be moving. Not at all. Their sun is slower than a snail on an hour hand."

"A what?"

"It's an old expression. Anyway, do you know if they have a canteen setup somewhere yet? I'm kinda thirsty."

Bevan grinned at me. "Of course you are. Right this way."

Three drinks later, I was feeling a lot better. The horse-piss they were selling wasn't exactly beer, but it did the job nonetheless.

"McGill?"

My tapper was talking to me again. This time, it was Primus Graves. He'd obviously been revived and probably had awakened with some degree of curiosity regarding his final moments.

"Hello Primus," I said in a cheery tone. "Bevan and I are having a drink in your honor. You died like a true Varus man, and I avenged you on the spot. It was glorious, if I do say so—"

"Shut up. I've got a fix on your tapper now—hold still, I'll be there in a minute."

The screen on my arm went blank. Bevan leaned close and frowned. "You don't think Graves will shut down this little watering hole, do you?"

"I dearly hope not. I'm not half-way to drunk yet, and I don't like leaving an important job unfinished."

True to his word, Graves arrived shortly thereafter. We'd managed to consume one more drink by that time, and I had a fresh brew waiting on a flipped-over crate for Graves the moment he walked in.

I offered it to him, and he sniffed it doubtfully. "Smells like varnish."

"As a matter of fact, sir," Bevan said, "it rather tastes of varnish as well."

Graves nodded, and he downed the drink. Then he sat on his makeshift stool and eyed us both sourly.

"I've been trying to catch up," he said. "You killed that witch Kattra after she nailed me, right?"

"With extreme prejudice, sir."

He nodded. "Of course you did. Then, Fike got pissed and ordered you into the alien town, at which point you torched the place?"

I began to protest, but he lifted a gauntlet to quiet me. "Whatever. Save it. Fike must not know you all that well yet, or he wouldn't have given you the opportunity to create more destruction."

"Uh... I guess not. You want another drink, sir?"

He shook his head. "Nah. We've got another mission—the three of us do, that is."

Bevan and I glanced at one another. We were slightly drunk and seriously baffled.

"Come on," Graves said. He sighed and climbed to his feet.

We followed him out of the underground bar reluctantly. Outside we met up with Fike and Primus Collins, who were walking and talking. Collins gave us a final sneer, then saluted Fike and walked off.

Fike then turned toward us. "It's been decided that we need to seek outside advice," he said. "Wait a second... are these men drunk, Graves?"

Graves looked us over. "Maybe Bevan is, but McGill always looks like that."

"Great... okay, you're relieved. I'll take charge of these two now."

Graves saluted and left. Bevan and I gave each other confused glances. Bevan looked worried.

"Come on," Fike said. "I'm taking you two with me as witnesses. We've got some explaining to do."

He led us to a set of gateway posts six bunkers down. The pigs were working hard today, encircling the Edge World town with puff-crete bunkers and freshly-dug trenches. This seemed odd as I knew the Shadowlanders were due to migrate in a week or two, when the sun crept too close for comfort.

Following Fike, we stepped through the gateway posts to God-knew-where. I did so without hesitation. After all, wherever I was headed, I'd probably seen worse.

Stepping out of the posts again, I knew in an instant where we were. The gravity was different, the air more sterile...

"This is Central?" I asked aloud. "Where are the resident hogs?"

"They have the night off," Fike said. "Actually, we used the VIP entrance. We aren't down deep in Central's vaults. This landing spot is for brass only."

There *were* hog guards at the exit of the chamber, but they were actually polite to Fike. There was no growling, no orders to fall to our knees or to show valid ID. Instead, two gentlemanly apes offered to help direct us to our final destination. They did look at Bevan and me like we smelled funny, however.

"Sub-Tribune Fike?" the lead hog said. "These two aren't upper tier…"

"Don't I know it. Don't worry, if they aren't housebroken, they're my responsibility."

"As you say, sir."

The hogs let us pass. We stepped out into the echoing hallways of the upper floors of Central. Windows—honest-to-God windows—showed stunning views of the clouds, a dozen neighboring sky-scrapers and flittering air traffic.

After less than a hundred more paces, we came to a set of big golden doors I knew all too well.

"You mean to tell me Drusus lives right here next to a set of gateway posts? He never even mentioned it!"

Fike laughed. "Of course he didn't. He'd have been crazy to let you know such a thing existed."

With my jaw hanging low, I followed Fike into the lobby, then the sumptuous foyer. Beyond these, we entered the waiting zone of Drusus' amazing office.

Occupying an entire floor of upper Central, it was prime real estate by any measure. In the center of it all was an aircar—a new one. This unit looked better than the old one. It didn't even bother with wheels, which meant it wasn't built to roll down normal streets. Instead, it had skids, fins, and God only knew what else.

The aircar attracted my attention immediately. I approached it, whistling loudly.

"Sub-Tribune Fike…?" Drusus asked in surprise, "…McGill? And who's this?"

Fike wheeled to gesture toward Bevan, who was lingering at the doorway. He looked like he was going to wet the carpet.

"This is Veteran Bevan, sir," Fike said. "He's an expert in alien-made products."

"All right, welcome all of you. To what do I owe this honor, gentlemen?"

"Praetor," Fike said. "Our mission has hit a snag. I felt it was necessary to come back to Earth and seek your advice."

By this time, I'd reached the aircar. I ran my hands along those long, low fins. The tips were like blades, and they sliced my fingers drawing a red line across them. "What a sleek machine!"

Drusus spotted me, and he cleared his throat pointedly, but I kept on walking around the vehicle as if mesmerized.

Drusus turned back to Fike. "Tell me, Sub-Tribune, what's the problem?"

"Tribune Turov was killed by a Shadowlander agent, sir."

"So?" Drusus shrugged. "Print out a new copy of her—unless the revival machines aren't working. Is that what you're here to report?"

"No sir, the enemy damaged a few of our machines, but the rest are operating fine. The trouble is they kidnapped Turov the moment she was revived. Using some kind of passcode, they got into the machine's software and deleted our backups of her. We can't print a new Turov at this point—she's effectively permed, sir."

Drusus blinked at that. "Hmm… that does put a different light on things. Have you tried—McGill?!"

I snapped my head around, and I found both of the officers were staring at me. With as much dignity as I could muster, I slid my lengthy person out from behind the wheel of the aircar and threw the door shut. The vehicle was of quality build—you could tell by the way the door crumped closed, rather than slammed and rattled.

"Sorry sirs," I said. "This sure is one fine piece of machinery."

"And I want to keep it that way," Drusus said crossly.

No doubt he was unfairly remembering some years ago when I'd had a disagreement with his previous model of aircar, and it had been slightly… disfigured.

"Get over here, McGill," Fike barked.

Sighing and leaving a lingering streak of blood behind on the hood, I walked back toward Fike and Drusus. I didn't even bother to ask if we could go on a little joyride. I could already tell the answer would be "no" before I even asked.

Bevan had taken a quiet seat at a circle of chairs, so I joined him and wiped a bloody hand on his pant leg. He glared at me, but he didn't say anything. He was too over-awed by Drusus. That's the trouble with an inexperienced man in my book. Bevan was too new to the Legions to know Drusus was just another piece of the brass.

"It gets worse, sir," Fike said. "I took command—I thought I could handle it. I tried to negotiate Turov's release, but all they did was hand over a hostage in exchange for our tribune."

"Another hostage?"

Fike showed him imagery depicting Kattra and her daughter Helsa. Drusus frowned at both of them. "They don't look all that dangerous."

"The older one took down Graves, one-on-one. The younger—she almost murdered McGill."

"Nonsense!" I called from the cushy comfort of Drusus' waiting area. "I was only baiting her."

"Of course..." Fike said. "Anyway, sir, the aliens are tough-minded, well-equipped and unwilling to surrender. McGill patrolled their main town just today."

"McGill did what? Good God, man. Did you order that?"

Fike looked a little sheepish. "Yes sir. I thought the natives would come to their senses."

"How many dead are we talking about? Hundreds? Thousands?"

"Hundreds, sir," Fike admitted. He'd taken off his service beret, and he held it in his hands. His eyes were downcast, studying the hat he was fidgeting with.

Drusus stepped away from him and looked thoughtful. "I can see it all now... A lack of leadership, a resistant enemy, and McGill in the middle of everything. I'm not surprised a series of negative events have transformed into a disaster. What can I do to help?"

"Well sir... you could print out a fresh copy of Turov, for one. I know Central must have a back-up copy in case—"

"Hold on right there, Fike. The point of this mission is to deal with Galactic encroachment on Province 921. We can't very well commit a serious violation of their laws a few days before they arrive, can we?"

"I suppose not, Praetor."

234

Drusus paced for a while. I could tell he was doing some hard thinking. I felt sleepy just watching him, and I began to slouch in that soft, comfy chair. How could the brass even stay awake with furniture like this under their butts all day?

"I could send out Deech..." he said, and I released an involuntary snort of alarm, "but," Drusus continued, giving me a reproachful glance, "she's not available at the moment for interstellar duty."

Sighing in relief, I slid back down in my chair.

Drusus snapped his fingers. "I know just the man. He's commanded the legion in the past, and he's been pestering me about a transfer for months now."

I blinked, wondering who he could be referring to. My mind was a blank.

"If that's all, gentlemen..." Drusus began, and even I knew we were getting tossed out of his office.

"One moment," Fike said. "I brought Veteran Bevan and McGill along for another briefing I felt they were the most qualified to give."

Fike turned the show over to us then, and we approached Drusus' planning table as a team. We played vids showing the fighting machines we'd battled on Edge World. Drusus was suitably impressed.

"You handled that ambush like a pro, McGill."

"Sure did... thank you kindly, sir."

"In fact, everything apparently went smoothly until you blew up the town with napalm."

"That wasn't me, Praetor!"

Drusus shook his head. "Regardless, I can see these machines are a serious threat. Bevan, what do you know about them?"

With a halting voice, Bevan told him about the enemy machines. He concluded with his suspicion that the machines were made in Province 926, rather than our own 921. Drusus seemed to find these details ominous.

"They're already dealing with 926... On one level, I can understand that. After all, in a decade's time, their planet will officially drift into Skay territory."

He paced around for a moment before continuing on. "There are two critical facts that make their actions problematic, however. For one thing, a decade is a decade. They shouldn't be trading with 926 vendors before they officially transfer into the hands of the Skay."

"And what's the second thing, sir?" I asked.

"The second problem is much more important from our point of view. We need to keep buying their revival machines *today*. We should have access to them for at least another decade. This action on their part might open us up to some legal trouble. The Skay can claim that the citizens of 91 Aquarii are already operating as if they belong in their province. It gives them legal ground to stand on."

Drusus looked up from his star maps to study us. His eyebrows were cinched up tight with worry. I'd often seen that look on the face of all my superiors. When I brought them news from the front lines, they never seemed happier. It was a rare day indeed that I left them in a more relaxed mood than when I'd arrived.

"McGill," he said. "I want you to question that captive from Edge World. Find out where Turov is being held."

"Uh... okay. I can try."

"Once you find her, you'll lead a mission to rescue her."

Drusus and I gave each other a serious glance. I knew what he was thinking. He knew Galina and I had a thing going on the side, and that we'd even been in love on and off for many years now. What's more, he knew I was probably the best teleporting commando he had. That combination of motive and know-how made me a natural for this mission.

I nodded in understanding. "She'll come home safe and sound, sir."

I heard a snort behind me. I knew that snotty sound well.

Slowly, I turned around. There was another officer present. I hadn't even heard him enter, probably because he was the naturally sneaky type. A man who I respected less than any of the others present.

"Winslade?" I demanded. "Is that really you? I guess the rumors are true!"

"What rumors, McGill?"

"Why, that you've volunteered to become the praetor's new secretary. That's what all the hogs are saying here around Central."

Now, I had no idea such a thing might be going on, but it stood to reason. Winslade looked startled.

"That sort of personnel assignment is up to Praetor Drusus, of course," he said stiffly.

Fike was trying not to grin. Winslade looked annoyed, and Drusus looked thoughtful.

"Winslade, I'm giving you an interim appointment. Your new post will make you the tribune of Legion Varus— temporarily, of course."

It was Winslade's chance to blink in confusion. His surprise might have been mixed with horror, too—it was hard to tell.

"This comes as a shock, sir."

"I'm sure it does."

Fike cleared his throat.

"Yes?" Drusus asked him.

"I don't see much logic in replacing one inexperienced man with another, sir."

Drusus nodded. "I've got more in mind than your service records. You're short one key commander out there with Turov out of the picture. You've already got your support legion to operate. You're good at that, and so there's no point in shuffling two people into new spots."

Fike looked glum, while Winslade still looked kind of shocked. For my part, well sir, I was grinning. Grinning big.

"There's more to it than that," Drusus said. "Winslade has been secretly working on the new armor McGill here brought back from Glass World. So far, we've yet to mass produce it. He can, however, provide a small commando team with superior gear."

Drusus reached a hand to his table. He replayed the vicious street fight with a practiced touch. He paused at the dramatic moment where one of my troops was made into a shish-kebab by an alien machine.

"With one of Winslade's suits," he said, "this sort of thing won't be happening again out there."

I had to agree with him. The secret armor we'd stolen from Rigel was amazing. If I was going to fight monsters like these combat-drones, I'd love to wear a suit of it.

-40-

Fike had gone back to Earth with a problem, and then he'd come back with a whole different one. I almost felt bad for him. Almost.

The first thing Winslade ordered was a full briefing. That was reasonable—but his reactions weren't. We held the briefing aboard *Dominus*, and although I did my damnedest to dodge out of it, I was dragged into yet another boring meeting.

"So…" Winslade began, interrupting Fike's briefing, "let me make sure I've absorbed these details, Sub-Tribune. Before you arrived at 91 Aquarii you were attacked and lost your commander, hmm? In spite of this *sick* error, you pressed onward, going so far as to allow this same assassin to return to your ship as a supposed hostage?"

"Well sir, first off, let me point out that I wasn't in command when the initial attack took place. However—"

"However, you still allowed a murderous saboteur aboard instead of insisting on Turov's return?"

"Not so, Tribune," Graves spoke up.

We all turned and saw Primus Graves at the doorway.

"Ah, back from the revival machines?" Winslade asked. "What, pray tell, do you have to add to our conversation, Graves?"

"Just this sir: I demanded the return of Turov. What's more, I demanded they submit to Earth's military protection. The Shadowlanders reacted violently."

239

"Right, right. I haven't even gotten to *your* disasters, Graves. All in due time. Please take a seat."

He did so, stiffly. I waved at him, but he wasn't in the mood. He glowered straight ahead, watching Winslade the way a snake watches a mouse.

"Back to it then," Winslade continued, turning his attention toward Fike again. "You managed to contain the planted agent, but only after someone named Daniels was killed—and McGill was nearly killed as well. I have all that down. At this point I'm going to offer a solution: Let's execute her."

The assembled officers blinked in surprise. Captain Merton was among them, and he raised a hand. Winslade signaled impatiently for him to speak.

"Sir... I don't think that would be wise. The locals are liable to kill Turov in response. That will perm her."

Winslade aimed a skinny finger at Merton. "That's exactly right, Captain. The situation is absurd. There is no equivalency between our captive and theirs. Kattra knows she can print out a new version of her daughter Helsa at any moment. That means she's not really a prisoner here at all."

"Well sir... but..."

"Silence. Listen people, your actions so far have been a series of abject failures. We're going to change all that."

My hand shot up. Sometimes it just did that, almost on its own. On other, worse occasions, I simply started blurting out words with no preamble whatsoever.

Winslade wrinkled up his nose like he smelled a shithouse, but he called on me anyway.

"Sir, I've got a better idea. Let's pull the same move they did on us."

"Explain yourself, McGill."

"I'll put on one of those fancy suits you've been working on, and I'll go down there and delete Kattra's daughter from their database. Then our hostages will both be real. They might be willing to make the exchange we've been asking for at that point."

Winslade narrowed his rat-eyes. I could tell he was seriously considering the idea.

Graves could tell too, so he got into the act with a sense of new-found urgency. "Tribune, McGill has no idea how to delete his own name from a tapper, much less repeat the magic trick the Shadowlanders performed on our revival machines."

"Not so, sir!" I boomed. "Natasha can reverse-engineer the hack. She can do anything like that."

Winslade looked at me, then Graves. He pointed a finger at me. "I like it. McGill, you've got twenty-four hours. Come up with a set of coordinates and a mission plan. If it looks workable, you're going in."

Graves and Fike both shook their heads and looked alarmed, but I ignored those naysayers. I stood up quickly.

"In that case, sirs," I said, "may I be excused from the rest of this briefing? I need to get right to it."

"Of course. Dismissed."

I waltzed out of the meeting with a broad Georgia grin on my face. Sometimes, I surprised even myself with my slick maneuvering. There was nothing I hated more than a long, rehashed meeting with no new information in it. With the careful use of a dozen words, I'd just escaped a small slice of Hell. Let the rest of them revel in it.

My first instinct was to find the officer's pub—but a nagging sensation caused me to take another approach. I went down to the labs instead.

Floramel and Etta had stayed back home on the Moon, but Natasha was down there in the *Dominus* labs. The place looked like a dungeon to me, but she liked it.

"James!" she said, smiling and excited. "I've got some real progress to show you."

"Huh? Okay..."

The truth was I'd kind of forgotten up until this moment that she had another secret project in progress. She'd been working on it for a long time, and I'd kind of figured by this time it couldn't be done.

She led me to a private office and turned on six kinds of anti-spy gear and VPNs, etc. After all that paranoid stuff, she brought up her software. She ran a few programs I couldn't make heads or tails of, until finally she had a bunch of symbols on the screen.

Her project consisted of listening in on deep-link transmissions. She'd figured out a year back how to see a transmission that was on-going, but now she was trying to translate it to know what was being said.

"They're using the Imperial alphabet. It's kind of hieroglyphic, but there are translation programs I can rely on. Here, check this out. Just yesterday a message was sent home from *Dominus* to Central. Using your suggested method of code-breaking, I came up with this."

Looking pleased as punch, she brought up some English words. Apparently, this was her translation of what had been sent.

"Barium-five, barium-five," I read aloud. "Water plant transmission, arch-down... Uh..."

"You see? Isn't that cool?"

"Heh... sure is. What the hell does it mean?"

She slapped my fingers away from the console in irritation. "I reported that our water recycling unit was down— even though it's not. Part of yesterday's transmission back to Central reported this false information. That's how I can tell my translation program is working."

"Huh?" I asked, scratching my ear with one finger. "I can't hardly make heads or tails of it."

"It's not perfect yet, James. It's a proof of concept, that's all. A serious advance."

I smiled falsely. "That's right, it sure is. I'm very impressed."

Natasha studied me for a moment, and I was worried. But then she smiled back, and I knew she was fooled. She honestly thought I was impressed.

"Okay," I said, slamming my hands together. "Now that you've got real progress in that department, I've got a new project for you to work on."

"What? But I've only just begun my effort here. This first breakthrough—"

"That's great, but it will have to wait. We've been given something more serious and immediate to do. Something official."

"Tell me about it."

I did, and as I spoke, her face registered fresh degrees of horror. "James... Twenty-four hours? I can't do all that!"

"Hmm..." I said. "Yeah... I didn't think you could."

"How could you be so insane as to tell the brass I could instantly hack alien hardware without even checking with me first?"

"Well... the truth is, I've got an ace in the hole."

Natasha licked her lips. She crossed her arms and leaned back, waiting for me to explain. I surely preferred the joyous expression she'd shown me earlier.

"There's something in Turov's quarters," I said, "something that can do the job for us."

A long time ago, I'd owned and utilized something called a Galactic Key. This object of power had been fought over for years, and it had finally wound up in Turov's hands. I'd let her keep it, as it was mostly trouble anyway.

Instead of naming it, I described what it did to Natasha.

"A universal hacking device? Something that works on Imperial technology?"

"It does. I've hacked revival machines with it before, in fact."

Natasha fell silent. She studied her desk for a time. "I've long suspected you had something like that," she said.

Then, with no warning whatsoever, she hauled off and hit me across the mouth.

"Hey! What's that for?"

"You know how much something like that would mean to me, don't you? But, just to get some favors from Turov, you gave it to her, not me. That is *so* like you."

"Now, hold on a minute. That's a very illegal piece of gear. If the Nairbs, Mogwa or Skay find out we've got it... well, they'll have one more good reason to perm the lot of us."

Natasha nodded slowly. "You're right about that."

"It's dangerous, girl. Giving that to you would have been a crime. I would have felt awful if you'd been permed over it."

She digested that thoughtfully, and at last she sighed. "All right. I forgive you. What do we do next?"

"We use the key to hack the Shadowlanders database, that's what."

"Hmm… let me see if I have the gist of your plan. First, you'll take the key and teleport down to 91 Aquarii where that silly siege is ongoing. Right?"

"Yep."

"Okay then… just do it. What do you need me for? There's nothing for me to hack."

I smiled. "That's not exactly true. Remember, I don't have the key yet… so I need someone to help me get into Turov's quarters. That's officially a crime-scene right now, see… not so easy to break-and-enter."

Natasha wasn't happy, but in the end she helped me. She was an accomplished hacker, and something easy like an officer's door lock was no problem. To get me into the area without raising an alarm, she turned off most of the security systems on Gold Deck.

Whistling, I marched past Veteran Daniels on Gold Deck like I owned the place.

"Hey! You there, McGill!"

I kept walking, making him follow me. When he caught up, I showed him my tapper. Natasha had cooked up some good-looking approvals for me to be on Gold Deck. They even had the right Fleet emblems and everything.

"Your orders do seem to be legit," Daniels said doubtfully. "I'm sorry, sir. Just doing my job."

"And you should keep right on doing it, Daniels. See you around."

Making my way to Turov's door, I tried the handle—but it was already hanging open. "Damnation, but you're good at this Natasha," I whispered to myself.

Stepping inside, I found I wasn't alone.

Someone stealthy was already there, so I didn't turn on the lights. I saw a figure in the dim illumination from the ship's passageway. Whoever it was, they were rummaging in Turov's desk.

Two steps, one roar, and a heavy fist swung down. The smaller man crumpled to the floor.

"You're under arrest, thief!" I boomed, standing over him.

I lifted the man to his feet and shook him. He didn't weigh much.

The lights went up then, having detected our movement—or maybe they'd responded to the noise. I wasn't sure how Galina had rigged her personal settings.

That's when I found myself nose-to-nose with a bleeding, angry, Tribune Winslade.

-41-

"Unhand me, you ape!" Winslade ordered.

I released him, and he almost fell on his ass again. Straightening up, he glowered up at me.

"Give me one good reason why I don't burn you down right here, McGill."

"Uh… because I was just doing my job, sir."

"Nonsense. Do you take me for an utter fool? I knew what you were planning the moment you came up with that cockamamie plan to go down to the planet and hack a revival machine. Not even Natasha can do that on a whim—but Turov and her little prize could."

Now it was my turn to glare. "Now see here, Tribune—"

"No. You shut up. I'm in charge here, McGill. Believe it or not, like it or not, this is my moment of legitimacy."

"So, you're after the key, huh?"

"That's right. I consider it to be the unofficial property of Legion Varus' commander. As such, I've laid rightful claim to it."

"Robbing Turov's grave so soon? Isn't this a little premature?"

"Not at all. Grave-robbing is best done while the grave is fresh—don't you agree?"

I was flummoxed. Winslade had been one step ahead of me all along. The feeling wasn't a pleasant one.

"Listen," I said, "I can't complete my mission without that key. You know that. Let me borrow it at least for tomorrow's jump."

Winslade huffed. "As if. You'll have to improvise."

"You know I can't—oh... wait a second. You don't *want* me to succeed. You want Galina out of the picture. You want Legion Varus on a permanent basis, don't you?"

Winslade shrugged. "The thought has occurred. In any case, if you would prefer it, I will relieve you of your mission. You won't have to make a suicidal attack tomorrow."

My eyes were narrow and dark as I regarded him. "So... do you have the key yet?"

"Of course I do. Now, I'm going to tidy this place up. Your new orders are to immediately vacate the premises and—"

I grabbed him. I knew he was lying. When I'd spotted him, he was obviously still searching for the key. He just wanted me out of the way so I couldn't stop him from finding it.

As part of our native-suppression gear, the quartermaster's had seen fit to issue wrist-ties to us. You never knew when you would need to take a captive on a mission like this, civilian or otherwise.

Before he knew what was happening, I had him hog-tied and face down on the deck. He made an awful racket and cursed up a blue streak.

"McGill, you're going up on charges this time! I will NOT suffer this kind of indignity at your hands again!"

"Now, now, Tribune. You know as well as I do that you're not supposed to be in here ransacking the place. Graves, Fike, the rest of the primus types—they don't trust you any farther than they can throw you. Not half that far, if the truth was to be told."

He kept on grunting and struggling, but my boot stayed planted on his spine. While he was down there, I searched him to be sure, before I went through Turov's desk.

"Huh..." I said. "Nothing."

"Get off, you oaf!"

"All right, all right," I said, standing him up like a ragdoll for the second time. "I'm real sorry about any indignities—"

"I'm not going to forget this, McGill. Not this time."

"That's real unfortunate, sir. I'll tell you what I'll do to make it up to you."

Winslade glared at me for several seconds.

"What?" he asked finally.

There it was. Winslade had pride, but never let it get between him and a good deal.

"Here it is: let's say I find that key before you do."

"You won't."

"But I know Turov way better than you do. I've got a list of other places I can search."

That was a lie, of course, but he didn't know that. What he knew was that I'd been intimate with Turov for years.

"So... what if you find it? You'll give it to me? Why should I believe you?"

"Because we're cutting a deal. Right now, just you and me. You get the key, but I get to use it one last time. I get to use it to go down and spring Galina."

"We don't even know where she is."

"That's right—but it doesn't matter. I'm going to erase Helsa, just the same way she did our girl. Then her mamma will cut a deal."

"After that string of unlikely events, you're promising to return the key to me?"

"That's right. Win or lose, you get the key. Scout's honor."

"Untie me immediately."

I hesitated only a moment, then I slashed the zip-ties and freed him.

Winslade snapped a needler into my face. "I ought to burn you down right now."

"Can't say as I would blame you."

He puffed for several seconds, then lowered his tiny weapon.

"All right," he said. "We've a truce, and we've got a plan. Now, where is that damned key?"

A slow smile split my face. "Come with me."

I turned my back on him and led him out of the office. I knew full well he might burn me down. I would have respected him more if he did so.

But I knew he wouldn't. He wanted that key far more than he wanted revenge. It was a weakness of the soul, just the sort of thing that plagued men like Winslade.

I led him down two decks, to a mid-deck zone. Technically, it served as our armory. Winslade never stopped rubbing at his bruised collar bone and complaining.

"If this is another of your goose-chases, McGill, so help me—"

"Just a few steps farther on, sir."

At last, we stopped about a hundred meters short of the ship's fire control center. There, feeling around, I found a compartment I knew would be there. I turned to Winslade.

"What is it now?" he demanded. "A fresh excuse? Are you needing more time, or perhaps you're simply out of lies, or—"

"None of those things, sir. I was just thinking you should step back a little."

Frowning, he did hop backward. It was just in time, too, as I'd fondled a catch behind a false wall.

With a groaning sound, a door opened up and clanged down between us.

"That panel is huge," Winslade complained. "I might have been killed."

"Uh-huh…"

We both stared into the revealed compartment. Inside was a dragon—an armored, self-propelled combat suit. It stood nearly three meters high, and it was made of shiny white metal—titanium.

"A *dragon*?" Winslade gasped. "How did it—Turov stashed it in here?"

"She does that," I said. "She's been hiding machines like this on ships for emergencies for decades. The first one I met up with was back on *Corvis*—remember that old ship?"

"Certainly, but which campaign?"

"Tech World. She drove it around the decks after we were driven off Gelt Station. I happen to know she found that experience exhilarating. Ever since then, she's been stashing fighting machines onboard starships whenever she can."

"All right… knowing her, I'm willing to believe that. But what makes you think she would stash the key here?"

I shrugged. "Can you think of a safer place? Let's have a look."

I climbed up the stirrups and opened the hatch over the cockpit. Rummaging around, I lifted a small pouch. I waved it around and grinned.

"Give that to me," Winslade hissed.

He had that small needler in his hand again. He was aiming right at me.

"Now, now, we had a deal, sir."

"Yes, and I might still honor it. But for right now, I order you to give me that object."

We had a short stare-down. Finally, I heaved a sigh and tossed down the key. He caught it after a single bounce in his off-hand. Cursing, he was momentarily distracted.

That's when I leaned into the cockpit of the dragon and touched an actuator. The battle machine's titanium fist jabbed forward, catching Winslade in the left ear.

He spun around and fell on the deck. He didn't get up again.

Climbing down, I tsked the whole time. He should have known better than to try a double-cross.

I plucked the key from his skinny fingers, then checked his carotid. I found a thready pulse. He was still alive, but he was going to have a hummer of a headache later on.

Grunting, I carried him up the stirrups again and stuffed his unconscious body into the Dragon's cockpit. The machine's interior had been tailored for Galina's small form, so it was a tight squeeze, but he fit without having to make any adjustments.

Sealing the false wall in place again, I left the scene at a trot.

Making my way down to Gray Deck a few minutes later, I told everyone my mission plans had been accelerated. Fortunately, they had some of Winslade's newest armored suits already available. I took the biggest one they had, forced myself into it, and put on a teleport harness.

Ninety seconds later, the world was a throbbing blue-white blob. I was on my way down to visit the Shadowlanders.

I hoped they'd be in a better mood than they had been the last time I'd met up with them.

-42-

The suit of armor I'd commandeered was much more advanced than the prototypes I'd tried out during the Glass World campaign. Back then, I'd worn what amounted to a layered stack of smaller suits made for Rigellian troops. It had covered me incompletely, but it had still been effective in stopping enemy weaponry as long as they didn't get lucky and hit one of the many cracks and splits.

The new suit wasn't perfect either, mind you. The helmet area was still vulnerable, for instance. Worse, there were a few ports and plugs that could be breached. But it would do fine for what I had in mind.

Armament was another issue. I'd chosen to pack one of the Rigellian shotguns along with a pistol and combat knife. Some might have suggested I carry a rifle for dealing with Shadowlanders at range, but I didn't like getting loaded down. Three weapons was about all a fella can realistically carry into battle if he wants to be fast on his feet.

The really important thing was my insertion point. Where, in that big mess of domes, huts and urns, etc., should I land? A good choice could mean success, while a bad choice would doom my mission to failure.

Intel told me where the enemy combat machines were stored, and where their command and control headquarters was—but I didn't care about any of that. I wanted to make this personal. I wanted to find their revival machines.

Reasoning that they'd be valuable and well-guarded, I chose to land near the center of their town. All I had the techs do was isolate a dome nearby that didn't have any life forms within ten meters—and I jumped.

Arriving in a crouch, I looked around, gripping my shotgun tightly. I became alarmed when I realized I was in the midst of two ranks of combat drones.

Suddenly, I realized why there hadn't been any life readings here: the place was full of robots.

Like me, however, the drones were motionless and kind of folded-up. They formed hulking dark shapes, most of them with blankets thrown over them to keep the dust off.

Lifting up a blanket, I took a peek. There were a few status lights on the unit I revealed. Most of them glowed yellow. The drone was charging.

It seemed to be shut down for the moment, and I considered disabling it—but I passed on the idea. There had to be twenty of these machines parked here, and someone was bound to notice if I started fooling with them.

Standing up in the middle of the throng of drones, I looked around. There was a Shadowlander tech nearby. He was monitoring the machines and eating some kind of nasty stew. It probably was made of that moss these folks liked so much.

Walking quietly, I approached him from behind. Something must have tipped him off, however. Maybe it was the swish of my black fibrous armor, or the rattle of a grenade on my belt. Whatever the case, he snapped his head around in surprise.

I had my knife out for a silent kill, if that was needed. The man's eyes widened and his spoon clattered to the floor. Without a word he reached for a big button on his console. I could only imagine that it would awaken the machines behind me.

My blade flicked out of my hand. It pinned his wrist to the console. The man howled a bit and struggled, but he managed to get to the console with his good hand.

I was rushing him, big stomping boots coming down in fast thumps—but I wasn't going to make it. I could tell that already.

253

The man touched the big red button. Behind me, a dozen machines stirred. They began that kind of slow wake-up process, the same behavior I'd seen them go through when they'd come up off the grav-carts in the streets. They must be rebooting, or something.

When I got to the console, I struck the operator in the head with the butt of my shotgun. He slumped over, but it was too late. The drones had all been activated.

"Shit!" I hissed out, tapping at the console.

It didn't respond to my touch. Every time I pressed an override or tried to get into a menu, it beeped and brought up some kind of security screen. I had no idea what the password might be, or even if the damned thing had a password.

Behind me, blankets began to slip away from the drones. They luffed to the mossy floor and the machines rose up, buzzing and activating their vision systems. Soon, they'd track me and shoot me down.

I considered running. I could have lit out of the dome and sprinted away. With luck, I might even have made it to the gates, what with my armor being hard to penetrate.

But that wasn't my mission. I wasn't here to make a fool of myself and get chased out of this Shadowlander town for a second time.

Then, I finally had an idea. It had been long in coming to that dusty gray organ in my skull, but at last, it had arrived.

"The key…" I said aloud.

Scrambling to get a hand into my armor, I managed to pull out the Galactic Key. It didn't look like much. It never had. The thing resembled a natural sea shell, all curved, smooth and shiny. There was no hint from its appearance that it had amazing hacking powers.

I applied the key to the Shadowlander interface, and the results were immediate. The security warnings vanished. I slammed my hand down on the same red button, but this time, it responded.

The drones behind me all froze.

I craned my neck around to watch. They didn't lie down. They didn't pull their sheets back over themselves. They just kind of stood there. Some were already in the middle of aiming weapons at me—but they'd all stopped functioning.

I breathed a little sigh of relief. "You dummies are going to have to wait to get a piece of old McGill."

Turning away from them, I took stock of things. So far, the mission had pretty much been a disaster. I'd failed to make any kind of a quiet, easy entrance. I had no idea where Galina was, and a score of evil machines had all marked me down for a quick death.

I sighed, freed my knife from the injured operator's pinned wrist and sheathed it. No longer held in place, the man sprawled on the mossy ground.

Right about then, it occurred to me that my plans so far could be called half-baked—or maybe even quarter-baked. The trouble had started once I'd clocked Winslade. After that unfortunate moment, I'd needed to get moving right away. I hadn't had time to figure out what I was planning to do down here.

Even now, Winslade was probably rubbing his head and getting himself all worked up. By the time I returned to *Dominus*, he was liable to be in a seriously ornery mood. Misunderstandings of this nature had gotten me into all kinds of trouble in the past.

"Gotta keep moving…" I told myself.

Taking a chance, I walked to the flimsy door of the big dome and peered out with one eye. What I saw was a busy street. Back aboard *Dominus* it had been nighttime hours, but here on 91 Aquarii, that's not how things worked.

It was always twilight here, never full dark or full light. At least, you never saw full night or full day if you were a Shadowlander. That was the whole point.

As far as we could tell, Shadowlanders didn't really sleep. They didn't have that entire circadian rhythm thing going, not in their strange lives. They rested when they were tired, but they didn't pass into an unconscious state like we did. To them, *we* were the freaks for hibernating on a regular basis.

Deciding that walking out into the main streets would be a mistake, I used my knife to punch a few eye-holes to look in other directions. To the west, I found there was another dome right up against the one I was in. It looked even bigger than the one I was in now, so I went for it.

Decisiveness was one of my strong points. Oftentimes, making any decision was better than doing nothing. This was definitely one of those times.

I used my knife to slice a narrow opening between the domes. The metal was quite thin, as the nomads had to carry it from place to place on a regular basis. In addition, my knife's edge was molecularly aligned. You couldn't find a diamond, shard of glass or a length of steel that was any sharper.

Cutting another eyehole in the next, bigger dome, what I saw inside surprised me. It wasn't a revival machine. It wasn't even a personal residence. Instead, it looked more like a throne room.

A central chair sat on a pile of carpets or blankets, or whatever they had to cover the ground. That was how nomadic people tended to live, with everything mobile. The whole town was built to be torn down and set up again every month or so. I guess it was a good thing Shadowlanders didn't sleep much. They had to be hard workers.

With a tearing sound, I cut my way out of one dome and into the next. But by the time I had gotten one leg into that chamber someone walked in the main doors.

It was a woman, and I knew her.

"Helsa, right?" I asked aloud. "What are you doing here, girl? You're supposed to be our prisoner."

Helsa froze. She stared at me, and her eyes slid around the room warily, looking for others. She walked into the chamber, drawing a weapon as she did so.

I made no fast moves. I just stepped all the way into the dome and stood there in my black armor, watching her.

"This is… awkward…" she said.

"Sure is. You're a cheat. Worse, you're a walking Galactic crime. The Skay, the Mogwa and the Nairbs, they're all on their way here, you know. What do you think they'll say when they find out about this gross violation of Imperial law?"

"I know that voice, that bulk…" she said, peering at me. "McGill? You're in that suit, aren't you? Why do you seem to haunt me?"

"You'd be surprised if you knew how many women had asked me that very question."

Helsa stepped forward four more paces, but I still didn't react. I recognized the weapon in her hand. It was a force-blade, switched off. Her mamma had used just such a weapon to kill Graves the day before.

Could a force-blade cut through my new body armor? I didn't *think* so...

"Why are you here?" Helsa demanded. "Are you actually alone? Such bravado... it's almost insulting."

"I told you I'm of a warrior breed."

"Yes, and I respect that. But you can't be here. You can't have witnessed what you have witnessed."

"No shame, huh? No honesty? No honor?" I asked, shaking my armored head and tsking at her. "I'm disappointed in you. I mean, sure you're nothing but a desert rat creeping around on a moss carpet down here on 91 Aquarii, but I kind of figured you were capable of keeping your word. But nooooo—"

"Shut up," she said, springing forward and thumbing her force-blade into life. It glowed and glimmered under my nose.

Naturally, she'd been walking up until she was close enough to pull her weapon out on me. I didn't even flinch.

"A sheer disappointment," I repeated. "You going to stab me now with that glow-stick, or what?"

"I don't want to. You're right... this is wrong. My mother ordered it, however. She's our sovereign. I can't disobey her any more than you can ignore the orders of your superiors."

I laughed. "You don't know me very well yet. I do, upon occasion, take certain liberties with the authority figures in Legion Varus."

Her mouth twitched. A hint of a smile. "I bet you do. In any case, you will be dispatched. Your memories will be deleted, and you'll—"

I reached out with a long, long arm. I did it fast, but she was faster. She flicked her glowing blade toward me.

My black-gauntleted hand grasped the force-blade in the middle of its sizzling length. Now, if I'd been wearing old-fashioned metal armor, or anything like it, I would have just

257

burned my hand clean off. But this stuff was the best personal armor humanity had yet to encounter. The fibers were impregnated with star stuff, and it was damned near indestructible.

A nasty smell erupted, and I could feel the heat of her blade. It wasn't burning me, not yet, but I got the feeling it could get hot enough to melt a bit and maybe even come through the glove. That process would take some time, however.

Surprised, Helsa tried to snatch her blade away from me. I let her take it, and I advanced. She slashed viciously, one-two-three times she drew a smoky line across my armored torso, but it didn't penetrate my suit.

Grinning, I kept advancing toward her.

"What are you wearing?" she panted out. "You sand-devil!"

"Just a little something our labs cooked up. You didn't think Earth became the enforcers of Province 921 by playing fair, did you?"

She tried to spring away, but I was already too close. She'd figured she could cut me down, but she'd thought wrong. Her overconfidence had allowed me to get within grabbing distance.

I clamped onto her wrists and shook her weapon loose. It fell to the carpets on the ground and burned a hole in them.

"Pity that," I said. "Come on, time to port out of here."

"Where are you taking me?" she demanded, her face registering horror.

"Why, back up to my ship, where else? We've got to get on the deep-link and report this to the Nairbs, pronto. They'll know what to do. If you're lucky, they'll only erase the Shadowlanders—but I doubt they'll stop there. With this kind of excuse, and what with the Skay taking over anytime now…"

Her eyes were tortured, and she looked like a wild rabbit caught in a snare. I didn't let up, however. She deserved it.

"You can't do this!"

"Yeah, yeah. People always whine when justice is done. I hear it all the time, but you have to turn a deaf ear and a hard heart to it."

"Please... my entire planet..."

"You should have thought about that before you pulled this bullshit move with the hostages and all. We didn't print out a fresh Galina Turov, did we? No, sir! We've got backups in our home data core at Central and all that, but we didn't break the rules. She's as good as permed as far as we're concerned. Too bad, but—"

"I'll get her back," Helsa said quickly. "I'll give her to you. Anything, McGill. Anything!"

Helsa twisted and writhed around in my grip, but I held on firmly. I wasn't about to let this snake get out of my hands again.

"Have her brought here, then," I said. "Right now. I'll take her back to *Dominus* instead, and that will be that."

Licking her lips and shaking a little, she used her tapper to transmit a message. Just in case, I revved up my suit. I could port her out of here in a flash if there was any more funny business.

A few moments later, two more women arrived. One was Kattra, and the other was Galina. They were both wearing those gauzy bed sheet type garments everyone seemed to wear on Edge World. Neither one of them looked too happy.

"McGill?" Kattra said. "I'm beginning to dislike you."

Galina's eyes roved around. I could tell she was thinking about trying to make a move. I hoped she didn't, as I had the feeling these alien ladies would kick her butt right-quick.

"I'm making a trade," I said. "I'm handing over your daughter for my tribune."

"That's unacceptable," Kattra said smoothly. "You already have my daughter as prisoner, and you—"

"No we don't. You made a frigging copy. She's right here, and unless you comply, I'll take her butt up to *Dominus* and report this matter to the Galactics. The Nairbs will be here any day now. They'll dispense justice upon their arrival."

Kattra's lower jaw jutted out. There was dark murder in her eyes.

She turned on her daughter in anger. "How did you let yourself be captured by this oaf?" she demanded. "You're an embarrassment to our entire world!"

259

"He has an impenetrable suit, mother."

"And you're the one who cloned Helsa," I said, jabbing a finger at Kattra. "That makes you the guilty party here. When the hell-burners begin to fall, sweeping away this strange world, remember that you personally brought it all down on yourself."

Kattra seemed to be catching on. She lowered her own weapons and bared her teeth. "Very well, McGill. I shall allow you to win this clash of blades. Don't dream that you will win the next."

Drawing her pistol, she aimed it at her daughter. Without a speech, she shot her dead.

I released the girl's hand, and she sagged down onto the carpets—which were looking worse for the wear by now.

"What'd you do that for?" I demanded.

"That's what you wanted, isn't it? Now, there's only one Helsa. She's aboard your ship. I would appreciate her release."

"Give me Turov, then."

Kattra hesitated, but then she passed over Galina. There were some jingling chains on her, and I could tell she wasn't happy about that. I put an arm around her, and she allowed it.

"Are you okay?" I asked her.

"No," she said sullenly. "I'm pissed."

I nodded.

Kattra watched us closely.

"You two are mates...?" she said. "I hadn't suspected it, but it all makes better sense now. Who else would come here and risk everything for such a vile woman?"

Fooling with my teleport harness, I set the destination. With any luck the suit would take us both home to *Dominus*.

"You have what you came for," Kattra said. "Now, you must release my daughter and promise not to tell any Galactic what happened here today."

"Hmm..." I said, thinking things over. "That's a tall order. I'm thinking you have to put more into the deal, seeing as we're the injured party here."

Galina was alarmed. "James, don't screw this up. Get me out of here before an army of drones marches into the dome."

"That won't happen. I switched them all off."

Kattra's eyes flew wide. "You what?"

"Hold on, hold on—forget about that. Here are my terms, Kattra. You'll tell the Galactics you wish to stay in Province 921 as long as possible. What's more, you'll ask for Earth to be your protector, and you'll sell your revival machines to us at a cut rate—say a twenty-five percent discount?"

"Twenty-five percent?! That's insane!"

I shrugged. "Okay, okay. Whatever. Make it ten percent off. Do we have a deal?"

Kattra's lips squirmed. At last, she nodded. "You have a deal, robber. Now, get off my planet!"

"Gladly."

With that, I activated the harness. Galina and I were transported up to *Dominus* in orbit above. I could feel her squirming next to me for a split-second, and it felt kind of nice. I was glad I'd gotten her back safe and sound.

-43-

When we arrived, Galina was all business at first. She demanded proper clothing and a sidearm. The techs on Gray Deck rushed to provide these things.

She fondled her pistol for a moment, looking at it in a loving fashion. This kind of alarmed me, as I've been shot by any number of superior officers. Sometimes, it had been for good reasons. On other occasions, it had been done out of petty spite.

"Uh…" I said. "Will that be all, Tribune?"

Galina looked at me thoughtfully. "No. I want you to attend a debriefing. Follow me."

What could I do? I walked in her wake, looking like some kind of a gorilla following his mistress. I was still wearing the combat armor as I figured it might still help me out today.

"Tribune?" I asked. "There are a few things that have gone on since you were kidnapped."

"I'm sure there are. That's why I'm taking you upstairs to be debriefed."

I chewed that over as we reached the elevator and rode it up to Gold Deck. I hated to be the one to tell the brass bad news, but I couldn't think of an easy way to slip away from her. If Galina got to her office and found it occupied by an angry Winslade with a banged-up head—well, things might not go so well.

"Uh..." I said. "I had to take certain liberties to get you back, see."

Galina halted. She slowly turned around. "You did?"

"That's right."

Her eyes narrowed. "No one ordered you to go down and save me, did they?"

"Well... not exactly," I said. My visor was open, and I scratched my face with one finger. Armored suits like this tended to be hot and kind of itchy. That went double after you'd almost died and got all sweaty. "You see, uh, the legion has a new commander."

Her eyes narrowed some more. They were pretty much slits by this time.

"Who?" she demanded.

"First off, Fike took over. He did some ops, got my unit slaughtered... well, anyways, he decided he didn't have the chops it took to run the legion. He walked through the posts and got another officer from Central."

Galina's eyes widened in alarm. "Don't tell me that bitch Deech is sitting in my office!"

"No, no, things aren't that bad. Drusus bumped up Winslade to the rank of tribune and then... well, he sort of gave him the legion to run."

Galina was in shock. I'd seen that expression on her pretty face before. But, as always, it didn't last long. Her mind switched to scheming again with fresh vigor.

"I see it all now. You decided you wanted me back, so you stole that suit and went down to the planet to find me."

"Pretty much..."

"Where is Winslade? Is he still alive?"

"What kind of a question is that, sir? Of course he is. I imagine he's off somewhere, taking a long piss or something..."

She checked her tapper. She looked up at me in alarm. "He's in my private armory! How the hell did he—oh..."

"What's wrong?"

"He's dead. I get it now. You murdered him and stuffed him in there."

"Well now, hold on, I didn't—"

Galina reached up and hooked a finger in my suit's chin strap. This surprised me. She tugged at me, pulling me toward her.

Wincing a bit, and not knowing quite what to expect, I leaned down toward her. To my utter surprise, she kissed me deeply.

My lips were in shock. They didn't really kiss her back, they just kind of formed a rubbery barrier for her to push against. She didn't seem to mind.

"Uh..." I said.

After a bit more kissing, during which I kind of woke up and kissed her back some, she finally pulled away and smiled at me.

"I love it when you go mad and kill for me," she said in a near-whisper.

It took me a moment for my brain to catch up, but it did so quickly enough.

"You do?" I asked. "Well... yeah. I had to do it, see. Couldn't sleep at night. I kept thinking about you down there on that planet, being abused or whatever."

At this point I was bent over at the waist, and she continued staring into my face. "I need one more thing from you, James."

"What?"

She put out her small hand. She made a grabbing motion.

"The key," she said. "Give me back my key."

My mouth hung open for a second. I'd kind of forgotten about the key, what with all the kissing and lying and stuff.

"Uh... okay. You knew I took it, huh?"

"Obviously."

With a hint of reluctance, I reached down into my armor to fish it out and hand it to her—but it wasn't there. With increasing alarm, I searched my pockets. The armor was a pretty tight fit. It shouldn't have been so hard to find.

Galina watched me with a flat stare. She folded her arms over her perky bosom "Are you really going to fake having lost it? Really?"

"Uh... Galina? I—I've got an awful confession to make."

She growled in sudden anger. That was just like her. She could blow hot and cold faster than a summer rainstorm.

"Don't try to bullshit me now! I'm very grateful for this rescue, James, but I don't plan on paying you for the service with the key."

I knew she'd willingly die a dozen times to keep that key. It had long been one of her aces she kept well up her sleeve. I didn't even know—didn't even *want* to know—all the skullduggery, hacking and blackmail she'd accomplished with it over the years.

Sadly, I shook my head. "You can strip me down and give me a barium enema. You won't find that key. I think I dropped it back in that throne room. I was fighting a couple of crazy women with force-blades, after all."

"You were playing with them!" she exclaimed. "You could have killed them both easily. You were essentially flirting with them, weren't you? Don't think I didn't notice."

"Yeah, well... I don't have the key."

To my surprise, she actually took me up on my offer. She had me searched, stripped down, then marched me down to the labs and had them fluoroscope everything. She even ordered a dozen techs to review every second of video the security cameras had made of me since I'd returned to the ship—but they found nothing.

After about ninety long minutes of this crap, she took me into her office and slammed the door.

"So," she hissed, "you really, actually, *fucking lost it?*"

"Yeah... it looks that way."

"The aliens have it then? They're not dumbasses, McGill. They'll figure out what it does, how it works—and where it came from!"

"Yeah... probably. But look, I only took it down there in order to save you. I used it, too. I disabled their combat drones, so I could get into their headquarters."

To prove my point, I played my suit's body cam vids for her. She saw me fight with the operator at the console, then watched as I used the key to disable the drones.

At last she heaved a sigh. "Okay. You screwed up—but you still did more than anyone else in this damned legion of snakes. Okay… I have to calm down."

"I've got just the thing for that."

I'd taken it upon myself to make her a powerful mixed drink while she was watching the vids. She took this dubiously, but she soon gulped it down. I gave her a second drink, and I had one myself. This put us both in a better mood.

"Do you think you could do a commando run again?" she asked me. "Like the last one—but to get the key back?"

"Do I *think* so?" I asked loudly. "I don't think so, sir, I *know* I can do it!"

I was boasting, of course, and I think she knew it. But she liked the boast, so she smiled at me.

Being a man who believes in seizing opportunities whenever they presented themselves, I slipped a long arm behind her and pulled her close.

She resisted, and I let her go in disappointment.

"I haven't bathed for days," she said. "The Shadowlanders are disgusting. They often go for a week without a shower."

"Well, they do live in a prefab dome city with no permanent—"

"Are you making excuses for the enemy again?"

"Uh… no sir."

"Good. I hate them. Now, if you will do me one final service today, James, I would appreciate it."

"What's that—?"

She'd turned away and walked into the bathroom. Curious, I followed her.

There, she fired up her shower and her clothes dropped to the floor in a heap. She looked great, and she didn't smell bad to me. Not in the least.

Her shower was impressive. It wasn't one of your typical, low-grav jobs that pissed a little warm water into your face. No, sir. It had a big head with a powerful spray. It had to be the best private bathing facility on *Dominus*—possibly the best in the entire fleet.

Without asking permission, I stripped down and climbed into the shower behind her. She had no objections. She didn't talk at all.

Soon, we both forgot about all the difficulties of our long day.

-44-

The next morning I was dragged into a command-level meeting on Gold Deck. I wasn't really interested, but the military could be like that: no one cared about your hurt feelings.

My body was kind of sore after fighting and screwing all day long yesterday. Stretching and yawning now and then, I fielded annoyed stares from a dozen others. They were all primus-ranked and above. To them, I was an unflushed turd—I just didn't belong.

I didn't care at all. They were just going to have to get over themselves.

"After the shit-show that went on in my absence," Galina began, "we'll have to take a new approach."

As she spoke, she moved to the central display and began working it with her fingers. She was freshly washed and done-up to look her best. I think she wanted to appear strong and healthy, just in case anyone who'd usurped her command position was still having lingering thoughts about taking another shot at it.

Fike wore a mask of stone on his face. You could sure tell he didn't like being lectured to by Turov. He reminded me of Graves that way, but he wasn't as good of an officer, or as tough.

"Here's our new situation," Galina continued, displaying the 91 Aquarii system with Edge World on the map near the central star. Nearby, no more than a dozen lightyears off, a blinking orange contact appeared. "This is the approaching fleet of the Galactics."

Everyone woke up and leaned forward.

"That close?" Fike demanded. "They're almost here."

"Actually, they've technically arrived. They're within scanning range now, so we must assume they're watching us. They're already dumping gravity waves in order to brake rapidly. Soon, they'll be orbiting this miserable planet with us."

"If I may, Tribune?" Graves asked.

She nodded to him.

Graves stood up beside her. "The alien formation appears to consist of a single Skay vessel. Accompanying them is a single Nairb ship."

"Those traitorous green snot-bags," I said suddenly.

Graves looked at me. "You have something to add, McGill?"

"Yes sir. The Nairbs work for the Mogwa. They must be turning against them if they're serving the Skay AI as well."

Graves shook his head. "That doesn't match our latest intel. To the best of our knowledge, the Nairb race serves all the Galactics as their bureaucrats."

"Oh… that explains a lot."

"When will they come into weapons range, Graves?" Galina asked.

"Tomorrow. We have less than a standard Earth day to prepare."

"That's unfortunate. Can we—?"

The meeting chamber door opened suddenly, slamming into the wall. A skinny, kind of drippy figure stood there. He trembled a bit, but he wasn't scared or cold. It was Winslade, and he seemed to be in a really bad mood.

"McGill…" he said, pointing at me and talking through clenched teeth. "There you are!"

"Primus Winslade?" Galina said sternly. "You're late. Come in and take a seat."

Winslade's mouth hung open for a second. That was pretty funny to me. I grunted out a short laugh.

Winslade's eyes snapped back to me. He seemed, if anything, more angry than before.

"So… McGill is the hero, is that it?"

"McGill did his job," Galina said stiffly. "That's more than I can say for most of you. Despite your shortcomings, I hereby officially thank you for your efforts, ex-Tribune Winslade. Your services as the temporary commander of Legion Varus are no longer required."

"Obviously…"

Winslade slunk into the conference room and slid into a chair. He sat right next to me, and he reeked a bit from the amniotic fluids of the revival machine. He made an effort not to look me in the eye, which was probably for the best.

"We have come to an arrangement with the Shadowlanders," Galina continued. "We will return their hostage, as they have returned me. When the Galactics arrive, they've agreed to inform them that their wish is to remain part of Province 921 for as long as possible."

Winslade looked stunned. "How did you get them to agree to that?" he demanded.

Galina glanced at me, then back to Winslade. "They've seen the light concerning who might make a better master. Earth, or the heartless Skay."

Winslade became thoughtful, but he soon waved a skinny hand full of stick-like fingers for attention again.

"Yes?" Galina demanded. "What is it?"

"If we can buy enough time, we might get them to relocate to a safer world—one deeper within Province 921."

Galina thought that over. "That would be the best solution. But why would they do it?"

"Think about this hellish planet—moving all the time because you're forced to? If they wait too long, they fry. If they move too far, they end up freezing solid—there must be somewhere better to live."

"I understand the nature of the planet, Primus. If you don't—"

"Excuse me, but until moments ago I was in command of this mission. In fact, I was in command of it for more hours than you've yet to log. If you don't mind, I'd like to explain what I've been working on."

Galina nodded sourly.

"There are three peoples sharing this world. They all hate each other. The only group we care about is the most advanced, but least populous group, the Shadowlanders. If we can provide them with a new and improved home, with improved stability, I think they'll go for it. If nothing else, they're already packed and ready to move."

Galina nodded. "I will consider your suggestion. After a study, I'll form a planning committee. After that—"

I didn't listen to anymore of her bullshit. She was lifting her leg on Winslade's idea, and everyone there knew it. Winslade looked sour, but he shut up.

After the meeting, I caught up with Galina alone.

"Not now, James," she said. "I enjoyed our evening together, but you can't expect to make love to me every minute. I have a campaign to run—thanks to you."

With that, she walked away down the ship's main passage.

Looking after her, I felt conflicted. Galina was in a very sweet mood toward me right now. Was it worth blowing it by pissing her off?

Sucking in a deep breath and letting it out again, I decided that it was. I walked after her and caught up in three strides.

"Hold on a second, Tribune. I wasn't about to suggest a nooner—as pleasant as that might be."

"What then?" she asked. "Don't tell me you've fallen in love with that awful Helsa creature—or her mother. Oh—don't tell me it was *both* of them!"

She was being sarcastic and jealous, but I ignored the whole thing. "I'm talking about a way out of this. A way to keep the revival machine supply available to Earth. If you think about it, the plan is ingenious."

"What plan?"

"Winslade mentioned it," I said, "but lots of people have been talking it over." That part was a lie. I hadn't heard anyone else mention any such thing—but I knew that if Galina thought it was general knowledge, she might bite. She hated Winslade and didn't want him anywhere near her legion.

"Hmm…" she said. "If that's true, and the idea works… I could take all the credit."

"Exactly. You'd be a hero."

She looked up at me again, slyly. "You must spread the thought far and wide. Get everyone talking about it. Use the grid—whatever."

"I surely will!" I said.

She caught me by the arm as I turned to go. I could barely feel her small fingers, but I stopped anyway.

"James… there's something else we need to work on. I want my key back. Remember that."

"Absolutely, sir. I wouldn't have it any other way."

"When are you going on that commando mission to get back the Galactic Key?"

"Uh… any minute now. I just had to attend this meeting, see, and—"

"Forget that stuff. Retrieve my property and make a deal with these irritating aliens. That's an order."

She left me then, and my fake grin faded away. I'd received some tall orders recently. First off, I had no idea how to get everyone thinking we should negotiate with the Shadowlanders. Legion Varus was a combat unit. If you asked any Varus man for any kind of solution, it was bound to start off with tramping boots and end with shooting.

My first stop was Helsa's prison cell in the brig. I came with the authority to release her—but I didn't do it immediately.

"Are you here to gloat?" Helsa asked me. "If so, it's unbecoming of you."

"Not exactly," I told her. I quickly laid out the deal we'd made with her mother and her clone.

Her eyes grew bigger and rounder as I spoke, but she didn't interrupt.

"Are you serious?" she asked. "You expect me to believe you bested my mother and myself in combat?"

"Yep. Here's the vid."

I tossed the evidence to her tapper from mine. She caught it and watched, aghast.

"So…" she said. "I'm unwelcome back home now."

"Why do you say that? Your mom killed that other Helsa. She's out of the picture."

Helsa shook her head. "My mother wouldn't have made a new copy unless she'd written me off. She has moved on and bonded with my clone. It would be for the best that I commit suicide."

Quick as a cat, she reached out and snatched my knife from my belt. I hadn't been expecting that, so she got away with it.

She backed away and placed the tip to her throat.

"Hey! Hold on! I've got a better solution."

She shook her head. "The Galactics are coming tomorrow. I'm evidence of a serious crime. I won't be a party to my own people's destruction."

"Yeah, yeah, I get that. But I've got a better proposal for you."

I laid out the deal that Winslade had originally described.

"You want the Shadowlanders to leave 91 Aquarii? Are you mad? This is our home."

"You share your home with two sets of angry relatives. Wouldn't you prefer a planet that wasn't full of dangerous barbarians? A place where you wouldn't have to migrate all the time?"

"Perhaps…"

"And, wouldn't you rather be the favorite daughter again? I think I can arrange that, too."

She looked at me doubtfully, but after a moment, she let my knife drift away from her long neck. A single droplet of blood ran down from her throat.

"Describe your plan to me."

I grinned, and I started talking.

-45-

The next day, the Galactics arrived, and they put on quite a show. We'd known about the single Skay that was coming—a massive ship that was actually an artificially intelligent being the size of Earth's Moon. What we hadn't realized was that there was another fleet. A task force of ninety Mogwa ships was trailing them.

That raised the stakes. These two Galactics had a delicate truce going. If they started firing live rounds at one another, all of that could blow up into yet another Civil War.

In between these two powerful forces, another squadron of five ships glided into orbit. These weren't warships, they were small private transports. They were Nairb ships.

I was minding my own business at the time of the arrival, marshaling my unit in our module. All the regulars had been ordered to confine themselves to their respective modules at that point. I suspected this was in case the Nairbs demanded a snap-inspection. The brass didn't want to take any chances. If anyone was up to something illegal, it wasn't going to be on full display for the aliens to see.

We were, however, allowed to watch the proceedings on our big vid screens. Accordingly, my unit was standing around like it was a New Year's Eve party in the main room of our module. We had a few beers in hand, but we were in uniform.

"Wow," Carlos said, coming to stand next to me. "This is something, huh big guy?"

"Sure is. I haven't seen this many ships in one place since the big battle at Clone World."

Finally, the images of the drifting ships vanished. They were replaced by an alien that looked like a big green seal. He was a Nairb, and an important one. He had some kind of silver circlet around his neck. I didn't know what the deal was with that, but I suspected it was some kind of rank insignia.

"Look at that," Carlos said. "He's like a queen, or something."

"Hush."

"Loyal slave-creatures of the Empire," the Nairb began. "It is to our infinite pleasure that we've been chosen to act as judges on this fateful day. We stand here on the precipice of conflict—but with appropriate legal action, it can and will be avoided."

"War?" Carlos asked. "Is he talking about going to war?"

"Shut the hell up!" I ordered.

Everyone had fallen quiet. The stakes appeared to be higher than we'd thought.

"First things first," the Nairb said. "We have two critically important personages here. One represents the Mogwa," here the Nairb moved a flipper. On his left side, looming over his head, Nox appeared. I would have recognized her poisonous black carapace anywhere. "The other represents the glorious Skay."

The Nairb moved the other flipper. On his right side, an external shot of the Skay appeared. It had a pockmarked surface, but the hull looked like it was still intact.

"Whoa," Carlos whispered. "That's an old warhorse. It must have been in some rough battles to look like that."

I didn't bother to shush him this time. After all, he was right. Why would the Skay send an elderly warlord of its race out here to Edge World? I didn't know, but it didn't seem like a positive sign.

"Now, who do we have present to represent the interests of the slave-races?"

Way down low, on the bottom half-meter of the giant screen, appeared the head of Kattra. "I am the leader of the

275

people who dwell on this planet," she said officiously. "I will speak for my world."

A moment later, Galina's face appeared down on that lower line-up, on an even level with Kattra. "And I'm from Earth. We are the Empire's local enforcers in Province 921."

That should be it, I figured. Altogether, with the Nairb in the center spot, there were five people in the online meeting. I yawned a bit, suspecting this might turn into a long and overly formal meeting where nothing of importance happened—but I was wrong.

Galina's face was under the Mogwa Nox. But then, under the Skay's ominous shadow, another face appeared. It was a familiar face, and it made everyone present gasp in astonishment.

"Tribune Armel!" I boomed aloud. "What the Hell is he doing here?"

It was true. Maurice Armel was a scoundrel of a man, a renegade legionnaire who'd traipsed off into the cosmos to seek his fortune as a mercenary leader in unknown parts of the galaxy. I hadn't seen him since the Glass World campaign, if memory served.

He was a Frenchman who embraced the worst of his heritage. He didn't like me, he didn't like the Empire, and he was willing to sell anyone out for a credit.

"This is inappropriate," Nox said. "Who is this person? Why are we saddled with an interloper?"

"Dear Grand Dame Nox, I am the enforcer of Province 926," Armel said. He struck a pose, standing proudly in combat gear. His thin mustache bounced over his twitchy mouth.

"Impudence," the Mogwa complained. "I object. The star system is still in Province 921's space. Therefore, no local enforcement from outside the province should be heard from."

"I object in return," the Skay rumbled, speaking up for the first time. "The purpose of these proceedings is to determine which province the star system belongs to. Therefore, our enforcer has as much right to be here as the Mogwa sycophant from Earth."

Everyone's eyes were getting big by now. The talks hadn't even begun yet, and they were stalling out already. What chance was there for peace?

"We are deeply *screwed*," Carlos said. "These two want to go for it. There's going to be a war, mark my words."

Things looked bad. Peace was a group decision. War wasn't. It only took one side to stand up and start shooting to kick things off.

The Mogwa queen appeared to be rattled. Her eyes roved over the scene with displeasure. "I propose that we remove both of these voices from the conference. They're useless and disruptive."

The Skay sat like a stone for a few moments. I knew it was doing some deep-thinking.

"Agreed," it said at last. "The opinions of slaves are not valid in this instance."

"What?" Galina squawked. "What does—?"

The Nairb flicked his flipper again in her direction, and she vanished. She'd been kicked off the feed. A moment later, the same fate befell Armel.

"There," the Nairb said. "Are all participants satisfied? If so, we can begin with—"

"No," said the Skay.

"What is it now?" Nox demanded.

"There are two more parties that must be considered in this matter. The bright-siders and the night people of 91 Aquarii must be heard."

Armel's spot and Galina's spot were replaced by two more aliens. I recognized them from the briefings. One was a mummy-like desert person known as a bright-sider. The other was definitely one of the black-eyed freaks from the icy side of the planet.

"What kind of fuckery is this?" Carlos demanded. "They kick all the humans out and reserve three spots for these losers?"

"It *is* their planet," I said, shrugging.

Right then, my tapper began to buzz. Galina was doing it. Her face looked up at me from my forearm, and she looked really angry.

"McGill, get up here to Gold Deck. We're losing control of this situation."

"I'd say we've already lost it," I remarked, but I was talking to my own arm hairs. She'd already closed the connection.

-46-

I hustled up to Gold Deck, and for once I found Veteran Daniels wasn't standing in my way. In fact, he urged me to hurry with big sweeping gestures. He must have gotten the word that I'd been summoned.

Turov was on the bridge, surrounded by the top brass. Graves, Merton, Fike and Winslade—they were all there. None of them looked even slightly happy.

On the main screen, the two Galactics were locked in a legal argument. It was pretty boring. Mostly, they were reading Galactic by-laws to one another. Neither seemed to be listening to the other. They were just reeling off historical precedents, legalese, and other crap like that.

"At least they're not shooting at each other yet," I said in a hopeful tone.

Galina's eyes focused on me like a pair of lasers. "McGill! About time you showed up."

If I'd been a sensitive man, I might have been upset by her harsh tone. After all, we'd just spent a lovely evening together, and before that I'd saved her pretty ass from purgatory. But that was Turov for you. She could be sweet enough in private, but she was a serious ball-buster in daylight. The psychs I'd dated called that "compartmentalization" and she was a master at it.

"Centurion McGill reporting, sir. What can I do for you?"

She took two steps toward me and threw a finger at the screen. "You were the last one to have contact with Armel. Back during the Glass World campaign—right?"

"Uh…" I said, feeling a trifle uncomfortable.

What she'd said was indeed a fact—but it wasn't a fact I thought anyone knew about except for me, Leeza and Armel himself. Apparently, someone had spilled the beans.

"Yes or no?" she demanded loudly. "Don't go playing dumb on me, I'm not in the mood!"

"No sir—I mean, yes sir. I did meet with Armel a year or so ago."

Graves and Fike glanced at one another. They both seemed irritated. Maybe that was because I hadn't reported an enemy contact. They were often disappointed in situations like this.

"All right, tell me, what does this fool have to offer the Skay? A forgotten army of Clavers? What?"

"Oh… right. He's got a saurian legion. I believe he mentioned commanding ten thousand of them—but that was just in passing, mind you. I didn't count tails or anything."

The group blinked, absorbing this.

Fike spoke first. "Not a serious force," he said. "If that's all he's got, we can take them. We'll outnumber them two to one from the start."

"Oh really?" Galina snapped. "We've suddenly been pitted against a professionally armed and armored legion with a competent commander—but that isn't the real problem?"

"No sir. We can take ten thousand lizards easily."

"Maybe, but he'll have all the alien freaks on this dirt-hole planet with him. Just look who else is on the screen!"

Galina pointed up to the big screen. It was true, the Shadowlanders had been joined by two other native groups. None of them seemed friendly to Earth.

Fike was startled by this idea. "You think the aliens will all turn against us?"

"You ensured that the Shadowlanders hate us," Galina told him. "Remember that punitive raid? With McGill at the head of it? Half of the eggshell domes and carpets in their crappy town burned down. Does that ring a bell?"

"Maybe we can get the others on our side, then," Graves suggested. "The rebel forces from the desert and the tundra."

"Maybe... but we can't even participate in this discussion. I'm extremely annoyed right now. Captain Merton, keep contacting the Nairbs and ask to be reinstated in this conference—with an unmuted voice."

"We've been doing so, Tribune. So far, they aren't even bothering to answer."

I was beginning to see the scope of the problem, and I understood why Turov was freaking out. She'd lost control of the situation. The Nairbs might rule damned near anyway they pleased—without our input.

"Hey," I said, "I've got an idea."

Several sets of unfriendly eyes shifted in my direction.

"What is it, McGill?" Galina asked.

"Bring Helsa up here. I think I can get to her mamma through her."

Galina narrowed her eyes at me. It was entirely unfair, but she didn't trust me around random alien women we'd only just met up with.

I thought that was just sour grapes on her part. Sure, I'd had a fling or two when the mood had struck me in the past. But that didn't mean I was involved with Helsa. In my opinion, she ought to give me the benefit of the doubt in these situations.

"Veteran Daniels!" she screeched. "Go get that alien bitch, and bring her up here!"

He hustled away, and I turned my attention back to the conference, which was still steaming along.

"Preposterous," the Skay was saying. "This isn't a matter of *if*, but rather *when* the star system in question becomes our property. Votes and other means of decision-making by the insects crawling over these rocky planets means nothing."

He was really well-spoken. I figured that's why they'd sent him out from the Core Worlds. He was an old, long-toothed Skay. He was probably too ancient to fight battles, what with that scarred-up hull of his, but maybe his AI was still cagey, still tricky in an argument.

"That is not what I was suggesting," Nox responded. "Votes are reserved for the Imperial Senate. Nothing like that vaunted process would be appropriate for these simple beings."

"What then? What kind of decision-making process are you suggesting?"

"Rules warning!" barked the Nairb.

Both the Galactics addressed his parliamentary concern, which had to do with proper wording and deference. All the Nairb seemed to be doing was slowing things down, but maybe that was a good thing in this case.

Helsa was hustled onto the bridge during this latest dust-up. I was frankly surprised. Had Daniels previously brought her up here under Galina's orders? That was the impression I had, as there hadn't been enough time to fetch her up from the brig level.

Helsa's eyes met mine, and she gave me a flickering smile.

I smiled back, but then I dropped that and turned away.

Galina was watching the two of us. *Damnation*, that girl was suspicious. I had to pretend like I didn't give two shakes about this alien girl.

Galina walked to me and simultaneously crooked a finger at Daniels. Helsa was brought near as well. "McGill," Galina said quietly, "work some magic, and do it fast."

"Uh... okay."

I turned to face Helsa. She looked kind of wary about me as well. She didn't know what was going on. "Helsa, I went down to your planet and had a nice chat with your mom yesterday."

"I gathered as much."

"Well, do you think you could contact her and get her to talk to us? On the side, I mean?"

Helsa's eyes flicked up toward the big screen. They widened in alarm. "Are those strange beings Galactics?"

"They sure are. Right now, they're deciding your people's fate—and mine."

"They can't do that. We're a free tribe. We're the best of the inhabitants of 91 Aquarii."

I laughed. "I'm sure you are, but that doesn't mean a stack of spittle to these nasty aliens. The Empire can snuff us all out like so many candles."

She looked back at me. "What do you want to say to Kattra?"

"Just that we need to make a deal—fast."

"Why should we prefer one invader over another?"

I pointed a thick finger at the Skay. "You see that cue ball up there? He's as big as a Moon and more than capable of leveling your fine planet. What's more, he doesn't give two shits about you and your people. Earth, on the other hand, just wants to do business as usual."

"Wait a second!" Galina said, putting up both her hands. She was looking up at the aliens, and listening to them. She seemed highly agitated. "What did they just say? Are they agreeing to some kind of insanity?"

"Sounds like it," Graves said. "I'm not surprised, really. A trial by combat—that's much more the style of Galactics. They find votes distasteful."

"Combat?" I asked. "Who's fighting who? I hope it's us against Armel. I'd really like to kill some lizards."

"Shut up, McGill."

We all listened in. They seemed to be ironing out the details.

"I ask," said the Skay, "who among the three peoples of this planet will stand with the superior beings known as the Skay?"

The burnt mummy-creature from the bright-side spoke up first. He had kind of a raspy voice, as if his vocal chords had dried out and become like leather shoestrings. "The people of the endless light will march with the Skay. We will sweep all that oppose us from our path. This is inevitable."

"Scheming bastards..." Helsa snarled.

The night-sider spoke next. He sounded kind of hissy, like the voice of a giant spider. "We speaks together, as we huddle close against the snows. We too, will march in the shadow of the Skay."

"It's a setup!" I hollered. "They're all in cahoots! They want to take your planet from you, Helsa! It's as clear as day!"

283

She looked alarmed. I could tell she didn't know quite what to do.

I reached out and latched my hand onto her arm. I tugged at her urgently. "Contact your mamma! Stand with us before they roll you all over with the help of that giant white rock out there!"

Helsa nodded. She began working her tapper in earnest.

-47-

A moment later, we saw Kattra flinch on the big screen. She glanced down furtively.

"She got the call!" I boomed. "Now, pick up you arrogant—"

"She disconnected," Helsa said. "I'm not surprised, she is in the midst of a critical meeting."

"Have you got some kind of emergency signal?" I asked her. "Something that would indicate she needs to pick up immediately?"

Helsa gritted her teeth. She worked her tapper again.

On the big screen, Kattra was clearly distracted.

"Shadowlanders!" the Nairb judge said. "What say you? What army will you stand with in this determination?"

"I... I must consult with my council."

"What?" the Skay demanded. "Is this dissembling a tactic? Delay and confuse? Is that the way of your people?"

"No, of course not. It is simply a legal formality. Will you give me the time to—"

"Thirty seconds," the Skay said. "I will wait no longer."

"Ninety seconds," Nox said. "I demand ninety seconds for consideration."

While they argued, I saw Kattra's face snarling out of Helsa's forearm. I stuck my big face in between the two women, who both seemed kind of worked-up about something.

"Hey!" I said. "Just McGill, here. I was wondering if I could offer you some help."

Kattra snarled at me. "McGill? I should have known you were involved in this somehow."

"I'm only interested in pleasing you, your high ladyship. Listen-up, because I think you're in trouble. If I'm reading my creepy aliens right, the night-siders and the bright-siders have teamed up against you. They're with the Skay, and they're going to take over your planet after it drifts into Skay space, if not sooner."

"How do you know this, human?"

I laughed long and loud. "Isn't it obvious? Even Helsa here got it—didn't you, girl?"

I drew my head back so Kattra could see both of us. We were kind of up-close and personal so we could both get into the tiny camera's pick-up range. It was like we were doing a selfie together, and I could tell Galina was getting annoyed—but she was just going to have to hold her water on that score.

"I think it's true, my Lady," Helsa said. "The two lesser tribes would never agree to walk the same path together so quickly. They hate one another almost as much as they hate us. I think they're all working together—against us."

"We humans call that a conspiracy," I said. "That's what this is, plain as day."

"So, what is your proposal?"

"Just like before—but we might have to do a little fighting together, first. Your army and our army—we'll stand together against these second-class upstarts that grub around in the low-rent parts of your planet. What do you say?"

Kattra looked thoughtful but unconvinced.

"Uh…" I said. "We're kind of running out of time…"

"There is too much dishonor between us," Kattra said. "You have clearly seduced and suborned my daughter, adding further insult on top of the assault you launched at my personal quarters. I would require atonement. Demonstrations of fealty. Definitive—"

"Hold on, hold on," I said. "We don't have time for any of that crap. The Nairb wants an answer. Will you stand with the Skay, or with the Mogwa?"

She bared her teeth. I could tell she was torn.

"Hey," I said, getting an idea, "what if I sweetened the pot for you? What if I gave you an invaluable gift?"

"What gift? There is no time, as you said—"

I lifted a big hand to stop her. "There is. The gift is already in your possession. I was thinking about telling you—but it was supposed to be a surprise."

Kattra cocked her head and stared at me quizzically. "What are you blathering about, human?"

Leaning close to Helsa's arm, I whispered loudly into it. "A Galactic Key. Look for it—I left it in your throne room. It's all yours."

Helsa pulled her arm away from my lips. She looked at me reproachfully.

But Kattra was still on the screen. Her look had changed. "I've heard of such things..." she said. "I must go now."

The connection died.

For the next minute or so, the Nairb called for the Shadowlander vote. No one answered him.

"Clearly, they have forfeited their choice," the Skay said. "I will wait no longer on the dawdling of a slave."

"I demand we extend the decision time," Nox said.

"What?" the Skay boomed. "This is an insult. This will not go unpunished."

"How long of a delay are you requesting, Governess Nox?" the Nairb asked.

"One hour, no more."

"Impossible!" the Skay complained. "I will give no more than three minutes."

The wrangling went on, and it took them five minutes to decide they'd wait for five more. I enjoyed every moment of that time, hoping against hope.

At last, the regal image of Kattra returned to the bottom center slot on the screen.

"You have forty more seconds," the Nairb said, "if you wish to reconsider."

"Not necessary," Kattra said. "We have rendered our verdict. We will stand with the Mogwa."

287

I whooped and hollered. It was a loud sound, and everyone there winced and glanced at me in irritation. I didn't care as I was too busy clapping my hands over my head and laughing.

"Very well," the Skay said. "I demand the right to deploy my enforcers to aid the righteous owners of this world."

"We demand the same right," Nox said promptly.

"Granted, in both cases," the Nairb answered. "The war will commence in forty minutes' time. All combat must occur on the surface of the planet itself—no bombardment or other interference will be allowed. Are there any other questions or statements to be made by the affected parties?"

"Just this," the Skay said, speaking up in the silence that followed, "you have chosen poorly, Shadowlanders. When we eventually gain control of your pathetic planet, we will grind the bones of every last creature in your tribe to dust. No matter what the outcome of this farce, you have chosen to die as a people."

"Your words are noted, Skay," Kattra said evenly.

She was a tough bird, I had to give her that. She didn't even flinch or piss herself. She just stared up at the Skay with those smoldering eyes.

-48-

"Forty minutes?!" Fike shouted. "We can't get down there that fast—all the lifters are on the surface now."

"Aw…" I said in disappointment. "Are you saying I can't fight in this war?"

Galina's eyes darted around the group. "Get into the drop-pods. All of you. I'll command the high ground from up here."

"I will stand at your side, Tribune," Winslade offered immediately. "You'll need a liaison to connect properly with the grunts."

She looked at him with unfriendly eyes. "I think I'd rather have you planetside, Winslade. Drop with the officers and keep my lines of communication open."

Glumly, Winslade followed the rest of us down to Red Deck. From there, we were fired out into space like so many screaming bombs. Inside half of an hour, I found myself standing on the mossy carpet of Edge World again.

I picked a fruit bulb, gave it a sniff, then took a bite. It wasn't half-bad.

Winslade came close to me. He was in a sour mood.

"That was quite an impressive set of verbal gymnastics, McGill," he said. "I only wish you'd managed to keep us out of it in the bargain."

"Aw now, you don't mean that, sir," I said. "I know you, old blood-and-guts Winslade. That's what the men call you, did you know that?"

"Really? That seems rather—"

"Hey, listen," I interrupted. "Do you have a cohort to command down here?"

"No… I was deposed as the legion's tribune, and unless Turov makes a change in the command structure—"

I lifted my tapper to my face. I activated it and contacted Galina.

"What is it, McGill? Don't you have an army to order around?"

"I've got my unit, yes sir. But Winslade here—he hasn't got any troops. Are there any dead officers he can replace?"

"McGill!? Damn you, man!" Winslade hissed at my side.

"No need to thank me, Primus," I told him. "I know how much you're itching to get into the action."

"Hmm…" Galina said. "Winslade was given the acting role of Tribune previously, but I think I'll put Graves in that spot now. I'll assign the third cohort to him, replacing Graves. Work together gentlemen—and do it right this time."

She closed the channel. I was left staring at my tapper, dismayed. I hadn't thought she would put him in charge of *my* cohort. I'd kind of figured he'd be given some other shitty job because she wasn't happy with him.

Lowering my arm, I saw Winslade's ferret-like features staring up at me. "So, we're working together again? How lovely."

"Yes sir, it will be a pleasure to serve. What's our tactical plan?"

"First, I'll contact Graves."

He walked off, talked to Graves for a moment, then walked back. He didn't look all that happy.

"He wants me to lead the cohort into that shoddy little town. You're to meet with these alien women you've been working so hard to seduce—by the way, how did you manage to get Kattra to agree to join us?"

"Uh…" I said, thinking of the Galactic Key. That part of the negotiation had been worked out without a lot of fanfare on my part. Both Winslade and Galina knew about the key, and they both wanted it.

"Listen McGill," Winslade said. "The last time we shared breathing space, you killed me. Do you recall that event?"

"Yes sir. That surely was an unfortunate accident on my part. My bad, as they say. I totally own up to it."

"Murder…" Winslade said, and he seemed to like the way the word tasted. "That's the word I'm thinking of. It has a nice ring to it."

Already, I knew where he was going with this. Now that he was my direct commander, he would find it easy to order me into a situation that would get me and my unit slaughtered. I could see it coming from a mile off.

"Possibly, there's been a misunderstanding," I said.

"A miscalculation, more like." He gave me a predatory smile. "You made the error, and you compounded it by lobbying for me to become your direct commander."

"Uh…"

"Do you wish to hear about your first assignment? Hmm?" Winslade asked. "It's going to be quite a challenge, I'm afraid."

"Now, hold on a moment. There's something else we need to discuss."

"I doubt that."

"Do you remember the Galactic Key we were both looking for?"

Winslade looked up suddenly. He blinked twice. "Yes, of course. What about it?" His eyes shifted from dark revenge to a yellowy shade. I thought that probably denoted a hint of greed. "Are you saying you're in possession of—?"

"Nope. Not any longer. The aliens have it."

He cocked his head to one side. His mouth dropped halfway open. "You gave these fools the Galactic Key? Are you mad?"

"Some would say so, yes. But using it, I was able to get the Shadowlanders to join us."

Winslade shook his head and gazed back at the makeshift town. "Such a waste… Does Galina know?"

"Uh… nope."

He looked at me speculatively. "What kind of scheme are you hatching, McGill?"

"A good one. A scheme that will help both of us."

"Let me guess: I get the key, and you keep breathing. Is that it?"

"Well… for starters."

Winslade and I soon had a truce going. It was a necessary thing, really. We couldn't very well run our troops effectively if we were gunning for each other.

For both of us, it was a relief. Sure, Winslade needed a good killing on the best of days, and he probably thought the same thing about me. But when you were sent into the field together to face an alien menace, well, it was way harder to concentrate when you knew your fellow officers were out to frag you.

We shook on it, agreeing to set aside our petty differences until such a time as we thought it was worth it to backstab each other again. I knew plenty of officers who operated within that kind of temporary framework. It was the Varus way.

"All right," Winslade said after I'd formed up my unit. They were all slumped over their rifles, looking bored. They had no idea that a major war was about to break out. "McGill, contact your girlfriend in that huddle of stinking domes. Tell her to come out here, rather than having us wait on her like a queen."

I wasn't sure how Kattra would take that, but I contacted her anyway. A dozen minutes later a group of Shadowlander agents walked out of the town. Behind them, around three hundred humping black shapes followed.

"What the hell are those things?" Winslade asked aloud.

"Oh… you haven't gotten up-close and personal with their combat drones yet, have you sir? What you see there is some of their best gear. Just wait until you see one of them stand up on their tripods, they're pretty impressive machines."

Winslade seemed appalled. He'd watched the videos, but as was so often the case, such representations failed to impress how wicked and deadly these prime examples of alien technology really were.

-49-

Helsa led the army of drones. She walked up to me and nodded. "McGill... you've done the impossible."

"How's that?"

"You've destroyed my people. I can't understand my mother's behavior. She's never made such a bold alliance before. I think it will lead to the destruction of all of us."

"Aw now, don't be so negative. You haven't really seen Varus fight yet. We can trash a lot of aliens—uh, I mean bright-siders and the like."

"I hope so. They aren't incredibly smart—especially the creatures from the frozen wastes. But they are more numerous than beetles on dung, and they don't fear death."

"Good to know. Is this your whole army? I was kind of hoping to have several thousand of you stand with us."

Helsa turned back toward her town. "Don't worry. When the time comes, more will engage in this great struggle."

"Okay..."

Winslade pursed his lips and eyed the terrain. "Graves wants our cohort to deploy on that high ground to the west. Do you think you and your lady-fair can setup her drone force among the rocks?"

"Sure thing."

I was pretty happy to be given the job of liaison with Helsa. I was pretty sure that Galina didn't know Winslade had assigned me such a specialized task. She probably wouldn't

293

have approved—but then, she'd decided to hide up on *Dominus*, above the fray. My daddy always said that if you don't show up, you don't get to run the church picnic.

Marshaling my unit, we marched together to an outcropping of rough stone. All around us more Varus units moved toward the same area.

Up close, the rocks were more impressive. Each towering stone was about as big as one of Stonehenge's upright sarsens back home, and there were thousands of them. The drones crawled into this cover like a mass of spiders. Once they'd found good firing positions they crouched quietly and disappeared from view.

I posted my own troops in front of the drones. Several more units of human troops from my cohort surrounded us. The drones would be a nasty surprise, rising up and tearing into anything that came at us.

All around the field of battle, similar defensive positions were taken. The word was that the enemy was already on the move. They were massing on the bright side of the planet with the mummy-looking guys in their floating chariots. On the night-side flank, which we were facing, the cold-weather types were also gathering into a vast horde.

"How long will it take for them to form an army?" I asked Helsa.

She shrugged. "Ten hours. Maybe twenty."

"That fast? Aren't they coming from all over the planet?"

She laughed at me. "No, not really. You see, no one can survive for long more than a few hundred kilometers from the Shadow Line. If you go much further out into either the desert or the tundra, you'll either fry or freeze. Even the natives can't handle it. They actually inhabit only a thin ring of land, like we do. It's just not as pleasant and temperate as our region is."

I nodded, understanding. Back home on the Moon, the temperature might swing up by two hundred degrees Celsius and then back again in a single day-night cycle. Without special gear, nothing could survive those extremes.

Looking west toward the night-side, I pondered the situation. "So... they don't live way out in the tundra? They just hug up against the best lands, the same as you do? Seems odd you guys don't share the livable space more evenly."

"They are allowed to exist," Helsa said sharply. "That is enough for them. The Shadowlanders are always generous, always thoughtful of our less fortunate cousins. We only kill them in their masses if they dare step into our moderate slice of the world."

"That's mighty considerate of you."

She didn't seem to detect my sarcasm, so I gave her an idiot's grin. That seemed to convince her, and she went back to marshaling her vicious army of robots.

When she'd left me, all three of my adjuncts approached—plus Bevan.

"These machines are amazing, McGill," Bevan said. "We could learn so much from dismantling one of them."

"You want me to steal one for you?"

His eyes flashed with greed. "If you think you could get away with it…"

"I'll give it a shot."

"Thanks, Centurion!"

Bevan walked away to spy on the combat drones. I let him go, as he was going to be pretty much useless in a pitched battle.

Leeson and Harris watched Bevan with suspicion. Barton was only interested in her own troops, however.

"Sir, could I ask a question?" she asked me.

"You sure can, but you might not like the answer."

Barton smirked. "I know that much. Why are we putting our light troops out in front of alien-made robots? Are we seriously going to use human beings as skirmishing troops for machines?"

"Yep," I answered immediately.

She looked unhappy, so I decided to give her a little more to go on.

"Look, you've fought these things before. They can rip through most formations. I'm hoping they'll make our jobs a lot easier. Even more importantly, I want them in the rear so the enemy doesn't know they're here. I want them to pop up and surprise the enemy when they come in close. At that point, it will be too late to run."

Barton nodded, eyeing the surrounding landscape. "I'll deploy my men as best I can, sir."

When she left, and the other two stepped close. Leeson laughed. "She's not so hot on you today, is she McGill? Where do you want my specialists to set up camp?"

I showed him a sheltered location on the northern side. He looked it over and had his weaponeers set up shells made of puff-crete. These would serve as pillboxes, with 88s inside each of them.

"They've got to be forward, and a little raised," Leeson said. "That way they'll have a good field of fire when the freaks show up."

Harris was the last to approach me. He looked concerned. "I think I should deploy behind the drones, sir," he said.

"How do you figure?"

"Well, after they roll forward, I'll come up behind them and fill in the holes in their line."

I looked dubious. After eyeing the field, I shook my head. "Nah. Station yourself behind Barton's lights. Team up with Leeson's auxiliaries."

"With those killer drones behind us, sir? Are you sure you want things that way? If the robots go ape, they'll cut down my entire platoon."

"I'll take that chance. Move out, Harris."

Grumbling, he walked off and gathered his armored heavy troops.

When I was alone, I checked my gear. It looked to be in order. The single upgrade I had going for me was a big one: I'd kept hold of my Glass World armor. It was shiny, black, and almost impenetrable.

"If we're out here on the west side, facing the ice-devils," a voice said suddenly. "Who's out on the other side facing those desert ragdolls?"

I knew the voice in an instant. It was Cooper, one of my two ghost specialists. Since I couldn't see him, I knew he was wearing his stealth suit.

Turning sharply, I spotted a pair of oval impressions in the sand. I thumped the butt of my big rifle down in the midst of them. Unfortunately, I'd guessed wrong. Cooper had already moved away from that spot.

"Ha!" Cooper hooted at me. "I'm one step ahead of you today, Centurion."

"That's a good thing. A ghost I can easily locate is useless. To answer your question, the Blood-Worlder legion under Fike is out on the eastern side. The bright-siders will attack his forces first. If he holds, and we do too, the town will be saved."

"Sounds easy enough. I'll go scout."

"You do that. Report back every half hour until something happens."

Cooper took off, and I began directing our defensive arrangements. As we were in rough terrain, we didn't build bunkers. Instead, we sort of glued together the spaces between the big rocks, connecting them with low walls of puff-crete. The enemy wasn't supposed to be heavily armed, so I had them build slits into the puff-crete to act as firing loopholes.

For a kilometer out, we had a reasonably open field of fire in every direction. It looked to me like it was going to be a good old-fashioned turkey-shoot.

Hours went by, and it felt like it should be getting darker or lighter—but it didn't. There was no detectable change in the twilight skies. It was kind of spooky, if the truth were to be told.

Finally, after nine long hours, we got word of contact to the northeast.

"Officers," Graves said in my ear. He was speaking on our command chat channel, which was only available to officers of the adjunct level and above. "An enemy force is approaching Fike's Blood-Worlder legion on the other side of town. Hold your positions. We're going to light them up with the star-falls we've been setting up in the center of our formation."

Shortly after this warning, the purple sky brightened and filled with white streaks. We all hunkered down, even though we knew it was our side that was doing the firing.

The star-falls sent bolts of energy in glimmering arcs toward the east. These arcs moved at a surprisingly low speed.

The artillery was energy-based, rather than using traditional explosive shells. It was able to penetrate various types of protective force-shielding that protected modern armies from missiles and aerial assaults.

Like meteors crashing in slow-motion, the first barrage rose high before dropping to the ground again. It smashed everything it landed upon. In the distance to the east, on the far side of the Shadowlander town, brilliant flashes flared into life. Each impact made you squint if you looked at it directly.

At ground zero, I knew the alien soil would be fused into glass. The radioactivity levels would spike in every crater. Anything within a hundred meters of each strike, shielded or not, would be vaporized.

The battle for Edge World had truly begun.

-50-

Cooper was the first to alert me to the approach of the enemy on my unit's position.

"Say again, Ghost? What have you got?"

"Bugs, sir. Zillions of them. They're—they aren't what I expected. They look like hairy beetles the size of cows."

Recalling my briefing and the ugly mug of the night-sider I'd seen conferencing with the Galactics, it sounded about right. "How fast are they moving, Ghost? Which direction?"

"Incoming toward your position, sir. I'd say they're moving at about thirty clicks an hour. They'll be there shortly."

"Go to ground and let them pass by, Cooper. Good reporting, McGill out."

I moved to contact Winslade, but Graves had already heard the news. He was on command chat again with the whole legion.

"The day-sider formation to the east took a hard shot. We killed thousands with our barrage—apparently, they weren't expecting that. The bugs to the west, however, are spreading out more and moving faster. They're trying to get in close before we can light them up—but they're in for a surprise."

Graves gave a dirty chuckle and cut the transmission.

Again, the skies split apart with the slow gleaming streaks of the star-falls. This time, however, the target troop formations were a lot closer to home. The glimmering trails lit up the air

299

right over our heads. We all ducked low, it was impossible not to.

"That's a low angle," Leeson complained. He'd wormed his way over close to my command post. "Graves must have them zeroed."

"He does," I said. "He's raining on their parade even now."

Once again, the star-fall salvoes came down with devastating effect. Watching through my HUD, I saw the enemy line obliterated as the evening air was ripped apart. Brilliant gushes of released energy struck a hundred times in their midst. The bugs—I could see them now via various tricks of optics, buzzers and the like—were reeling. Some groups kept approaching, but others split apart and ran around chaotically. I was reminded of ants that knew they were burning alive. They ran with increased vigor, but soon fell and curled up. After that, they were cooked to ash.

"Nice shooting, Graves!" I whooped. "This might be easier than I thought it would be!"

The enemy attack was broken. I watched as the bug-like night-siders split up and ran in random directions. A few of our snipers popped shots at them with snap-rifles, but they were at such extreme range I doubted we got any hits.

"We're not even going to need those robotic freaks Helsa brought out here," Harris told me.

"I hope you're right. Keep a sharp eye out for infiltrators."

The enemy fell back and disappeared into the low hills to our east. Intel reports suggested they hadn't given up yet—not by a longshot. They were still out there in their thousands, gathering strength.

We took a few hours to rest and eat. All the while we chowed on dried rations, more reports of massing troops came rolling in. Apparently, the enemy wasn't done yet.

"How many are out there?" Harris asked me. "And don't say millions. I don't want to hear that."

"Uh… no one knows, not even the Shadowlanders."

"Well, if they've always been so damned numerous, why the hell haven't they overwhelmed the Shadowlands before today?"

Helsa was nearby, and she heard what he said. She came near and answered his question.

"They've never worked together before. Neither have they come in such numbers. Normally, we've been able to keep them down by beating small armies decisively. We've always known... well, they control much more of the world than we do. They've always had the numbers..."

"What kind of numbers?" Harris demanded angrily.

Helsa shrugged. "Ten times our count, I would guess."

"You mean with night-siders and the dumbass sun-mummies combined?"

"No, I mean each of them."

"Twenty to one, then?" Harris demanded. "That's just sweet. That's great. This is such bullshit! We haven't even seen Armel yet. He's letting them probe us. He's out there, watching on some buzzer feed channel. He's counting guns and heads—and he's laughing about it all, too."

"Then he got an eyeful today!" I boomed, determined not to let Harris turn a victory into something ominous—even if he was probably right. "We whipped their tails for them. It's my guess they'll try one more big attack—maybe a coordinated effort—then they'll give up and run for home."

"I very much hope that you're right," Helsa said, then she sauntered off.

Harris and I watched her walk away. Harris whistled. "You sure can pick 'em, boy. You always could."

"You got that right."

Time wore on. Right about when we were beginning to think they weren't going to come at us again—they began to advance.

This time, they weren't all choked up and approaching in a tight mass. They came in a widely dispersed pattern from every direction.

Graves countered by bombarding them at random with the star-falls. He punched a hole in every thin wave they sent—but they were determined. Suffering horrid losses, they kept on coming closer.

The mummies coming out of the east landed the first blow. They seemed to be faster-moving than their strange

301

brethren from the cold side of the planet. The lines that reached close enough to fire on Fike's Blood-Worlders launched what looked like a mortar attack.

A thousand lights like fast flares rose up and came down again in the midst of Fike's trench lines. The strikes were incendiary, and they lit up a lot of good men who burned alive from the inside out.

"That's phosphorus!" Harris declared, watching the vid feeds. "Or something like it. Nasty stuff."

A few minutes later, it was our turn. The night-siders got close enough for our small arms to reach them, and we obliged with a hailstorm of power-bolts, snap-rifle rounds and belcher fire. Hundreds of the enemy fell thrashing—but the rest kept up their advance.

"McGill!" Barton called into my ear. "Something's happening back at the town!"

"That's not our problem. Adjunct Leeson keep 88s ready to fire the second they get a little closer…"

As if they'd heard me and sensed the imminent danger, the beetle-like night-siders rose up as one and charged us.

"Holy shit," Harris said. "Look at them run!"

It was true. The enemy must have been crouching and crawling slowly before. Either they'd figured that was safer, or they were only able to move fast for a short period of time. Whatever the case, they were now moving much faster.

"They're running thirty clicks an hour—forty!" Harris declared.

"Leeson, it's time to open up!" I shouted. "Give them a good taste with the 88s!"

All along our line, I saw other units begin to beam the enemy lines that were nearest to them. Leeson, however, was still holding his fire. I gritted my teeth. I wanted to order him to fire—but it was his call. That's how I ran my unit. After all, he'd been fighting for Legion Varus when I was in diapers.

At last, the sickly green beams came to life. Two of the 88s began to sing, one to my left and one to my right. Each reached out with their deadly rays and began to sweep toward the other.

The bugs were cooked in their shells. They reeled in shock. Making an odd, desperate whistling sound that I could just hear over the din of battle, they ran around in random circles for a moment before falling in a shivering heap.

We killed a thousand—two thousand. I dared to let the corner of my mouth twitch up, the beginnings of a grin. They weren't going to make it to us.

"*McGill!*"

My head snapped around. That voice—it was Barton. She was in trouble, or freaked out, or something. That cry had been so long and desperate…

I saw it then. How could I have stayed so focused on the charging enemy right in front of me for so long? It was every commander's job to pay attention to the whole battlefield, to get the bigger picture and decide what to do about it before it twisted around and bit him in the ass.

Barton was pointing her long arm at the town behind us—which was in flames. Somehow, the enemy had gotten past us, into our center. Could Fike's sub-legion have failed us so utterly? I didn't know, but I had to find out.

-51-

"All cohorts," Graves said, speaking over command chat. "Break off one unit from your defensive positions and send it to the center, on the double."

Winslade's voice spoke up next. "What's happening, Graves?" he demanded. "Is it treachery, or a bombardment, or—"

"I'm not sure, Winslade. There's fighting going on in the dome city. I've tried to contact Kattra, but I'm not getting a response. I repeat, all cohorts—"

Another voice broke in, talking over him. It was Galina Turov.

I knew she'd been overseeing the battle from above. She'd let Graves handle the fight up until this moment. She must be seriously worried if she was going to step on his operational toes now.

"Fike!" she called out. "What is your status?"

"The enemy have engaged us, but I believe we're winning for now. Our losses—"

"I don't care about losses. Graves? Are all your defensive positions holding?"

"Yes, Tribune. For now."

"All right, then I approve of your plan to pull back a reserve force. You should have thought of that earlier. Whatever you do, don't let the enemy destroy my star-falls!"

That thought was a grim one. I hadn't even considered it, but she was right. The star-fall artillery troops were basically a few hundred lightly armed specialists that were trained to run the big guns. If a real combat unit got into the middle of them… well, it would be a slaughter.

"Winslade," I said, speaking over tactical chat, which didn't hit the whole legion, "I'll go. My zone is pretty much clear now, anyway."

"Not alone, you won't," Helsa told me. She passed me by and trotted away, vanishing among the rocks. She had a determined look in her eye.

"Negative, McGill," Winslade said. "Hold your position."

My eyes slid after Helsa. Coming to a decision, I trotted after her.

Her step was light and quick. Mine was heavy and thumping. Due to my longer stride, I soon caught up.

We ran to where the combat drones were still crouching. Helsa signaled the twenty odd handlers she'd brought with her to ride herd on her robots. With a wave and a whistle, she had them all up and marching in a minute or two.

"Uh…" I said, watching her and her team work. "What are you up to, Helsa?"

"I should never have left her. I was a fool."

"Huh…?"

Lifting my tapper to my face, I contacted Winslade again. "Sir? I think we have a problem. Helsa and her combat drones are pulling out."

"What? Stay right there, McGill, and I'd better not find out this is *your* doing!"

"No sir, I'd never—" I stopped talking, because he'd cut off the connection.

"Helsa?" I asked. "Where are you going, exactly?"

"Can you truly be so ignorant? I was told this was the case, but I didn't place much credit in the claim. I attributed such statements to petty jealousies and malicious jokes—but after spending the day with you, I'm no longer certain."

"That's right. I'm six kinds of a moron. Border-line retarded on a good day. But if you're planning on taking your drones back to the city, I think you ought to at least tell us you're doing it."

She narrowed her eyes at me.

All around us the drones were up now, stretching their pointy-legs and whirring.

"Don't try to stop me, McGill. You'll only gain yourself a quick trip through a revival machine."

"Don't I know it," I said easily. "So you are making a run to your home town?"

"Obviously. Stand aside."

I weighed my options. Winslade had said I had to stop her. I could do it, of course. I could kill her fast and maybe—just maybe—survive the onslaught afterward. After all, I was wearing my Glass World armor.

Heaving a sigh, I tossed the idea aside. What would be the point? I was pretty sure that killing Helsa wasn't going to get these combat drones or their handlers to calmly return to their posts and support us in any upcoming action.

After watching me for a moment to see what I'd do, she nodded to me and ran off. A few hundred drones and drone-minders rushed after her.

Winslade showed up about then.

"McGill, damn you, man! I told you to stop her!"

"Right, sir. I'm on it."

Unslinging my morph rifle, I took careful aim. I even flipped up my long-range reticle to zoom in on Helsa's back.

Just when I was about to squeeze off a shot, Winslade shoved the muzzle of my gun down.

"Are you insane? I didn't order you to shoot her!"

"Uh… how else would you suggest I stop her, sir? She's moving fast, and she didn't show any interest in listening to my thoughts on the matter."

Winslade released a little growl. "Very well. Go after her. Take your whole unit—minus Leeson and his artillery. We'll have to hold the enemy back without your help."

"Very good, sir."

I began running after Helsa. Using my tapper, I summoned my unit to follow.

There was a whole bunch of grumbling to be heard. Harris was the loudest, he never liked a sudden change of plan.

Soon, however, Barton and her lights caught up with me. With my gear, I couldn't outrun them. A moment later, I slowed my pace and let Harris and his heavies catch up.

"Barton, keep up with Helsa if you can."

"It will be a challenge, sir. She's really moving."

"Don't I know it."

We ran hard for about twenty long minutes. That's hard to do in full kit, even when you're in shape—which my troops were.

"They're stopping. That crazy bitch is stopping at last," Harris panted. His breath blew over his mic in blasts.

"McGill—?" Barton called out. "Helsa is right ahead of us—her drones are lighting up!"

"Good God, what is she shooting at?" Harris demanded.

I soon saw what the fuss was about. Up ahead, a firefight had broken out. Graves and his brigade of star-falls were there, and they were under attack.

At first, I thought Helsa was going to fire on Graves with her combat drones—but then I saw the real enemy.

Boiling out of the dome city, hundreds of figures raced toward Graves and the drones. The figures were humanoid—but not human.

They were taller than men, and heavier. Each of them wore a combat harness, a heavy rifle—and behind every trooper dragged a long, scaly tail.

"Armel's saurians!" I roared over command chat. "All units, the lifters are under attack. Armel has gotten behind our lines somehow."

"McGill," Turov said. "Graves appears to be dead. You've got to save those star-falls. Get them aboard a lifter if you can."

"Roger that, Tribune."

Fortunately, I wasn't alone. Helsa had led me here at a dead run, but there were lots of other units converging on this spot to help. They'd all be here in five to ten minutes.

But in an all-out fire-fight, as any veteran could tell you, five to ten minutes was more than a lifetime.

"Unit," I called out over tactical chat. "Get in among the star-falls. Protect them at all costs."

Helsa wasn't listening to me, naturally. Her concern was the dome city. She advanced to meet the saurians, providing the perfect distraction. Barton reached the star-fall brigade just as the saurians began laying down fire on them—but that soon stopped.

I could tell that the saurian commander had orders to destroy the star-falls, but Helsa and her drones could not be ignored. The robots whirred and rose up, standing tall on their tripod of legs. They began to methodically beam the saurian troops into smoking ruin.

Wheeling to face this threat, the saurians returned fire. They weren't heavily armed, fortunately. Each one wore a teleport harness and carried a heavy-rifle—that was pretty much it.

The bad thing was they had the numbers on us. I had to estimate Armel had thrown a full cohort into this thrust for our heart. Worse, the saurians were well-trained. They put up a good fight. They threw grav grenades, then they raced in close and flipped over the combat drones. Their broad backs heaved with scaled muscle.

In the meantime, I gathered my troops and had them take cover among the star-falls.

"You want to try to turn these cannons on the enemy?" Harris asked hopefully.

I frowned at him. "At this range, we'd blast the drones and the lizards to fragments—hell, we might even blow ourselves up."

Harris nodded and gave me an up-down twitch of his bushy eyebrows. I could tell he didn't give a single shit about the drones. He wanted to save his own skin.

"No," I said after considering it for a moment. "Barton, have your snipers pick off a saurian whenever you can. The rest of you hold your fire until we can tell who's winning."

The struggle went on for a full minute. After that, the two sides began to separate. I could tell right off what was happening—Helsa was withdrawing, heading toward the dome city.

Now, I could understand that. She wanted to see what kind of damage was going on back there. She wanted to save her town. But I was sorry to see her go.

The saurians broke off, not following the Shadowlanders.

"Shit," I said, "Harris, about that idea of yours…"

"I've been working on it, Centurion. Just give the order."

Baring my teeth. I nodded. "Fire one blast—one star-fall. Go!"

He rushed away, and the saurians turned to face us. All along, while they'd been battling the robots, Barton had been sniping. They were finally going to get their revenge, and they knew it.

"Turov?" I called. "Come in, command."

"What is it, McGill? Have you defeated those damned lizards yet?"

"Uh... not exactly. Helsa took off on me, and my reinforcements aren't here yet—the saurians are about to rush me."

"Oh fuck... McGill, don't let them destroy my star-falls!"

"Roger that, sir."

I disconnected. She was no help at all. I'd kind of been thinking she could order a bombardment or something—but that was against the rules, I remembered. We'd agreed to keep the conflict going entirely on the surface of the planet. No broadsides, no air support—no nothing.

"Harris!" I shouted. The saurians were firing now, and the crack of their big rifles was startlingly loud. The big bullets struck all around us. Stones split, and the sands jumped. The star-falls were being punched through with holes.

Star-falls weren't overly tough and difficult to destroy. Being energy weapons, they were relatively delicate. They weren't made of heavy metals. Complex circuitry, portable fusion generators and polymer projection cones—that's pretty much all they were. The saurian bullets weren't sophisticated, but they could punch a hole into our artillery pieces from a hundred meters off, no problem.

"Fire in the hole!" a tech screamed.

Everyone threw themselves prone, except for two of Barton's light troopers. The big, slow blast of energy dazzled everyone's eyes. Purple splotchy afterimages lingered, and they couldn't be blinked away.

When I could see again, I noticed the two light troopers were gone. One smoking boot, that was all that was left. They'd gotten in the path of the star-fall projectile.

The ball of energy flew dramatically at the saurian line. They tried to dodge—but their doom wasn't *that* slow. It flew at something like the speed of a fastball back home.

The jagged sphere of energy splashed down in the midst of the enemy. A hundred or more were struck dead. Another hundred were burned and left rolling around to put out flames. Others staggered in shock. Into this mess, we fired a hailstorm of rifle rounds.

The enemy losses were terrific, but it wasn't enough to stop them. They'd had a thousand men, and now they'd been reduced to half that—but they still outnumbered us five to one.

Those saurians who'd managed to rush wide, who tried to flank us—they survived. They came sweeping in now, firing and advancing.

We returned fire, and although I expected to be wiped out, I was surprised at how many of us were still alive. We were all under cover now. Both sides were fighting on our bellies, hugging the ground in any shallow depression we could find to hide in.

"They're really shitty shots, sir," Harris laughed. "Blind as bats if you ask me."

"Maybe that ball of lightning you threw into them blinded them," I agreed.

But then I had a sudden, terrible thought. I looked up and back, over my shoulder, at the star-falls.

Many of them were damaged. They looked like big light bulbs with black star-shaped holes punched into them.

"They aren't shooting for us," I shouted. "They're destroying our artillery!"

"Huh… You're right. But if we hold on the cavalry will be here soon."

In the near distance, more human units were approaching from various angles. Already, they were laying down suppressive snap-rifle fire from range.

I glanced again at the star-falls. Another one shattered and sagged. Then a saurian stood up and threw a grav grenade. He'd wormed up close enough to do it. The blue strobing ball of light fell into our midst. Two of Barton's men and another artillery piece were destroyed.

Snarling, I decided I'd had enough.

"3rd Unit!" I roared. "All heavies, stand and charge the enemy! Lights, hold your position, and keep sniping!"

"Oh shit…" I heard Harris say.

A moment later, what remained of my command rose up and charged.

I was proud of my men. Sure, they weren't happy about my orders—but they obeyed.

311

Thirty-odd heavy troopers sucked their last collective, ragged breath. They all cursed my mamma something awful—but they charged.

-53-

I took a big round to the guts right off—but that didn't do the trick. I was blown backwards onto my butt. I groaned back to my feet again and shivved a surprised saurian. He must have thought I was dead—and in truth, I might have been out for a few seconds due to shock. I'm not exactly sure.

Running my sizzling force-blade into the charging lizard, I shoved him off with a boot and then met two more. They shot me and stabbed me—but nothing went through my armor. I killed them both, and I was left reeling and growling in pain.

I decided right then and there to put a note into the suggestion box back at Central concerning this armor. In my opinion, they needed to put more padding under the outer layer. Sure, it couldn't be penetrated, but you still *felt* it when you got hit. Anyone who doubts me could try putting on a suit and having some folks try to beat them to death with hammers. That's what it felt like to be shot over and over again.

By this time all the lizards were in close, and the fighting was right in the midst of our star-falls. More humans were arriving as well—but the enemy ignored them. They were busy destroying our artillery.

All of them were, that was, except for two reptiles that seemed hell-bent on killing me. Maybe I'd stepped on someone's tail, I don't know. I've discovered over the years that aliens often seemed to take a powerful dislike to old McGill. Go figure.

One of the saurians held me down, and the other tried to kill me with a gun, a knife, then a force-blade. They even set off a grenade under my back.

This last effort cracked my lower spine, I'm pretty sure. I writhed weakly in agony on sand that had been transformed into crunchy glass.

Using the last bit of brain-power I had left, I forced myself to lie still. After all, any sane person would believe I was dead. Playing opossum wasn't even a stretch, as I felt like death warmed-over by now.

One of the saurians leaned close. His big nostrils flared. His snake-eyes examined me, cocking his head to look at me first with the left eye, then the right. He fingered my armor and said something hissy to the other fella.

I couldn't pass up the opportunity. I drove my blade into his right eye-socket, and a gush of nastiness flowed out.

Seeing this, the second lizard lost his nerve and fled—but he ran right into a squad of nine heavy troopers in armor. Fike and his people had finally arrived in force. They cut the last of the saurians down, and thirty seconds later all of the enemy were dead.

Deciding I liked where I was, I stayed low and spent my time trying to breathe. I had some broken ribs, maybe a few cracked vertebrae... It wasn't anything I hadn't felt before, but I wasn't excited at the prospect of standing up right then.

Finally, a familiar voice came near. It was Sub-Tribune Fike himself.

"...what an unholy mess," he said to one of his butt-boy aides. "This is a shit-storm of amazing proportions. Only McGill could—oh, there he is."

Boots crunched nearby.

"Looks like they fought to the death, sir," said the young adjunct at his side.

"Yeah, well, they failed. More than seventy percent of our star-falls were destroyed. We're not allowed to call back to Earth for more equipment, you know that, right? This is a disaster."

"What should I do with McGill, sir?"

"Strip off that armor and recycle him. I'll phone home in the meantime."

The adjunct came near, and he began to tug at me. I decided I'd played opossum long enough.

"Hey there, Adjunct."

"Whoa! Holy shit—you're alive, Centurion?"

"Last I checked. Help me up."

The man did so, and I tried not to show how much it hurt. I leaned on a wrecked star-fall and tried to look nonchalant. I didn't think I could walk on my own, but sometimes that feeling would pass if you gave it a few minutes.

"McGill?" Fike said in disbelief. He crunched closer to me and peered up into my faceplate. "Are you okay, man?"

"Right as rain, sir."

He shook his head. "I'll be damned. Too bad you survived. I'd trade your carcass for one more star-fall."

"You're all heart, Tribune."

Fike ignored me and went back to cataloging the damage. I watched him go, and when he was out of sight I began to limp toward the grounded lifters.

The adjunct fell into step beside me. His helmet said his name was Clane. "You're wearing that new armor, right?" he asked me.

"Bingo, son. Give me a hand, will you?"

Clane threw a shoulder under me, and I limped faster.

"You'd better not let Fike or one of his bio goons see you like this, Centurion," the adjunct advised. "He'll recycle you for sure."

"Don't I know it... Hey, that's one of my dead medics. Get me to his bag."

The medic was Carlos, and he was in three pieces. I searched the biggest chunk that was left of him and found a satchel. A few minutes later, I had my chest piece off. I was spraying on salves and injecting myself with stimulants. My cheeks reddened as my blood-pressure increased.

"That's better... I can breathe now."

Adjunct Clane whistled. "You've got some big bruises... looks like you've been playing the part of a punching bag."

I looked at the kid for the first time. I kind of liked him. "Where are you from, soldier?"

"Texas, sir."

"You mean Texas Sector?"

"I guess so…"

I smiled. The folks from Texas had never completely given up on the idea they were something special. "Listen up, if you ever want to fight in a real legion, give me a text. You can die in style with Varus. I'll see to it."

The kid blinked a few times, but then he smiled. "Thanks, sir. My parents got me this position to prevent exactly that kind of scenario—but I might take you up on it someday."

Clane walked away, and I put my armor back on my sore body, easing it down over the injuries. I didn't want anyone else to see how banged up I really was.

After a cocktail of drugs and a few minutes to stretch a bit, I was able to walk almost normally. It was time to take stock of things.

The first thing I did was a headcount. I had a grand total of thirty-five living troops left in my entire unit. Almost all of them were out hugging rocks with Leeson and Winslade. After making some harsh judgments, I shot two of the wounded and patched up the last one who was still with me—it was Della.

"I'm surprised Cooper didn't make it," I said.

"We moved around behind the enemy when they engaged the rest of 3rd unit," she told me. "When the enemy charged the star-falls, we attacked from behind, killing one straggler at a time."

"Good work… for a ghost."

"That's what we're supposed to do," she said with a hint of defensiveness in her tone. Most of the legionnaires didn't really like ghosts. Sure, they were skilled and vital to the unit. They did recon work no one else could, but they always seemed like dirty killers to the rest of us. Mostly, they snuck around and knifed unsuspecting enemies. They were assassins, not soldiers.

"Damned straight it is," I said, agreeing with her heartily. "A kill is a kill!"

Della gave me a grateful smile. "Anyway, we were stealthed, but Cooper got between a lizard and the star-falls. He caught a stray round and perished. After that, I was careful to stay behind the last saurian in their ranks."

"Well done. I'll report in to Winslade while we march back to our position in those damned rocks."

She vanished again, but I knew she was nearby. I could see her small footprints puffing into existence off to my left.

"Winslade? This is Centurion McGill reporting, sir."

"McGill?" he called back a few seconds later. "How did you get a priority revive?"

"Uh... I didn't, sir. I never died."

"What? I thought it was a wipe-out... Oh yes, that armor I made for you. Pretty effective, yes?"

"It is that, sir. I'd only make one request: add some more padding on the interior. I got banged up like a rat caught inside a clothes dryer."

"Hmm... You'll have to pass that on to Central personally. I'm off the project."

"Right, sir. Where do you want to post my unit?"

"First, what happened to the combat drones? I don't see them in your vicinity."

"Uh..." I said, looking off toward the dome city. I saw a curling column of black smoke rising from the center of the place, but there was no sign of Helsa and her minions. "I kind of forgot about all that in the excitement."

"You what? Those machines are your charges, McGill. Turn right around and head into the town. Find Helsa, and bring her to heel."

"Uh... that's a tall order, Primus."

"Then you'd better get cracking."

The channel closed, and I cursed. Della's empty footprints came near.

"What's wrong?"

"We've got to find out where Helsa went."

"Oh... I wouldn't think you'd mind that order."

There she was, getting slightly jealous over nothing. That was typical for Della. Every once in a while, we had fling, but it never lasted. We'd even had a kid together once, my

317

daughter Etta. But she always took off again before too much time had passed.

Still, despite all that, she didn't like me orbiting another female. Talk about frustrating... I felt my heart beginning to pound in irritation, and I opened my big mouth to say something rude.

But I stopped myself. She and I were the last living members of my fateful charge. There was no sense in having an argument now. Besides, I suspected it was the pain in my ribs and the medications in my bloodstream that were making me feel a little ornery.

Forcing a smile, I looked to where I knew she was.

"Listen-up, Della," I said. "I've got a plan..."

-54-

I marched into that dusty, smoking little town as bold as you please. The happy-juice I'd shot into my arm helped with that—but mostly, it was just my natural swagger.

Shopkeepers, citizens and the like scattered before me. I couldn't blame them for fleeing. After all, I was an armed alien in black armor, and they'd just had a small army of saurians appear in their midst and tear the place up.

Walking across the town, I soon found the trouble-spot. In the dead center of the camp was the dome they kept their drones in. I recognized the area, if not the dome itself, as it had been knocked flat.

"Huh…" I said to Della, putting my big hands on my hips and surveying the damage. "Good thing the combat drones weren't here, right?"

Della was there at my side, of course, but she had the good sense not to answer. She was, after all, my insurance policy.

The few citizens who'd had the balls to follow me didn't respond either. They didn't wear universal translators, and I don't think they were terribly interested in my opinions anyways. I got the feeling they were trying to figure out how to kill me and get away with it.

The dome beside the flattened one was the seat of Shadowlander government. There was some damage here as well. The eastern side was scorched and kind of crispy.

I stepped up to the front doors and threw them wide. Inside, a team of aliens were huddling and whispering.

These guys always looked like they were planning to do a man harm. They were leaning close together, but the second I appeared they said a few more inaudible things then melted away.

In the center of the huddle was Kattra. I could tell right off she wasn't a happy camper.

"McGill..." she said, as if she was cursing the sun or something. "What gives you the right to barge into my town again? I thought we had an arrangement. You stay outside our city and protect it. We don't want to see you here—none of your kind are welcome!"

"No? Well now, that's a crying shame."

I walked in and made myself at home. The queen-lady and her crowd of councilors glared malevolently.

"Listen Kattra, I'm here to check up on you. We saw the smoke and all, and we got worried. The top brass of my legion ordered me to find out what's what."

"They could have simply called."

"They probably have been, but I don't think you've been answering."

Kattra glanced down at her tapper, which was indeed brimming with unanswered messages.

"We've been attacked, and we repelled the invaders at great cost. Your job was to protect us from precisely this kind of event. From my perspective, you Earthmen failed completely."

"Yeah, well... you can't go to war without expecting to take a few casualties. I'm sure the damage is nothing your revival machines can't handle."

The swarm of sycophants behind her shuffled about angrily at that. They made a few outraged bleating sounds. I didn't know what they were saying, but I passed on turning on my translator because I already knew I didn't care to hear their comments.

"You continue to make jokes at our expense, I see," Kattra said. "I should expect nothing else. Humans naturally heap insults following grave injuries."

I frowned. "Uh… Did I miss something? I mean, you got a few of your domes knocked down and all, I get that. But your combat drones are mostly intact, right?"

"That doesn't begin to describe our losses. The enemy saurians came here to do us grievous harm. They partially succeeded."

"Oh yeah?" I asked while looking around curiously. "What did they do?"

"You truly don't know? Your spies are everywhere, so I assumed—but no matter. The saurians teleported into the middle of our town."

"I got that much."

"Once here, they attacked the dome where we keep our combat drones first, destroying it. Obviously, they knew where to strike."

Kattra looked at me suspiciously. Right then, I got the idea that she thought I might have tipped them off. That was a rude assumption on her part, but I guess I could understand it.

"Next," she said after I made no reply, "they moved toward our production facilities."

"You mean they wrecked your revival machines?"

"No. It was much worse than that. They damaged the equipment we use to *build* revival machines."

"Uh-oh… shit-fire, that's bad!"

"Yes, it is. It was a critical strike landed at a weak point to do maximal damage. They attempted to cripple us by destroying the very basis of this planet's economic livelihood. Only true barbarians would do such a thing."

I kept quiet, thinking of a half-dozen races that might do exactly that—including Earthmen. There was no point telling her about all that, however, as she'd probably figure it out on her own in good time.

"What can I do to help?" I asked.

"You can slay these monsters!" she said. She stood tall and spoke with feeling. "They must not be allowed to make another attempt. The first wave lost their harnesses when they attacked and died—but not all of them were lost. Many of the devices were programmed to return, and hundreds did so, even if their owner was nothing but a corpse."

I nodded at that. It made sense. These teleport rigs often had timed recalls on them. I remembered that Natasha had been whisked away by just such a timed trap when it went off on the very first teleport suit we ever found.

"We do plan on defeating Armel, if that's any consolation."

"It is no comfort at all."

"Right... well, you should know that he hit us pretty hard, too." I proceeded to explain that Armel's troops had overwhelmed our defenses and destroyed most of our star-falls.

Kattra was aghast. "Those artillery pieces are irreplaceable."

"That's right."

"And you were using them to great effect to hold back the enemy hordes."

"Hmm... yes. The next time, they'll probably be able to get in closer."

Kattra began striding around on her carpet, thinking hard. "They'll come back. I've placed Helsa and her remaining drone force on guard duty at the manufactory, but another suicidal attack can't save our equipment. Not completely. If we suffer much more loss, we won't be able to grow another revival machine."

"Can't you just save the blue prints or something?"

She laughed at me. "The creation of each revival machine is as much an art as it is a feat of engineering. The core components of our machines are grown organically. We *do* tack on an electromechanical control system, but the plans for such details aren't unique."

"Great... well... I've got an idea that might help. That's why I came here."

She narrowed her eyes. "What idea?"

"How about we strike the next blow before they do? How about we take the fight to them, before they regroup and hit us again?"

Kattra's eyes slid around in thought. "I like your idea. How can it be done?"

I grinned. She was a bloodthirsty one all right. She'd just been given a black-eye, but instead of crying about it she was

322

already dreaming of revenge. That was the kind of woman I could sink my teeth into—figuratively speaking, of course.

Turning to my left, I snapped my fingers. Della dutifully appeared out of thin air.

The delegation of suck-ups hissed and carried on. Kattra, however, eyed Della thoughtfully.

"We have specialists like Della, here. We call them ghosts. We also captured maybe a hundred or so of the teleport harnesses that Armel's troops left behind when they ported away. Not all of them escaped or returned their dead masters to headquarters."

"So what?" Kattra asked. "Where will you go with these captured harnesses—assuming you can operate them at all?"

I smiled—no, I grinned. I grinned widely.

"Remember how they work? They're set to automatically return home. That means every control chip on every one of those harnesses has the destination coordinates of the enemy base recorded inside. Surely, one or more of these rigs can be hacked to give up that vital information."

Kattra stood suddenly. The gaggle of wimps that surrounded her shuffled back instinctively. I got the feeling she might stab any of them that pissed her off, and that she'd done so randomly in the past. I couldn't say that I blamed her on that score.

"I like how you think, human. You're not intelligent, but you have the cunning of a predator in the night. I will take this idea—and you, with your stealth suits and impenetrable armor—you will aid us?"

I nodded, and I kept on grinning. "I'm down for some revenge myself. I owe old Armel and his gang a kick in the pants for sure."

Kattra's face transformed. All along, she'd been looking at me like I was a stinking shit-house rat.

But for now, she was beaming. It was a wicked expression, but overall I considered it to be an improvement.

-55-

"How do we accomplish this miracle?" Kattra asked me.

We were standing over a messed-up pile of teleport harnesses. Some of them had blood on them, some were slashed and hanging—none of them were in prime condition.

I knelt and poked around in the pile. "This is all you've got?"

Kattra frowned. "There must be forty units there. Are you a tech, or not?"

"Nope, not really."

She made a sound of exasperation. "What's the use of this nonsense then? We can't hack them quickly. They're imperial-made, from the Skay side of things. They don't—"

My hand shot out, and I gripped her arm. She looked shocked. A blade appeared in her hand.

Just as fast, Della appeared and stepped close. She was armed too. She looked pissed off, but I wasn't sure right away who she wanted to kill more, me or Kattra. I suspected it was a combination of both.

"Is this some kind of a sex-attack?" Kattra asked me. "I've heard that your males were aggressive, but this timing seems—"

"No, no," I said, laughing and letting go of her. "I just was struck with a thought. You said these rigs are of Imperial design, right?"

324

"Yes, imbecile. I don't understand why my statement might lead you to assault me, but—"

"Look, look. It's important, because we can get the coordinates quickly if you're right. Get out the Galactic Key I gave you."

She eyed me for a reluctant second or two, then she produced the key. I was glad to see it was unharmed.

I reached up a hand, making grabbing motions.

Kattra showed me her teeth, but she finally placed it in my hand. "I would assume you only wish to steal it back and flee—but I think I know what you might be planning."

Nodding, I leaned over the best-looking of the teleport rigs. I touched the device to the harness lock, and sure enough, it unlocked immediately. The straps clicked and fell open.

Next, I put it on. Running the key over my tapper and the interface wire on the harness, I plugged it into my tapper and right off, the screen on my arm lit up.

I whistled long and low. "It works! This unit is out of battery power. In fact, by this error code I think the battery must be defective. Here, I'll pull a battery out of one of the other units…"

Working for a few minutes, I soon had a half-charged kit that was fully functional. In fact, an indicator light on the control pad was blinking. The suit was already trying to return to its point of origin.

"Frisky computer on this thing," I said, holding down the override button. "Della, give me your stealth suit."

"What?"

The two women looked at me in surprise.

"What did you think? That you were going with me? We only have one stealth suit. Besides, we have to do this fast before they get their act together. Come on, Della."

While I rudely snapped my fingers and made twirling motions in the air, indicating she should hurry the hell up, she took her stealth suit off, and I pulled it over my head. She seemed almost as reluctant to part with her invisibility mesh as Kattra had been to let go of the Galactic Key.

Speaking of which, when I was shimmying into that tight mesh and activating it, Kattra suddenly released an un-ladylike squawk.

"McGill! You have my gift! Don't you dare—"

"Sorry," I said, taking my thumb off the override button. The suit immediately began to throb, and the room filled with glimmering blue light. "I need the key to do this mission properly."

"This is a base trick," Kattra complained. "I find myself yearning to kill you yet again."

"You should get used to that," Della suggested.

A moment later, I was a ball of energy. I couldn't hear the women any longer, and that was a solid relief. They both seemed to be all fussed-up about something or other.

Steeling myself, I jumped through space for less than a second. That was a good thing, as I didn't want to end up way out in the middle of nowhere.

When I appeared with a glowing afterimage effect bothering my eyes, I realized right off I was still on Edge World. That was a blessing—but it was the only one I was getting today.

The world was *bright*. Very bright, and painfully hot. Reaching up with a hiss, I closed my visor. That made an audible click.

Two saurian heads turned when they heard that click. One of them gargled something and pointed to where I stood, invisible. Five more heads turned after that.

I was surrounded. I'd appeared in the midst of an encampment of sorts. All around me were hot, stinking saurians wearing nothing but harnesses and weapons. Their big scaly balls dangled low as they all swung around to look at me. Unlike lizards back home, these reptiles kept their prominent genitals on the outside of their bodies.

Naturally, I knew that saurians liked it hot. They were from a hot world, one that averaged around sixty degrees C most of the time. To them, the bright side of Edge World must seem pretty homey.

Freezing in place for a few seconds, I dared not move. My hope was they'd forget about the glimmer of blue they must have just seen, and the click of my visor slamming shut. For a few seconds, as they stared and puzzled, I thought maybe my simple plan was going to work out.

But then, one of those damned lizards let his curiosity get the better of him. He was an officer—a centurion—and he stepped steadily closer. He shuffled over the burning, blinding sands in my direction. His big feet left monstrous prints in the dust.

Footprints.

I glanced down in alarm, and I immediately saw that, sure as shit, my feet had created some very human-looking footprints. The glaring light, the fine, sifting dirt—the environment made this effect stand out. It would be obvious to anyone who looked at the sands under me that someone was standing there, or recently had been.

But fortunately, none of these dummies had looked down. At least, not yet.

The lizard centurion was looking right through me in fact, but his approach was unerring for all of that. If he kept coming, he'd soon walk right into me.

Then I saw him throw his snout high and watched him sniff the air. That's when I knew the nature of my problem. Like many creatures, saurians had a better sense of smell than any human had ever possessed. The centurion knew something was wrong because my scent was lingering in the vicinity.

Getting desperate, I readied myself to strike and run. With luck, the enemy would be confused. I knew that wouldn't last long, however. Each step I took would leave a very clear footprint behind.

It was one thing to have a single set of human prints appear in the dust, it would be quite another to have these prints appearing in rapid succession, leaving a little sound and scent behind with each step I took. They might even figure out I was stealthed and start running after me.

Still, I braced myself to attack, as I didn't have a better plan. Under the stealth suit, my combat knife slid quietly out of its sheath, and I gripped it tightly.

"Centurion," said a familiar voice. "Why are you not ready for the second wave? Don't you retarded lizards know I'm not paying you to make eggs with one another?"

It was Armel. He was right here, supervising the commando attacks personally. That only made sense, as teleport suits didn't come cheap. He wanted to make sure his lizards didn't waste them.

Armel came walking up from my right, I turned my head, but I didn't dare to make a sound or twist my feet around.

The centurion sniffed the air again, full of suspicion. He reached up and touched the translation device at his throat.

"There is something wrong here. A bad-scent. A bad-sound."

"What kind of scent?"

The big nostrils twitched again. "Human."

Armel snorted. "You're smelling me, you cold-blooded moron. Now, stop wasting time. Are your troops ready for the second attack?"

At last, the centurion turned away from where I was standing. He looked at Armel, and I could be wrong, but I wasn't seeing any love in his eyes as he gazed at his commander.

"My warriors are ready. They will die honorably."

"That's not what I want. I want you to kill that bitch-queen of theirs. Kill her daughter as well, if you can catch her. With Kattra out of the way, we shall sweep the rest of Varus aside with our next assault."

"As you command, Tribune."

Armel made a flipping gesture with his hand, urging the centurion to get on with it.

There weren't as many lizards teleporting out this time. On the first attack there had to have been five hundred or more. This time there was less than half that. Most likely this was because we'd damaged too many of their teleport rigs, or because Armel didn't want to risk more of them on an assassination mission.

I felt an urge to teleport back and warn Kattra. She wasn't expecting the enemy to come for her personally.

While the lizards assembled in ranks nearby and began a countdown, I reached up to the control pad with a stealthy hand. If I could teleport out first, I could warn the Shadowlanders.

Unfortunately, my rig didn't light up. I touched the pad—then I pressed it harder and even gave it a little shake.

But nothing happened, because my rig's battery was out of gas. *Damn.* I hadn't had time to recharge it—or at least, I hadn't taken the time.

"Unit, away!" Armel shouted. "Fly with my blessing, and kill that witch!"

He was in fine spirits. He threw his arms high, like a shaman saluting an elder god. All around him, the desert lit up and pulsed with blue light that was even brighter than the glaring eye of the sun overhead.

When they'd all gone, I rushed him. My feet crunched on the sands, but it wasn't much of a sound. What with the sighing winds and the recent hubbub of the teleporting lizards, I doubted he would even hear me.

I ran up behind him, blade lifted high. I planned to grab him by the air hose and stab my blade into the seam of his armor under his neck. With a hard thrust and a bit of luck, I could kill him before he knew what was happening and called for help. After all, one assassination deserved another.

My plan almost worked. I got close, but he began to turn around to see what the sound of tramping boots might be behind him.

Altering my grip, I decided for a frontal thrust. He turned his body, and I could see his confused expression inside his faceplate. He didn't get it—not quite.

Reaching Armel, I rammed my blade into that crack where his helmet met his chest piece. By anyone's account, I'm powerful man. To make sure the blade went home, I held my knife in both hands.

It must have looked quite shocking, coming out of thin air, a glittering blade making a deadly thrust. His eyes flew wide.

My knife chunked into him. He stumbled back, arms wheeling, and he went down on his can.

Smiling, I glanced at my silver blade, expecting it to be wet with his blood—but it wasn't.

Looking back down again, I saw Armel struggling back to his feet. He was cursing something awful.

"Assassin!" he called out. "You will pay for this evil act!"

That's when I decided to toss caution to the wind. Sure, there were other saurian troops around. A few dome-shaped bubble tents sat no more than a hundred meters to my west.

But I didn't care. He had to die. If the assassins he sent to kill Kattra succeeded, the best counter I could muster would be killing him. If our side would be disrupted, well, so would theirs. They probably wouldn't even order the next attack until he crawled out of whatever revival machine he had operating out here in this sunbaked hell.

With a single motion, I threw off my stealth suit. Lifting my morph-rifle, I aimed it at him.

At point-blank range, with my weapon set for close-assault mode, it could spray a shocking amount of power bolts. Steel, titanium—any such normal material would be penetrated and burned through.

I released a long burst, blowing him right off his feet again. He was lifted up and tossed back this time. He landed in a sprawled position, and he rolled onto one side.

Assuming he was dying, I approached him.

To my surprise, he turned to look at me. He wore an angry expression, but there wasn't any blood riming his teeth.

"McGill," he spat. "I should have known." Painfully, he got his feet again.

That's when I noticed something I should have seen right off. Any *fool* would have realized....

He was wearing black armor. It was cut in a different style, but there could no longer be any doubt as to its nature.

Armel was kitted out in a full suit of impenetrable armor from Glass World.

330

-56-

"McGill?" Armel repeated. "Do you know that you are, without the slightest doubt, the most irritating man alive?"

"That's what everyone tells me, Tribune."

I considered spraying him down again, but I passed on the idea. Already, the camp had to be alerted. Shooting him a few more times would be fun, but it wouldn't accomplish anything.

Instead, I walked over to where the lizards had been kitting up. I dug into a pile of harnesses and found one with a fully charged battery. This wasn't hard, as they'd obviously been recharging their rigs since they'd returned from their last attack.

Seeing what I was doing, Armel followed me. He shot me in the back. The bolts spanged loudly on my back plate, but they couldn't penetrate my armor any more than I could get through his. He emptied his magazine, but all I did was stagger a few steps.

"You done fooling around, Armel?" I asked him.

"I don't believe it…"

He walked up and examined me. "This is not our make… has Earth done this?"

I laughed. "Why did you think we went to Glass World in the first place?"

He lifted a black-gloved finger and shook it under my nose. "Don't worry. I can kill you. Just give me a moment."

I slid the battery pack into place and put my thumb on the control pad. In the meantime, Armel calmly searched among the teleport harnesses at my side.

"You will not escape," he said. "I will not have it. I will not be humiliated by a retarded ape yet again."

"Uh..." I said, growing kind of curious.

He was digging around, and he pulled out a charged harness, the same as I had. He didn't put it on, however. He held it in the air and worked the controls. Baring his teeth, he adjusted the coordinates on the rig carefully.

"You know," I laughed, "you've got me wondering what you're up to, but I just don't have time to see what kind of shenanigans you've got in mind, Armel. Maybe next time."

Armel straightened. He'd finished his preparations. His hand was on his control pad, as was mine.

"No time, eh?" he asked with a nasty smile on his face. "Such a pity, but I understand completely. Please, be my guest and proceed."

I thumbed the teleport launch button—but nothing happened. Frowning, I looked down at the rig.

Armel cackled at me. "Such a fool. Such a moron. Your idiocy would embarrass a macaque. Even those who shit in their hands and throw it at others would not claim you."

"Uh-huh..." I said. But as I watched him, a light bulb went on inside my dim brain. "You must have some kind of security system on these, right? Biometrics?"

"Something like that. The point is, you'll never be able to—"

He broke off as I produced the Galactic Key and ran it over the control pad. All of a sudden, it lit up.

"What are you doing? What is that device—?"

"Sorry Armel, but I've got to be on my way now."

Grinning at him, I pressed the button. The world began to shimmer.

Armel's face lit with an insane fury. I knew that expression, I'd seen it before on a lot of people faces—especially women. He was really pissed off.

It was a crying shame, as I would have liked to continue our little talk and seen if he'd really come up with a way to penetrate a suit of impenetrable armor. But it was too late for all that fun stuff. Once the teleportation process began, I was sort of in-between two locations. I wasn't exactly with Armel on that lonely stretch of desert anymore, nor was I back at the Shadowlander town, either. I was somewhere in-between.

Just as I blinked out, I saw him thumb the activation switch on the rig he'd been fooling with. Then he dropped it on the ground, and it began to flash blue as well.

I didn't get the point of all that. After all, he wasn't even wearing it. Where was he sending it to?

That's when I felt something—something kind of funny. When I say funny, I mean sick-like.

I'd felt this sensation before—and it wasn't anything good. Something had gone *wrong* inside my guts.

Arriving back at the Shadowlander camp, I found myself in the middle of a pitched battle. The dome that served as Kattra's throne room was in flaming tatters. Around my feet a half-dozen bodies were scattered. They were Kattra's counselors, and they were all dead.

Farther away were the lizard commandos. Half of them were dead, too. They'd run smack into Helsa and her combat drones, which she'd wisely brought back into her home town to protect her mother.

Unfortunately, her mother Kattra hadn't survived, but the lizards weren't doing all that well either. They were dying off fast. The drones were just too wicked, too powerful.

Naked except for their weapons and teleport rigs, the saurian commandos had destroyed a few drones, but now they were surrounded and overwhelmed.

The first thing I did was take a staggering step. I felt a sickening pain in my guts when I did so.

Oh. I'd almost forgotten. That strange feeling I'd experienced as I'd left Armel's side... In one horrible second, I knew where the other teleport harness had gone to.

Looking down, I saw the teleport harness I was wearing, still looped over my armored body. But there was something else, too. A black bulge in the armor that covered my guts.

It was another harness—the one Armel had been fooling with. He'd reprogrammed it to jump into my body even as I was making good on my escape.

I've suffered this kind of injury in the past. One time, I'd teleported into some hog back at Central, mixing up his organs with some of mine. On other occasions, I'd merged up my boots with other people's boots. One time, I'd gotten my helmet stuck in a roof.

Anyway, this time it was bad. The harness had merged up with my body. It was all up inside me, and I could feel it. I was having trouble breathing, and walking was pretty much out of the question.

Deciding to let myself fall on the ground—after all, that's what my dying body wanted to do right about now—I made wheezing noises. Focusing as best I could with the moments I had left, I unslung my rifle and aimed it into the circle of fighting lizards that surrounded me. They all had their backs in my direction. All I could see from the ground was big fat tails with assholes underneath.

Pulling the trigger on my rifle, I shot them down. It took a few seconds for them to realize the ambush was coming from their midst. When they finally did see me, lying on my back and hosing them down with power bolts, they fell on me, snarling and stabbing with knifes.

They shot me, stabbed me, chewed on my limbs—but of course, nothing penetrated my armor.

The combat drones marched closer, taking the opportunity to burn the last of the survivors down.

"Halt program!" said a girl's voice.

Rapid footsteps approached. A face—a kind of pretty one—leaned over me. It was Helsa herself, and she looked concerned.

"McGill? You're back?"

"Yep. Too bad I couldn't save your mother."

"It could not be helped… but you're hurt, aren't you? Are you shot?"

I coughed, and I felt my organs swelling with blocked blood vessels. "Worse than shot. I'm a goner. Tell my people they'll need to revive me, okay?"

334

"I will do this," she said, and I expected her to run off—but she didn't.

"Will you open your visor?" she asked. "I can't get it open."

"A combat visor wouldn't be much use if you could," I said.

With a painful flick of my fingers, I got the visor to open up. Air stinking of saurians and blood filled my nostrils, but it seemed to smell good to me anyway.

"That's better," I said.

"Yes," she said. She was on her butt now, with my head cradled in her lap. It was a nice way to go out, as I measure such things. "You fought like a warrior, McGill. I will be forever impressed."

"Mighty kind words, Miss. Too bad we're surrounded by these stinking lizards."

She smiled. "My people have a saying: a dead enemy always smells good."

I coughed and smiled back. "That's a wonderful sentiment. Poetic, even."

Helsa smiled again, then she surprised me. She bent close, pressing her face to mine.

She kissed me, and it was a long, deep and soulful affair.

But by the time she took her hands from my sweaty cheeks and straightened up, I was a dead man.

-57-

When I woke up, I'd just been birthed by a revival machine. I was on a lifter, I could tell that much. This was no surprise as our lifters were all grounded, and the legion brass had seen fit to leave our revival machines parked aboard them.

The next thing I noticed were the lights flickering in my eyes. I hated that. Couldn't these bio people just run a wand over a man or something and know if he was okay or not? What year was this, after all?

"What have we got?" asked a stressed-sounding female bio.

"He's a solid eight."

"Good enough, get him out of here."

Hands grabbed me by the biceps and hauled me off the table. I growled in my throat, but I didn't punch the guy. He was just following orders, and besides, I was getting the idea that something was wrong.

Staggering—almost slipping on my wet, bare feet—I groped blindly for the uniform lockers. Someone threw a coverall into my face. It didn't hurt or nothing, but it did piss me off.

"What's wrong with you people?" I demanded. "Can't a man get the time of day after dying a hero?"

The bio girl laughed sardonically. "You're a hero, are you? Where'd you die—ah, Centurion?"

"Right in the middle of that dome city!" I shouted. For emphasis, I threw a hand out hard, pointing into the distance. That hand—I will always and forever insist it was by accident—smashed into the orderly's left ear. He crashed to the floor, cursing.

"Hey man, I'm real sorry about that," I told him. "You want a hand up?"

"You'd probably land me in the grinder," the orderly said. "You're half-blind and as clumsy as a Blood-Worlder."

"A smart man would stand well clear in that case."

Straightening, I noticed the lights were flickering again. The whole place was shaking, in fact.

"Uh…" I said. "Is something going on?"

"We're under bombardment," the bio said. "I thought that was where you came from—plenty of dead are out on the perimeter."

Concerned now, I dressed as quickly as my rubbery fingers would allow and staggered out of the place.

"McGill!" called a sharp voice behind me. It was Winslade. He marched after me on springy feet. "I've been looking for you—where's my suit of armor? Don't tell me you lost it!"

"Well sir," I began, but he put a hand up in my face.

"Don't bother. The details will only further ruin my day. Come on, we have to get a force together and march on the enemy positions."

"Huh? Where are they?"

He pointed into the distance, off to the north. "You see those cliffs? On top of them is a high plateau. A table-land people once called it. In any case, Armel has moved troops up there with plasma mortars. The first thing they did was shell our remaining star-falls. Now that the enemy has the high ground and an advantage in artillery, they're raining down destruction."

Looking around, I saw two burning lifters. That couldn't be good, I had to admit.

"Sir," I said, "gather up all the men you can. I know a few of them are back in the dome city. I'll go fetch them."

He looked at me with slitted eyes. "This better not be an excuse to chase some alien tail, McGill. I'm on to you. Be back in fifteen minutes, or else."

I trotted away, assuring him that fifteen minutes was ample time. After another dozen strides, I glanced back to see he had begun pestering one of our weaponeers.

Slowing down to a walk, I ambled into the middle of town. The place was a wreck. It had taken some mortar hits as well. Apparently, Armel wasn't any happier with the Shadowlanders than he was with Legion Varus.

Reaching the center of town, I cursed when I found my suit of armor was missing. I tried to talk to a few of the combat drones, but they didn't even look at me. They didn't seem all that bright, even for robots.

"McGill?"

It was Helsa. I turned around and gave her a hearty smile. "That's me!"

"How did you get back here so fast? After a hard death, most of my people take a day off to contemplate their place in this universe."

"A legionnaire has no time for that kind of crap," I told her. "We're reborn with a rifle in our hands, and we're sent right back to the front."

"Your words are truly disturbing."

"Uh… speaking of equipment, where did my suit of armor go?"

She looked surprised. "*Your* suit of armor? Is that why you came back to the site of your death?"

Smiling, I walked up to her and snaked a long arm around her waist. "Not just that. I was hoping for another kiss."

Helsa was startled, but she was still smiling a little. I half expected her to knife me or something—but she behaved herself.

"You're a madman. This is no time for mating. The enemy is at our gates."

"Listen," I said, keeping hold of her, "if I go up there and wipe out those lizards who are dropping bombs on us, will you have dinner with me afterward?"

338

She made a puffing laugh and shook her head. "So forward! Our men simper and beg. It's strange to be accosted in this manner. When I kissed you earlier, I thought I was being aggressive—but you have put me to shame!"

"That's me. Shameless McGill. What do you say—about the date?"

"I… I say yes."

"Good." I kissed her a good one, and she really did seem surprised. Maybe it was true that the men in her culture were all wimps. It seemed like a terrible waste, as the girls were mostly cute, if a little rough around the edges.

When I let go of her, I asked for my armor again. She sighed and led me to a cabinet.

"Here," she said, pulling out the big lumpy suit. "We'd kind of hoped to keep this and study it—but it would never fit any of our people. Our men don't grow so big."

"Thanks a bunch."

I put on the armor and checked the pockets… sure enough, the Galactic Key was there.

Feeling a bit better about the cruel universe, I raced back to where I'd left Winslade. Unfortunately, he'd already set out toward the defensive position we'd held since yesterday. I ran after him, cursing and panting.

When I got to the cluster of column-like rocks, I found the rest of my unit and my entire cohort were deployed there. Winslade was in a terrible mood, and the rest of them weren't much happier.

"All right, 3rd cohort," Winslade said, speaking to every commander under him. "We've drawn the lucky short straw today. Three cohorts will be performing a sudden assault effort on that table-like rock formation to the north. 3rd cohort is one of the three formations chosen for this mission."

Squinting, I gazed off toward the distant cliffs. Everyone around me did the same. Climbing those walls looked damned near impossible. The cliffs were sheer, but there was a winding path that ran around to the rear of it.

"Who's the crazy?" Carlos asked. "Is it Winslade himself, or is Graves plotting our destruction again?"

"Both of them, probably," Harris commented.

Harris was in a grim mood. So was Leeson, and even Barton looked sour. That was unusual for her, but I guess this planet was beginning to wear her down.

"We can't tolerate this endless bombardment," Winslade continued. "But we can't simply abandon the defensive positions we've set up around the Shadowlander town, either. If they draw us off into an all-out attack, we'll destroy the force up on those cliffs, but we'll leave the town open to another assault. Possibly, that's their real plan—but it doesn't matter. We have our orders. We will do, and we will die, until it is done."

"What a tool," Carlos muttered.

I thought about cuffing him, but I passed. After all, he was kind of right.

"Two cohorts," Winslade continued, "will make a pincher movement around the west and the east side of the cliffs to the rear of the rock formation."

As he spoke, my helmet's auto-mapping battle computer drew the plans out on the inside of my faceplate. It was distracting, but I tried to pay attention, and I restrained my natural urge to swipe it all away.

"A final cohort to engage will join the assault once the other two are at the top, behind the enemy. At that point Graves has authorized the use of a single lifter. They'll fly up there and attack the enemy from the opposite side."

"That's got to be us," Carlos whispered. "Please let that be us!"

"Our job has been assigned," Winslade went on. "We shall march around the western side to flank the enemy. After reaching the heights, we'll engage and the trap will be sprung. With any luck, we'll wipe them out about six hours from now."

"Six frigging hours?" Harris muttered. "Shit…"

"That's a long walk," I agreed.

We started off as soon as the briefing was finished. As it turned out, the target enemy was farther away than they looked. We walked across open, mossy lands lit by the purply skies for a long time before anything happened.

For the first two hours, we marched steadily toward the goal. The lizards on top of the mountain took no notice of our approach. They kept bombarding our main encampments, dropping sizzling balls of energy on top of the cohorts.

Each cohort and lifter was covered by a shimmering shield of force—but these defensive systems could be overwhelmed. Now and then, a warhead got through and killed a squad or two. Sometimes, equipment was destroyed. Twice, even the Shadowlander's town was hit. That caused fires and no doubt numerous civilian deaths.

"These bastards don't quit, do they?" I asked.

Winslade had dropped back to march with my unit. I didn't know why he did that—we didn't like him any more than the rest of the troops did—but maybe he felt more at home with 3rd Unit. That was just our good luck, I supposed.

"Pray that they stay fixated on breaking Graves' static defenses," he said. "They're letting us get rather close. With any luck, we'll be hugging those cliffs and at a bad angle for blasting in another half hour."

We marched onward for maybe ten more dull minutes—but the situation didn't last. The enemy bombardment of the legion's entrenched positions suddenly stopped.

"They've ceased fire," Harris said. He came up to me, grinning. "Maybe they've seen the light. Maybe they see us coming, and they know it's time to pull out and forget about popping off at our shielded positions."

I didn't answer. Instead, my long neck was craning. I stared upward at the high cliffs and the dark sky behind them. It seemed to me that I could make out a few figures on the rim up there.

"Barton!" I roared. "Switch out your gear, turn your lights into snipers! See if you can pop a few lizards on the cliff up there."

She was way ahead of me. She'd already anticipated this possibility, and she'd long ago ordered her people to switch to their longer barrels. Giving a single order to kneel and fire, all her troops began taking careful shots. We were still at extreme range, but hits were still possible.

Other units took notice of what we were doing, and they did the same. Soon, hundreds of rifles were cracking loudly in the twilight sky.

"They aren't even shooting back!" Harris said elatedly. "This is gonna be a turkey-shoot. I can taste it."

I glanced at him, but I didn't say anything. I didn't see any reason to crush the spirit of the only man in the unit who had a morale-boost going.

"Spread out, Barton!" I ordered.

She relayed the order, and her lights scrambled over rocks and bushes to new positions.

Winslade walked up to stand next to me. His skinny arms were crossed over his bony ribs, and he looked at me quizzically. "You're stretching out your lines? The lizards aren't even returning fire yet."

"Uh-huh…"

It took about another minute, during which several of those distant figures on the top of the cliff fell. Sometimes, they even toppled over the edge and tumbled down, tails whipping around hopelessly, trying to regain their balance. During these rare occasions, the troops whooped and hollered like they'd won the pennant.

It didn't last, however. Suddenly, the whole upper rim of the cliff seemed to erupt in green fire. The blaze of light started off bright and only grew brighter. The plasma mortar warheads arced only slightly. They grew bigger and bigger, swelling with alarming speed.

"Take cover!" I shouted.

A dozen throats took up the cry. Men scattered and scrambled everywhere, trying to find cover—any kind of cover.

Then, the barrage that those bastards up on the cliffs had fired directly at us began to land. We were at point-blank range for mortars, so there hadn't been much time to do anything.

The ground jumped under my feet. It heaved up and bucked, and I half-fell, half-dove into a crevice. Seeking cover, I wormed deeper still. Others all around me scrambled and crawled over one another. We were like rats trying to escape stomping boots.

When the big energy warheads landed, men disappeared—a dozen of them at a time. It was as if they'd been swallowed by the ground itself. There was nothing left other than a crater and a few grisly scraps.

The crack in the ground I'd dived into suffered a direct hit. All around me, troops were torn apart. A young woman I didn't even recognize was one of them. She died in a melting puddle of sand that ran like lava for a moment, then transformed into crusty glass.

Scrambling back to my feet, I checked my vitals. I was hot, lightly irradiated and freaked out—but my armor had kept out the worst of the blast.

"Hot damn…" I said. "This stuff is gold."

Someone moaned aloud next to me. I looked around until I found the source of the sound. It was Winslade.

"Those vicious reptiles," he said. "They decimated my command!"

"Can you stand, sir? Can you walk?"

"Yes… I think so."

"Then we have to run for it, Primus. They'll be loading back up for another barrage."

"Of course they will—help me get to my feet, McGill."

I hauled him up by one skinny arm. I stood him on his boots and half-dragged him over the rocks. Soon, he cursed me and batted my hands off him. Using the same method, I grabbed every able man I could and got them up and running.

Those who were too injured I ignored and left behind. There wasn't anything I could do for them, and honestly, letting them perish in the next strike was probably for the best.

Harris was one of those I left behind, and he cursed a blue-streak.

"You cold-hearted mother!" he called out behind me. "I've got one leg left, and I can still outshoot you!"

"Sorry, Adjunct," I called over my shoulder. "Unless you can outrun me, I'll catch you back at camp in the morning."

"You aren't sorry! You're enjoying this, McGill!"

Harris was up and hopping in my wake. I had to give him that: he didn't give in to death easily. He hated dying, he always had.

About then, I saw Barton moving to help Harris. "Dammit, girl! Leave him! We've got a cliff to climb!"

But it was too late.

"Incoming!" someone up ahead screamed.

Damnation. I'd miscalculated. They'd taken so long to fire the first time, I'd figured we had a few minutes—but no, of course not. The first long wait had given them time to aim and get the range right. Now that they had us zeroed, the salvos would only take about two minutes to come in.

"Take cover!"

We were down again, and we tried to find cover, but there wasn't much to be had. Fortunately for me, the lizards had decided to nail the same spot as before, finishing any survivors. Those of us who'd gotten moving quickly were only knocked off our feet by the rippling series of blast waves hitting us in the back.

Those that had been too slow, however, weren't so lucky. Harris and Barton were both killed. A lot of our weaponeers died as well, as they couldn't run quickly in their insanely heavy kits.

One exception was Veteran Sargon. He usually operated in Leeson's platoon, serving as the top noncom to ride herd over the other specialists. Being a big man, even for a weaponeer, he'd managed to move his metal-covered body over the ground faster than the others.

He threw himself down in a gully beside me, and the moment the blasts stopped shaking us, he was up and running again.

"Centurion," he said, "we've got to keep moving. We've got to run all the way to the shadows under that overhang."

Sargon pointed ahead toward the base of the cliff. I nodded in agreement, and I raced away close behind him. Winslade, Leeson and maybe two dozen others followed us.

It was pathetic. We'd lost most of my unit, and most of Winslade's cohort. Graves was going to be pissed.

After three more crashing barrages from the lizards, we reached the base of the cliff. Walking around it, we were out of range of the mortars above. They simply couldn't angle downward enough to hit us here.

Winslade hugged the shadowy stone walls with his skinny sides heaving.

"We've got to keep moving, Primus," I told him.

"No. We'll wait here for a few minutes. I'm tired of playing the fool."

I looked around at my cluster of survivors. Sargon shrugged and leaned against the cliff wall. Leeson joined him.

"Forget about taking a piss," I said. "Give me a full rundown. What have we got left? Troops, specialists, gear—the works."

Leeson muttered something about his ass, but he began tallying up what we had left to work with.

"Nice dodge, McGill," Winslade said. He'd gotten to his feet again, and his rodent-like eyes were surveying the landscape.

"Uh… what dodge is that, sir?"

"Looking busy. We have to have some reason to be hugging ourselves here while others are starting the long spiral up to the top."

I turned and looked around. Sure enough, several more units were indeed shuffling on by as we delayed. All of them looked tired and hurt.

Suddenly, I got an evil suspicion.

345

"Sir? You aren't lingering down here just so more of our troops get in front of us, are you?"

"Of course I am. I'm not a fool—and you aren't either. Stop pretending, it's tiresome."

After we'd taken stock of everything, I found we'd been hit pretty hard. We had no medics, no techs, only a dozen light troopers, twice as many heavies—and that was about it. The only weaponeer with a working belcher was Sargon. At least he was good with his weapon.

Our helmets crackled after we'd screwed around for another few minutes. It was Graves.

"Primus?" he called. "Winslade, why aren't you moving? Don't tell me you're dead, I can see your vitals on the screen in front of me."

"I'm feeling better, sir," Winslade answered. "Thanks for inquiring. We took a hard blow out there on those rocks. We've regrouped and we'll be—"

"Just get moving, dammit. You'll be at the rear of the formation now as it is."

"A pity..."

Graves signed off, and we got going. Winslade set the pace, and he wasn't moving terribly fast. We stayed in sight of the unit ahead of us—but just barely.

"This is humiliating," Leeson told me. "The rest of the boys up ahead are never going to let me live down this chicken-shit stuff."

"Probably not," I admitted.

After nearly an hour of hugging the cliff, we made it to the rear escarpment. We were able to begin the long spiraling climb at the back side of the tableau, and we were still way behind the most forward troops.

"Have you got any ghosts left?" Winslade asked me.

"Negative, sir. Cooper and Della are both dead."

"A pity... Della is quite likeable. That fiend Cooper, however... never mind. You'll be my scout when we get to the top."

My helmet rotated, and I eyed him. "Why's that, sir?"

"Because you've got an impenetrable suit of armor on, you oaf. Had you forgotten?"

"Oh… right. I'll move to the front ranks."

Clanking along, I found myself to be in better shape than most of the men. Almost everyone had suffered some form of injury.

As we climbed up higher, it seemed like the sky was brightening. It was an odd effect, as you expected the angle of the light to change with the rising sun—only, in this place dawn took weeks to crawl over the land. The angle of the sun never changed. It was like taking the longest morning walk of my lifetime.

At last, we got close to the top of the cliff. I could tell because a shower of explosive pellets came raining down from above.

The first casualty was Leeson. Either he'd been careless, not hugging the rocky cliffs, or the saurians had orders to shoot officers first.

Three cracking shots rang out, and he went spinning off the narrow pathway. His body bounced and thumped all the way to the bottom.

Everyone else shouted in alarm and hugged the wall of the cliff. Only I leaned out, trying to get a glimpse of the enemy.

The rocks jumped and smoked next to me, making me duck back under cover. Yep, they were officer-hunting today.

"Light troops! Put down some sniper fire on those smart-ass lizards!"

Barton's recruits were well-trained, if a little shaky. They stepped into view and began plinking away at the saurians above us. Unfortunately, as any gunman can tell you, being on top of a cliff was way better than being at the bottom when it came to surviving.

The two sides exchanged shots for a full minute. One of our recruits died in the process, and I couldn't tell if we got any hits.

Regardless, I used this precious time to advance up the cliff. Reaching out with my big hands, I pulled myself up the rocks, like an orangutan heading for the treetops. Soon, I was able to get a bead on one of them.

Blam!

347

I was hit. Right in the chest—but the big round didn't penetrate. Still, I was spun half around, and I almost fell. As we were about two hundred meters above the rocky floor of the valley, I wouldn't have survived the drop—armor or no.

But I managed to catch myself and take a one-handed potshot back at the surprised lizard who'd nailed me. It was he who was blown off his scaly feet. He did a rolling, bouncing tumble all the way past Winslade and the rest to crash down in a bloody pulp far below.

I went back to climbing again, and I managed to down two more lizards. They hit me one more time, but again, my armor held. The rest of the snipers retreated.

"Come on up!" I shouted to the men below.

They climbed after me, and eventually Winslade caught up. He was breathing hard. "You're a master of stealth, McGill," he complained. "Why didn't you just blow a horn or something to let them know you were coming?"

I grinned, but I kind of felt like tossing him off the cliff. He seemed to sense this, and he stalked on by sourly.

The sad thing was we were down to just two squads of infantry, mostly heavies. For leadership, we had Winslade, myself and Sargon—that was it. We needed everyone we had left, so I couldn't afford to shank Winslade—not now.

The rest of the way to the top went smoothly. That was mostly because other groups had forged the way ahead. Their broken bodies were scattered here and there on the rocks. As we passed them by, we looted gear and ammo as needed.

"You have to admit," Sargon said as he came near, "Winslade's bullshit has kept us alive so far."

"Yeah... but we're not here to stay alive. We're here to kill the enemy."

"Amen, brother. How are we going to do it?"

I gazed doubtfully up to the top of the cliff. It was alarmingly close. There was sporadic fire up there, and I knew the lizards were under continuous assault. They had to be getting low on troops as well.

"Here's the deal," I told Sargon, "when we get to the rim, I'll call Graves. That's what they're waiting for, a final distracting attack from our side."

"That's what any man in 3rd Unit is best used for—a distraction."

Using my HUD, I scanned the region. Several other units were in position now, near the top like we were. They were all waiting among the rocks for Winslade to arrive and give them new orders. He was gathering everything we had together, a wise move.

Soon we reached the rim, staying low so the lizards couldn't take a potshot at us.

"This is it, sir," I told Winslade. "It's not getting any better than this."

He nodded, and he contacted Graves. "We've taken heavy losses, but we're finally in position. You can begin your invasion."

"Not good enough," Graves said. "Hit them now with everything you have left. That's an order."

Graves dropped the channel. Hissing, Winslade bared his teeth. He turned on me like it was all my fault.

"A few short hours ago," he hissed at me, "I was in command of this operation. I should never have helped you free Turov."

"Well… yeah…" I said, and I trailed off. From his point of view, he was right.

"Grenades out, troops!" Winslade commanded. "We're going up and over the top of this final ridge. I want every man-jack of you to carry and toss a grenade at the enemy. Don't let any of them survive."

There was a ragged, tired cheer of "Varus! Varus!"

Taking a deep breath, Winslade stood up.

We all followed him, and our hearts surged. Sure, he was just one skinny man with the heart of a weasel, but he'd been ordered to die like the rest of us—we all knew it. If he was going to lead this action, we'd follow him.

Winslade reached down to his chest and activated his body-cams. This would broadcast the action live over command chat. Any officer who cared to could watch. That was against regs, but I doubted anyone would give him a hard time about it.

As he activated his grav-grenade and stood tall, I have to admit, I figured he was going to fake us out at the last moment. It's a sorry state of affairs that a centurion would have such a firm lack of faith in his primus, but there it was.

But Winslade didn't chicken out. His spine was straight as he vaulted lightly over the rocks. Reaching the rim he threw his one and only grenade.

A few hundred others followed him. We were the ragged remains of a dozen units, but we all roared until our throats burned.

When I passed over the last rocks, coming out of cover—I was rudely surprised.

The mortars were there waiting for us. They were all lined-up, perhaps twenty of them. Fat-bellied and aiming their black muzzles on a flat-trajectory, I had only a second or two to realize it was a setup.

Then, the saurians operating the big guns fired them all at once.

-59-

It's said that Napoleon Bonaparte broke the back of the Royalists in Paris with the careful use of forty cannon, using a "whiff of grapeshot" to decimate a force that outnumbered his by six to one. Well, today it was my turn to be on the receiving end of artillery used at a point-blank range.

Lying on my back, coughing up blood, I found myself shocked to be alive at all. I'd taken a blast, but my armor had kept me alive—barely.

All around me, hundreds of other Varus troops were dead or dying. Oh sure, we'd gotten off a few grenades and destroyed a cannon or two—but overall, we'd gotten our clocks cleaned.

Breathing was difficult. Each sucked-in gasp seemed to hurt more than the last. I just lay where I'd fallen, on my back, staring up at that purple sky. There wasn't much going on inside my brain, other than shock and a ringing sound that rattled around in loops.

A figure came near after a minute or so. I saw him stand over me with his hands on his hips. He shook his head and eyed me in distaste.

"We meet again, McGill," Armel said. "Why do such moments always seem to end in death for one of us or the other?"

"I'm not sure about that, sir," I grunted out.

"You fought well, but you were outmatched. My saurian troops have made me proud today."

"That's right. Your toy lizards played us every step of the way."

He bent forward, narrowing his eyes a little. "Praise? Honest praise from the mouth of a scoundrel? You surprise me."

"A man gets what he deserves in the end, that's what my mamma always said."

Armel laughed. He threw back his head and grabbed his gut. "You can't know how pleased I am to see you dying at my feet. That last time you got away, and I was cheated. Today, I want to feel the joy of watching your life completely pass from your oversized, apish body. Today—"

A lizard showed up behind him about then. Saurians were as tall as I was and bigger-boned. This lizard was one of Armel's officers, and he towered over the human.

Armel turned on him angrily. "What is it, you cold-blooded brute? Can't you see I'm speaking to the enemy commander?"

The translation light flashed at the saurian's neck. "My apologies, Tribune, but a ship approaches from the south."

"A ship? What ship?"

Right about then, I saw a shadow looming up behind both of them. It was bigger than Armel, and bigger than his lizard—way bigger.

"Turn the cannons!" he shouted wildly. He raced off, leaving me on my back like an overturned turtle. "Turn the cannons, fools!"

The saurians worked, bulging their scaly arms and shoulders. The fat-bellied cannons wheeled slowly around. I was surprised they weren't automated, but maybe old Armel didn't have access to the good stuff. Sometimes, when you were a homeless mercenary selling your sword among the stars, you had to make do.

Watching with interest, I saw the big lifter come down to land behind the saurians. It was a ballsy move on Graves' part. After all, if Armel had left a few of those big guns aimed out over the valley, one direct hit would probably destroy the lifter—and that was a serious chunk of credit to lose.

Armel put in a good effort, mind you. He beat the hunched shoulders and triangular skulls of his troops with a walking stick. Each blow caused a shower of sparks, which told me the stick was more than a cane—it was an oversized shock-rod.

But it did no good. Before he could get his fat cannons turned around, the lifter's anti-personnel turrets opened up and began to blaze. Showers of power-bolts flew from a dozen gun ports, tearing into the artillery brigade. The mortars were destroyed, the saurians were destroyed—even old Armel himself was blown to fragments.

After that, the lifter landed and troops poured out. They walked from body to body, executing survivors.

It didn't take long for one of the troops to reach me. He raised the muzzle of his weapon to aim right into my faceplate, but then he halted.

"Centurion?" the man asked in surprise.

"The name's McGill," I managed to rasp out.

"I'm sorry, sir. I thought you were a saurian. Your armor looks different and… well sir, you're kind of big."

"No problem, Specialist. Could you do me a favor?"

"What's that, sir?"

"Call your commander over here."

A couple of rough minutes passed after that. I was kind of feeling shivery and sick. I figured I must be all broken-up inside, but I didn't let myself die. Not yet.

Finally, a primus showed up. It was Graves himself.

"Hey, sir," I said weakly. "Good to see you."

Graves glanced at his tapper. "Your vitals are shit, McGill."

"Yes sir, and you're all heart to notice. Did you see that broadcast? Did you see how Winslade sewed on some pretty big balls at the end of this death-march?"

"Yes. Yes he did—it was quite surprising."

"Uh… was it your plan, sir, that we would all die and give you the shot at hitting Armel in the flank?"

"It all worked out better than I'd hoped it would."

"That's good to hear, sir. Good to hear."

"Now McGill, I'm retiring you. You'll be debriefed in a few hours—make that tomorrow. Get some sleep, you've earned it."

"You're all heart, sir. I've always said it."

Without further ceremony, Graves shot me in the chest.

"Ouch!" I complained. "I felt that one."

Muttering, Graves lifted his pistol again. He fired until his magazine was empty.

"Jeez!" I said, groaning and half rolling onto my side. "Did my dog take a shit on your lawn, sir? My ribs are broken, and you're not helping any."

Graves sighed. "That armor is a little too effective. Open your faceplate, Centurion."

I hesitated. A part of me wanted to survive, and I entertained a few fantasies about being carried down to camp in that big lifter. Letting go of such pipe-dreams, I opened my visor.

Maybe I'd get a chance to meet up with that little bio I'd met the last time I'd died...

Fresh, dry air rushed into my face. It felt kind of good.

Then Graves finally shot me dead.

-60-

Coming awake the next day, I lamented the rough nature of my fate. It seemed to me that I'd died an inordinate number of times on this planet. I was beginning to get a negative view of the place. Walking out of the revival chamber, I painted one wall with the slime on my hand.

My first action after revival surprised even me. I decided to go down to visit the quartermaster, the guy who distributed equipment. After all, I'd had some pretty special gear on my person this time around. I'd really like to get it back.

"Quartermaster?" I asked.

The prim non-combatant centurion nodded. He had a lipless mouth and a mustache that was too big for his face. "What is it, Centurion?"

"Any chance you've seen a special suit of armor?" I asked him. "One tailored to a person of my unusual dimensions?"

He began working a tablet as I talked to him. "McGill, James," he read aloud. "Centurion, 3rd Unit, 3rd Cohort. Gear to be issued: one morph-rifle in serviceable condition. One—"

I put a big hand between his eyes and his tablet. That earned me a scowl.

"I know what's on the screen, Quartermaster. What I'm asking is if you've recovered a very special piece of armor. It's black, it's form-fitting, and it will take a direct hit from an energy bolt and shrug it off."

His face soured. "That doesn't sound like regulation equipment, McGill. I'm sure you've been briefed on the dangers of bringing privately owned items onto the modern battlefield. My files are replete with—"

"Look," I said, leaning a little closer to him. "I'm not talking about my granddaddy's wetsuit from the Unification wars. I'm talking about an experimental piece of armor that's invaluable, issued to me personally from the labs under Central."

His eyes widened a fraction at the mention of Central's labs. They were a secret, but everyone knew about them.

"Do you have a serial number? A requisition sheet? A—"

"No. I've got none of that stuff. Like I said, the armor was specially issued—"

"Well then, I'm sorry. I can't help you. Nothing matching your description has crossed into my possession."

Gritting my teeth, I nodded. "All right. They told me upstairs you were a serious tool, but you've certainly proved everyone wrong today. Thanks much, Quartermaster."

He glared at me as I exited his lair, but I didn't give him a kind word. He could shoot me in the ass for all I cared.

Stomping and grumbling, I went up to see Graves. That turned out to be harder than it should be. After annoying a squad-full of noncoms and petty officers, I finally made it into his office.

Graves was squatting in a low, dark bunker full of computer tables and coffee mugs. As usual, his office had very little in the way of adornment. When I stepped into his lair, he didn't even look up.

"Centurion McGill, your unit is waiting for you at your assigned gathering point."

"Yes sir, I get that, sir."

Slowly, he looked up from his work. "Then what are you doing here? There's no need for you or Winslade to brief me. I saw the whole thing. If it's praise you're looking for, go find an underling to give it to you."

"Huh? Oh... no, sir. That's not it at all. It's just that I've become kind of attached to one of my pieces of gear, see..."

He smirked. "Ah, I get it. This is about the armor. You like wearing it and playing the hero, don't you?"

"As a matter of fact I do, sir."

He nodded. "Do you have any idea how many primus-ranked officers requested that I transfer that armor to them?"

I blinked in shock. "They can't do that, sir! I got that issued to me fair-and-square from Central itself. If they want a suit, they'll have to talk to the nerds about it."

Graves nodded. "That's what I figured you'd say, but something else helped you in this case—most men can't fit in that suit. It's adjustable, but too big for most."

I felt a surge of relief run through me. "That's great news, sir. Where can I pick it up?"

Graves looked down at his desk again. "You can't. It's been assigned to Sub-Tribune Fike. He happens to be close enough in general weight and dimensions to wear it—but I think it looks stupid. The sleeves and legs are too long."

"Aw, come on! Fike can't just steal my armor!"

"He can, and he already did. After Winslade broadcast that fight up on the plateau, everyone wanted something that would keep them alive under unbelievable conditions. Recently, human commanders of a sub-legion have been ruled to possess a rank half a level below their assigned positions."

"Uh…"

"That means," he said patiently, "that a sub-tribune overrules a primus like me. I'm only an acting tribune—I don't actually possess the rank."

"That's bullshit! I'm talking to Turov about this."

Graves stood up and shook his head. "I don't want any more of that kind of nonsense out of you on this campaign, McGill. Do you hear me?"

"Loud and clear, sir. The idea has flown right out of my head. Don't even think of it again, and I won't dare mention it."

Graves eyed me coldly and kicked me out of his dark office. Once I was out in the twilight of Edge World again, I cursed up a blue streak.

Naturally, that armor was priceless to a man like me—but that wasn't the only problem. Something of even bigger value was in one of the pockets: the Galactic Key.

Sighing, I realized I had to contact Turov. She wasn't going to be happy, but then, she rarely was when she was out commanding an army in the field.

"Tribune Turov?" I said, dictating an audio message to her in a cheery tone. "How about that battle up on the hill? Pretty nice work, if I do say so myself. As an aside, however, I have to let you know about something Fike took from me... something of *yours*, I mean."

That was all I said. That was all I had to say. If she listened to the message—and I knew she would because she couldn't help herself—she'd know instantly what I was talking about.

Whistling, I headed for the officers' mess. It was nothing more than a dugout with a few barrels for stools, but it was heaven as far as I was concerned.

My tapper began buzzing before I had my first homebrewed beer halfway down. Chugging the rest real quick, I opened the channel and put on a happy-face.

"McGill?" Turov asked. "You don't mean what I think you mean, do you?"

"Uh... about what?"

"The key, you moron!"

"Oh, that. Unfortunately, Fike pulled rank, and he—"

"What do you mean he pulled rank? What kind of bullshit is this? He's a sub-tribune, a zoo-keeper with big ideas."

"Don't I know it, Tribune. But you see, Graves explained to me that according to the new regs, Fike outranks him."

"That's nonsense. I put Graves in overall operational command."

"You sure did, and a wiser decision has never been made. But—"

"Wait... that doesn't count for something like a personal preference, does it? Technically, Fike has superiority. What a bastard. How did he find out about the key?"

I shrugged. "As far as I know, he doesn't know the key exists. But he wanted my armor, see. When I died, well, I left it in my pocket."

"Very thoughtless and sloppy of you, James."

That kind of surprised me, as I didn't know how I was supposed to figure out when I was going to die and hide the key or something.

"I'm sorry about that, Tribune," I lied. "I truly am. It's a damned shame."

"What are you talking about? Go get my property and return it to me. That's an order."

"Uh… Fike kind of outranks me, sir. By a lot."

"And…? So what? Kill him if you have to. Or arrange one of your farcical tricks. I don't care—just get it back."

She closed off the channel. I sighed and then drank another beer. I found the second didn't taste as bitter as the first one had, so I drank five more. That did the trick. With a few pretzels to soak it all up, I was feeling pretty good.

-61-

Sometimes, inspiration comes from an odd place. Today, as I slumped on a makeshift table, taking gulps of crappy-tasting beer—I got an idea.

"Bevan!" I said aloud. "He'd *love* this shitty beer."

That was my first thought, so I contacted the guy, and he came out to see me.

"Hey mate," Bevan said, climbing onto the stool next to mine. "Say... you've been at this for a bit, haven't you?"

"Yep. Try the dark brew. It's from the bottom of tank, they say, but you'd never know it by the taste."

Squinting, he did as I suggested. "Lovely and awful all at once."

"Agreed."

"Say McGill, where's that fancy suit of armor I saw you in just the other day? Did you lose it?"

"I was ripped off. Fike has it now."

"That's a shame. I wouldn't think he'd be tall enough..."

"Hey, Bevan? You're a materials man, right? Could you make me a new one? Artificially, I mean?"

Since I was kind of drunk and kind of pissed off, I proceeded to explain to him how the armor was made. "...so you see, it's kind of a weave made with Vulbite spit and stardust."

"Absolutely fascinating," Bevan said, and I knew he meant it. "If I could examine a sample in my lab—"

"You've got a lab?"

"Yes. That's why they brought me out here, don't you know?"

I blinked at him stupidly. "But... what are you working on?"

Bevan considered my question. At last, he decided to answer it. "I'm a last-ditch attempt to fix Earth's problem."

"How's that?"

"You know these Shadowlanders make our revival machines, right? Well, if we lost our supplier... we might have to construct our own."

"That's what you've been up to all this time? Trying to make a bootleg, knock-off revival machine?"

"Shhh... keep it down. But yes, that's it. So far, I've had little success. The technology isn't just a chemical process. It's very odd and organic. Essentially, the revival machines use an organic computer with incredibly complex molecular chains to read DNA then reprocess cells on the fly. It's amazing technology. I'm wondering where the Shadowlanders stole it from originally."

I squinted at him, digesting his statement. "You don't think they came up with it all on their own, huh?"

"Gods, no! It's unthinkable. I believe they got the original technology from a Galactic."

"Ah..." I said, thinking that over carefully. "There is one race that could master such a thing: the Skay."

Bevan brightened. "You know, you might have something there. They're masters of weaving together biology and machines. They seem to be odd hybrids themselves. They've mastered their own genetics, certainly."

I thought that over for a few minutes, but my brain was kind of foggy, so I ordered another beer. That helped, because I started getting ideas.

Standing up, I almost pitched forward, but I caught myself. "I should have eaten a bit more..."

Leaving the dive bar and Bevan behind, I made my way over to Fike's encampment. That was quite a walk, as it turned out. He was clear on the other side of the Shadowlander town, camping with his Blood-Worlder legion.

Being a bit drunk, I bought some food as I passed right through the middle of town. Shadowlanders looked at me like I was some kind of freak, but I didn't care. I just grinned and ate their weird moss-fruits and walked on.

When I got to Fike's encampment, I threw up outside his command bunker. That made me feel a lot better. Wiping my mouth, I walked down the dusty steps into his oversized spider-hole.

The one cool thing about running with a Blood-Worlder legion was how roomy the bunkers were. The ceilings were four meters high instead of the standard two, which meant I didn't have to duck.

Swaggering down the passages, it wasn't hard to find Fike's office. He was in there, proud as a peacock, with a line-up of Blood-Worlder troops in front of him.

"That's right. I *do* want you to strike an officer. In fact—that's an order."

He started off with a slaver. They were tall, skinny freaks that were stronger than they looked. The first man in line dubiously unfolded his lengthy limbs in a wind-up punch that crashed into Fike's belly.

The sub-tribune whooshed, but he didn't go down. Instead, he laughed and stood tall with my black suit of armor on. Right off, just looking at him, I knew that he'd cheated. He'd added his own padding. That was probably done in part to fill the empty space in the armor, in addition to making it more comfortable.

"See?" Fike demanded. "This stuff is tough. Now, who's next?"

I raised my hand, but Fike waved me off irritably. "I see you, McGill. This exercise is intended to build morale, not damage it. Now, stand aside."

Willingly, I walked around to one side. From that standpoint, I could see all the action—but Fike wasn't staring right at me.

Next in the line was another type of Blood-Worlder, a heavy trooper. If slavers were sticks of spaghetti, these guys were the meatballs. They stood about three meters tall, but they were hugely broad and strong.

362

When the confused man stepped forward, Fike ordered him to strike, slapping his armored gut.

I, off to one side, made a different suggestive gesture. The Blood-Worlder glanced at me, but he didn't say anything.

When the heavy trooper stepped up to the plate, I figured it was fifty-fifty he'd follow my suggestion. As I had nothing to lose, I watched with interest.

To my delight and Fike's shock, the Blood-Worlder brought his basketball-sized fist down on Fike's head. It was an overhand chop, and I couldn't have done a better job myself.

Fike went down like a sack of grain. He lay there, groaning. To my mind, it was all Fike's fault. After all, he should have been wearing a helmet.

The Blood-Worlder stepped from side-to-side uncertainly. Fike rolled onto his side and groaned.

I stepped up, grinning broadly. I put my hands on my knees and looked down at Fike.

"Well done, sir!" I told him. "That was highly morale-building. This man will never forget the thrill of this moment."

"Fuck off, McGill."

I praised the Blood-Worlder, who looked kind of upset and worried, until he walked off-stage. The rest of the line-up behind him sensed the fun was over and melted away as well.

"That dumbass nearly brained me," Fike said when he managed to stand. "You can't know what a daily raft of disappointments I endure while working with these morons."

"Aw now, that's not fair, Tribune. He was just doing his best. The next time you do this exercise, you might consider wearing a helmet. I mean… it's safety first, right?"

Fike grumbled and rubbed at his neck. He was going to be sore in the morning, I could tell.

"What do you want over here anyway, McGill?"

"I just thought I might drop by to pick up my property, sir."

"What? I thought that was settled. The armor is mine. I know there are size differences—I'm not blind—but rank does have its privileges. Be assured that when we get back to Earth, my custom suit should be ready. I'll return this suit to you then."

"Huh? Oh… no, no, sir. There's some kind of misunderstanding. I'm not talking about the armor. There was a small, personal item in the pockets, sir. That's what I'm looking for."

"A personal item?"

"Yessir. If you could just let me—" I reached for his pocket, but he slapped my thick fingers away.

He fished in the pockets himself. He dug out the Galactic Key. He looked at it curiously. "What's this?"

"That's a prime specimen, sir. A seashell from my home district's best beaches."

"Why the heck would you carry something like this into combat?" he asked, tossing it into the air and catching it.

His careless behavior made me want to squint and wince, but I did neither. Instead, I grinned. "A lot of people wonder how I've gotten so lucky over the years. The secret is right there in your hands. This item is a bona fide talisman of good fortune."

"Talisman? Are you mentally-challenged?"

"Some do maintain that, sir. But the proof is in my personal records. Haven't you ever wondered how I manage to survive so many insane missions?"

Fike laughed. "What I've wondered is how you've managed to get yourself killed so damned frequently. I think I understand that better now. Here."

He pitched the Galactic Key high into the air, and I scrambled to catch it before it hit the ground. This made Fike laugh again and shake his head in amusement—which caused him to grimace in pain and grab at his neck again.

I caught the key, fortunately. I dove for it for a good reason. Any normal shell would have shattered when it struck that stone-hard floor—but the key wouldn't. I didn't want Fike catching on to its strange nature.

Once I had the key in my hands, I stuffed it away and said my goodbyes. Fike looked after me suspiciously. He was still rubbing his neck, and he was still wearing my armor.

But I had the key in my possession. By my scoring, I was halfway done with old Sub-Tribune Fike.

-62-

Sauntering out into the twilit world, I decided Fike hadn't yet seen enough of old McGill. Accordingly, I didn't head off to the other side of town where my legion was camped. Instead, I wandered the trenches and firebases, talking to Blood-Worlders and squids at random.

Unsurprisingly, this gained me the attention of various sub-legion officers. Two of them, both squids, approached me while I chatted-up some slavers.

Now, when I say I was having a conversation, you have to understand that this was a highly one-sided affair. Slavers only talk occasionally, and heavy troopers are even quieter. As far as I knew, the giants—one of whom was standing over my shoulder drooling and listening to me—never talked at all.

I didn't let any of that bother me. Country folks seemed to come in two flavors, those that talked your ear off and those who were practically mutes. I just figured these boys were like the latter persuasion, and it was very familiar to me.

"Centurion McGill?" an alien voice said from behind me.

I glanced over my shoulder and spotted the two squids. I quickly checked their nametags, but I was disappointed. Neither of them were on the very short list of squids I knew personally.

"Uh… Sub-Centurion Foam?" I said. "What can I do for you?"

"You can answer my questions."

"Okay, shoot."

The squid flinched some of his many arms, touching his large sidearm with fluttering tentacles. Then, he seemed to do some thinking as his translators burbled what I'd said, translating it into squid-talk.

"Oh... shoot has a colloquial meaning? How disappointing."

"Are you going to ask me a question or not, squid? I'm busy talking to these here soldiers."

Sub-Centurion Foam let his limbs slip and slide over one another for a few seconds. I don't know how these big aliens managed to keep their limbs wet all the time, even in a dry climate, and I don't want to know.

"Your pointless behavior is exactly what I wanted to discuss. Possibly, you are unaware of the moronic nature of these beasts. They are literally incapable of conversation."

"Aw now, you shouldn't talk like that about your own loyal troops! If a human commander would dare speak to another human that way... well sir, let me just say you'd be calamari by sun-up."

The squid didn't seem to get my references. After he blinked his overly-numerous squid eyes at me, he spoke again. "Another non sequitur. I'm finding this conversation to be tedious."

"Move along then, squishy. No one asked you anyways."

I turned my back on him, ignoring Foam. The squid and his sidekick lingered, however. A few minutes later, after I'd finished telling a funny story to the curious slavers, I whirled around to frown at the two squids again.

"What are you two doing hanging around? Do you like my stories?"

"We have alerted Sub-Primus Churn to your presence. He instructed us to await his arrival."

"Churn? Hot-damn! I'm surprised Hegemony hasn't permed his ass by now... Did you know he's my favorite squid of all time, now that Bubbles is dead and gone? Did you know that?"

"There is no indication that Sub-Primus Churn shares your feelings about this relationship."

"I bet. There he is!"

It was the moment I'd been hoping for. Churn was a devious Squid. All of them were, actually. They were half-rebellious on the best of days.

"Churn!" I boomed out, throwing my arms wide. "You made sub-primus? Congrats!"

All the squids backed up a bit when I lifted my limbs. For most aliens, that was a fighting stance—a physical challenge. Their numerous limbs squirmed over the ground around them for a few seconds.

"Don't ink yourselves, boys," I said, lowering my arms again. "I didn't mean to scare you. I'm just happy to see Churn, here. After that disaster back on Storm World, I'd figured he'd have been replaced by now."

"Disaster?" Churn asked me.

He slithered up, joining the other two. The full trio of massive squids eyed me with distaste, but I pretended not to notice.

"Yeah, sure. Your legion got wiped out, remember? Didn't you die in the mud way back then?"

"Yes, but I was revived."

"Ah... really? Wasn't Armel your commander at the time?"

Churn looked uncomfortable. Squids pretty much always looked like they needed to take a shit, but I could tell the difference. When you were really getting to one of them their eyes began to roam around strangely. These boys' eyeballs looked like those of a horse in a lightning storm.

Churn spoke at last. "Armel... Yes. There was a brief period during which I served under that human."

"Brief, huh? What was it? Five or six years? Damn, how long do you squids live? Never mind, I don't care. I'm just surprised you caught a revive that early-on in the legions. Old Armel must have liked you."

"Tribune Armel is a traitor to Earth," Churn said carefully.

"He sure is... but do you still talk to him, sometimes? Just for old time's sake?"

"Certainly not. That would be treasonous behavior."

"I guess that it would. Anyway, what can I do for such a high-ranking squid?"

"It would be better if this were coming from Fike himself, but I'm here to ask you to leave our encampment."

"What? Fike is kicking me out?"

Churn fidgeted for a few more seconds before responding. "No—but he has ordered me to ask you to leave."

"Ah, I get it. He didn't have the balls to come out here and do it himself, huh? So, he sends his most repulsive sidekick. Well, since you're only making a request, I'm feeling free to ignore it."

I turned back around to the slavers, who were looking kind of uncomfortable at this point. After all, they had four officers in front of them, and things weren't going smoothly. They were smart enough to understand that when the brass started shooting at each other, it was often their unfortunate asses that caught the bullets.

For my own part, I was working the single piece of squid psychology that I understood well. Cephalopods were, by culture and genetics, only able to understand master-slave relationships. They didn't really have friends, or enemies. They did sometimes make temporary alliances, but usually they simply obeyed their superiors until such a time as they felt they could get away with pulling a move and killing their boss. Should such a moment arrive, they usurped their rightful commander and became the new leader.

This pattern of behavior meant no squid could ever really relax. They knew that everyone below them was gunning for them. Everyone was seeking their senior officer's destruction for selfish advancement.

As a result of this natural paranoia, if you acted confident enough around them, they were always nervous and off-balance. It was only when they felt utterly confident that they might dare an assassination attempt. An uncertain squid was by nature a less dangerous squid.

Sitting on the back of a switched-off pig, I kept telling stories. Pretty much all of them were bullshit, but I did have a moral to each tale that I gave them at the end.

"…so you see," I finished up, "if you play stupid games, you win stupid prizes."

I looked around at my listeners. The squids still wore their pissed-pants expressions—but the slavers were in a different zone. They were soaking it all in. I was the prophet on the mount to these boys.

Reluctantly, the single Blood World heavy trooper raised his ham-sized hand. I was impressed. He hadn't said a damned thing for nearly an hour of bullshit.

I called on him immediately. "You there, tell me what you think."

"Stupid games… stupid prizes?"

"Ah, I see. I can tell I should make the point of things more clear to you. See, the idea is that when a man does a dumb thing, a bad thing happens to him."

"No prize?"

"Well… no, you *do* get the prize. You get a *bad* prize. You get the bad prize because you were dumb."

The heavy trooper squinted hard. I could tell his thinker was going to hurt by morning.

Right about then, another familiar face showed up. It was Sub-Tribune Fike himself.

"Hello, sir," I said to him. "Are you feeling kind of hot in that suit of mine? Your face is a little red."

"McGill, what are you still doing out here? And no, you're not getting this suit back. You can forget about that."

"About what…? Oh! No worries there, sir! That's the furthest thing from my dull-witted mind. No sir, I'm afraid I'm here to inform you of an unfortunate situation."

"What situation? I'm contacting Graves. You need to get out of my camp. You're stirring up trouble, and—"

"Just hear me out for a moment. This is about treachery. Underhanded assassination is in the works."

Fike stopped. He stared at me fixedly. "What are you talking about?"

My thick finger came up, and it aimed at Sub-Primus Churn. "See that squid? I know him. He's up to no good. In fact, he's in league with one Tribune Armel."

369

Fike snarled. But he didn't snarl at me. Instead, he turned on Churn.

"Sub-Primus? Is this true?"

Churn worked his beak-like mouth a bit. It clicked and burbled in surprise. The translator at last began to speak for him.

"There is no way this being could know whether or not I've had dealings with Tribune Armel."

Fike cocked his head. That wasn't a good answer, but it was the kind of answer I expected from a squid. They didn't always know what to say when you called them out. They tended to get fixated on some detail that wasn't directly the point of an accusation. The slightest error in a statement—the kind of slipshod error I made on an hourly basis—drove them crazy.

"See!" I shouted. "He's as guilty as sin! He's not even bothering to deny it!"

"Denial is unnecessary when there is an absence of proof," Churn said.

Fike turned to me. His anger was gone. He was concerned now instead. "McGill, I know you've had run-ins with cephalopods in the past. That kind of bigotry isn't appreciated here in my outfit."

"Far from it, sir. I'm only trying to do my civic duty. You recall back during the Clone World campaign? When Sub-Centurion Bubbles became a turncoat?"

Fike nodded. I knew he remembered the day well. He'd nearly been killed by Bubbles and his allies, the Claver clones. In fact, he even shook my hand after I helped bail him out of a deadly combat.

"Well sir, I've got a nose for squid treachery. I know when they're going bad—and I know someone has been feeding Armel some good intel. How else has he managed to strike at us so effectively in every situation?"

Fike turned slowly back around toward Churn. "Sub-Primus, you are hereby relieved of command until this situation is resolved."

Churn clacked his beak at us, but he was arrested and hauled away. I waved goodbye, but he didn't even have the decency to wave back.

During this time I was all smiles, but Fike worked his tapper furiously. At last, he turned back to me and wore a grim smile. "McGill? Guess what? You're working for me now."

"Uh... how's that, sir?"

"You're only a centurion, but you'll have to fill in for Churn as a sub-primus."

"Really? What's the hurry, sir? Seems like you've got quite a load of squids running around the place that might be better qualified—"

Fike shook his head. "With this kind of treachery in my ranks, I'm not promoting another cephalopod. I've got to keep a sharp eye on the ones I've got left. And as to timing, the enemy is inbound right now."

"The bright-siders?"

"Exactly. They're attacking. They'll be here in force in less than an hour. I want you to take command of Churn's cohort. You'll be posted out there."

Fike made a vague gesture toward the eastern desert region.

"Wonderful..."

Fike swaggered away, and Churn's officers looked at me expectantly.

"What are your orders, Sub-Primus?" the one named Foam asked.

"Uh..."

Right then, the heavy trooper leaned close, and his dead-pig breath washed over me as he spoke.

"...win stupid prize?" he asked.

I nodded. "Yep. You've got it. You've really got it, big guy."

He looked happy, and I was happy for him—sort of.

-63-

It turned out that I'd been placed in charge of a front-line cohort of stinking Blood-Worlders. I'd worked with these boys before, so I wasn't completely in the dark as to how to handle them. The key was to give decisive orders and understand their various strengths and weaknesses.

In every Blood-Worlder legion, the majority of the men were heavy troopers like the smart ass who'd recognized the award of a stupid-prize to me just minutes earlier. His breed was big, dumb and obedient. The only bad thing about them was they came in inseparable squads.

Each of these squads was made up of nine brothers. They were actually blood-related, and they changed personality after they watched some of their kin die. They went totally ape at that point, becoming wild berserkers.

All the Blood-World types had quirks like that which you had to watch out for. With this in mind, I had to position and prepare my troops for battle very carefully.

I made Foam my exec, as he was the only squid I really knew. Sure, he was seriously evil—and he hated me—but it's best to work with the devil you know, I always say.

"Hey! Foamer! I want a skirmish line of slavers two hundred meters out. Put all the heavy troopers into the main trench lines, and keep the giants in reserve."

"The enemy will attempt to kill a few of our heavy troops," Foam said. "This will cause them to leave their entrenched positions."

"Don't I know it! If Armel understands one thing, it's how to face a formation of crazy Blood-Worlders. Why did you squids breed the heavies to go ape when they were attacked, anyway?"

Foam looked startled. "That was never a goal of the breeding process."

"Why'd you do it, then?"

"Genetic manipulation is far from a perfect science. Turning on one genetic marker often activates others, which results in less desirable traits being introduced."

"Huh…" I said. "So it was an accident? That's just grand."

"Yes, it was sub-optimal. Humans fight primarily with ranged weapons. An overwhelming urge to charge into close-combat can—"

"Yeah, yeah, I know. Shut up and hustle the men into position."

The squid left me, his limbs flapping around as he hurried. It was kind of weird to give a half-ton space-squid orders, but there it was. I'd been placed in charge of this menagerie, and it was time to see if I was any good at it or not.

Using optical enhancers and satellite shots relayed from *Dominus* above, I watched the enemy approach. They were fast, and they seemed to have learned a thing or two since our last run-in. They weren't all bunched up as in previous attacks. They came on in staggered lines, with at least three meters of empty space between each man.

I didn't have any light troops, but I did have some slavers. They were way up front, hugging the ground. They aimed long rifles and began popping off shots way before I thought they should.

"Are they even in range yet?" I demanded of Foam.

"The evidence is clear."

He flicked a video from the front lines over to my tapper. I was immediately impressed. "The slavers are actually getting hits. Not many of them, but they have the Bright-siders ducking already."

"Shall I tell them to stop, Sub-Primus?"

"No! Keep it up. Let them come to us with early losses. What about our star-falls, Foamy?"

"No supporting barrage is incoming," the squid officer answered. "Command ops says the inbound hostiles are too widely spread out to be damaged effectively by our remaining artillery."

"Shit..."

As the slavers kept sniping, the front rank grew ragged, then frayed. There were holes to be seen, and I dared to smile.

Then the enemy finally began to return our withering fire. The smile on my face drooped. They were lancing at my slavers. Every now and then, one of my big skinny boys lit up in lavender flames.

"Pull them back!" I ordered. "Pull the slavers back!"

Foam gave the order, and I winced as they withdrew toward our trench lines. Five, ten, thirty of their humping forms were transformed into living torches. Maybe half survived long enough to dive into the first trench line.

"Tell the heavies to keep their heads down. Don't stand and fire until the enemy is in optimal range."

"Sir, my battle computer simulator indicates this is a tactical error. The enemy will be able to close—"

"You'll shut up and follow my orders until such time as I'm dead in the dust. Is that clear?"

"As clear as seawater, sir."

I glanced at him. Was Foam getting mouthy? It could be, but that would be unusual for a squid. They generally followed orders intently unless they meant to turn traitor on you, then they went all the way in that direction. Squids weren't variable, they were binary in their behavior. It was all or nothing with them.

Going back to the buzzer feeds and scopes, I watched as the bright-siders came into the range of our entrenched gunmen, then swept past that vital point. They were closer than a kilometer now, and still moving fast.

The first rank had folded into the second, but they didn't seem any less determined. Hell, if I had troops that were that hard-charging, I'd have been proud as punch. As it was, I had to hand it to the enemy, they didn't fear death, hell or high-water.

"The enemy is at six hundred meters range, sir," Foam said.

"Prepare to stand!" I roared directly over the cohort tactical channel.

Roars and grunts swept the field. Nearly a thousand over-sized brutes hunkered in their trenches, leg muscles quivering and ready.

"Four hundred meters..." Foam said in an even tone.

The enemy was *fast*. They had to be running at thirty clicks an hour, maybe more than that.

"Stand and fire at will!" I shouted.

Even as I finally gave the order, I felt I'd waited too long. By the time my line of big dumbasses stood, sighted and fired with a crackling roar, the approaching enemy rank was about three hundred and fifty meters out.

The effects of that first volley were devastating, however. Damn near a thousand big rounds reached out and punched huge holes in the charging line. The enemy was shattered. They fell, they rolled, and they died by the hundreds.

Some kept coming, however. They fired as they ran, too. Jets of flame-like plasma lanced from them toward my cohort.

"Duck!" I screamed. "Put the men down in the trenches again!"

"That would be most—" Foam began.

I put the muzzle of my morph rifle into his face. His evil squid-eyes rolled over me, the gun in my hands, and the situational displays in our rearward trench line. I didn't even have a command bunker, but I didn't care. I hated dying in bunkers, anyway.

Foam wisely stopped arguing and relayed my orders faithfully. The heavy troopers hunkered down again.

For the most part the enemy fire rolled over them. Some were torched, and they ran around like headless chickens. Their brothers croaked in dismay—but they didn't break and charge. Not yet.

"One hundred meters…" Foam said in an almost accusatory tone.

"Stand and fire again! Tell the men to fight at will, hand-to-hand if they want to!"

If it was possible, which I doubted, Foam's eyes seemed to spread open even farther than before. He was clearly shocked by my unprecedented tactics. He passed on my commands, however, and every confused noncom squid in the trenches gave my orders to the men.

The heavy troopers stood, released another crashing volley, then at long last, they lost it. They'd already started getting pasted. Fifty or more were dead, another few dozen were burning alive—it was enough to put the fear of God into anyone.

As with all men of their simple kind, they didn't react with fear and run away—far from it. They charged—eyes wild, blubbery lips parted and drooling. They used their heavy pistols and thick, single-edged cutlasses. The two lines met in the open dirt, and carnage erupted immediately.

The third rank of the enemy swept close, right on the heels of the first two, who were half dead or more at this point. They stopped racing toward us and stood tall. Their skinny arms lifted what looked like long-range flame throwers.

That's what they were, essentially, according to reports from the field. They projected a tube of force down which a gush of flaming liquid was squirted. A fine line of flame, no thicker than a flashlight, shot down that narrow force field until it struck something. The target was instantly painted with a slurry of substances—something like burning napalm.

These weapons were nasty, but short-ranged and not terribly accurate. As a result, my heavy troopers and the bright-siders they struggled with were hit without distinction. Like a thousand candles on a birthday cake, they lit up in a hellish inferno.

"Release the giants!" I shouted. "Have them run to the right flank. We have to take down that rear line at all costs!"

Foam's beak rattled, and I saw the giants behind me stir. They stood tall—impossibly tall. They were the most human-looking of all the Blood World soldiers, if the largest and dumbest. They had heads that were too small for their bodies, but they could fight with a savagery no human in history had ever possessed.

"Swing right! Swing right!"

The giants milled for a moment, confused by the flames and rising column of black smoke. The field of battle was almost obscured from view now.

Growling in frustration, I began to march in the direction I wanted them to go. Behind me, the giants took note and followed. There was only about fifty of them, but the ground shook with their collective heavy tread.

Coming around to the flank, we finally had a clear field of fire. The rear rank—the last of the bright-sider army—stood tall and beamed lines of heat into the flaming mass of struggling forms. They were killing their own men as often as they were mine—but they didn't seem to care.

"Fire!" I shouted, and I mag-dumped my morph-rifle into the enemy line.

The giants, each activating their personal bubble-like shield, fired from the hip. Their projectors gushed, putting out energy akin to that of an 88 light artillery piece. Sweeping side to side, they destroyed the surprised bright-siders.

A few of the enemy turned and lit us up as well—but their weapons weren't effective against the giants and their shields. They could only put a sea of rippling flame down, blistering my men's feet. The napalm slid right off the protective bubbles of force without reaching the skin of my giants.

After less than a minute of exchanging fire, the bright-siders finally broke. My heavy troopers, undeterred by horrible wounds and high losses, charged out of the blackened smoke and ran after them. My giants thundered in pursuit as well, trumpeting and hooting with their bass voices. They sounded like a herd of charging mastodons.

"We should call them back, sir," Foam advised me.

"No. Let them have their fun."

In the unforgiving desert, where the sun was just a simmering gleam on the horizon, the giants and the heavies caught up with the bright-siders. They tore them apart, limb from limb. Swords hacked and flashed redly in the sunlight. The giants released horrible grunts of excitement and even ecstasy. They sounded like a herd of rutting bulls to me.

For us, the battle was over.

-64-

Later that day, Graves contacted me. He was all smiles.

"I've reviewed your cohort's vids. That was impressive, McGill. Even Fike says you behaved competently—and he hates you."

"He sure does," I said, dumping a bottle of water over my head.

"I always thought you'd missed your calling. You should have accepted the job of sub-primus when Drusus offered it to you."

"Why do you say that, sir?"

"Because you understand these apes. You get how their minds work."

"It takes one to know one I guess."

Graves laughed. "That's right. Anyway, you held your position on one of the hardest hit flanks. You had no defensive terrain or infrastructure, other than a few trenches—but you held."

"Permission to return to the Varus side, sir? I'd like to rejoin my unit."

Graves hesitated, but then he nodded. "Permission granted. I'm rejecting Fike's transfer request."

His words came as a shock. I had no idea that prick Fike had tried to transfer me permanently. I supposed it was sort of a compliment—but still, you'd think the man would have at least asked my opinion.

I didn't let any of these thoughts show on my face, which stayed slack and stupid. It's been my longstanding opinion that overall, everyone prefers a dumbass to a smarty-pants type.

"That's excellent, sir," I said. "Thank you."

Graves broke the connection, and I stood up wearily. "I'm moving on, Foam. You fought well today."

He eyed me oddly for a moment before answering. "You are a good commander, Sub-Primus McGill. You kill the enemy with zeal."

"Thanks, Foam. You were a good exec. Give my regards to your new sub-primus, whoever he might be."

With that, I trudged my weary way back to Legion Varus and 3rd Unit. Along the way I met up with someone I didn't expect to see outside her town walls.

It was Helsa. She was looking lean and fit. Her sheer robes flapped in a sudden hot breeze coming from the bright-side deserts. That wind… it pasted her clothes to her body. I could tell right off that she didn't believe in any kind of undergarments. I doubted her people even knew what they were. As a result, every sweet curve and detail was outlined for the roving eyes of a man like me.

"Uh… hi there."

"McGill…? You're walking alone on a battlefield. Why?"

"Because the battle is over, darling." I waved vaguely out sunward. The burning eye known as 91 Aquarii was threatening to peep over the horizon. Was there a slight change since yesterday? I thought that it was a smidgeon brighter. It had been around a hundred hours since we'd arrived here, and even on Edge World the morning sun had to rise eventually.

Helsa fell into step beside me as I continued walking toward Varus. I didn't ask her what kind of skullduggery had led her to me. Clearly, she'd tracked me somehow. The Shadowlanders were six kinds of tricky, and they had tech all their own. It wasn't surprising they could find one man out of twenty thousand, even on a confused battlefield like this one.

"I've come with an offer," she said.

"How's that?"

"We must strike our camp soon and move on. The dawn is coming. Have you seen the three banners that fly at different heights over our city?"

"Uh-huh, I guess I have."

"When the sunlight touches the highest flying banner, it is time to begin our preparations. When the lowest is bathed in our sun's light, we must move on. It is our way."

"Even in the middle of a battle?"

She shrugged. "Our sun never stops creeping. It doesn't rest for death, joy or sorrow. Neither do we."

"Okay... Did you say something about an offer?"

"Yes. We would like to end this siege. We think you're the man to do it."

"Sure, right... but how?"

Helsa stopped walking and peered up at me. The lustful wind clawed and luffed at her clothes, and I enjoyed the view. She didn't seem to notice the way an Earth-woman would have. I suspected her wimpy males weren't into ogling women.

"We've been plotting. We believe we could do to Armel what we tried to do to your legion—that is, we could sabotage his revival machines."

"Yeah...? Well, he's got plenty of lizards. You might slow him down some with that tactic, but—"

"That is why you are important to this plan," she said. She reached out a hand and tapped a finger on my standard-issue armor. "There are many saurians in his army, but only one commander. You will kill Armel after we've disabled his machines."

"Ah..." I said thinking it over. "That might just work. Without Armel to lead them, those lizards won't know which end of their own tails to suck on."

Helsa blinked. "You describe an odd visual, but I think I understand your meaning. Will you do it?"

"Uh... do what?"

"Lead a teleport-strike on Armel, of course."

"Oh... I could, I guess, but I'd need a harness."

"We've got a set of them. A team of agents will go with you."

I thought it over. "I wish I had my armor still. That would make this mission a lot more attractive."

Helsa frowned and examined my breastplate. It was shiny metal, rather than the sleek black of the Glass World suit I'd worn the last time we'd met.

"Yes... this is different armor. How did you lose such an advantage?"

"Well, I died up there on that plateau. When I tried to get my armor back, I found out old Fike had snagged it."

"He can do that?"

"He's got the rank. He says he'll give it back when Central finishes making his own set."

"In other words, he's a thief."

"Pretty much, yeah."

"Thieves are dishonorable," Helsa said, frowning.

I thought about mentioning that she was a self-described assassin—but I didn't. Maybe assassins were honorable in her culture—in fact, I had a hunch that they were.

Helsa began to pace. I stared at her and even moved sideways a few steps now and then to improve the view. The wind kept fluffing and dragging her clothes around, and a man had to work to keep up with it. She didn't seem to care at all. She didn't even notice my fixation.

"We will take care of this," she announced at last. "But you must commit to our strike on Armel's camp if we succeed."

I thought about it for half a second, then I grinned. I grinned big.

"Little lady, you've got a deal. Can we seal it with a kiss?"

She appeared quizzical. "A kiss? That is a gift for the dead and the dying."

"It is?" I said, thinking of the kiss she'd given me days ago. I had indeed been flat on my back and in the throes of death at the time. "Well... I tend to die a lot. Why don't you advance me one for the near future?"

Helsa smiled slightly. She stepped closer.

That was all the invitation I needed. I swept her up and laid a big one on her. She seemed to like it. When we parted and she stepped back, I looked around in surprise.

There was no one there. Nothing but the winds and the sifting sands. She'd teleported out on me. Damn, but the girl was a sneaky one.

-65-

Hours later, I was asleep in my bunk. My eyes opened when I heard something odd. Lurching to my feet, I reached for a blade, groping. My fingers found the hilt, but before I could draw it, I felt a much smaller hand wrap over mine.

"Shhh," she said.

It was Helsa.

"Damn, girl. You shouldn't go sneaking around in a Varus man's bunker. I've killed for less, many times."

"I believe you, but I have something for you."

She opened a big bag, and a heavy suit flopped out. It took me a moment to realize it was an empty suit of fine Glass World armor.

"Hey! That was quick!"

"We saw no reason to delay. Dawn creeps closer every hour. We must strike camp soon."

"Uh… yeah. This thing is all wet inside—is that blood?"

Helsa hesitated. "Possibly…"

I looked up. "I didn't tell you to kill Fike!"

She shrugged. "You didn't tell me not to."

"Girl, you're going to get me into trouble. I can't go strutting around in this armor now. People will notice."

"Excellent. In that case, there's nothing to keep you here. Let's strike now."

She reached out a hand, and in it was a teleport harness. It was a wicked thing, with narrower straps and a lighter battery

384

than Earth rigs usually had. I suspected it had a shorter range, no more than lightyear or so.

"Is it charged and targeted?"

"Of course."

"If you guys know Armel's address so well, why haven't you taken him out yourselves before this?"

She smiled. "Who's to say we haven't tried? The trouble is his revival machines are under heavy guard. We can't get to them—and he keeps returning to life."

This was kind of funny to me. It had seemed to me that our side in this struggle had been taking all the punches. But if these agents had been plaguing good old Armel by killing him now and then, he couldn't be enjoying the experience.

"You want me to bust in and finish his equipment, huh?"

"Think of it as a repossession. After all, we built his machines in the first place. That's why we attacked your ship in an attempt to destroy your machines. If you read the licensing agreement carefully, your ownership is revoked if you use them to attack our planet."

"Really? Huh… that's downright diabolical. I like it."

"Will you go with me then?"

"Right now? I need a shower and some breakfast to fight my best."

She seemed a bit put out, but at last she agreed. We stuffed the bloody armor under my bunk like we were hiding a body, and we walked to the officer's mess.

After a bit of arguing and a lot of cold looks from various ladies, I got Helsa into the place. She had her first-ever meal of eggs and bacon—and she loved it.

"This is the offspring of an animal?" she asked, poking at her third egg before scarfing it down. "I had no idea Earth animals were so flavorful."

"They're tasty, all right."

We ate with gusto, but when we were just standing up to leave, a figure appeared in the doorway. It was a pissed-looking Sub-Primus Fike.

His hair was sticky, and at his back were a half-dozen heavy troopers. Nobody looked like they were in a laughing mood.

"There she is, having breakfast with McGill. I should have known. Arrest that woman!"

Fike pointed at Helsa, but she didn't run off. Instead, she handed me that stringy teleport harness. "You know what to do," she said, and she gave me another peck on the cheek.

Two massive paws reached for her—but they closed on nothing. There was only a bluish swirl of light. She'd popped out again.

I was impressed. The Shadowlander teleport harnesses were more refined than ours. There was a lot less flashing and strobing—you just stepped in or stepped out of existence.

Fike had his hands on his hips. He glared at me and panted.

"Have you been running, Sub-Primus? You seem all out of breath."

"It figures you were at the bottom of this, McGill. I should have known you'd be so petty as to hire alien assassins—"

"Now hold on a just minute, sir. I fought for you and held my position. After that, I trudged all the way back to my own outfit across the desert. You can check my tapper's location services—I've been in bed all night."

"I know all that. I've already checked. But some sneaky alien agents broke into my bunker and stole my armor. Now I come here and find one of their top people having breakfast with you. What are the odds that's a coincidence?"

Throwing my hands up with my palms out, I shrugged. "I don't rightly know, sir. But I don't believe in coincidences."

"I don't either."

Fike spent the next hour on his tapper, paging through my location data. Just like I'd said, he found I hadn't been much of anywhere. I'd spent most of my time stretched out on my bunk.

"See? I wasn't anywhere near your camp. Are you satisfied now, sir?"

He eyed me with vast distrust. I gave him my best dumbass stare in return. I really poured it on, doing my best to ooze ignorance.

Disgusted, Fike threw his hands up and marched out. At the door, he turned to regard me one more time.

"If I find out you've got my missing armor, McGill, I'll have you flayed alive."

"Been there and done that, sir," I said, "but you have to believe me, I don't know what happened. Maybe the aliens were curious about the armor and wanted to steal a sample to copy or something."

Fike growled and marched out. His army of meatballs followed him. They knocked over a few tables, and people were left behind cursing in their wake.

Harris wandered over to me after he'd gone. "That was just plain rude," he said.

"Sure was."

I sat down and moved to finish Helsa's plate. Unfortunately, the girl was a pig. She ate everything. I guess living on moss and moss-fruits all your life left a person with a deep hunger.

Harris eyed me for a few seconds and sat down in Helsa's spot without being invited. "So..." he said. "You stole back the armor, right?"

"Naturally."

Harris released a deep belly-laugh. It rumbled out of him, and it went on and on. I didn't even look at him, but I was glad I could entertain my subordinate officers now and then.

An hour later found me strapped up in my armor and ready to launch. The goop had been hard to wash out, but I hadn't wanted to spend a mission squelching around in Fike's internals.

The skinny harness was wrapped around my armor, and it just barely fit. With a worried expression, I fondled the ignition button.

A buzzing started under my armor about then. It was my tapper.

I almost pushed the launch button on the harness. After all, the incoming call might be some nosy superior or other—maybe even Fike himself. If any of them caught sight of me wearing this kit, well sir, they were likely to jump to some conclusions.

The buzzing was persistent. It didn't let up, as if the caller was hitting the transmission key over and over—really leaning on it.

What convinced me in the end to answer was the fact my arm didn't just start talking by itself. My superior officers had the power to force my tapper to open, making contact with them unavoidable if they really wanted to push it.

But this determined person didn't do that, meaning they probably weren't high brass.

At last, I sighed and took a peek. The call was coming from Specialist Natasha Elkin.

I opened the channel, and she stared out at me. "James? What are you doing?"

"Listen, Natasha, I don't have time for—"

"Are you going on some kind of mission? If so, don't do it."

My finger had been hovering over the launch button, but I moved it away a fraction. "Why not? What do you know about it?"

"You remember that task you gave me, to figure out how to listen in on deep-link calls?"

"Yeah."

"Well... I've gotten better at it. I didn't tell you before because... you know... it's a serious crime, and everything."

"I get that. What did you overhear?"

"Your name. Someone has been talking about you."

I laughed. "That's nothing new, girl! I've got all sorts of people who like to talk about me. Some hate me, some love me—it's a mixed bag."

"No James, it's not like that. The people talking—one of them is from the Shadowlander town."

"Yeah? Huh..."

"Right. And the other party to the call, well, it took me a while to figure that out. I didn't have his deep-link rig's ID on my list of known stations, you see."

"You've been tracking deep-link station numbers?"

Natasha shrugged shyly. "This listening-in thing—it's become something of a hobby."

"That's wrong and dangerous, girl. But go on and tell me anyway. Who's on the other end of these secret phone calls from the Shadowlanders?"

"Tribune Maurice Armel."

-66-

After Natasha told me who the Shadowlanders were talking to, well sir, I got kind of angry.

"Are you telling me they're traitors? That they're talking to the enemy? They're selling us out?"

"I don't know, James. All I know is that someone in their town is communicating with the enemy. Does that mean they have a spy in their camp? Maybe. Does that mean the whole alliance is suspect? Maybe. All I know is that *something* is happening."

I began to pace and curse. Fike's blood was pooling up in my left boot, which I hadn't cleaned properly, and it was starting to squelch with every step like churned butter.

"We've got to tell somebody," I said finally.

"How can we? We're not supposed to be listening in. No one even *knows* we can do that! If you tell them... I don't know what kind of trouble I'd get into."

"Doesn't matter. Graves has to know—or Turov."

"You tell them with your name on all of it. Leave me out of the story."

I laughed. "So, I'm supposed to tell them I hacked into a deep-link machine solo? I think they might have some doubts."

"You're right... they'll know it was me."

Natasha looked glum, and I was real sorry about that, but I just couldn't let this pass. Treachery was one of those things that really stuck in my craw. What's more, Helsa had been leading me on the whole damned time. I was even beginning to wonder if she'd known I was leering at her out in that desert. By damn, she was one tricky woman.

"Where do you think that teleport suit would have jumped to, James?" Natasha asked me.

"I don't know, but I bet it's somewhere unpleasant. An alligator pit, maybe. Or maybe some lonely spot on this planet where I'd either burn up or freeze to death."

"Hmm... What if we decided to handle this ourselves?"

"What do you mean?"

Natasha shrugged, and she looked a little shy. "What if we rigged something up and sent it to them? A little surprise?"

I stared at my tapper, and I considered the possibilities. I began to grin.

"All right. I like that. One dirty trick deserves another. But what if it leads to the Nairb ship? Or our ship? I don't want to cause any mayhem where we don't want it."

"Right... I'll put a computer chip on it. A few if-statements, that's all it would take. It won't go off if the package arrives in our territory, or off-planet."

Smiling at last, I started nodding. "Okay. Let's rig-up the biggest bomb we can steal from armory. They'll get the message, loud and clear."

"I've got just the thing. Come over to the lab in Gray Bunker as soon as you can."

She dropped the channel, and my tapper went dark. As I marched across the camp, I got another call.

This time, it was Helsa.

"James?" she said, and she sounded kind of sweet. That was a change. The woman had never spoken to me in a gentle tone before—not even when she'd kissed me as I lie dying in her arms.

"Helsa! It's just the person I wanted to talk to. Is this harness functional? I tried the button, but nothing happened."

She blinked twice, then frowned. "Are you really the imbecile they say you are?" Suddenly, she caught herself and forced a fresh smile. "But no—of course not. You're just confused. You must press the safety lock at the same time as the transport button. There are only two buttons, after all."

"Ohhhh, I get it! Thanks a million!"

She managed a fluttering smile. "Don't keep Armel waiting. There aren't many hours left before the dawn touches our domes."

"Don't you worry your pointy little head."

This last comment made her frown a bit, but she managed to push that expression away and turn it into a smile again. I was reminded of the poor attitude she'd exhibited when we'd first met. I now suspected that was her true personality. Everything else was just an act.

After she signed off, I grumbled rude things about Shadowlanders and made my way to Gray Bunker.

Most of our encampments had some form of lab accompanying the base. That wouldn't have been the norm for armies of the past, but we faced unknown aliens and environments on a regular basis. There always seemed to be a surprise or two in store in the areas of science and technology.

Natasha greeted me at the bunker entrance. "This way— hurry before one of the techs sees you."

She led me down spidery tunnels that leaked dust from a thousand years back onto my armor. She trotted into the last lab on the bottom floor, and I followed her, shutting the creaky door behind us.

Looking around, I immediately liked the dark cubby. It had real possibilities. "You sure you didn't bring me down here just to have your scandalous way with me?"

She gave me a twisted frown. "Get that thought out of your head, James. We're on a mission. Can you stay focused?"

"Uh…" I said, watching her putter with a football shaped object on her workbench. "Is that what I think it is?"

"A small A-bomb, yes."

Now in my time, an A-bomb wasn't a poor-man's excuse for a nuclear weapon. Far from it. An A-bomb came with an antimatter warhead, which meant it released more force than normal fusion warheads when it converted itself into a ball of expanding energy.

"But… what if the harness just goes to one of our own bunkers—or the middle of their town? We don't want to kill their whole population."

"Don't worry. It's got an onboard computer. When the system figures out where it is, it won't detonate unless it's at least fifty kilometers from here."

"Hmm… Okay then. Let's do it."

Never having been a man who liked to overthink these things, I began arranging the harness to encircle the football-sized bomb. I had to cinch it up and then some, working to take the slack out of the straps. It wouldn't do for the bomb to roll away just as we were launching it.

"Hey," I said, getting an idea. "What if we attached a camera, and we have it transmit what it sees?"

Natasha looked up at my grinning face. "Are you sure you want to see that?"

"I sure as hell do!"

She sighed and went back to working on the weapon. Soon, she had something rigged up. The camera was so small it was like a coin she'd pasted on the side of the bomb.

"Just don't show me the file if… if it's really bad," she said.

"How could it be bad?"

"I don't know. What if this lands in a nursery or something? We don't know what we're shooting at, James. We have no idea at all."

That gave me a moment's pause. I realized she was right. Sure, the odds were this would land in a trap of some kind. Something that would neutralize me and make me Armel's prisoner. Maybe he wanted my armor, I don't know.

But there was a chance, a small chance, that this would appear in a populated area. Was it really right to take the risk?

I sighed and took the harness off the bomb. "We can't do it. Not with a booby-trapped switch. I'm sure your script is perfect, but…"

Natasha stood up on her tiptoes and kissed my cheek. "I'm glad you couldn't go through with it. The longer I've been thinking about it, the less certain I've become, in fact…" She broke off, watching me in concern. "James? What are you doing?"

"I'm stripping off my armor and strapping this on."

"You're going to fall into their trap?"

"Sort of. The bomb is a kind of conversation piece. If I don't like what I see, I can press the detonator—or not."

Natasha looked worried all over again. "This is crazy."

"A bit."

"Why are you taking your armor off?"

"I don't want it to get vaporized, or scuffed up, or something."

"Right… well, don't set off the bomb until you're sure it won't kill any civilians, okay?"

"You got my word," I said with an absolute certainty she seemed to buy. It made me marvel when people who knew me well accepted my random statements. It was as if they hadn't been paying attention for decades.

In Natasha's case, I knew it was sheer sweetness. She couldn't have blown up a town—not even a town full of mummies—and so she figured I couldn't do it either.

That thought made me sigh and doubt myself all over again. I almost scrubbed the entire illegitimate, haphazardly planned operation.

Then, however, I remembered how Helsa and Armel had played me. How they were probably out in the desert somewhere, cackling with excitement, taking bets on when that idiot McGill would fall into their hands.

Showing my teeth in a tight grimace, I activated the harness and teleported away.

-67-

The teleportation experience was a bit odd using the alien light-weight harness. It kind of... tickled.

That's right, it made every individual hair on my body stand up at attention, as if I'd been run through a dryer without an anti-static sheet thrown in.

Such minor discomforts were soon forgotten, however. When I arrived at my destination, I was all ready to squint in bright sunshine and get blasted with heat—but that didn't happen.

Instead, I was hit with a chilling effect. The skies were as black as a coal pit, with a scattering of brilliant diamonds sprinkled all over. There was no moon, as Edge World didn't have one, and that fact just made it all the darker and colder.

A whole bunch of somethings slithered around me. At first, I could sense them rather than see them. I knew right off by the sound of leathery pads rasping over frosty rocks what they must be—the spidery night-siders.

"Back, back! No, you fiends!" a familiar voice said. "Don't eat him... not yet."

It was Armel. It took a second for my eyes to adjust enough to see him. My breath blew out in white blasts, and I almost shivered. When I sucked in a fresh puff of air, it burned my lungs it was so cold.

"Damnation, Maurice," I said. "You should turn up the heat a notch."

"Funny, very funny. You always play the fool, McGill. But I'm disappointed. Why aren't you wearing your armor? I was certain you'd bring it to meet with me today."

"Not a chance."

"Why not?"

My hands fidgeted over the bomb. I was already considering setting it off. After all, I didn't care if we were in an inhabited area. I didn't think these frosty spiders loved their young, or each other. It might be for the best to dust off the lot of them.

"Because I knew this was a trap," I said.

"Really? And you came anyway? Is this some new level of ignorance, or do you have a plan?"

"Sure do. You see this thing here?"

I hefted the bomb. It could have been my imagination, but the half-seen spiders around me seemed to react. They didn't like the look of my toy.

"What is that?" Armel asked in a dead tone.

"I think you already know."

"You will be permed, McGill," he warned. "No one can confidently revive a suspicious case here. You remember that the Galactics are watching, no? The Mogwa, the Skay and the Nairbs."

"Then they'll bear witness to my death, and I'll catch a revive all the faster."

"No, no, no," he laughed. "It doesn't work that way. None of the Galactics give a shit about you. They'll tell your legion nothing."

"Well then, I guess you and I will go to Hell together."

I don't think Armel liked that comment. Maybe he'd miscalculated. I couldn't see his face, as it was pretty dark, but I got the idea he wasn't convinced he could avoid a solid perming either.

"There is no need for this animosity," he said after a pause. "Let us part ways. I'll simply go back to my lodge— they have no tents here, you must have lodges built with heavy leathers. I will retrieve a charger for your harness. Then you can be on your way without—"

"Stand where you are, Armel," I said firmly. I could see he was backing up, moving away from me and my circle of growling spiders.

"But McGill, surely an imbecile such as yourself is capable of grasping the fact that your harness hasn't got enough charge to leave this place. The battery is whisper-thin. It was calculated to take you out to this spot—and no farther."

"I believe that. Helsa is as devious as they come. She wouldn't leave something like that up to chance."

"Very well then, we are in agreement. I'll simply return to—"

"You're not going anywhere if you want to keep breathing. I'm in charge here. If I drop this bomb, or I release this trigger, the whole area will go up. These spiders will finally get the warm-up they've been dreaming about."

Armel sucked in a breath. "Very well then, we are at an impasse. Will you kill us now, or later?"

"Later. I want some information first."

"I'm in no mood to give it."

With my left arm clamped over the bomb, and my left hand holding the trigger, I drew my pistol with my right. I fired a bolt, which punched a hole into the nearest spider.

The monster didn't seem to like that. None of them did. They went into a kind of frenzy, and they began hissing and bubbling and carrying on. The one I'd shot sank down, shivering and flowing out stinky liquids, but the others surged closer.

One of them clamped his mandibles on my right boot. Another snapped at the gun in my hand. I lifted this to fire again.

"No! Hold it! Cease, you fools!"

Armel stepped closer, waving his hands over his head. He beat back his spider-friends with the butt of his pistol. Growling and rattling their mouth-parts, they retreated with poor grace.

"Bad-tempered spiders you've got here," I said. "You should burn out these nasties, Armel. They all look like something that should be on the bottom of my shoe."

"You half-wit animal!" he complained. "You're not fit to die among any of these people. Why didn't you wear your damned armor?"

I laughed. "You wanted it that bad, huh? Don't worry none, it wouldn't have fit a skinny little fop like you anyway. Now listen, we have to come to some kind of arrangement without killing each other this time around. We've done it before in the past, why not today?"

"Because it isn't just your armor I wanted by bringing you here, McGill. I want you out of the way. You've caused my legion and my clients a great deal of harm. Now, answer a question for me."

"Okay."

"How will Graves finish this? How will he go for the kill and take the battle to my legion?"

"Uh... I don't rightly know."

"Are you serious? You expect me to believe that? You can't win a war by staying on the defensive forever. You must know something."

"Well... the truth is, I'm drawing a blank, here. Graves is kind of annoyed with me, see, and Fike... well, I think Fike outright hates me."

"Of course he does. I'm a fool to think I could get information from a rutting field-animal such as yourself... it would be easier to squeeze blood from a turnip. You are a dolt, McGill. A growth on the hindquarters of an unpleasant animal."

He stepped closer, so I took a firmer grip on my bomb.

"Helsa was right," he said, blowing bad, steamy breath into my face. "You have nothing to offer. You know nothing, and I'm done with this conversation."

To my total surprise, he reached toward my bomb—and he set it off.

-68-

When I was revived again, I came out of the chute laughing. I tried to explain what was so funny to the bio-people, but they didn't seem to have any sense of humor.

"Has he got a brain-warp or something?"

"I don't think so, Specialist. His numbers are passing."

They were both male voices, so I didn't want to hang around. They got me up and off their table in good time.

When I walked out of Blue Bunker, I was holding myself up by one hand on the walls. Since I'd skipped taking a shower, I left a slimy trail on everything I touched, a trail not unlike that of a garden snail.

My tapper was buzzing and talking to me, but I didn't care. I headed to the door and walked outside.

To my surprise, it was kind of bright outside. How long had I been dead?

"McGill reporting," I said, answering the most persistent caller. It was Graves.

"You're late for the briefing, McGill."

"Uh… I've been kind of busy playing dead, sir."

"That's no excuse. Get over here to Gold Bunker, on the double."

He disconnected, and I went into a shambling trot. By the time I reached Gold Bunker, I could walk straight.

Off in the distance, I saw something I hadn't expected. The Shadowlander town—it was mostly gone. The buildings had been dismantled, and there was an ant-like procession of people heading west and away from their slowly rising sun.

"Huh… I must have been dead for a week," I commented to no one in particular.

Marching down the steps into Gold Bunker, I was directed toward the big conference room. I threw open the door, and it banged into the opposite wall. There were no seats left, so I stood in the back.

"There he is, back from his beauty rest," Fike said. He stood at the front of the chamber next to Graves. "I hope you enjoyed your little siesta, McGill."

"I surely did, sir. Nothing like the peace of the dead."

Fike turned back to Graves, who was messing with a com-link.

Tribune Turov showed up on the big screen when Graves finally finished fooling around. She scanned the audience, landing her pretty eyes on me. They narrowed to slits.

"There he is at last. Is it true that you detonated an antimatter bomb on this planet, McGill?"

"Uh…" I said, looking around and noticing a large number of unfriendly stares. "I might have at that."

She nodded slowly, but before she could continue Fike jumped in.

"He destroyed a suit of specialized armor, Tribune," he complained. "For that alone—"

"Stop whining about your armor, Fike. You'll get a new suit eventually. Besides, he's done far more damage than that. The Galactics have ruled that the detonation of an antimatter device was a violation of their rules."

"How so?" I asked.

"For the same reason we're not allowed to bombard the planet from orbit. You're supposed to prove the comparative strengths of your ground forces, not annihilate four percent of the planet!"

"I didn't annihilate anything… Not exactly."

"Tens of thousands were killed, McGill."

"But Armel pulled the detonator tab himself. I wasn't even going to do it."

"You took the bomb out there to the night-sider camp. No one believes you didn't plan to use it—especially not the Nairbs."

I opened my mouth to protest further, but I stopped myself. I wasn't going to win anyone over with a loud argument.

A siren sounded then, making us all jump. Galina moved to the big screen on the back wall.

"Shut up, everyone. It's the Nairbs. They've reached a consensus."

Baffled, I watched as the green seal-like creature appeared. He looked prim and maybe even a little proud of himself.

"Humans. This is an announcement, not a conference. After reviewing recent activities and weighing complaints and statements from both sides, I find you to be in violation of the initial parameters for this contest. Accordingly—"

"We wish to file a grievance," Galina interrupted.

The Nairb looked annoyed. "That is improper at this juncture. I have yet to pronounce my ruling."

"McGill did it!" Galina shouted, pointing at me. "He operated without authority when he bombed the night-sider camp!"

"That is also irrelevant. We can't be expected to track each of you vermin as individuals. Legally, your designation is that of a herd, swarm or hive of creatures. Guilt must be shared when weighing a matter like this."

"Hey, I object," I said.

The Nairb raised a flipper to silence us all. "This is entirely out of order. I will now mute your audio input and pronounce my verdict."

We fell silent because there was nothing better to do. The Nairb drew himself up to his full height, which was less than a meter tall because he was shaped like a seal, and continued.

"The contest has gone poorly. Both sides have been accused of violations—teleport harnesses, high-powered bombs and the like. Worst of all has been the frequent use of revival machines. These allow both sides to keep replenishing

401

losses, and the contest has therefore devolved into an endless slog.

"Neither the Nairb Inspector's Guild nor the two senior Galactics present wish to see this contest drag on. We have, unfortunately, been unable to declare a clear winner. Accordingly, we've decided to resolve the conflict with finality."

We dared to look at one another with hopeful eyes. Galina seemed to have been under the impression the Nairbs were going to throw the book at us, but fortunately, Armel had cheated at least as much as we had. On top of all that, it was only obvious that the Nairb couldn't make a quick arbitrary judgment against either side. Two Galactic races were on the verge of war, and neither of them was going to back down.

"The human legion known as Varus will face Armel's force of saurians on an open field. They will be roughly equal in numbers and armament. If either side is destroyed, or routed from the battle, they will be declared the loser. That is our judgment, and it will not be swayed by bleating pleas."

The Nairb disconnected, and the officers all looked at one another in shock.

All of them, that was, except for me. I was all smiles, and I pumped my fist in the air.

"We're gonna kick their butts! You watch, people. Armel and his lizards will be slaughtered!"

No one else seemed as confident or happy as I was, but I didn't care. I did a little victory dance while people stared at me glumly. If you ask me, they were all a bunch of nervous nellies.

-69-

After the meeting broke up, I headed down toward my bunk and pulled out a long box. Inside, I found a very special suit of armor. I had to spray it out again, as the special funk Fike had left inside was still detectable to a discerning nose like mine.

A few minutes later, I stood tall and proud, wearing the armor they'd made under Central just for me. With a fresh feeling of confidence, I strode toward the caravan of nomads that were still streaming by our encampment.

I didn't see anyone I recognized at first, but there were at least a hundred and fifty combat drones marching along with the rest of the Shadowlanders. Seeing them gave me an idea.

"Hey! Hey, you!"

Trotting alongside the marching drones, I finally spotted a half-familiar face. I chased after a member of the inner council of suck-ups. I'd seen him before, a throne-sniffer who'd fawned all over Kattra. He was skinny, with big dark eyes that got a lot bigger when I rolled up on him.

"Hey," I said, "where's Helsa? Or Kattra?"

He showed me a set of yellow teeth. "Our Lady has moved on, but her daughter is at the head of this procession." He indicated the long, long line of marching combat drones.

I thanked him and pressed into the herd. A plume of dust rose up, churned up by around fifty thousand sandal-wearing feet. They didn't seem to have too many vehicles, and those they did have were being used to carry their mobile structures and other goods. Anyone who was fit had to walk.

"Helsa?" I asked when I saw a familiar head of tousled hair.

She turned slowly in my direction. Her face, which started off kind of sour-looking, moved straight on into outright anger. She stepped out of the procession and stood to the side of that long line of drudgery.

"McGill? What gives you the gall to come here and pester me?"

"Huh? I thought you liked me."

She laughed. "Unbelievable. I didn't think it could be true, but apparently it is. You are an idiot."

Helsa began walking again, and the winds whipped up her sheer clothes to flap and hug her form. This time she made an effort to cover up—pulling her flowing cloak with both hands to cover her charms. I was sad to see that.

"Come on, you owe me. I took out Armel, just like you wanted me to."

She stopped again, and she wore a look of astonishment. "You thought that's what I wanted you to do? To teleport there with a bomb and incinerate a population?"

"Uh… is this a trick question? I certainly *did* think that. What's the matter? Did you expect me to port out there and fight him bravely, one-on-one?"

She shook her head. "No, I expected you to die."

"Oh… well, I did do that."

"This conversation is at an end. We must withdraw from this place before the sun touches us directly."

"Why? Will you melt like a bunch of vampires or something?"

"No, we will not melt, but we will be shamed. It is our right, our permanent privilege to stay within the best slice of land on our world. If we don't move with it now, we'll be no better than bright-siders within a month's time."

I didn't quite get what her problem was, but I could see that these monthly migrations were very important to the Shadowlanders. Their self-worth was all wrapped up in the idea that they owned the best slice of perpetually moving real estate on this arid planet, wherever that spot happened to be located at the moment.

"Okay, I'll tell you what. I'll just take your combat drones. What have you got here, like, two hundred of them? That would be a nasty surprise for old Armel. I could chase him off the planet with such a force."

"What is the point, McGill? The interstellar currents are driving us into Skay territory anyway. Winning this battle—even if it were possible—will only keep us in Province 921 for another few years."

"Right, exactly. Time enough for us to evacuate your people and find a new home for the lot of you."

She laughed bitterly. "You really think that's what we want? To become vagabonds among the stars? I'd rather live with the night-siders!"

"You already are nomads. Is it so hard to move one more time?"

"We're nomads on a world we know. A world we love. We have no trust that you or your government will place us somewhere where we'll be happy."

"Well… you've got a valid concern there."

She stopped again and stared up at me. She looked like she was trying to figure me out. Her pretty face went through a series of emotions.

"We had a deal, Armel and I did. You ruined that deal."

"What deal? Did he offer you a place in his legion? He likes to do that with women."

Helsa opened her mouth, then closed it again. She turned and hurried away, but I followed her.

As countless pissed-off women from my sordid past can attest, I have a shockingly long stride. If you want to out-walk old McGill, you'd better be ready to up and run for it.

"Say," I said. "Are you telling me everyone is right about what they say about you?"

She stopped and turned. Her head was lowered dangerously, and she stood in a fighting stance. I knew I was pissing her off something awful, but I pretended not to notice.

"*Who* is saying *what* about me?"

"Well... pretty much everybody. There's Armel, for one. He's got an awful big mouth under that mustache, you know."

"What did he tell you?"

"You know... the usual. All about how he nailed you on his first try, and how easy you were. He said you were just like tons of other dumbass, yokel girls on other backwater planets. He laughed about some kind of deal he'd made to save you and your people. About how all you had to do was give up some sugar, and help him trap that big, old badass McGill—"

That was as far as I got before she slapped me. It was a good thing too, because I'd almost run out of insulting bullshit to tell her.

Her slap, actually, was more of punch. There were knuckles in there, and I felt them all. I caught her hand quickly before it could be withdrawn.

Helsa had a blade out in her other hand, pressed up against my belly, but I was in my black armor, and I didn't think she could scratch it.

"Let go of my hand, human."

"What's got you so angry?"

"You're lying. You're dishonoring me with your grip and your words."

"I'm not lying. Armel set off that bomb, not me."

I let her go. She rubbed at her wrist.

"More lies. Armel told me of your savagery, your appetites, and your habit of constantly lying."

I was a bit alarmed. I'd kind of hoped Armel hadn't dumped on me, but it made sense that he had.

One of the truly advanced elements of telling whoppers had long ago been mastered by my humble self. When you're telling a string of misleading details, you make sure that one of them is stone-cold true. That way, when you can prove it, people generally believe the rest of your story.

Lifting my tapper, I quickly found the last vid file from my previous existence. I was lucky, in that my tapper had successfully recorded a stream of video that lasted up until the moment of my demise in a fireball of vast proportions. Our networking was getting faster every year, it seemed to me.

Running my finger along, I went to the end, then ran only the last thirty seconds. I shoved my forearm under her nose, and she sneered—but she couldn't help but watch.

Armel and I talked, then he came close, and he reached in and set off my bomb. It was as plain as day.

"See?" I said. "He never planned to follow-up on any promises he gave you. There will be no crown of gold, no silk cushions, no—"

"Shut up. He promised nothing of the kind. He guaranteed that we'd find peace and prosperity under the Skay."

I threw back my head and hooted with laughter. I howled as if she'd told me the funniest thing I'd heard all day.

She stabbed me then, repeatedly, but she couldn't breach my armor.

"Stop that," I said, brushing her off.

"No one laughs at Helsa of the Shadowlanders!"

"Are you sure about that? Armel's laughing. He set off the bomb that made the Nairbs call us cheaters. That's why we're about to fight them to the death in your shitty desert. And you know something else? You are one ungrateful woman."

I turned away and walked away from the road. I headed back toward our encampment. I was surprised to see we'd gone pretty far from our huddle of bunkers. These nomads took their marches seriously.

I heard slapping feet in the dust behind me. Despite my trust in my armor, and my devious plans, it took all my willpower not to turn around and face her—but I managed it.

Helsa fell into step beside me. "Did he really laugh at me?"

"I'd swear on a stack of bibles," I lied.

"That dancing sand-devil. He must be cut down."

"Uh… what'd you have in mind?"

She stopped and pointed over her shoulder. Turning and looking, my eyes widened.

Two hundred combat drones, maybe more, were following her. They all stopped and stood silently, watching us both with their roving cameras. Right then, I was glad I hadn't tried to grab her again or anything.

"These automatons will serve you until you leave our world—but don't take too long to do so."

Helsa turned away and hurried back to join the endless, dust-churning masses that were her people. I watched her go, and I felt sorry she hadn't hung around for another few hours. After all, we could have celebrated our rekindled friendship with a bottle of wine and a soft bunk.

Ah well, I guess some things were just not meant to be.

-70-

The creeping mosses of the Shadowlands curled and blackened every day along the line they called Dawn's Edge. On most worlds, this border between night and day moved quickly, but not so on Edge World. Here, the line moved with the determined slowness of a minute hand on an old fashioned clock, the kind most people couldn't make heads or tails of these days.

As Dawn's Edge crept over the world, the delicate mosses died, unable to withstand direct sunlight. The stuff had evolved with a peculiar weakness to both full day and full night. It could only survive in the eternal purply twilight that existed in-between and much longer than seemed natural.

It was along this line that we met with Armel's forces. They came out of the east with the creeping dawn. We formed ranks to meet them right where the Shadowlander city had so recently been dismantled.

The battlefield had been chosen by the Nairbs precisely for its flat, featureless nature. In their desperate efforts to please two implacable enemies, they'd selected the most neutral stretch of land they could find.

Turning my wandering eye upward to the heavens, I saw a startling sight. Edge World had a moon today—the first in its entire history.

It was the grizzled old Skay, of course. It rode low in the north sky, hovering a hundred thousand kilometers over the planet's pole. That was freaky and ominous all by itself, as no natural satellite can sit over a planet's pole for long. They must orbit in a continuous circular flight, falling forever around their master's gravity-well.

But such minor rules of physics had never bothered the Skay. They were terrifying beings, artificially intelligent and alien in every sense of the word. They were artificial of the mind, but with fleshly parts as well. Their gigantic selves were collectively spaceships, colonies of bizarre life forms, and a single unique individual all at the same time.

Graves walked up to me as we waited for Armel's vast army of saurians to approach. "The Skay has come close, lowering itself to get a good view of the action."

"Yep," I said, "looks that way."

"What will it do if it loses? Do you think it will retreat and give us this planet?"

I thought that over. "Probably. The Skay are wily old bastards. It will figure that it can't really lose, that in the end it will have this star system anyway, once it drifts fully into their territory."

Graves almost seemed disappointed. "You don't think they'll attack the Mogwa over it, huh?"

"Nah. Humans and Shadowlanders are small-potatoes to them. They won't get into another war over one little lump of dirt out here on the frontier. When they come to fight again, it will be over something bigger."

Graves nodded. "Hmm... You're probably right. Ah, I see that you've managed to snag Fike's armor again."

"What? That's sheer slander, Primus! I had a fresh set sent out from Central, I swear. If Fike has misplaced his gear, I can't be held responsible for that."

He chuckled. "I don't care. Fike's been getting kind of big for his britches lately anyway. Well McGill, good luck on the field of battle today."

We shook hands, saluted, and separated.

Harris walked up to me, having witnessed the entire exchange. "I have to admit, Graves is a class act," he said. "He always was."

"That's true."

We watched together as the enemy ranks formed ahead of us. Their long lines of metal armor and banners approached, forming a dark mass in the distance. They were saurians from Steel World, and they numbered in the thousands. On average, a saurian was around double the weight of a normal human. They would be very intimidating when they engaged our forces in close combat, which was their favorite tactic.

"Seems unfair that our Blood-Worlders aren't allowed to stand with us," Harris said.

"Yeah... hey, tell Sargon to keep our colors straight."

As our senior noncom, Sargon had the sacred honor of holding 3rd unit's flapping banner. In years past, that honor had fallen to Harris, but that was no longer the case as he was now an officer.

"I'll see to it, Centurion."

Harris walked away. During the quiet moment that followed, I reviewed the enemy forces. It was clear they'd copied our approach to warfare. That part wasn't surprising, as they'd been trying to form their own mercenary legions since I'd first joined up with Legion Varus.

This time out, they looked stern and professional. They'd been serving under Armel for years now, and he'd probably taught them all he knew about how a legion was supposed to operate.

Armel... that traitor. He was a serious foe. I'd often wondered what had happened to him over the years. Back during the Clone World campaign he'd worked for Claver. When that operation had gone haywire, he'd formed this lizard legion and moved on to serve Rigel.

Today, here he was, working for the Skay in Province 926. We'd had no idea as he'd taken his saurian band outside of Province 921, where Earth held the rights to all mercenary contracts. By selling his legion to other planets in far-off regions, Armel had skirted all kinds of trouble with the Galactics.

After eyeing the enemy for a time, I moved my field of view to the torn-down town itself. The Shadowlanders were gone, but you could still see all their cast-offs. There were still a few hungry scavengers, broken pots and some flattened

411

domes, but that was about it. There wasn't much to mark the place as the center of Shadowlander culture. I knew there were other similar nomadic towns, but none were as grand and important as this one.

"What are you looking at, Centurion?"

It was Kivi. She'd come up to stand at my side, and she stared at the enemy formations with at least as much concern as I did.

"Have you got your ground-drones and buzzers out there patrolling?" I asked her.

"Eighty percent of them are deployed, sir."

"Good. Any sign of enemy scouts or infiltrators?"

Kivi glanced at me. "That would be cheating. Couldn't we get them disqualified for that?"

I shrugged. "Maybe—if the judging Nairbs would dare to upset either of the Galactic sides with a trivial ruling."

She nodded. "They're in a tough spot. No matter how this goes, one of these Galactics won't be happy."

Kivi wandered off, she was attending to her drones and spying devices. After perhaps five minutes, she came back to me with an odd look on her face.

"Centurion? I'm getting some strange readings out there."

"Out where?"

"In the center of the field. In the region where those flattened domes are. Do you think—?"

"Ignore that, Specialist. It's probably just some gear the Shadowlanders left behind."

She nodded vaguely, shading her eyes from the slanting light of dawn. She kept staring toward the center of the battlefield which was right about where the domes were. Her frown lingered on her face.

"You don't think there's something out there, do you sir?" she asked me at last.

"I said forget about it, Kivi. File no reports. Tell the other techs from the 2nd and 4th Units to leave it alone, too."

Kivi stared at me for a few seconds. She knew me well, and she wasn't a dummy. For a short time, I thought maybe she was going to call Graves or something.

But at last, she looked away again and nodded. "I'm sure it's just junk, Centurion. Not bombs or anything like that. Something like that could get our side into trouble, you know..."

"That's right. That's why nothing of the kind is out there. Move along, Kivi."

She scooted at last, and I breathed a sigh of relief. The sensation was short-lived, however. An artificial horn blew, calling upon us to prepare. Shading my eyes and zooming in with my helmet's optics, I could see the army of saurians. They were hulking black figures with the bright sky outlining them from behind.

The enemy legion was finally on the move, advancing toward our position at a steady marching pace.

-71-

Armel's plan was clear from the start. His saurian troops weren't better trained than our men, nor were they any better equipped—but they did outweigh us. If I had to guess, I'd say he had a few more tails and snouts deployed than we had noses on our side as well.

In short, they outmatched us. Therefore, rather than getting fancy about it, he'd decided to march right down our throats and fight it out to the death, man-to-lizard.

Our troops were much more varied in skills and armament. That's because our legions were supposed to be able to function in a wide variety of environments. We had light troops with light weapons in case skirmishing was in order. We also had bigger guns—small artillery that could be placed on high ground to command the enemy's likely approaches. The rest of our number, about half, was made up of heavy infantry.

Now, all that might sound pretty good until you carefully consider the situation at hand. In this battle, we were on flat ground, and we weren't allowed time to find the best positions to set up artillery. Our lights were just plain outmatched by the enemy, and even our heavies were outweighed by the saurians.

"Hmm…" I said, watching them approach. Right off, I was worried, and I contacted Graves. "Sir? We need to get a move on. We should meet them mid-field."

"Thanks so much for the strategic advice, McGill. Now, shut up unless you've got critical intel for me."

Graves disconnected.

A few moments later, he gave his first orders. "All units, all cohorts, send in your lights. Harass and skirmish. Do not engage in close combat, but don't let them run you off too easily. Buy us some time."

Shaking my head, I turned to Barton. She was pale. She knew the odds—but she rushed out there anyway. "Any special orders, sir?" she asked me.

"Nope. Just give them hell, and try to come back in one piece when Graves calls you off."

Barton nodded and raced away. A line of lights, a full platoon, raced after her.

"By damn," Harris said from my right. "They've got heart, don't they?"

"Won't be enough today," Leeson said from my left. "Those lizards are going to mow right through them."

"Got your 88s set up yet?" I demanded of Leeson.

"No sir—almost."

I waved for him to get going. He trotted back to his specialists and walked the line, checking them all personally.

Then I turned to Harris. "Let's put your heavies right behind the weaponeers. No sense getting hit in the ass with some blue-on-blue."

"My thoughts exactly, Centurion."

We positioned the heavy troops behind the light artillery—two 88s and a dozen belchers. It didn't look like much, and it wasn't.

Still, we took heart in the fact we weren't alone. We were one unit of about a hundred. Together, we could throw a hell of a lot of pain downrange when the time came.

Armel's forces were ninety percent heavy infantry, but he did have a contingent of troops with mortars to the rear. When our lights came forward and began peppering his line with fire, he had his rear brigade shower them with smoking black spheres.

Each of these spheres contained an acidic smoke. It was nasty stuff, I could tell you from experience. It could eat through a suit, dissolving polymers and choking the victim inside.

415

The wobbling spheres came down in an erratic spray. A dozen of them landed nearby, and the battlefield was partly obscured. Light troops were enveloped by the vapors. Soon, they were running, falling and finally melting on the stained ground.

"Bastards…" I muttered, beginning to pace.

"You should get down, sir," Leeson suggested. "They have snipers too."

"Get ready on those 88s!" I shouted back at him. I was wearing my black armor, and I didn't care if I did catch a round or two right now. Maybe it would save one of my men who wasn't as well protected.

Leeson shrugged and went back to his charges, rushing from man to man in a crouch.

Our surviving lights were on their bellies by now. They were sniping away at the saurians who kept marching forward into the fire. Now and then a lizard went down, but it wasn't too often. Judging by the red names that kept popping up on my HUD, we were taking losses in the neighborhood of two to one.

Losing patience, I called Graves again.

"Sir? I'm sorry, sir, but it seems like a fine time to light up the field with our star-falls, doesn't it?"

"Can't do it, McGill. The Nairbs outlawed that during the meeting—didn't you catch that?"

"Uh…" the truth is, I barely listened to the briefing.

"Get off the line and fight your damn battle!"

Graves disconnected again. Right about then, our lights broke ranks. The saurians were almost on top of them. They fired their heavy rifles, catching our running troops in the back now and then.

When Barton got back to us, panting hard, I ordered her to take her people to the rear and start sniping. She nodded, too out of breath to speak.

Without saying much, I counted heads. She'd lead thirty-six out and come back with nineteen. That was pretty bad, even by Legion Varus standards.

Already, the saurians were cracking shots at us. There weren't any hits, but they were still a couple of kilometers off.

"Leeson! Fire at will!"

I ordered the rest of the unit to hug the ground. We hadn't been allowed to dig trenches, but there were natural divots and contours in the land. Even the blooms coming out of the carpet of mosses offered some cover.

As always, Leeson took a damnable long time to bother to fire. The enemy had picked up speed by now. Saurians troops could charge fast and hard, but not for long. Armel was clearly holding them back until he got close enough—that last kilometer—then he'd order his men to rush us.

By this time, we were all plinking away. Our heavies were armored, and they could take anything short of a direct hit. Once, I caught an explosive pellet in the ribs. It staggered me, but I didn't go down.

Carlos rushed to me, but slapped my ass quickly, declaring me fit to die all over again. I pushed him down as more vapor-spheres began to fall on our line.

"Barton! Leeson! Pull back everyone in light armor!"

They didn't need any further urging. Almost a third of my troops fell back and soon were obscured by the drifting acidic clouds.

"Leeson, dammit, are you dead?"

"No sir, don't worry. It's almost game-time."

I gritted my teeth and cursed for ten full seconds. Leeson knew his weapons well—better than I did. Even though some of the units on our flanks had opened up, he wanted maximal effect.

When he finally did fire, he achieved his goals. The sickly green beams reached out, cutting right through the drifting black clouds to touch the approaching ranks.

On both sides of my unit, other weaponeers had begun to fire their belchers and 88s. The range was kind of extreme, but the enemy was undeniably thinned out.

That's when the enemy decided to change the tempo. Armel had chosen this critical moment to close the gap between our two armies as quickly as possible. In everyone's estimation Varus had superior ranged fire, so it was time to take the fight to us, up-close and personal.

Every enemy throat on the battlefield released a terrific blast of noise. Taken altogether, this alien cry was deafening. Half-howl and half-roar, it swept the mossy plains and made every human cringe.

The saurians were charging us at last.

They came out of the black smoke and dust like a herd of wild beasts. Each bounding step took them higher and farther than any human could have managed without technological aid. Somehow, knowing they were managing this feat with just their own muscles powering every churning step made it all the more intimidating.

"Jesus!" Harris said. "Look at them come! It's like a field full of giant hopping locusts!"

He wasn't far from wrong. The enemy charge was disheartening, both their numbers and their eagerness seemed overwhelming. The bounding saurians were in a frenzy now, and they'd soon meet our line and break over it.

Leeson finally gave the order to fire. His twin 88s hummed and swept from both sides of the field toward the middle. The light of them was unnatural, and the wide beams filled the air with the smell of ozone. This was quickly replaced by the stink of charred flesh and an oven-like heat.

The front ranks of saurians were caught and destroyed. They burned as they continued to run until they collapsed in a heap of gray ash. After the beams swept over them, however, the ranks that followed came on, undaunted.

"We need more elevation," Leeson shouted. "I can't stop them, McGill. Not all of them. Should I pull back the 88s?"

"No—hold your position. Give 'em everything you've got."

"Yes, sir!"

That was it. I'd just ordered Leeson and his men to die. They all knew it, but they stood their ground anyway, furiously working their weapons. They spit into the dust and cursed my name—but they kept on firing.

Twice more the 88s sang. On either side of 3rd Unit, the centurions ordered their most valuable troops to the rear—but I used a different tactic.

418

"Heavies!" I shouted, raising one improbably long arm into the sky. "Up and charge them!"

"Say what?" Harris squawked.

"You heard me!"

Already, his men were scrambling to their feet. Harris got up with the rest, releasing a stream of bad words and shoving aside anyone who came near him. He hustled to the front, rushing past the 88s and weaponeers to the front line.

Just as he got there, the first saurians arrived. They were a bloody, dirty mess. Some of them were shot, many were scorched. Many had stumps for limbs, but they came at us anyway, seeking to tear us apart with a mouthful of sharp teeth if they had to.

Harris' men were rocked backward by the impact of the enemy charge, but they weren't soft. They had powered exoskeletons, metal armor and morph-rifles set on assault mode.

Their guns ripped the air, chugging out thousands of power-bolts. The ragged enemy ranks were destroyed.

Long before we could think about declaring any kind of victory, however, the second wave came bounding toward us.

Standing tall, I shielded my eyes and I gazed over the tops of countless heads. In a brief gap in the dust and smoke, I was able to see a kilometer or two across the field of battle.

What I saw way out there was spirit-crushing. There weren't just two waves coming. There weren't even three— there were *four* of them.

We'd taken out the first chunk of Armel's army with artillery and ranged fire. They'd been annihilated. But now, the rest of them were about to land on us. We couldn't hold—there was no hope of it.

The battle would soon be lost.

-72-

It should be said at this point that I've never been a man to take defeat lightly. In my long and storied lifetime, I figure that my competitive nature has probably gotten me into more trouble than any of my many other character flaws.

Today was no exception. As I reviewed the situation, I saw it was clearly hopeless. What's more, it always had been. Since we'd landed on this creeping sundial of a planet, we'd been abused by Armel and every living being who cared to call this rock home.

To me, that seemed just plain unfair. When faced with an unwinnable situation, well sir, I felt clear of mind and soul to take unusual action to rectify the perceived injustice. What's more, I felt fully justified to take any manner of action I saw fit.

In this case... I decided it was time to cheat.

Helsa had given me something a day earlier: the keys to her small army of combat drones. Taken by themselves, they weren't all that much. Just a few hundred deadly robots, more or less.

But, when coupled with a few other advantages, they could be an important factor on the battlefield. One of these advantages was the simple fact that I'd ordered them to bury themselves in the loamy soil near their old stomping grounds, at the center of what used to be the Shadowlander town. The other advantage was they were now positioned behind the last saurian's flapping tail.

With a sense of righteous destiny, I pressed the activation button on the controller Helsa had seen fit to leave with me.

At first, nothing special happened. I bared my teeth and squinched up my eyes, trying to see the center of the field past all the raging lizards and whatnot. Then I recalled that these drones liked to take their time while booting up.

My troops were experiencing a brief lull in the fighting, but it wasn't going to last long. Most of them were wandering around, carrying the wounded to the rear and generally looking stunned.

"Prepare to hold back the second wave!" I roared. "Lights, advance and take up morph-rifles if the heavies fall. Leeson, move your weaponeers forward with their belchers. Stand fast, boys!"

They all hastened to obey my orders. More than a few groaned at talk of a second wave—but they were game. They took up positions and continuously fired into the billowing smoke and dust that now blocked everything from view.

Most maddening of all, I could no longer see my combat drones. Were they engaging or not? I had no idea.

The second wave was brutal. They were a lot fresher and most were uninjured. They came on with a vengeance, but we met their fury with a shocking amount of firepower. Saurians staggered to our lines, dead on their feet. Still, they often managed to land a blow or unload a magazine at point-blank range before they toppled at last.

This time the fighting was hand-to-hand before it was over. We won, but at least half my troops were dead or dying. On our flanks, 2nd Unit and 4th Unit had all but collapsed.

Harris wormed his way over to me, and he slapped me on the back. "That was some good fighting, McGill. But we both know we're screwed now."

"Yeah... probably."

Harris laughed. "I saw those waves back there. We've only stopped half the saurians, and that doesn't even count Armel's ball-throwing reserves in the rear. We're toast, and you know it."

"Yeah..." I repeated.

Every second my eyes roved over the scene, looking for a break in the storm of dust and smoke. Where were those damned drones? Irritably, I pressed the activation code several more times. There was no visible effect. I cursed and waved Harris away irritably.

Climbing to my feet, I began to march toward the center of the battle field. Maybe the damned remote had a small range, and the drones hadn't gotten the signal.

"Where are you going, Centurion? Sir?" Harris asked, but he was talking to my back.

"Take command, I'm going to check on something."

"What the fuck...?"

I broke into a trot, then a dead run. I plunged into the smoke and dust, leaping over bodies and debris that came at me seemingly out of nowhere.

The third wave of saurians rolled up about then, meeting me in a ragged line. They seemed surprised to find a human out here, but when I slammed into them, they attacked me, snarling.

Force-blades sprouted out of my black armored sleeves. The armor was lighter than any normal heavy trooper wore, and more flexible, but it still had the capabilities of our standard-issue heavy suit.

I slashed and thrust at them. They looked at me like I was a madman—which I pretty much was. Getting over their surprise, they shot me a dozen times.

I stumbled and went down to one knee, but then leapt up again. Deep cuts from my blades disemboweled two of them, those who'd thought they could rush close and finish me.

They'd thought wrong. I was fine, if a bit banged-up. With the new undercoating of soft stuff I'd put into the suit, it was hotter inside but much better at protecting my body.

Pellets splashed and exploded over me. I was tossed off my feet again, and a saurian planted a big three-clawed foot on my chest.

That was a mistake. The last thing I wanted was to be pinned down. I cut off that offending foot with a single burning slash and stood up again.

Three saurians encircled me. They'd been left behind by countless others. Most of the wave had probably never even known I was here, what with all the smoke and confusion.

The trio rushed me together. That was bad. There had to be five hundred kilos of lizard coming my way, and although I'm a big man, I was about to be rolled back on my can. If they just sat on me, there wouldn't be much I could do.

I took a chance then. I grabbed the only grav-plasma grenade I had off my belt, activated it and dropped it on the ground.

The lizards barely noticed. I got a few nicks in as they closed with me, having figured out by this time that the armor I had on wasn't being pierced by anything they threw at it. One lizard's arm hung by a thread, and another had lost his tail.

But then they were on me. They bore me down on my back, forcing me to lay supine.

The truth was, I didn't fight quite as hard as I could have. After all, the grenade's timer had to just about be up.

Snarling and hissing with pleasure, they crouched on my body, biting the legs and punching the belly. It wasn't pleasant, but nothing penetrated.

Boom!

The grenade went off, and the lizards were treated to a front-row seat. Their tails were lifted up, and their underparts were showered with shrapnel. This was done with such suddenness and force that they were sent flying right over me.

One of them, the guy with the dangling arm, did a perfect "one" flipping ass-over-teakettle onto his back about three meters off. He struggled to rise for maybe two seconds before slumping down in death.

The others were squirming and grunting, wishing they were back in their mamma's egg-sack... or wherever they'd come from originally.

Standing up, I found I was sore around the groin area. But everything was still intact. "Sorry boys, but I've got to run."

I took off as fast as I could toward the center of the field. When I got there, two things confused me. For one, the fourth wave I'd spotted earlier had never materialized. For another, I found the holes I'd placed the drones into—and they were empty.

"Huh…" I said aloud, standing in the midst of a swirling firefight with my hands on my hips. "Might as well keep going and see what's what."

Trotting fast, I headed toward Armel's line. I don't rightly know what I expected to see—but I knew those drones had to be out here somewhere. If I could find them and help them do some more damage, so much the better.

That's when I began to find bodies. Lots of them—all saurians. A dozen lay dead, tails-up, in that weird pose so many of them die in when stricken hard. There were a lot of parts missing, blown clean off.

I began to grin and trot faster. This had to be the work of my drones. It had to be.

The smoke and dust cleared enough for me to make out what was happening nearby. A pitched battle was occurring, and I could see the combatants clearly.

On one side were around eighty robots. The rest had been knocked out of commission. Surrounding these was a desperate mass of struggling forms—they were lizards, but they didn't have armor on.

I realized at last what I was looking at. The combat drones had found Armel's reserves, the scaly pricks with the mortars that had been showering us with all those acid balls all day long.

Without hesitation, I joined my robots. We killed those damned lizards for the next ten minutes or so—every last one of them we could find.

73

Armel showed up about when I ran out of lizards. This was kind of a surprise, as he was usually the chicken kind of officer, the kind who stayed well behind the front lines.

But not today. He came up out of nowhere, and he belted me one in the back of the head. I was surprised by this as well, as my robots didn't do shit to stop him.

Then I recalled that I'd ordered them to kill saurians—not humans. I'd done that just in case some of my own men showed up. I didn't want anyone from Varus to die in a blue-on-blue accident. After all, my people might then shoot at the robots, thinking they were the enemy.

When Armel showed up, however, he was definitely the only human in sight. The rest of my people were doubtlessly hunkered down in some blood-and-mud filled hole on the other side of the battlefield.

"So, it is you!" Armel growled in a raspy voice. "I knew it the moment these metal monstrosities showed up. It couldn't have been the Shadowlanders. They would never be so full of treachery and deceit!"

Having been knocked to one knee, I stood up and turned around. The blow hadn't put me out, despite the fact Armel had landed it with the butt of his combat rifle. My helmet had absorbed the shock nicely.

Armel was wearing fancy armor, too. This surprised me.

"Hey! Where'd you get a suit of the good stuff, Maurice?"

"From Rigel of course. I have you to thank in that regard, you gave me the idea after impressing me a week ago."

I nodded. "Well, that will even things up some I guess…"

Armel formed two stabbing blades of force, and I did the same. We were both going to be pretty damned hard to kill as long as we kept our suits on, so we squared off and circled.

We jabbed and slashed at one another, drawing smoky lines across each other's breastplate—but nothing went through.

"You are a fool, McGill. You have lost this planet by cheating."

"Nonsense. We faced your lizard-legion and won, fair and square."

"Then where did this mass of murderous robots come from? Answer me that, you lying ape!"

I threw my hands wide, and I took a long step backwards. There was a heavy crunching sound under my left boot. The sound was, in fact, from the control box that Helsa had given me. I'd dropped it when Armel had belted me, and now I'd stepped on it. Rotating the heel of my boot from side to side, I made sure the box was ground into dust.

Oh sure, I'd considered ordering the robots to kill old Armel, but that would have been a mistake. If I proved now that I was in control of them, well sir, the Nairbs never looked kindly upon rule-breakers like myself.

"I honestly don't know where they came from," I lied. "They must have been left behind when the nomads took off."

Armel's mustache squirmed over his lip in rage. "You are so full of shit it's amazing it doesn't squirt from your ears when you smile at me like that!"

"Now, now, try to keep your brain turned on for one second. Notice that the robots aren't attacking you? Or me? They're just killing lizards."

Armel's eyes slid from side to side. "You have programmed them for this."

"Nope. I'm not smart enough. All I do is kill people and wreck things."

Armel lifted a gloved hand to his helmet. I could tell I'd planted a dark seed of doubt in his mind. "It is a trick. It's always a trick with you."

"The way I figure it, it was just chance. We fought over the center of the old Shadowlander town. They always parked their robots right here, in this same spot. Last time they saw your lizards, they were attacking their town. Maybe they were set to hate reptiles, or maybe they—"

Slam! Armel had bashed me one in the helmet. My head rolled to one side, but I rolled it right back. I grinned at him.

"Stop it with your absurd lies," he said. "You've obviously destroyed my army with outside help. I won't listen to any more—"

Deciding to test out his suit's quality, I swept up my boot and slammed it into his balls. He wasn't expecting that, as I was still grinning at him like a two-bit fool. I did that a lot with enemies, it kept them guessing.

I was gratified to see him wince and snarl. He didn't go down, but I could tell he'd felt my ten kilo boot all right. You just try wrapping up your jewels in some foam rubber, and then let your buddies beat on your crotch—it's no picnic.

"You fiend," he said, baring his teeth and stumbling back a pace. He was still on his feet, but he wasn't a happy camper.

"Sorry about that. You really should try putting some padding under your armor. Sure, a bolt won't penetrate, but—"

"Shut up. You have lost. I've filed a complaint with the Nairbs, and they have agreed to take up the case. They will never stop their investigations, and the Inspector hates you personally."

"Yeah… that's true. But it doesn't change reality, Armel. What's your explanation for what happened on this battlefield today?"

"Subterfuge. Sabotage. Backstabbing and cheating. All of these words describe the incident accurately."

"What's your evidence?"

He straightened his spine up some and pointed a gauntleted finger at me. "What are you doing here alone? Why have you broken ranks and raced across a bloody battlefield?

427

Because you obviously knew what was happening here. You *knew*, and that is proof enough."

"Hell's bells," I said, slapping my black breastplate. "Are you blind, old man? See this here? I'm wearing impenetrable armor, same as you. We're the only two men on this sad-sack planet who've got this kind of personal protection."

"So what?"

"So, that's why I'm here. I raced across the battlefield because no one else in my legion could pull it off. If we'd all had this kind of armor, why, we'd have cleaned your clocks by now, robots or no."

Armel's shifty eyes did some shifting then. He was thinking it over, and I could see that he could understand the logic in my bullshit. I was laying it on thick, mind you, but I've found over my long lifetime that when you lied you had to go whole-hog. There couldn't be a hint of doubt in your mind, or the other guy would detect it.

In fact, my absolute certitude concerning my fabricated version of events was working some magic on Armel's brain. I could see it. He wasn't sure what had happened.

Finally, however, he got his second wind and stepped closer. He wagged a finger in my face. I hated that almost as much as a kick in the nuts.

"It doesn't matter," he said. "Not today. This battle was compromised. The Nairbs will surely see that and rule in my favor. They aren't as impartial as they would like you to believe they are. Their hatred for you, McGill, will cause them to stray from their stance of neutrality and award me the victory by default."

I blinked at him for a moment, wondering if he was right. Then, I faked another kick.

He hopped back comically, and covered his gonads with both his gauntlets. Laughing, I turned back toward the west, and we went our separate ways.

74

My normal expectation after a victory of the kind I'd helped achieve today was to be lauded as a hero upon my return to camp. Today was no different. I arrived with a big grin and a laugh.

"We beat their scaly asses!" I shouted. "Legion Varus has swept the field clear of saurians! The battle is ours, brothers and sisters!"

At first, everyone who heard me hooted back their encouragement. The grimy remains of my own unit rushed up from their hiding spots, clapping me on the back and marveling at the completeness of my kit.

"That armor is unbelievable," Leeson said.

"It's more than that, it's frigging unfair," Harris said. "Why does McGill get a suit, while we get squat?"

I clapped him on the shoulder, letting my hand land quite hard. He staggered a half-step and glared at me.

"Because, my friend, rank and honor comes with certain privileges. But don't worry, as soon as these go into mass-production, I'll order a suit for each of you."

That promise put a damper on all complaints. It was total bullshit, of course. We couldn't make many of these suits. It just wasn't practical. At this point, they had to be made by hand, and we only had about seventy captive Vulbites who could do it.

The Rigellians had thousands of suits, naturally, because they'd been allied with the Vulbites over a long period of time. They therefore had billions of individuals crafting them, rather than a few dozen.

Still, none of these pesky facts needed to be shared. Everyone was in a great mood, and I hated to needlessly bring people down. It just wasn't my way.

Another figure appeared then, a skinny man with a pair of thin sour lips to match his stick-like limbs.

"There you are, McGill," Winslade said. "Do you realize that Graves ordered me to come out here and find out what happened to you personally?"

"Uh…" I said, and I looked down at my tapper. Sure enough, there was foil tape wound all around my arm. I'd done that when I'd decided to run off by my lonesome toward the enemy lines. After all, fielding thirty-odd calls from Graves and other officers would have been mighty distracting.

All of that was a big deal to me, but I wished I'd managed to remember to take the tape off when I'd left Armel and returned to our side of the field.

Damn.

Wearing a distracting grin, I put my hands behind my back and began picking at the silvery tape.

"So good of you to come out and check up on me, sir," I told Winslade. "We're all fine and dandy here. I'll investigate my tapper malfunction and—"

"Do you realize," Winslade interrupted me, "that you've been reported by the enemy? To the Nairbs, I mean?"

"Uh… you don't say? Isn't that just like Armel? He's always been a sore loser."

Winslade eyed me suspiciously. I swear that if he'd been born a barn-rat, instead of just looking like one, he'd have been one of those smart bastards that refused to set foot in a baited trap.

He shook his head. "I don't know what you did out here, McGill. I simply hope and pray it wasn't so heinous an act that we've been disqualified."

"I'm as pure as the wind-driven snow, Primus sir, and that's a fact."

He made a puffing sound and walked away in disgust.

He had me worried, however. So far, both Armel and Winslade had their radar up. Now, that could all be because they knew me well and were accustomed to my shenanigans, but the Nairb Inspector was no fool. He'd spent years chasing after the infamous border-bandit named McGill. Any hint of impropriety was bound to be taken as just cause to launch an investigation.

Hmm...

Determined not to allow everyone's negativity to spoil my celebratory mood, I marched my unit back to our bunker. We'd been assigned a puff-crete rabbit-hole a few kilometers to the west of the old Shadowlander campsite.

Unfortunately, there wasn't much to be pleased about at the bunker. When we'd built it a few weeks back, the sun had never reached the place. Now, however, it splashed over the shell-like walls with blazing intensity. Even though the light looked like a pleasant sunrise, it wasn't cool outside—it was hot. I supposed that if dawn lasted for weeks back on Earth, it wouldn't be cool at that time of day either.

Still, I managed to break out some hooch and pass it around. We drank, grimaced, spat and drank some more. It was time to celebrate the day's hard fighting. Those who had died, fully half my unit and more, had already been reborn. They were wandering back into the bunker with haunted eyes. At least we were able to tell them we'd won the battle. That brought a smile back to everyone's face.

My tapper had started buzzing before my first gulp, and by the time I'd belted down several more, it was just about bursting.

"Can't you put that on vibrate or something?" Carlos complained.

"I think it is on vibrate."

"Hot girl, huh?"

"Only the best know my ID."

Carlos laughed and turned away. I consulted my arm—and I saw it was as I expected. Graves had flooded me with messages over the last hour or so.

Sighing, I began to tap at them. I was bored before I could swipe them all to trash. They were all saying pretty much the same thing:

Report in.

Get your ass up here to Dominus.

There's a problem, report in.

The Nairbs are using your name, and they don't sound happy.

That last one had come from Galina. I tapped on it, and I answered.

On my way, sir!

That was a dumb move, as my tapper lit up immediately with an incoming call. As she was a couple of ranks higher than I was, I couldn't block the transmission. I couldn't even choose not to answer it.

"McGill? What are you doing, you fuck? Get up to *Dominus* or I'll have you shot and revived on my Blue Deck."

"Yes, sir. Good to see you survived the battle, sir."

That last was a smart-ass barb, and she knew it. She'd pretty much avoided setting foot on Edge World since we'd arrived.

With a last shout-out to my troops, I clapped backs and shook hands all the way to the bunker's exit. They cheered me, and I walked out into the bright, slanting sun.

A few minutes later, I walked through some gateway posts they'd set up over at Gold Bunker, and I was transmitted up to *Dominus*.

Walking the passages, I soon found there was a meeting in progress on the bridge. Stepping onto the command deck, I expected to see a Nairb's face, swollen up all out of proportion on the central holo-screen.

But that wasn't what I found at all. Instead, I saw a huddle of real live Nairbs. They were barking up a storm from the front of the room. The translators couldn't even keep up.

"...and it is further noted that the accused have continued to dissemble," one of them said as I walked in. "They've made no effort to locate, arrest or otherwise produce the named perpetrator."

"Perhaps you humans have misunderstood Galactic Law," squawked another one. "The absence of a criminal in no way prevents his prosecution from taking place. Your efforts to hide the beast and protect him from justice will not prevail."

"Uh…" I said, stepping up to the squad of green seal-like creatures. "Hello, Mr. Nairb. I'm sorry to keep you waiting, but I've been down on Edge World winning a battle, see—"

"Incorrect!" said the first Nairb. "The battle was not materially won."

"This is possibly a new count," said another. "Review the bylaws, I demand it on behalf of the aggrieved party. All attempts to deny a charge automatically triggers another count of—"

"Whoa, whoa!" I said, laughing a little nervously. "Hold on, boys. That's not what I meant at all. I was just trying to explain that I was down on Edge World fighting, and it took a bit to get up here. No offense was intended, honorable sirs."

"We are not capable of taking offense from such a lowly creature as yourself, McGill. In fact, suggesting such a thing is an insult."

"Uh…" I said, deciding to pass on the idea of pointing out the contradictory nature of the alien's statement. They seemed all puffed-up and pissed-off enough already.

75

In my long and storied life, I've pissed off all kinds of people. Most of them were probably women—but aliens had to be a close second place.

"Now that the McGill is here," the Chief Inspector said, "we can continue with the core of our investigation. I will question the defendant personally."

Turov's eyes slid toward me. She had that scared, angry, pleading look on her face. She often wore that expression when authority figures demanded explanations from me.

Finding her distress to be distracting, I tried not to look at her.

"What a fantastic opportunity for all of us," she said, "we all want very much to get to the bottom of this matter and move on."

The Nairb zeroed in on her. "Are you suggesting we should increase the pace of our investigation?"

"No, no! Not at all, kind and thoughtful Nairbs. I'm simply looking forward to the just conclusion of these proceedings."

The top Nairb gave her a long, disapproving glance, and then he turned back to me. "I've waited for this very moment for so long, McGill-creature. It is blissful for me to place you under arrest and under oath. Know that, inferior being, your every utterance is now being recorded and transmitted to the

Galactic Core via deep-link. No one will interrupt us, no one will—what are you doing, beast?"

While he'd been speaking, I was pecking at my tapper continuously. I needed help, and I got it fast in the form of Natasha. All I did was patch her into my audio feed, so she could hear what I heard. At the same time, I muted her voice and lowered my arm.

"Sorry about that, sir. What's your first question?"

The Nairb ruffled himself like an upset bird. He didn't have any feathers, but when he gave himself a shake, it kind of puffed-up the goopy liquids in his body, making him look bigger for a few moments. I found the whole process to be just a tad disgusting, actually.

"The bailiff will restrain the accused if it attempts any further disrespectful conduct during this trial."

"Uh…" I said, looking around. I almost laughed when a bigger than average Nairb approached. He must be the bailiff. I hoped he didn't try to restrain me, or anything. I might accidentally kill the fool.

"Now," the Inspector continued. "Let us move on. Did you or did you not, McGill, place unauthorized robotic defense units in the middle of the prearranged battlefield?"

"Absolutely not, sir."

"Very exciting. Self-confessed conspiracy, making false statements to an Inspector—this is unexpected and refreshing."

"Glad I'm making your day, sirs. But I don't quite get where you came up with this charge of premeditation?"

"From your own words, ape-creature. You stated that you didn't place the active weapons systems on the battlefield—but we know that you did. Lying to an official inspector is a crime. Just as importantly, if your words *are* true, it would indicate you had an accomplice smuggle the drones into place. That means an expansion of the entire case. Thus, a conspiracy is born."

"But, wait a second. You can't have that both ways. Either I set up the drones or someone else did. If I didn't place them there, then I'm not necessarily in cahoots with whoever did the deed."

"Cahoots? Is that an animal-noise?"

Before I could answer, they set to chattering among themselves for a few minutes. At last, they came up with an answer.

"Ah yes, I see it here on our audio-recognition scans. It's an obscure colloquialism. McGill, you will refrain from using bizarre terms in the future. Doing so might open you up to an obstruction of justice charge. You will not succeed in delaying these proceedings with such tactics."

"I apologize, Your Honor, sir. That wasn't my intention. What I meant to say is that if I didn't have anything to do with the placement of the drones, there can't be any conspiracy."

"False," the Nairb said primly. "I can see you're a neophyte when it comes to Galactic Law. Conspiracies do not require actual acts or participation. They can be entirely derived from intentions. Therefore, if you were aware of or even simply in support of an illegal act, it makes you an equally guilty party by association."

"Uh… you mean it's a thought-crime?"

"Yes! That describes the situation perfectly. I'm glad you can comprehend your legal peril, McGill. It makes these proceedings so much more pleasurable."

"Hmm…" I said, sneaking a quiet glance at my tapper. I saw Natasha was still there, but now she was looking freaked out. With one finger, I tapped a few words. *Deep-link. Fix it.*

Before the nosy Nairb could start accusing me of some new fanciful violation, I looked up and grinned. "Sorry sirs, you used some funny words there, and I had to look them up."

"Nonsense. There was nothing obscure about our statements. They were perfectly translated. We're confident that the collection of animal-noises you call a language, as obscene and guttural as it is, was flawlessly—"

I laughed. "I'm sorry, sirs. I just meant that I didn't understand all your words—not even in my language."

"Ah! Ignorance and under-education! We understand that excuse, and we're not surprised by its use in this instance. Is there anything else you wish to say, beast, before your sentence is pronounced?"

"Pronounced? But… we haven't really had a trial yet. You haven't heard our side of the story."

"Unnecessary and counterproductive. We know implicitly of your guilt. This interview was merely for the purpose of explaining the situation, and frankly, it was an attempt to find grounds for additional charges. Fortunately, you've given us several more to append to our already robust list. The court is in your debt for that service."

"Uh... you're welcome... but may I ask how you know that I'm guilty?"

The Nairbs talked about it for a few minutes, putting their nasty heads together and doing some squawking. At last, they turned back to me and all the other sick-looking humans who stood around the bridge with shocked looks on their faces.

"Your request is approved. Witness exhibit A."

Here, the prissy Nairb took over our holotank and began displaying the battlefield as it was a day or two ago.

I was surprised to see myself front and center on the stage. An audible groan went up from the officers surrounding me, but I didn't look at them.

On the hologram, I walked onto the scene, moving across the open area where the Shadowlander town had once been. Just a few discarded items lay strewn about, the collapsed domes prominent among them.

We all watched as I worked a small device. As I did so first dozens, then hundreds of combat drones rose up from the dirt. They stood ominously tall, like massive, skinny-legged beetles. Dirt dripped from them, and they scanned their environment with evil intent.

Smiling and waving for them to crouch down again, I pressed more buttons. The monstrous robots sank back into their holes. Small scooping devices sprouted from the robots and worked to cover them up. After they were all hidden again, I walked among them and kicked dirt on the few antennae and shiny black surfaces that were still visible. In some cases, I even overturned a carton or dragged a piece of trash to hide any sign of the drones.

While this damning video played, the humans on the bridge gasped and carried on. They seemed to think it was a pretty big deal that the Nairbs had such clear evidence of my alleged crimes.

I ignored everyone and worked my tapper. With the crowd being well and truly distracted, I was able to send several key texts back and forth. At last, Natasha's face on my tapper nodded, and she gave me the thumbs-up sign.

The last thing she did was send me three fateful words: *signal is jammed.*

The Nairbs let the video play out, then they turned to me in triumph. That nasty Chief Inspector fellow looked particularly happy with himself.

"Are you convinced now, McGill-creature? At last, your decades-long criminal career has come to a just end. What's more, I'm applying for an extinction permit. It might take some years before the sentence is executed, mind you, but it will come. Let me assure you of that."

"I'm sure it will, sirs. You've done your homework this time. There's no escape for heinous humanity this time."

"James!" Galina said, unable to keep quiet any longer. "Is that all you have to say? You've caused this all to go to shit. You've been caught, and you don't even seem to care."

"Well sir, what would you have me do about it?"

She looked so pissed it didn't even bear thinking about. Her fists were at her sides, shaking and squeezing the air. Her eyes were squinched tight, and her lips were all pulled up from her teeth. She looked like a rabid dog. She really did.

"Fix this, you asshole."

Galina didn't utter these words lightly, let me assure you. She'd said something similar, I recalled, long ago. Once we'd been on the roof of Central, and she'd given me the same order when I'd been faced with Xlur and his demands for our self-execution.

Nodding and smiling, I walked to the nearest dumbfounded marine on the bridge. He was looking at the Nairbs, who were replaying the part where I'd buried the drones personally like mines set to go off later on the unsuspecting saurians.

Slamming closed my helmet's visor, I grabbed the marine's weapon. I turned with purpose toward the delegation of Nairbs.

Before anyone knew what was happening, I flipped the morph-rifle to assault mode and held down the trigger. A spray of power-bolts began to hose down the aliens.

At first, they seemed to be in shock. The Bailiff was the first to explode into a steamy gush of fluids, then several others fell.

The rest all began running—but there wasn't really anywhere to go.

The marine I'd disarmed finally got into the action. He tried to take back the gun I'd stolen—but all that did was get him the butt of his own rifle rammed into his belly. He went down on his can, but he wasn't through yet. He drew his pistol and dumped the magazine into my back.

It was a good try. In fact, I figured I owed the boy a beer if and when we ever had the opportunity to enjoy it. Unfortunately, I couldn't afford to let him get lucky, so I gunned both him and his partner down.

Several other Fleet pukes joined in after they saw the marines were shot, but my armor was impervious to their small-arms fire. Try as they might, they could only make me stagger and stumble now and then as they blazed away with their sidearms, pumping hundreds of bullets and power-bolts into my body.

In the meantime, I kept busy by walking around the bridge, messily murdering the Nairbs. More marines arrived at last, however, and they charged me as a group. They managed to pull the rifle from my hands and pin me on the deck.

"Tribune," I called, lying flat on my back. "I'm just following orders—and you know it."

Galina came close and looked down at me. "This is a bad one, James. Do you really think you can fix this?"

I nodded. "I think so—leastwise, we've got a shot. One out of a hundred—maybe better."

She grimaced, then took a deep breath. When she straightened up, she walked to where the last small group of Nairbs were huddled.

The Chief Inspector himself was still alive, and he'd squirmed his way into the middle of his underlings. He doubtlessly planned to use them as shields.

"Turov," he said. "This doesn't bode well for your species. We're expanding our investigation, invoking the shared-guilt clause of Galactic Law. Somehow, you've interrupted our communications, but that won't be the end of these proceedings. It will only be the beginning."

Galina nodded vaguely. "Did you just say, Inspector, that you couldn't communicate with your ship?"

"Are your auditory organs impaired? That's exactly what—"

She drew her slim pistol and shot him. That was it for the rest of them. The last handful of green snot-bags began shrieking like rabbits in a snare. They humped and flapped their way around the deck in desperation.

One by one, Galina chased them down and shot them all. She cursed the whole time, while I laughed until my belly hurt.

-76-

With her slim sides heaving, Galina walked up to where I was lying on the deck. I looked up at her, still pinned down by a half-dozen confused Fleet boys.

She aimed her pistol at me, and I laughed from inside my impenetrable suit of armor.

"What's that going to do?" I asked her.

With a grim expression, she bent down and reached for my gorget—that was the metal ring that locked my helmet onto my special suit of armor.

To my surprise, it popped right open at her touch. I glanced down, and sure enough, she had that damned Galactic Key in her palm.

Her face split into a grin, and she put her slim-barreled pistol into my face. She pressed the muzzle up against my right nostril, in fact. It burned there as the barrel of her weapon was still hot after shooting all the Nairbs.

"Ow," I complained.

"Hurts a little, does it? I'm sooo sorry."

She said this in a nice tone, but she kept on burning my nose with her gun anyways. I got the feeling she wasn't actually sorry—not in the least.

"I take it you didn't like how I killed the Nairbs, huh?"

"Why would you think that?"

"Well..." I said, "for one thing, you didn't look happy when you were gunning down the rest of them."

"I wasn't happy, and I'm not happy right now."

"Yeah? So why did you do it?"

"I only did that because I had to, you moron. You'd already killed half of them. Letting the other half go would have been even worse than our present predicament."

"Uh... so you agree that we're committed now? To my plan?"

"Yes," she said, "we're executing your plan now—if you even have one."

"In that case, you should probably let me get up. It's time to kick-start phase two, Tribune."

She considered her options. The muzzle of her long gun left my nose for a few seconds, but then she jabbed it back down into my cheek. It felt like she was putting out a cigarette on me. "Tell me what your plan is, first."

My eyes slid up to the glaring ring of Fleet pukes. They looked like they wanted to murder me. Probably, they were still upset about how I'd treated the crewmen who'd gotten in my way during my killing spree.

"I can't. Not with this clown-posse standing around."

Galina bared her teeth, but she nodded. She stood up.

"Stand him on his feet and get out of here—all of you."

They hustled off the bridge. Even Captain Merton was kicked out. A little bit of public slaughter had a way of setting people's minds straight about who was in charge.

I smiled at Galina and waved at the smeared remains of Nairbs all over the deck. "Reminds me of old times, huh? You know this must be the biggest stack of Nairbs I've ever murdered—and that's saying something. I bet that's true for you too, huh?"

"Shut up. Have you got a plan to get us out of this, or not?"

"I sure do. First off, Natasha has blocked their communications. They mentioned it, didn't they? She's straight-out jamming them."

"Natasha... right, that ex-girlfriend hacker of yours. But James, what about the Deep-Link broadcast they were doing?"

"Huh?"

Alarmed, she walked up to me and grabbed my arm. I couldn't even feel the desperate squeeze of her fingers through my suit. "The Deep-Link, you fucking idiot! They were transmitting directly to the Galactic Core!"

"Oh right! That…" I said, enjoying the sight of a little bit of panic on her face. I'd played dumb to get her to freak out. After all, she'd burned me for a mite too long with that gun of hers. "Don't worry about that," I said. "She blocked the Deep-Link too."

Galina squinted at me. "I didn't know that could be done."

I shrugged, not offering any more information. It was a secret that Natasha and I shared. We'd managed to come up with a method of tapping into Deep-Link transmissions and listening to them. Once you've managed to tune in to any given signal, jamming it is relatively easy.

"All right," she said, "I'll have to take your word for it. What do we do next?"

"Now we go talk to Nox, naturally."

"What? Are you crazy? She'll know she's lost her Nairbs. She'll know this wasn't any accident. She'll revive her green bastards and sic them on us again, with extra charges this time."

"Yep, probably. But we're not going to let her do that. We're going to cut a deal."

"What do you mean?"

"Let's go down to Gray Deck, and I'll explain. We've got to move fast."

She followed me off the bridge. Out in the passages, tons of freaked-out officers, both Fleet people and Legionnaires, thronged the place. They peppered us with questions, but Galina shoved them aside with a growl.

"You're all useless! Get out of my way, fools!"

We marched to the lifts, then rode down to Gray Deck. When we got there we found two teleport harnesses with full charges, strapped them on, and ported out.

We arrived aboard the Mogwa ship a few seconds later. We'd broken every protocol in the book by popping directly into the Governor's headquarters—but this was go-time.

"Hiya Governor Nox," I said brightly.

443

Startled, she turned around to face us. Her nasty feet-hand things churned on the deck.

"Is this an insurrection?"

"No sir, not in the least. We're here to help you out of this predicament."

"What are you talking about, creature? Turov, restrain your beast."

"I wish that I could, Governor. I really do."

Nox was kind of a scaredy-cat, even for a Mogwa. But she forced herself to relax and appear confident.

"There had better be an excellent reason for this intrusion, humans. My ship carries hell-burners, and I'm not afraid to use them."

"I'm sure that it does, sir," I said smoothly. "But hear us out, we've got an offer you're going to want to take advantage of."

One of Nox's hands strayed toward her tapper. I'd picked up a rifle along the way, and I lifted it to aim in her general direction. She got the idea and lowered her appendage again.

"All right," she said. "Describe your offer."

Smiling, I did so. While I spoke, Galina began to look more and more alarmed. By the finish, she released an inarticulate squawk of rage.

"James! Is that it? Is that all you have? No one would go for that deal! Earth won't approve it, either."

I glanced at her, then I nodded toward Nox.

The Mogwa seemed pensive. She spoke at last.

"Your statements are interesting. Your species is far too clever. I can see now why so many administrators who've had the misfortune of venturing out here recommend we cleanse the province completely."

"It is always good to start off fresh," I admitted. "But the truth is, no one is ever placed into the events of history at the beginning. You're now responsible for whatever goes on out here. Anything bad that happens in old 921 will reflect on you and your career—forever."

Nox didn't like my words. She didn't like them at all—but that didn't change the facts. She'd been given responsibility for this province, and it was her baby now. In the eyes of the

Mogwa back home, anything that happened out here was all her fault.

She began to pace the deck. Her six feet tapped in an odd pattern.

"This is the sort of thing that happened to Xlur, isn't it? Maybe he *did* commit suicide."

"What's your answer, your lordship? Yes or no?"

"It's yes, of course. But you already knew that, didn't you, McGill? I'll keep my eye-clusters on you in the future. You're not the kind of danger I expected to encounter. I'd calculated there would be great physical peril—but you humans are political as well."

"That's right. We're like monkeys screaming in a tree. You never know what you might catch when you look up at us."

Nox was annoyed, but she was also thoughtful. She turned away from us and activated her ship's communication console. At once, it flared into life. With a swipe of one of her many limbs, she expanded a portion of the local stars.

A single bright crescent appeared and it became rapidly larger as she zoomed in. It was the Skay, looking for all the world like an errant moon.

She tapped the image, and a signal was sent. Moments later, a channel opened.

"Mogwa," the Skay said. "Why do you disturb me this way? We have agreed that all communications will be intermediated by the Nairbs."

"That's true, Citizen of the Skay. But the Nairbs have suffered… an accident."

The Skay was silent for perhaps a second. "I see," its artificial voice said at last. "I shall rejoice then. They obviously ruled in my favor, so you had them put down."

Nox looked over her shoulder at us. Galina chewed on her fingers, while I gave the lady Mogwa a polite wave.

She turned back to her screens. "What you say is untrue, but I know I'll never convince you that matters went otherwise. We are at an impasse."

"Not so. You have forfeited, first by cheating and now by attempting to remove the judges. Neither of these attempts will succeed."

"Uh... Governor?" I said. "May I speak to the nice Skay, sir?"

Nox glanced at me again. "Well... I don't see how things can become worse."

Galina looked alarmed, and I thought for a second she was going to tell the Mogwa not to let me do it, but instead she just bared her teeth and watched as I approached the big image of the Skay. She looked more than a little bit sick, and her fingernails went to her mouth again. They were going to need a fresh coat of paint after this, I'll tell you that much.

"Mr. Skay, sir. This is James McGill. I'm sort of a—well, a professional negotiator in this province."

"You are in *my* province, McGill. You have no authority here."

"Ah-ah, that's the rub. Right there. We're not in your province quite yet. It will take another decade to get there."

"We're attempting to speed up the process. Your absurd behavior has been helpful in this lone regard."

I wasn't sure, but I figured I'd just been insulted.

"How's that, sir? I didn't—" I began, but Lady Nox finally lost it.

"No, you cunning animal!" she said loudly. "I'll not allow your nonsense to continue!"

Glancing back at her, I figured at first I was going to have to calm some hysteria—but it was far worse than that.

Nox had a weapon in one of her many hands. It was a black tube, and I didn't even want to know where she'd pulled it out from.

"Uh..." I said.

Without so much as a word of explanation, she shot me in the face. I was still wearing my armor, but after Galina had removed my helmet, I'd never thought to put it back on.

Those were the breaks, I guess. I died pretty much instantly.

-77-

You could have painted me nine kinds of surprised when I was brought back to life an unknown time later. That lady-Mogwa had killed me in such an unexpected and decisive manner, I'd kind of figured I was permed, or leastwise that I'd be reprinted from some old back-up file. I wouldn't be remembering my rude ending if that were the case.

But I *did* remember. I remembered the whole thing. To me, Nox had exhibited a bad attitude. Her behavior had been just plain rude. To my way of thinking, I'd been trying to save her bacon, and I hadn't deserved to be killed for that.

"McGill? McGill? Can you hear me?" It was some kind of bio, and the guy was poking at me.

"Yeah…"

"Okay, he's good. Get him off the gurney—he's to be sent directly down to the brig."

I was hustled off Blue Deck and dragged to the lowest decks aboard *Dominus*. At least I was happy to learn I was back aboard my legion's transport ship.

I recognized a few faces as I was hauled away. I smiled and waved whenever I saw a familiar legionnaire—but no one smiled or waved back. I'm no fortuneteller, but even I knew that was a bad sign.

The brig on any big ship is pretty much an offshoot of the sewer. Whoever designed ships always put some cramped holding cells right next to the waste processors. My tiny prison

447

was hot and steamy. It stank to high-Heaven, and I hated the place.

A few hours later, a familiar face showed up. It was Natasha.

At first, I thought she'd come to see me, but then I noticed her hands were manacled behind her back. I felt bad about that. It wasn't the first time she'd gotten caught up in one of my schemes and punished unfairly for it.

The guards shoved her into my cell and slammed the door. She sat beside me on a metal pallet that hung from the wall.

"Hey, at least we've both got some company!"

She looked up at me slowly. There were tears in her eyes. "What did you *do*, James?"

"Aw now, don't go crying. Things will be okay."

"No. No they won't. We're to be executed right after the deal you made with the Skay is consummated."

"Uh…" I said, confused. "But I didn't make any deals with the Skay. I talked to the Mogwa-lady, sure, but before I could offer up anything that made sense to that moon-sized stick-in-the-mud Skay, Nox killed me."

Natasha shook her head. "I don't know what to believe. I guess it hardly matters. We're both going to be permed soon, anyway."

"Why'd they bother to revive me if they just plan to kill me?"

"I don't know. It's a bureaucratic thing."

I nodded, as I was used to that kind of answer. But I didn't buy it. Not completely. They were probably holding old McGill in their back pocket, like an old-fashioned ace card— just in case.

As our tappers were disconnected from the grid, I played crappy games on mine. Natasha seemed bored too, and she spent hours swiping and poking at her arm. Finally, however, she whooped.

"I got through!"

"Huh? What game are you playing?"

"No, no… I got through the security grid. I'm online."

"Oh…"

Together, we studied her screen. Natasha was quickly able to determine where and when we were. The news was disappointing.

"Nine days..." she said. "They kept us dead for nine long days."

"So what? I skipped two years once."

She looked at me wonderingly. "What should we do, James?"

I thought about it. "Get onto the ship's grid. Log in with someone else's ID, and get into the traffic up on Gold Deck."

Her tongue slipped out and vanished again nervously. "What if they find out?"

I laughed. "We're up for a perming, girl. What the hell does it matter now?"

My logic was unassailable, so she dug into hacking. She finally managed to get into a few secret accounts other techs kept for these kinds of emergencies—all of her own had been ferreted out and erased.

"Who's account are you in now?" I asked when she finally got a visual from the bridge to come up on her arm.

"It's Kivi's."

"Does she even know you hacked her?"

Natasha smiled shyly. "No. She'd shut it down if she did."

I grinned, and we watched events unfold. What we saw bored us at first—but then we became alarmed.

Dominus was in orbit over Earth. Watching the main viewscreens, we saw what had to be our Moon swinging into view. The transport was aiming right at it.

At least, that's what it looked like. But then I noticed that there wasn't just one moon, there were two of them.

One of them was way too far off, but it was moving closer every minute.

"That's that evil-looking Skay—or a different one. It's hard to tell. He's sneaking up on our Moon."

"No he's not," Natasha said, sounding lost. "He's repossessing it. James—he's hauling it away."

We watched in horror as the Skay closed slowly with our Moon and began to do strange things. It was weird, seeing a twin to our own friendly satellite up there, fraternizing with an alien stranger.

"How could he do that?" I demanded.

"Some kind of gravitational manipulation, I imagine. Kind of like applying an anti-gravity clamp onto an object. He's making it lose all inertia, and probably severing its gravitational link with Earth."

"Uh... that's got to be a bad thing, right?"

Natasha swiped and tapped at her arm furiously. She brought up news reports from Earth. The stories were all awful. There were tidal waves, hurricanes... our coastlines were being wrecked on one side of the planet, while on the other side the ocean had almost stopped moving. It was turning into a million square kilometers of still pond-water.

"Will this destroy the world?" I asked.

"No... some places will be devastated, especially the coastal cities. But then, the oceans will probably start to die. There will be mass aquatic extinctions. The jet-stream might quit flowing, or it will change its behavior. The Moon swings around Earth all the time, and it makes our world churn. A lot of what we call weather is due to tidal shifts."

She looked kind of sick, and I couldn't blame her.

"Listen, can you get us a line out to somebody on Gold Deck?"

Natasha slid her eyes up to meet mine. "James..."

"Come on. I know you can do it."

"Who do you want to talk to?"

I thought over the list of possible suspects. There was Turov, Graves, Captain Merton...

But then, I knew who it had to be. The one fellow who would be willing to try anything to fix this mess.

Winslade let his tapper buzz at least six times before answering the call. That was probably because it said it was coming from Kivi. He couldn't have cared much about whatever she had to say at this point.

"Kivi," he said, his face popping up. He looked angry and scared. "Stop pestering me with these incessant..."

He trailed off, seeing Natasha's face. I took that moment of confusion to horn in on the meeting, sticking my big face in sideways. I gave old Winslade a wave.

"Hey, Primus," I said. "I just wanted to let you know we've been released, and we're coming up to help in any way we can."

"What? That's nonsense! McGill, if you've killed more of my guards, so help me—"

He tapped at his arm, and I watched his big finger slapping on the screen while he did it. Then he went back to frowning again.

"You're still in the brig? I traced this signal back—and why are you using Kivi's account, Tech Specialist Elkin? That is an unconscionable breach of security."

Natasha began to sputter excuses. She was a great tech, but she was useless in creative situations like this one.

I grabbed her arm and pushed my face into Winslade's view again. "Listen up, sir. We can fix this. I swear on my mamma's bible we can. But we can't do it from down here in the brig. Can you spring us out?"

Winslade's eyes slid around like a cephalopod who was considering a bribe. Finally, I saw him walking away from the bridge. He took the conversation out into the passages where he could continue talking to us privately.

"McGill, it's too late for your special brand of foolishness. A deal has been struck, and it's being carried out right now."

"What deal, sir?"

"Nox left the Nairbs dead in her revival queue, claiming there was some kind of problem with the processing. She even blamed the Shadowlanders for sabotaging it."

I laughed. Nox was a tricky one—even for a Mogwa.

"She refused to revive them," Winslade continued, "and she pressed her claim on 91 Aquarii, insisting that Legion Varus had won the day, fair and square."

"It was anything but."

"Obviously. Anyway, the Skay was forced to either go to war or back down. It chose a third option."

"Uh…" I said, thinking that over. "What third option?"

451

Winslade hissed and pointed over his shoulder wildly. "That nightmare of tectonic destruction that's going on in Earth's orbital field right now, you ignoramus!"

"Oh! You mean it insisted on towing away the dead Skay ship?"

"Exactly."

"Huh... Well, okay. That gives us an edge."

"How so?"

I shrugged. "You'll just have to trust me on this one. I can see the way out. It's as clear as day."

Winslade narrowed his eyes to slits. He looked like a highly suspicious house pet. "What is your imaginary solution?"

"No way am I giving it up now. You're not going to take the credit while we rot down here in this cage."

Winslade bared his teeth. "This isn't the time for such selfishness, McGill. Our world will be forever changed after this day. You *must* tell me your harebrained idea."

I could tell I had him on the hook. All I had to do was reel him in.

Winslade's weakness was his sense of desperation. He was a man who'd try almost anything when the chips were down. He also knew me, and he knew my crazy plans frequently bore fruit.

I puffed air at him and went back to playing a game on my tapper. Winslade bitched at me for a few more minutes, but finally, our cell door popped open.

Standing up, I grinned down at Natasha. "Come on. We've got work to do."

She followed me out of the place, apologizing to the confused and angry-looking guards. That was just like Natasha, she was always worried about people's feelings, even if they were her sworn enemy.

A few minutes later I met up with Winslade in the passages just outside the guarded entrance to Gold Deck.

"You can't go any farther," he said. "You're due to be executed online within a few hours—that's part of the deal they made with the Skay."

"You mean that big cue ball actually insisted on witnessing my execution?"

"Yes, it certainly did. Can you blame the thing? You have a unique way of charming aliens and ladies everywhere you go, McGill."

"You can say that again. Sometimes, I impress even myself. Now, stand aside Mr. Primus, sir, if you want to save the Earth and the Moon."

"You can't just walk onto the bridge, McGill. They'll shoot you down—dammit, *I'll* shoot you down!"

He drew his pistol and aimed it at us. As we were unarmed, all we could do was glare back at him.

"That's a chance I'll have to take, Winslade," I told him. "You can shoot me in the back right now, or you can follow along and explain things to Graves, or… or I guess you can just skedaddle and hide someplace. It's all up to you, sir."

Not giving him another glance, I strode on by. I don't mind telling you that my back crawled a bit when he was behind me. He was a natural-born backstabber.

But in the end, he didn't shoot me. At the entrance to the bridge area, I glanced back over my shoulder. Winslade and Natasha were nowhere to be seen.

They were both pretty smart that way.

-78-

When I walked onto the bridge, I was ignored at first. Not even the two marines at the entrance could be bothered to toss me a sneer.

Maybe that was because of the amazing spectacle that was playing out in three-dimensional holographic splendor in the middle of the chamber. Everyone had their heads tilted back just so they could take it all in.

On the display, our beloved Moon was front and center. Behind her, sneaking up like an old letch in a locker room, was a badass Skay. It was the same old bastard I'd seen before out at 91 Aquarii, I recognized him by his worn out, pock-marked hull.

As the two bodies got closer, our Moon began to... well... crumble a bit. Chunks of gray-white material, looking like fine dust on the screen, drifted away into space. The disruption grew steadily. Soon there were dust devils of the stuff, rising up in violent, twisting cones like tornadoes. The skinny tips of these whirling maelstroms were all touching down on three points of the Skay's face. The broad cones—they were lifting off from the Moon itself.

"What the hell is it doing?" asked a familiar voice.

Surprised, I tore my eyes from the fantastic scene, and I spotted Drusus. He had his head tilted way back, so he could look up at the disaster unfolding in giganto-vision right above us all.

I hadn't even known Drusus was aboard—but it made sense. Whenever there was triple-decker, six-star red alert with Varus' name all over it, the top brass generally blamed him and sent his sorry ass in to fix it. I suspected that was because he'd been the original tribune. When something like this happened the politicos and other suck-ups down on Earth seemed to assume it was all his fault anyway—and maybe there was a grain of truth to that. He had to be at least partially responsible for Varus and its general infamy.

"As best we can tell, Praetor, the Skay is exerting a gravitational field. It's... it's sucking up all the surface debris from the Moon."

"Makes sense, I guess," Drusus said in a defeated tone. "I don't know how else they might go about hauling our Moon out of Earth's orbit. I'd hoped it would be beyond their technology, or at least that we'd have years to come up with some plan of action—but it doesn't look like that's going to happen now."

"They're taking immediate possession of our Moon?" Captain Merton asked. He seemed to be incredulous. "May I remind you, sir, that Earth Fleet stands ready to defend our territory. There are fifty ships with armament comparable to *Dominus* in the Solar System. Perhaps this is the appropriate time to stand our ground."

Right then and there, I decided I liked Merton. I always had to some degree. He was an honorable man who was just trying to do his job. Often, Galina or some other legion brass type spent time spitting on him—but here he was, still ready to throw down and die for our Moon. That had to tell you something.

Drusus sighed and looked at Merton seriously. "I appreciate the sentiment, Captain. Unfortunately... there will be no valiant last stand here today. The Mogwa have shown no interest in defending us. Our entire fleet might or might not win a conflict with this single Skay. Even if we did, we would be announcing war on a Great Power, with no one to back us up."

"But the Mogwa hate the Skay, sir," Merton said. "They've fought several wars with them. If we give them an excuse—"

Drusus shook his head. "It's not happening. I've talked to Nox and others—they aren't interested. They think of us as whining babies. The actual suggestion I got from them was to find or build another artificial satellite if we liked this one so much."

"Really?" I squawked out loud. "Is that even possible?"

Pretty much everyone in the place craned their necks to gawk at me. This included the two slack-jawed marine chumps that had spent the last two minutes standing next to me without even noticing.

Instantly, four hands landed on my person, two on each side. It was all I could do to keep myself from slamming them onto the deck—but I managed it.

Sure, I could have probably put both of them down. A few slips of the wrist and some quick footwork—but no. I wasn't wearing any fancy armor today, and I wasn't even armed. I'd be dead in less than a minute, and all my plans to help Earth keep her beloved Moon would be dashed, probably forever.

"Uh..." I said, glancing at either marine, "thanks for the thought, boys, but I'm not looking for a date."

"McGill...?" Drusus said, and from his tone, I got the feeling he wasn't happy to see me. In fact, it sounded like it made him even more depressed. "Who ordered your revival?"

"I wouldn't rightly know, sir. I just woke up in the brig, and I got bored down there, see, so... I left."

Drusus nodded tiredly. He accepted this explanation at face-value, and I was glad for that. Winslade had helped me get this far, after all, so I didn't want to finger him as my benefactor.

"Well," Drusus said, "seeing as this is mostly your fault, I guess it's only fitting that you watch the greatest injury ever perpetrated upon our green Earth."

"Now hold on, Praetor sir. I don't agree with that."

He folded up his lips and eyed me. "This isn't your fault?"

"No sir! I accomplished my mission out there on Edge World. I led Legion Varus to victory, the only way it could be achieved."

"Meaning... you cheated."

456

"An offensive way to describe it, sir... but... yes. We won though."

Drusus nodded. He put his hands behind his back, clasping them together. Then, in a predatory fashion, he began walking over the metal deck plates in my direction.

Finally, when he got close, he violently flung a finger up toward the Skay. "Look at that! Do you call that a win for Earth?"

At this point, the whirlwinds of transferring matter were increasing. The two heavenly bodies, similar in size and general appearance, were only about two thousand kilometers apart. It was like they were kissing or something. I couldn't even figure out how they weren't slamming into one another— the Skay had to have incredible control of itself.

"Looks like that Skay is about to mount up and ride on our old girl, I'll admit. But sir, we can still revive our people. We've got plenty of machines left."

"For another decade, maybe," he said. "But long before that, the politicians will start hoarding all the revival machines we buy for themselves. After that—we'll lose 91 Aquarii permanently. It's inevitable."

"What about contacting Claver?" I asked him.

"We tried that. They don't have a supply, and they don't want to sell us any of their units. Once these machines we already have wear out, we're going back to permadeaths for everyone."

That little speech seemed to dampen the mood even more than the theft of our lovely Moon. Everyone aboard *Dominus* had died more than once. We were pretty attached to our revival machines, as we liked continuing to exist. The idea of losing them... well, it was a death sentence for everybody.

"So..." I said, "would you be happier if we'd let the Skay take our revival machines now, and allowed us to keep our Moon instead?"

Drusus dropped his eyes and studied the deck. He shook his head. "It's a hard choice. I know it's not fair to expect Varus to win every time—but somehow, everyone back here on Earth had been hoping for a better outcome."

"And... what if I could give you that outcome, sir?"

Drusus didn't tilt up his head right away. He was still studying the deck plates.

Behind him, however, my words sparked movement. Three people exchanged glances then walked up behind Drusus. One was Graves, another was Merton and the third was Turov.

Up until now, these three wise monkeys had kept their damned mouths shut. But they knew a con when they saw one. They knew I was working my worst McGill-magic on their commander, taking advantage of him when he was down and hurting.

"Praetor Drusus," Graves said, speaking up first. "Let me take the prisoner back down to the brig. I'll make sure he doesn't escape again."

Punctuating his true meaning, he drew his sidearm and pointed it at me.

Drusus shook his head, but he kept studying the deck plates between my size-thirteen boots.

"The Fleet is still closing in," Captain Merton said. "We *can* take effective action. We've beaten a single Skay before."

"That's not good enough. Years from now, they'll send out a squadron to crush us. It might take them decades, but they're machines. They'll never forget it if we break our word and attack their brother now."

"But we've beaten them before, sir! We can do it again."

Drusus glanced at Merton. "We did that under the guise of defending the Mogwa. We were therefore exempt from direct guilt. If a master orders a slave to act, no one blames the slave. At least, not a machine."

Merton compressed his lips and stopped talking. It was clear he wasn't going to get his way.

"Sir?" Galina spoke up next. "Do you know what I think?"

He glanced at her. "What, Tribune?"

"I think that if you really want to get out of this, you'll have to give McGill's insane idea a shot. Either that, or forget about it and accept our new fate with a moonless sky forever. You'll have to decide quickly, however."

She gestured toward the big hologram. We all turned to look.

Chunks of the moon were now flying from the surface—crags of ancient rock that had been there for countless years, splintering into pieces.

Drusus winced as if physically struck. After staring for a few moments, he turned around to me.

"Can you really do something, McGill?"

"Absolutely, sir! You're gonna be sooo happy. I promise."

He looked sick, but he nodded and turned toward the two marines. "Release him."

"This is a mistake, sir!" Graves said, breaking with his longstanding tradition of accepting his superiors' judgments without any back-talk.

"The Fleet can do it, sir," Merton said. "Just give us a chance."

Drusus looked at each of them, then he turned back toward me.

"McGill, don't screw this up."

"That's simply not possible, sir. Don't you worry about a thing. First off, I'll need a teleport harness with two extra batteries and a powerful transmitter. I'd really appreciate it if Fike would return my personal suit of armor too, if you don't mind."

Fike, who'd been standing around at the back of the bridge being quiet, cursed a bit at the mention of his name. Apparently, he'd gotten cozy in my armor again since my most recent demise.

"That can be arranged," Drusus said. "But I'm really hoping you aren't planning to kick off a new war."

"No sir! I'm going to prevent one. Oh, and one more thing…"

"What's that, McGill?"

"Does anyone have an A-bomb handy? Nothing dramatic, just a few gigatons will do the trick."

-79-

To my mind, my plan was simplicity itself. First off, I had to get the Skay's attention. After that, everything should go as smooth as glass.

At least, that's what I hoped.

My opening move was to teleport to the Skay's surface. After that, I spent a few minutes broadcasting on various channels. I knew it could hear me, but it was arrogant—sinfully arrogant.

Most big-cheese aliens are like that. They think that they crap ice cream, and you're nothing but a dung beetle. This general attitude went double for Galactics of any kind. In my long adventures, I'd determined it was even worse with the Skay.

Now, I had to give them at least a partial pass. After all, there was a significant size difference. Humans like me weren't even insect-sized to a Skay. We were more like an amoeba. To understand how they thought of you or me, try to ask yourself how much care and concern you have for any of the approximately forty trillion microflora that are living inside your body right this moment. That's right, humans carry around about two kilos of bacteria at all times. We don't think about that fact much, but there it is.

The Skay don't think much of us, either. We're less than fleas to them. So and therefore, it was no surprise when the

Skay ignored me. Accordingly, the first thing I had to do was get the monster's attention.

If I'd been commanding a threatening Armada or an entire planet, sure, the Skay would have answered me. But as I was nothing but a speck on its hindquarters, it didn't even bother trying to scratch me off.

After I made polite inquiries for a solid ten minutes, I followed up by cursing and whatnot. After that, I finally gave up. It was time for the antimatter bomb I'd brought along on the trip.

In my slice of the universe, A-bombs aren't rare, but they aren't exactly commonplace, either. They offered up the most extreme yield of matter-to-energy conversion possible. When antimatter encountered regular matter, there was complete annihilation on a one-for-one, particle-for-particle basis. Consequently, the modest football-sized bomb I had tucked under my arm could release no less than 2 gigatons of force.

Two gigatons was a lot. More than the sum total of all the fusion bombs set off on Earth throughout history.

Trudging along in a spacesuit, I moved to what I considered to be a good starting spot. This Skay was an old bastard, a veteran of countless conflicts. As such, he was kind of scarred-up on one side of his otherwise smooth, gray-white surface.

"You're gonna listen to me, old boy," I said to myself, huffing and puffing inside my helmet as I bounced and skittered over the giant's hull. "Just you wait."

I figured that planting the bomb in the middle of the most dented spot was my best bet. It should be mentioned that I didn't expect to *kill* the Skay, or even to breach his hull. It took more than one A-bomb to do that. It took hundreds if our previous encounters were a good guide. We'd tried to fight the Skay before with such weapons, and it had taken a *shitload* of punishment to kill just one of them.

But killing the Skay wasn't really my goal. I was just trying to kick him in the ass and get his attention.

Whistling badly, I switched on the bomb's timer. Once it was ticking away, I promptly teleported to the far side of the monster, over near its mouth. Then, I waited.

461

It didn't take long. If the Skay had been a normal planet with an atmosphere, the blast might well have sent a shockwave, a dense blast of air, all the way around to where I'd placed myself. But there was no air on the surface of a Skay. It was just like the Moon in that regard.

What there was, however, was a reverberation sent through the massive hull. That raced around the surface and vibrated my feet. It was numbing, like when you beat a baseball bat on the sidewalk until it breaks—it hurts your hands.

The vibration buzzed up through my boots and made my bones ache. I stumbled around and fell on my knees.

"TINY CREATURE! WHAT HAVE YOU DONE?"

I pointlessly put my hands up to cover my ears—but there was a helmet in the way.

"Jeez! Turn it down, Mr. Skay!"

"You dare threaten me? You think you can destroy *me*, the immense demigod of a thousand conflicts? Know you, mortal sub-insect, that I was alive and warring when this Moon of yours died. That I have presided over the explosion of a dozen suns, the death of countless trillions of puny irritants like you, and—"

"Hey, hey," I said, "settle down, Master Skay. I'm not trying to blow you up. I just wanted to talk to you."

"Impudence has no comparator to your case."

"That's probably true..." I admitted. "But hey, listen, I want to make a deal with you."

"There is no need. No human possesses anything of interest to me. My existence is almost incomprehensible to your microscopic brain. Even speaking theoretically—"

"Yeah, yeah, I got all that. But listen to my offer: I can allow you to take over 91 Aquarii *today*. Right now, with no waiting around for the star system to drift into your space. What do you say?"

Silence reigned for several long seconds. "What you say is impossible. I have no record of your authority. I have no reason to trust, negotiate, or—"

"Jeez! What's wrong with you people? Here I am, trying to offer up a fantastic bargain, and all I get is talk about what

462

can't be done. Let me tell you what *can* be done: I can send you back to the Core Worlds as a winner. As the Skay that came out to this dismal frontier and returned in triumph."

Again, the Skay hesitated. I knew I was tempting him something awful.

"Your thought-processes are illogical and far-fetched. However, you have intrigued me enough to give you a warning: speak quickly, for you don't have long to exist."

"Huh...?"

I looked around, suddenly feeling kind of exposed out here on this bright-lit cue ball-like surface. I looked north, then south, but I didn't see a thing.

Of course, there wasn't going to be some cloud of dust rising on the horizon. If he'd sent a flying drone out, or even a galloping predatory hunter-killer—there wouldn't be much warning. Whatever monstrosity the Skay had sent out to find me would simply plunge over the horizon and do its worst. There wouldn't be any sound or much time to react.

Still, I couldn't help looking this way and that. It made me a bit nervous, and I don't mind admitting it.

"Are you still alive, you absurdity?" the Skay asked.

"I sure as hell am. I'm alive and well, and I'm getting ready to deliver my next love-tap. This one will be sixty-seven times the size of the last one."

"Sixty-seven times? An antimatter warhead of that capacity would outweigh your estimated mass."

"Yeah well... you'd better calculate again! Or instead, you could just listen-up for a second."

"You are wasting your final precious moments of existence."

"Okay, okay. Here's the deal: we're the enforcers in Province 921. You're the local authority in Province 926, right?"

"Stating the obvious is no less of a waste of time than—"

"Right, okay. The Nairbs judged that you lost the contest on Edge World—but they're gone. So is Nox—her ship has left the province. What if we both—"

A shadow fell over me at that moment. It was a really *big* shadow, and it had come from the east. Had I looked in that direction? I wasn't sure—but it didn't really matter.

A massive construction of metal and meat fell upon me. It lowered a pair of jaws that yawned bigger than my helmet. The jaws were lined with bright metal teeth. Each curved titanium fang in that massive maw was thicker than my thumb and twice as long.

Instinctively, I threw up my left arm. It was going for my head, to chomp down on my helmet. If I let it do that, I was probably a goner.

Accordingly, I let it take my arm instead. The massive jaws crushed down—but the fangs couldn't penetrate my armor. Instead, they crushed the bones inside to jelly.

I shouted and carried on—but I didn't die. The thing picked me up, shook me with its powerful neck, and tossed me across the barren surface of the Skay. I rolled and tumbled for a long time, being in low-gravity and all.

"Have you had time to consider my offer?" I asked loudly.

"You're still alive?"

"Yes, of course. I'm setting off my next bomb in a few seconds. I'm glad you sent this creature out here—I needed more mass to merge up with the anti-matter. I wasn't sure if the star matter of your hull would work right or not."

"Your understanding of quantum mechanics is poor," the Skay admonished.

When I finally stopped rolling around and grunting in pain, I saw the beast lumbering toward me. It looked me over, probably deciding what part to chomp on next. Using my good arm, I reached to the teleport harness—but I hesitated.

"This is your last chance, Mr. Skay. Will you take possession of 91 Aquarii and give us back our Moon? You'll be able to return to the Core Worlds as a winner, not just a loser towing some ancient trophy."

"Your analogy is weak. All Skay win, all the time. There is no other acceptable option."

The big monster dipped its big ugly head again. Obligingly, but not without a grimace, I shoved my boot up into its mouth. It began chewing and grinding away. My foot was mangled-up something awful. There wasn't anything more than pulp left from the shinbone on down.

Feeling a sick explosion of shock and a hot trickle of blood running down my leg to wet my balls in a gush, I knew I didn't have too long left to keep bargaining.

My one good hand gripped the teleport harness return button.

"Last chance," I gurgled. "Is it a deal, or not?"

"The Mogwa would never approve of your suggested trade."

"Doesn't matter," I slurred. "There are no Mogwa here. They don't come out here for decades, sometimes. Humans are left in charge in their absence. We're making our own deal. Do you want 91 Aquarii right now or not?"

A few more seconds went by before I saw the monster stop chewing on my foot. Confused by its inability to eat me, it decided to bulge up its neck muscles again—or neck motors, whatever. It whipped its neck around, and it gave me a mighty heave. Due to the low gravitational pull, I flew up into space.

Twirling and tumbling, I spun up so high I just about reached escape velocity. But then the Skay's gravitational field caught me again, and I began to fall.

Spinning like I was, I knew I couldn't afford to land and be struck by the kind of force that was coming my way. I'd be way past hurt, I'd be stone dead in an instant. After all, body armor only does so much to protect a man.

Grasping desperately, I managed to get ahold of the teleport activation button. I pushed it down, hoping against hope that the mechanism would even work at this point.

To my relief, the spinning universe began to pulse and turn blue-white. I vomited, and I grinned—I was going to escape.

"*Agreed.*"

At that moment, as I was teleporting away and slamming back down onto the surface of the Skay in the same instant, I wasn't even sure I'd heard the Skay's single word.

But I *had* heard it.

Then I vanished. I'd teleported away with a big grin. I couldn't remember arriving back on *Dominus*. I must have lost consciousness by then.

Best of all, I'd done it all at about the same time.

* * *

There were instruments beeping in my ears. It was annoying.

"He's awake. Ask him—ask him now before he passes out again."

My eyes fluttered. I couldn't believe I was alive—but I wasn't in a regular revival chamber. I was on an operating table, and there were cold fingers and surgical steel pressing my numerous injuries.

"Oh... shit," I said. "I don't feel so good."

"McGill?" Graves said, poking his craggy face into mine. "What did you do out there? What the hell did you do?"

"I fixed it, Primus. I fixed everything."

Big hands grabbed my shoulders, and he shook me. "The Skay is leaving. It's ignoring our every hail. How did you do it? What did you tell that thing? Where's it going next?"

"Uh... can I get a flesh-printer going, or something? I don't think I'm a hundred-percent right now."

"You arrived on Gray Deck in a mangled state. You're not going to make it, but Drusus hasn't approved you to die yet. We filled you with happy-drugs to keep you breathing for a few more minutes."

I laughed, and I spit up some blood. "You're right. I do feel kind of high. That's downright considerate of old Drusus."

Graves shook me again. I got the feeling that there were several bio-people fluttering around me. They began poking me through the secret holes they'd built into my suit. I would have to remember to plug those up with some pot-metal or something in the future.

"Talk to me, you idiot! We know you cut a deal with the Skay, but we have to know what it *is*."

I shook my head. Old Claver had once given me a secret to a long life. He said I should always leave a hostile audience wanting more. That my last act should always be to tease people, to give them a good reason not to perm me.

466

"Sorry sir," I said, "you'll have to ask the next version of McGill. This one is finished."

Graves bared his teeth at me like a dog. He dropped me back onto the table.

"All right. Recycle him."

"Head-first or feet-first?"

"Whatever you feel like."

That was a disappointment. Even full of drugs, going into those spinning blades feet-first was no picnic. I struggled to lift my head to see the bio-people—but I couldn't do it.

At last, an angelic face rose up into my hazy field of view. "James? You look awful."

It was Dawn, the girl from the Moon base I'd dated for a time.

"Hey, Dawn? Are we on the Moon?"

She laughed. "No, the Moon was evacuated days ago."

"Oh... that's right."

"I'm going to have to kill you now. Sorry."

"That's okay... Hey? How about a date when I get back?"

"Are you sure you won't get permed or anything?"

"Nah. Graves loves me."

"I can tell."

I felt a tiny sting, and I began dying. I reached out a big clumsy hand—the one that still half-worked. "What about that date?"

"Sure, James. Just go to sleep now."

I did as she asked, and I died for reals this time with a smile on my face.

-80-

When I came awake again, I was circled by smiling faces. Drusus was there, Galina was there—even Graves.

Graves wasn't smiling, mind you, but you can't have everything.

"Wow," I muttered when my mouth worked right. "This is an honor—uh, that is if you guys are really happy to see me. Not just enjoying a few brews before the perming party, or something...?"

Drusus laughed. "Hardly. What you did out there—it was unbelievable. The Skay just turned around and withdrew. It let go of our Moon and even gave it a nudge so its orbit wouldn't decay."

"You don't say? Wow. I didn't even ask for that!"

They chattered a bit while I climbed into the shower they had installed—and I realized at that point I'd been revived in the VIP chamber. That was another shocker. Legion Varus didn't have this kind of spacious, clean and luxury-minded setup for any other revival room. Just this one.

After taking a few minutes, I climbed out and stood in the buff with my hands on my hips. "Say, how about we all go down to the officers' lounge and celebrate?"

"You might want to put some pants on first," Galina suggested. She handed me a uniform, and I pulled it on.

468

Laughing, we all walked out into the passages. I was in the lead, with Drusus at my side. Galina and Graves brought up the rear.

"The one thing we'd like to know is how you did it," Drusus said. "What kind of trick did you use? Did you have some intel? Some secret you threatened to release?"

"Uh..."

"It had to be something good," Galina chimed in. "Something powerful. Something like threatening to tell the Mogwa that the Skay have genocidal bio-weapons... Right?"

"Oh..." I said, reaching up a finger to scratch under my ear. "Didn't you guys hear the conversation? I was broadcasting for all I was worth just to get the big cue ball's attention."

"No, no, we couldn't," Drusus told me. "Not after you set off the bomb. There was too much radiation, see. Lots of EMP interference. I must say, the use of an A-bomb to get the attention of a Skay—that was a unique solution. I doubt such weapons have ever been set off to start peace-talks before."

"Heh, nope. Probably not."

Inside, my guts were just starting to do a slow roll. These guys didn't know. They didn't know about the deal I'd made to get our Moon back. That meant all this love-and-biscuits routine might be... premature.

Glancing over my shoulder, I snuck a look at Graves. He didn't look happy. He'd been the only one who wasn't talking, laughing, or clapping me on the back. Maybe that was because he'd known me longer than any of them. Besides that, he'd always been a "trust-but-verify" kind of guy.

"Let's get that drink before they close for the night!" I said, and I set off at a ground-eating pace. They all had to struggle to keep up.

All of them, that was, except for Graves. He let himself fall behind. He didn't seem to care.

When we got to the officers' club, I immediately bought a round for everyone. That was only good policy, the way I figured it. When you had to deliver startling news, it was best to do so when your target had an adult beverage in their hand. In this case, I suspected they might need two of them.

"...but let's get back to the point, McGill," Drusus said. "You haven't answered my questions yet."

"That's true," I admitted. "Sometimes, a man needs to have a secret or three. After all, I just woke up from yet another revive. That reminds me, do you ever have dreams when you're dead? I had a doozy this time around. It was about this one-legged duck, see—"

"McGill," Galina said, interrupting, "you're dodging again."

My eyes slid around from face to face. They were beginning to suspect something was wrong. Turov and Drusus were at least—but Graves? Well, I could tell by the scowl growing on his craggy face that he was beyond the point of having suspicions. He damned-well knew something was up.

This was a critical juncture. When a man like me is faced with a difficult moment, my natural urge is to lie my ass off. That's just how my brain is wired. Never admit anything, delay the day of truth until it wasn't possible to put it off any longer—then come up with a new dodge. I'd lived by that simple creed all my long and storied life.

But this was different. Oh sure, I could probably get away with some tall tale about how I knew the Skay's aunt was really his mother, and how we'd both loved the same kind of puppy when we were young—any kind of horseshit that came to mind.

But that wouldn't solve things for long, no sir. After a few days, a week tops, the Shadowlanders were going to be calling Central to ask why they had their extra moon back in orbit, and why it was demanding they all fall on their knees in the moss and start worshipping their new god.

Even knowing this, I wanted to start lying. I seriously did. What a few glorious days I might live. Galina already thought I was some kind of hero. That would probably result in some nice rewards for me. On top of that, Dawn had promised me a hot date as well. You might think that entertaining two women might not be workable, but a man with my skills could probably manage the situation to everyone's satisfaction...

"McGill!"

It was Galina, she was standing tall now, and she had put her second beer down. She'd obviously been talking to me, and I hadn't been listening. Not at all.

"Uh… sorry. Could you repeat that last part?"

She put her hands on her hips in disbelief. "Seriously? You didn't hear a word I asked you?"

"Uh…"

"McGill," another voice spoke up for the very first time.

It was Graves, and he had his drink on the table in front of him. It was utterly untouched. His face was like stone.

"Tell us the truth, Centurion. Tell us what we don't want to hear. Whatever it is, we're all going to find out soon enough."

My mouth fell open for a bit. Then I worked my lips silently for a few seconds more. It was as if I'd been struck dumb.

That's a peculiarity of my make-up, I'm afraid. Lies always come to me in a glib, easy rush—but not the cold truth. The truth was always a struggle to get out at times like this.

Taking in a deep breath, I nodded to Graves. I leaned forward in a conspiratorial fashion. The rest of them—except for Graves—leaned closer to hear what I had to say.

"It all started back when I went to the Core Worlds," I began. "That was a long, long time ago. More than a decade back by now. Anyways, I learned some things back then. Things that I never told you about during the numerous debriefings."

"Like what?" Drusus asked.

"Like secrets. Dark things… In the case of this Skay, see, I happened to have heard of him. He's all scarred-up, right? Did you notice that?"

"We could hardly have missed it," Galina said. "Get to the point, James."

"I am, I am, I swear it. See, I found out that the Skay, because he's kind of famous, even among the Mogwa… First off, you have to understand something. The Skay people, well, they kind of have their own ways of mating. Of sharing software and making new, little Skays."

"Little Skays?" Drusus asked doubtfully. "Are you telling us a Skay is capable of growing in size after it's constructed?"

471

"What? Oh... no, no, no," I laughed. "I didn't mean that literally, I'm talking kind of figuratively, here. I mean their minds start off young and have to grow. Anyways, the old Skay that we dealt with today had a baby Skay, see. Not a little one, just a sort of a spawned one with a similar mind."

Galina rolled her eyes at me. Drusus seemed intrigued, but old Graves was still giving me that same flat stare. I tried not to even look at him. Damnation, that man was hard to crack.

"So, I learned a secret." Here, I lowered my voice and leaned even more forward, nudging my beer with my chest. "That big old Skay—he's not the daddy of the little Skay he thinks is his. That's the secret. I told him about it, and he was so grateful that—"

Graves suddenly stood up. His chair slammed back on the deck behind him.

His face had a clear look of disgust on it. He was holding his pistol in his right hand, and it was leveled in my direction.

"Excuse me, sirs," he said. "But if McGill dares to utter one more word of this horseshit story, so help me, I'll blow a hole in him the size of his lying mouth."

Drusus and Galina blinked at him for a second or two. They both looking shocked. Then their eyes narrowed as they absorbed his words.

Together, all of them stared at me. There was nothing soft or considerate left behind in any of those three faces. Not anymore. They were all suspicious and pissed off.

"Uh... ah, shit. You're not going to like this..."

Then, I told them the truth. Not all of it, mind you. In my version it was all the Skay's idea. He'd worked me, abused me, and downright forced me to agree to the crazy trade of our Moon for Edge World.

Long before I'd gotten to the finish line, all three of them were drinking. They were glum-faced, and Graves ordered another round—and another after that.

Everyone got drunk, but no one laughed or smiled. It wasn't that kind of a drinking-binge. It was the other kind, when you feel sick, and you want to bury it all.

472

Galina had her fist pushed up into her cheek, which was kind of pink-looking. She was a little bit drunk, if I had to guess. I'd seen that look often, but probably never when she was also depressed.

"So... you traded away our revival machines so we could keep our Moon. That's what you're telling us, isn't it?"

"What? No, no, no! That's crazy-talk! We're not going to lose our revival machines. We'll just have to relocate the Shadowlanders to... some other planet. Then, they can keep making our favorite product."

Graves slowly shook his head, Drusus narrowed his eyes at me, and Galina hiccupped.

"You've made these arrangements?" Drusus asked me.

"Huh?"

"I'm asking you if you've talked to Kattra and Helsa about this."

"Oh... I'm sure I mentioned it once or twice. They seemed to think it was a good idea."

Drusus started massaging his face. "McGill... you're talking about a mass-emigration. Moving an entire population to another planet."

"That's right. It's been done before. Hell, they're already nomads! It's a perfect solution!"

473

Drusus sighed. "It might be, if we had a decade or so to work it out. Try to think, McGill. You're talking about thousands of individuals."

"Uh-huh."

"Maybe millions. They don't even know they're moving yet, and they have—what? A week?"

Here, he turned to Graves, who nodded stoically.

"A week?" I said, laughing. "Why do they have to move that fast? The planet isn't even entering Province 926 for ten years maybe."

"According to the old rules, yes. But you promised the Skay immediate ownership, right?"

"Uh... maybe. I don't think that part was clear."

"Apparently not. Graves, what's the Skay's last estimated course?"

He leaned forward. "The alien is headed directly for 91 Aquarii. It clearly intends to take immediate possession of the star system. His estimated arrival is... just under six days from now."

My jaw sagged low, and I gawked at them. "Really? You guys think the Skay got it wrong? You think he's going to go right out there and move into their orbit again?"

"That's why he came out from the Core Worlds, McGill," Graves said patiently. "The reason he took your offer was because it gave him an immediate win. He can now go back home and brag that his mission has been cleanly completed ahead of schedule. That's a no-brainer for any AI being."

My mouth was still hanging open as I looked from one of them to the next. Galina helpfully reached out a hand and applied a few fingers to my chin, shutting it for me.

"Uh..." I said. "Maybe we could renegotiate?"

They all groaned and leaned tiredly over the table. "To do so now might spark the very war we've all worked so hard to avoid," Drusus said. "We're in a much weaker position at this point, as the Mogwa have left with their Nairb representatives. We're dealing only with one recalcitrant Skay."

"Yeah..." I said, thinking hard. "Well then, there's only one thing to do."

They all looked at me. There was a total lack of confidence in those stares, and I felt they were being a tad harsh on old McGill, but I kept that complaint to myself."

"What do you propose, Centurion?"

"I'm going to have to go right out there and make things right."

They stared at me—well, that's not exactly right. Galina's eyes were closed now, and that fist she had shoved up into her cheek seemed to be the only thing holding up her head. Graves was just gazing into his beer as if he might find solace at the bottom.

Drusus, however—he was doing some serious staring. Finally, he nodded.

"All right," he said. "We'll teleport you back to Edge World. But please—don't start a fresh interstellar war, McGill."

"Don't worry about a thing, Praetor sir. You haven't got a problem in the world when old McGill is on the case!"

He nodded glumly, and I left the bar. Once out in the passages, I started to run. I had a lot of work to do, and I had to hop on it right now.

My first stop was Gray Deck. Even Central had a Gray Deck, and so I checked out the goods. After haranguing people who weren't interested in helping for about half an hour, I started making some calls—but I didn't call Drusus. Sometimes, he could be as big a stickler for rules as your average hog—or even a Nairb.

Nope, what I needed was a rule-bender, so I contacted Etta, my daughter.

"I didn't even know you were back, Dad."

"I sure am. Why don't you come up to Gray Deck for a minute, honey?"

She hesitated. She had a woman's intuition now, and her senses were telling her something was wrong.

"You're not going on *another* mission, are you? Not so soon…?"

"Hell no! I'm just having an argument with the hogs up here, and I was hoping you could help me sort things out."

"Dad, I'm kind of a hog myself now. You realize that, right?"

"Now girl, you can't go talking about yourself like that. You're not a hog, because a hog is a uniformed member of Hegemony, Earth's so-called combat forces. You're not a hog at all. The proper term for you is *nerd*."

"That's a big relief, Dad."

"Anytime... So, when can you come up?"

Etta eventually arrived and walked warily onto the deck. As I was standing there in my all-black Rigellian armor, she got kind of suspicious right off.

"You said you weren't doing a mission today."

"That's right—well now, hold on, I *am* teleporting out to Edge World. That's why I'm here. But it's not a combat mission. I don't intend to die or anything."

Etta looked kind of confused and suspicious. Sometimes I wished she'd never grown up and started doubting her daddy.

I pointed to the head honcho. "If you could just tell this hog here—ahem, that is, this uh, kind of portly gentleman—that I should be allowed to go to the coordinates of my own choosing, I'd be grateful."

She looked at the pissed hog I was talking about. I'd been kind by calling him portly—in truth, he was fatter than a waffle house waitress.

"What's he want you to do, exactly?" she asked.

"He's got some coordinates from way out on the edge of the province. We're not allowed to cast people that far without authorization. I can't even turn on the machine without full confirmation and—"

"We don't have time for all that," I interrupted. "I keep telling him."

Etta looked at me. "Do you have authorization to be transported to these coordinates, Dad?"

"I surely do. Just, uh... not on me."

Etta sighed. She reached out with her lanyard and ran it over the equipment. Then she gave it some biometrics, using her eyeball for a retinal scan, then her finger for the prints. At last, the machine beeped and turned its indicator lights green.

"There we go," I said, smiling. "You see, hog? I told you I had friends in high places."

"Whatever," the tech said, and he waddled away.

"Say," I said to Etta when he was out of earshot. "I just need one more thing."

"What?"

"A set of gateway posts. Mind you, I'm just borrowing, not stealing. Don't worry about it, I'm good for them! Ask anybody."

Etta heaved a big sigh. "Okay. They're in those lockers over there. Just grab a pair of them and get into the casting couch. Activate the machine when you're ready to be cast to the coordinates you typed in."

I started toward the lockers and rattled the doors.

"Wait until I walk out of here," Etta hissed at me. "I'm not even going to watch this."

"Hold on... could you help me open these locker doors first?"

With poor grace, she opened the locker. I pulled out a fresh set of gateway posts and smiled. This was going to be easy— really easy.

-82-

I appeared on a windswept plain. Bright light shone directly out of the east.

The thing was, I knew right off I couldn't be in the right place. The Shadowlanders lived in the perpetually purply half-light on the cusp of Edge World—not in the permanently brilliant sunlight of the bright side, or the freezing gloom of the dark half.

"Hmm…" I said, checking the coordinates. They were right, but something was…

"Oh yeah!" I said aloud, after doing a bit of thinking.

The world had moved on. It had rotated at its slow, walking pace toward the east. That meant I was at the same spot I'd been before, but it had rotated enough to put me in the sunshine.

Turning, I faced myself due west. With the slanting morning sun on my back, I began walking.

Soon, I found signs the nomadic Shadowlanders had recently traveled the path. There were discarded items, dead bright-sider warriors with moss growing over them, and even the remnants of human defenses. I trudged past our abandoned bunkers and puff-crete walls for a time, then came to an open road again.

It was all nine kinds of spooky, what with everything being so empty and derelict. It was like walking on a planet that had seen the apocalypse and kept right on going.

After I'd marched for a full hour, I spotted a team of bright-sider outriders. They appeared on the horizon out to the north, then vanished again. They were clearly watching me.

Damn. I'd kind of hoped to find the Shadowlanders without having to kill anyone. I had my morph-rifle of course, which I unslung and checked. It was loaded, charged, and ready to go.

But I knew I couldn't fight an army. I had two gateway posts on my back, banging and clacking with every step. They had to weigh forty kilos or so, but it was the awkward bulk of them that made things tough on me.

I considered dropping the posts. I could make better time and fight more freely without the burden—but I passed on the idea. I didn't have time to fool around and find another set of posts. I had to do this entire mission without any extra delays. Timing was everything.

Grumbling, I marched onward. Soon, the sun behind me had lowered until it was a half-disk. That was a good sign. If I could get to the Shadowlander camp before—what was that?

Something crashed off to my right, to the north. I wheeled around and brought up my rifle. I almost released a spray of bolts—but something told me it was a trick.

Call it a dead man's intuition—that was what we legionnaires called our instincts in moments like this. We'd been tricked and killed in combat so many times over the decades, that you just got to where you had a feel for an ambush when it was coming your way.

Accordingly, I whirled in the opposite direction.

A half-dozen bright-siders were racing toward me from the south. They were mounted on cat-like animals—beasts that had padded feet and made little sound as they closed with the single dumb-ass human that dared to walk in their territory.

Without a moment's thought, I lit them up. Some people might say it was a hasty action, what with the war being over and done. These boys might be bringing me flowers or something—but I always said it was better to be safe than sorry.

The lead mummy was indeed sorry almost immediately. He was knocked from his mount by a burst of fire. The second went down a moment later, doing a header over his dead cat's pointy ears.

I shifted my aim, but I wasn't right on with the third guy before the rest reacted. They didn't run for it. They split up and spread out, coming from opposing angles, converging.

I could have given them a break if they'd turned tail and run, but they weren't that kind of warrior. They had balls, I had to give them that, even if said balls were probably shriveled-up and wrapped in bandages to protect them from their blinding sun.

My rifle hammered again. Two more went down—then the last two were on me.

Firing wide-mouthed guns that looked like blunderbusses, they knocked me around with big shells. They were forty millimeter rounds more or less, if I had to guess.

The first one hit me in the thigh and would have taken my leg clean off if I hadn't been armored. The second one hit me square in the chest, and that was the bad one. I was tossed back, coughing and gasping.

I had impenetrable armor and lots of padding, but the shock of that heavy round still went through it all. I more than felt it, I ate it.

Spinning and falling onto my face, I tried to lever myself right back up again, but I couldn't do it.

They jumped on me. Two of them rode on my broad back. Fortunately, they didn't weigh much. It was kind of like having two wrapped-up versions of Winslade grappling with me.

I tried to do a push-up, and I managed to get my body off the dirt, but the combined weight of the gateway posts and two scrabbling fifty-kilo mummies kept me from getting to my feet.

The two mummies gave it their all, I have to say. They growled and screeched and clawed at me. They stabbed me with rusty knives and fired a few more pellets into my ribs, point-blank.

But it was like two starving peasants were trying to work-over an armored knight. They couldn't get through, and I didn't play nice.

My combat knife was in my hand. I cut one mummy's leg off for him, then turned on the other guy.

Rising slowly, painfully out of the dust, I faced the last man. He looked at me, crouched low, baring lots of yellow teeth that looked like they'd seen better days. He did some practice lunges, but he was clearly scared.

"Go on now," I told him, gesturing toward the east and the brightening sun. "Get on home to your mamma."

I'm sure he didn't understand my words, but he got the sentiment. With several snarling words sent my way, he trotted to his mount and climbed aboard. Then he rode off toward the east, vanishing in the light of the rising sun.

Checking my gateway posts, I figured they weren't too badly banged up. I shouldered them painfully and set off toward the west. My hip was kind of hurting, but I forced myself to walk on it.

As I kept going, I tried to do what little math my brain was capable of. The answers I came back with weren't encouraging.

Sure, we'd only been gone about ten days. That meant the darker twilight regions weren't all that far ahead—but I was still in trouble.

After all, I had to figure that the Nomads wouldn't just stop walking when they reached a dark zone and set up camp. No sir, that wouldn't make any sense. If they did that, they'd have to tear it down and set up again too soon.

Nope, the nomads would keep going. Logically, if they did this once a month, they'd have to go a twelfth of the way around the planet's surface before they'd stop and set up their little town.

"Shit…"

I stopped walking and my sides were heaving. I looked off to the west, then the east, then back west again.

Walking wasn't going to do it. I'd die of starvation long before I caught them. They had vehicles and they might be a thousand kilometers away. By the time I caught up, they'd be moving again.

Putting down my gear, I sat on a rock and took stock of things. I had a teleport harness, two gateway posts and my armor. My only serious power supply was in my morph-rifle,

481

unless you counted the small suit battery that ran my HUD and whatnot.

The battery in my rifle wasn't strong enough to power up the posts. That took enough juice to light up a city block.

Nope, it had to be the harness. There was no other way.

I eyed the thing dubiously. I'd had a lot of experience with such devices, but that didn't mean I knew how to program one accurately. My big problem was navigation. I'd never been accused of being a math wiz.

Still, I had to try. It was that or die out here with aliens beating on my starving, stupid ass.

Heaving a big sigh, I took my best shot. I estimated the planet's curvature, my current position, and the probable distance I'd have to go to find them after I got there.

This kind of blind jumping was terribly dangerous. In the past, I'd merged up with all kinds of things—ceilings, floors, other people's bodies...

But there was nothing else to do. I did my best, taking a full hour to work on my tapper. At last, I came up with some decent numbers.

During this process, I naturally looked up every few minutes. Mostly, I stared off to the west. I was worried that the single mummy-boy I'd let go would return with a hundred of his cousins, bent on revenge.

Why had I let that skinny bastard go?

No one came my way, however. Maybe I'd put the fear of the legions into their barbarian brains.

Splicing wires that sparked white on contact, I got the battery port to accept power from my rifle and soon had a charge I thought would do the trick.

Gritting my teeth and praying hard, I activated the harness.

-83-

I missed.

My landing spot wasn't *way* off—in fact, if I hadn't been left screaming and pin-wheeling my arms in the air, I might have been proud of myself. After all, as a rank amateur at this game, I couldn't expect miracles.

By all rights, I should have permed myself. The possibilities were endless. I might well have popped myself right out of the atmosphere, even shooting myself into the local sun, or meeting any of another dozen disastrous endings.

But my tapper's mapping functions had given me some pretty reasonable coordinates. The trouble was I'd aimed a little too high.

I'd been paranoid, see. I could calculate the curvature of this world fairly well with the help of my tapper and dead-reckoning, but I couldn't be *sure* there wouldn't be a rise in the land at my exact point of arrival.

What if there was a hill at that spot? Nothing too grand, just a hundred meters or so of stacked dirt? That would mean I'd pop into existence buried in the middle of a thousand of tons of earth and stone. I'd be buried alive, unable to move, waiting to die...

That fear got me to nudge up the estimates my tapper had given me. Consequently, I didn't appear on the ground level, I popped out a good fifteen meters above the planet's surface.

Falling out of the sky, I howled on the way down. I tucked my head, pulled up my legs, and formed a ball.

Thusly braced for impact, I punched into the roof of a building. It wasn't a very sturdy roof, but it did stop my fall. Made of thin aluminum plates, the dome collapsed and I kept falling. When I hit the hard ground at last, I felt a few ribs crackle. I'd be sore in the morning, that was for sure.

Climbing to my feet, I found a full family of Shadowlanders surrounding me, confronting me. They were chattering words at me and seemed really pissed off.

Looking around, I tried to get my bearings. It appeared I was in the middle of some kind of family gathering. As there was a broken table under my boots, I had to figure I'd interrupted them at a meal.

"Aw now," I said, "I wrecked your dinner, didn't I? I'm real sorry about this. Luckily, no one seems too badly hurt."

One of the women gestured wildly toward the head of the table.

Turning painfully, I squinted—and I groaned aloud.

A dead oldster sat there, crushed by the roof I'd brought down on their heads.

"Damn," I said, "I'm awful sorry about that, ma'am. I'm sure you can revive him though, right?"

They pretty much chased my ass out of the place. It was a good thing I was wearing armor, or all those kicks to my hindquarters would have hurt.

As I deserved the punishment, I didn't fight back. I just kind of waded through the angry mob, accepting whatever abuse they felt like dishing out. They were all standing behind me, cursing in their strange language and rubbing at their bloody knuckles. My armor wasn't as forgiving as I was, after all.

Whistling a tune, I marched through the town. I soon came to find out it wasn't the same town Helsa and Kattra were from. It was a smaller outfit, a village of sorts that handled moss-wrangling, or some such thing.

They were able to tell me which way to go, and I trudged off into the twilight. After another few hours of marching, I reached what passed for a capital city on this planet.

484

If I thought I'd received a cold welcome the first time I'd marched into this town, I was in for a shock. These people positively glowered at me. Could they have heard about the incident with the family and their dead patriarch? I wasn't sure, and I soon lost interest anyway.

Finding the dome closest to the center of town, I walked in like I owned the place.

Kattra was there, with her squad of suck-ups circling around. She looked at me with vast disdain.

"How is it you dare to impose on us again, human?" she demanded. "Haven't you killed enough of our people? Haven't you—?"

"Look," I said, cutting her off. "We don't have much time. Listen closely."

I explained the situation to her, and she looked like I'd fed her a dog turd and forgot the mustard.

"You've got to be joking. The Skay is coming back here? How did this happen? We've negotiated in good faith—the Galactics can't do this. They can't go back on their word!"

"I know, I know," I said sympathetically. "It's not fair. Not fair at all. But sometimes they just do crazy things like this. Maybe the Skay reported back the deal he made, and his home government rejected it."

"That's incredible... no, it's unprofessional. I won't stand for it."

"Uh... how's that?"

She got up off her throne, and she walked toward me. "We watched you shortly after you arrived, McGill. You fought a squad of bright-side scum single-handedly, and you slew them all."

"You saw that, did you?"

"Yes. It was very impressive. Earth soldiers are tough, even vicious. We know how to do battle—but we're not in your league."

She was walking around me now, running her hands over my armor. Now, I'm six kinds of a moron—just ask anybody— but I can tell when a woman's buttering me up for something awful.

"Those are mighty kind words, Kattra. But—"

485

"Just listen for a moment. You and your people must stand with us, we can't beat the Galactics alone. Together, we can begin a rebellion."

I thought that over for a second, and I nodded. "We surely could. In fact, we've considered that more than once. There's this little problem, however—it's the Mogwa and the Skay. They'll come out here and crush us."

"But not for years. Maybe centuries. In the meantime, we'll live gloriously. Isn't it better to live a short, proud life? I would rather fight on my feet than to grovel and lick the boots of Galactics forever."

I heaved a sigh. I felt for her, I really did. I'd had just such feelings in the past, and I knew, at some point, I was going to go out that way. It was my destiny.

"I do feel that way. In fact, I've rebelled in countless ways. I've killed Mogwa—lots of them. I've killed Skays as well."

She smiled. She reached up and tried to open my helmet.

Just then, off to my side, I saw Helsa. She was stepping close on my six. She was coming at me the same way the mummy-people did. These Edge World types were all kind of sneaky, and they reminded me of various predators back home.

"Get out of that armor," Kattra said, still touching me. "I will service you—and my daughter will as well."

"That's uh…"

My big head swiveled this way and that. I noticed that the suck-up team had vanished. Just Kattra and Helsa were in the room now, and they were putting moves on poor old James McGill.

Now, a better man would have shrugged these two off. He'd have known this offer couldn't be on the up-and-up. It just couldn't.

But I'm a deeply flawed man, so I took my helmet off.

The two ladies both smiled up at me with those weird, big, predatory eyes.

-84-

They moved on me. They came in real fast—but I was ready.

I caught Kattra with my left hand, and Helsa with my right. My big fingers could almost touch my thumbs after going around those two long necks—almost.

"Ladies, this is kind of rude. I'm a guest here, aren't I?"

Hissing and scratching my armor with their blades, the two of them went at me like buzz saws. Fortunately, the good Lord saw fit to give me the arms of a gorilla, and they just couldn't quite reach. Still, I found myself wincing away from the glittering arcs their weapons cut through the air.

"I'm becoming offended," I announced to them, giving them both a light shaking.

That settled them down, and they switched to working on my fingers. But that was even more hopeless than trying to shiv me. My hands were like steel collars, each pinning one ornery woman.

At last they stopped struggling and glared at me, panting.

"Damn, ladies. I once gave a pair of housecats a bath at the same time, and they were less trouble than you two."

"As the ruler of this planet, I demand that you unhand us, McGill," Kattra said.

"I will, I surely will. But first, you have to tell me why you're trying to kill me this time around."

487

Helsa released a bitter laugh. "You must be joking. You doomed our world. The Skay is coming here to take possession of our planet and our entire people. Death is too good for you!"

"Yeah... I can see that. Okay, I'm going to let you go, then I'm putting my helmet back on. Can you two keep yourselves under control for that long? I've got a solution to all your problems."

"That's not possible," Kattra said.

"What is it?" Helsa demanded. "Another antimatter bomb? Perhaps you wish to irradiate another vast swath of our homeworld?"

"Nope, nope—this is even better."

Slightly curious, they stood back while I carefully fastened my helmet into place again. Then I walked them outside and showed them the gateway posts.

"You see these babies? They're aligned with Central back home. All I have to do is power them up and any and all of your people can walk straight to Earth."

The two women stared at the contrivance.

"You're out of your mind," Helsa told me.

I laughed. "That's funny, coming from you two."

"We can't simply leave our home planet," Kattra said. "We can't give up everything we've ever known. We can't—"

I threw my big arms wide, and they both jumped a bit.

"All right then! Just sit tight. Wait for the Skay—he's coming. In the next few days, you'll have a new moon up there in the sky."

Pointing up at the heavens, I let them ponder that, then I turned to walk out.

"Where are you going?" Kattra demanded.

"I'm leaving—I'm going back to Earth. My work here is done. I told them you were too proud and shit-off stupid to save yourselves, but I had to give it a whirl. Now that that's over, I can go talk to some smart people."

Kattra showed me all of her teeth and got in my face. "You are the idiot here. Not us!"

"That's what people keep telling me," I admitted, "but the proof says otherwise. Here I am, offering you freedom from slavery. Freedom from serving a giant machine intelligence. And it all stands right here in front of you."

"In your province, we'd serve the Mogwa instead," Helsa said. "How is that better?"

"Oh, it's better. You've already been doing that all along. They've pretty much ignored you, right? That's not how it is with the Skay."

"How would you know?"

I laughed, and I lied big. "Because I've dealt with the Skay out in Province 926 many times. They're vicious bastards. Heartless machines. They don't even give the people a reason when they perm an entire species on a whim. It's just BOOM! All over in a flash."

They were blinking and breathing hard. They were trapped, and I knew it. The devil you know is always better than the one you don't.

Kattra turned desperate eyes toward the gateway posts. "How could we do this?" she asked.

"No, Mother!" Helsa urged. "Don't listen to this man. He's a fiend!"

Kattra waved her back. "McGill? Answer me. You've brought a gateway that spans no more than a meter. We can march our people through it, but not our revival machines, our gear, our manufacturing vats—"

"Don't worry about any of that. Here's how it will work."

I proceeded to tell them how we'd gotten the Blood-Worlders to Earth the first time. How we'd first used this small gateway to bring through all the components of a larger one, a unit with a broad ramp that you could drive a truck through.

After telling her all this, I got an idea, and I dug deep in my tapper's history files. These days, they never seemed to run out of space. I found files showing the Blood-Worlder invasion of Earth, and the day we'd shipped them all back to Nova Scotia by the thousands.

"You see that? Heavy troopers two at a time. Giants walking through without even having to duck. It's more than possible, we've done it before. All you have to do is give the word—but don't wait. That Skay is coming."

I made a show of looking up at the sky, examining the horizons as if I expected to see the gray-white disk of the big Skay floating into view at any moment.

"I will... I'll step through your contrivance. I will see Central. I will see Earth—then I will decide."

"That's more than fair, Ma'am."

Helsa seemed less happy about it than Kattra was, but about an hour later, I had them both following me through the powered-up gateway posts. They looked around in shock as I gave them the nickel tour. We walked through the upper floors, examining the sights. They were the most shocked by the vistas out of Central's windows.

"This structure... it's impossibly huge."

"Nah," I said. "It's no big deal. All our cities have two or three of these."

My lies had the desired effect. They were overawed. As nomads, they'd never seen anything as grandiose as a bustling metropolis. They were hicks from the sticks in comparison, and they both knew it.

As we'd come out at the upper levels, very near Drusus' office, it was only right that we visited the big man himself.

Now, some might say that Drusus is everything I'm not when it comes to diplomacy. He greeted them warmly and gave them gifts. He showed off his new aircar, his big desk and his row of statues—busts, he called them.

Afterward, Helsa approached me. "This man, Drusus—he's weak. He's not like you. I could have killed him a dozen times since we got here."

I nodded. "That might be true. He's more of a political animal. A leader and a thinker, not a killer."

Helsa grabbed my bicep. "I prefer killers."

"Is that right? Say, have you ever tasted alcohol? Beer, wine...?"

She shook her head, and I smiled. I smiled big.

"Would you like to see the city? The streets, the shops, the restaurants?"

"What are these... restaurants? The word does not translate."

I laughed. "Girl, you are in for an experience. Come on."

490

We snuck out, leaving Drusus and his minions deep in negotiations with Kattra. They were going over possible worlds for emigration, rules of conduct, even lower prices for Earth on future revival machine sales. After all, there had to be something in it for us humans.

Before we left Central, I saw Kattra's team of underlings scurrying about. They'd come through the gateway posts from Edge World in her wake. They would draw up the details, the fine print. All that stuff made me want to yawn.

In the meantime, I showed Helsa a real city, with real amenities. To her, our people were rich beyond imagining. Even though her folk had a valuable product to sell, the realities of endless warfare with two other tribes, plus the fact they had to pack up and move all the time, had kept them in a relatively primitive state.

I assured her that once they had a nice, normal world under their feet, a place where they could set down real roots, their civilization could flourish and grow to heights they'd never imagined.

By the end of the night, Helsa had been schooled on a wide variety of adult beverages, but she wasn't to be easily outdone. She schooled me as well in various bedtime activities I'd been thinking about since I'd met her. We rented a fine hotel room with a view of the sea, and we spent the night together.

We did have one bad moment, around about midnight. She'd strayed to the balcony and stood there, buck-naked in the evening breezes. The night was lovely and warm, wetter than she was used to. Her nose was up, sniffing the air, which was full of a dozen unfamiliar scents.

The trouble came when our Moon came out from behind the clouds. She screeched at it, pointing and crying out in terror.

I wrapped myself around her, and I assured her there was no danger. It took a few minutes, but at last, she relaxed in my enfolding arms.

"That Skay is dead?" she asked.

"That's right. It's a dead one."

"Why is it there? Why do you allow such a ghastly mass of death to ride in your skies? Do you use it to scare children?"

"Uh… sometimes. But to us, it's a trophy. We Earthlings killed it, you see. Centuries back."

She looked at me with big, big eyes. "Really?"

"Scout's honor."

Helsa sighed and melted against me again. "I like being with a fearless male. I think I will like it here on Earth."

I smiled, and I gently rested my chin on her head. We gazed up at the Moon, which had been misunderstood by humanity for countless generations.

The only thing I regretted about this campaign was that new disillusionment. The people of Earth would never again be able to look up into their night sky and feel the same way about its mystery and beauty.

Books by B. V. Larson:

UNDYING MERCENARIES
Steel World
Dust World
Tech World
Machine World
Death World
Home World
Rogue World
Blood World
Dark World
Storm World
Armor World
Clone World
Glass World
Edge World

REBEL FLEET SERIES
Rebel Fleet
Orion Fleet
Alpha Fleet
Earth Fleet

Visit BVLarson.com for more information.

To Listeners!

The Audiobook version of EDGE WORLD, performed by Mark Boyett, will be released on Audible December 15th, 2020!

Printed in Great Britain
by Amazon